THE
MOSES
RIDDLE

To my Grandmother Donna, without you I never would've met . . . our mutual friend.

If you keep doing what you're doing, nothing will change.

— Marvin Herb, January 17, 1991

This is a work of fiction. All the characters and events portrayed in this novel are either fictitious or are used fictitiously. Any similarity or resemblance to actual persons, living our dead, events or locales is entirely coincidental.

The Moses Riddle

A Thomas McAlister "Treasure Hunter" Adventure

First Edition: 2005

For more information visit: www.huntkingsbury.com

THE
MOSES
RIDDLE

Book I of
The Treasure Hunter Series

HUNT
KINGSBURY

P R O L O G U E

Three thousand years ago on the dry, sandy plains of Egypt, Abubaker, a historian, documented a temple restoration at the Necropolis of Saqqara. One day, Abubaker observed the arrival of a man with a long silver beard, accompanied by a contingent of armed guards. The guards were stationed around a cart, pulled by oxen, which carried a large square object covered by hide. The bearded man entered the temple of Unas and stayed inside for two days. The guards remained outside. Abubaker noted this peculiar incident in his journal, thus capturing a secret journey Moses made to Egypt. This was the only time Moses returned to Egypt after the Exodus, and the trip was not documented anywhere else, not even the Bible.

At the end of the temple restoration, Abubaker's notes were stored with all the others in the general archives building in Cairo. When the Pharaoh, Amenophis III, died, Abubaker's notes were buried with him in his tomb, to serve as proof to the gods of the civil good deeds Amenophis III performed during his rule. The notes remained in the Pharaoh's tomb, undisturbed, for over three thousand years, until the tomb was discovered by a young archeologist named Thomas McAlister. Many of the documents removed from the tomb stayed in Egypt. But some of them, including Abubaker's notes, were entrusted to the man who found them, and they remained with him, undeciphered and all but forgotten, until a life-changing crisis brought them to his attention.

In the gray light of pre-dawn, DJ Warrant, special agent for the FBI, started the ritual. It was a private, sadistic little thing, that he'd only done two other times in his career. To let in more light, he separated the shabby hotel room curtains until they were about a foot apart. Sitting at the badly chipped Formica table, he withdrew his M1911-A1 World War II-issue service automatic from its holster. Holding it in front of him, he pushed the button to eject the clip. It sprang forcefully into the palm of his left hand.

As he'd done the other times, he flicked the first bullet, a big 250 grain .45 hollow-point, out of the clip with his thumbnail. He then took out his Swiss Army knife, opened the nail file, and slowly, deliberately, carved the initials TM into the soft brass on the side of the shell. TM: Thomas McAlister. When he had the letters just right, he brushed the brass filings away, placed the shell back into the clip and the gun back into his holster. It was done. The bullet was addressed. He felt better already. The knot in his stomach relaxed.

At this point, it was only symbolic. It was too early to need to kill McAlister. If his intuition was right, however, and McAlister had gotten away, the need might arise soon. The need wouldn't come from his employer, the U.S. government. No. It would be a greedy, dark, personal need. He had only been tricked two other times in his career. Only two other times had he felt the shame of exposed failure, and the lust for concrete revenge that had followed. In both cases he'd addressed bullets and, in both cases, his lust for vengeance had been quenched. His problems had disappeared. Forever. As he thought of all the ways to dispose of a human corpse, thousands really, the edges of his mouth curved upward to form a reptilian smile.

DJ was a walking case solver. He'd solved more cases for the FBI than anyone else in the agency's history. In crime fighting circles he was a legend. But despite his auspicious past, and the knowledge that the recently addressed bullet was inside his .45, riding comfortably on his hip, inwardly he was terrified. Little jolts of fear pulsed uncontrollably throughout his body. The same helpless jolts of fear you'd feel if you saw your child snatched up by a passing van, or if you were pushed by a stranger off a cliff.

DJ had two rules when he had someone under surveillance, and he never broke them. First, he watched vigilantly for changes in the individual's routine, because a change usually meant that he or she was getting ready to run. Second, he demanded that his surveillance teams have either audio or visual contact with the subject at all times. If either of those rules were broken, it usually meant trouble. Thomas McAlister, the archeologist currently under surveillance, had just broken the first rule, and his own surveillance team had broken the second one.

It was only mildly disconcerting that McAlister did not wake up and go downstairs for coffee at his usual 5:30 a.m. Men were prone to oversleep. But the fact that he had not made any noise *at all* for over two and a half hours was chilling. It basically meant that McAlister was no longer in his house. That he had gotten away. That DJ had been outmaneuvered.

People are noisy creatures. Though not in any FBI manual, DJ knew that the average person sneezed once every eight hours, coughed every six hours, and yawned two to three times a day. On average, men urinated every three to four hours, and one in every five men snored. McAlister snored intermittently, but DJ's team hadn't heard him all night. He should have been awake by now, and despite the fact that men averaged fewer words per day than women, two thousand words versus seven thousand for women, McAlister hadn't said a single word or made the smallest sound for two hours and fifty minutes.

DJ's encyclopedic knowledge of these statistics and anthropological facts, and thousands more like them, helped him solve cases. He could expound on the history of modern ballistics, explain the phases of bodily decomposition, and tell you the names and detailed personal histories of the FBI's ten most wanted. It was as if he'd been born with the knowledge. But, if you asked him his daughter's middle name, he'd look at you with a blank stare.

DJ's current quarry was Thomas McAlister, an unemployed Egyptologist who had supposedly found an amazing treasure. DJ had been briefed on this assignment a week ago, by his direct supervisor Chief Hargrove. From the start, this case had been different. Hargrove had held the meeting in a highly secure section of the Pentagon.

At the meeting, Hargrove had been extremely nervous. DJ had spent a lifetime observing people, he knew when someone was on the edge, and when their nerves were frayed. Hargrove had exhibited all the signs: trembling hands, an odd timbre to his voice, and worst of all, his repeated insistence that this was the most important case they'd ever worked on together. He had almost pleaded with DJ to complete it successfully. "It'll make or break us," he'd said over and over again. "It'll make or break us."

Hargrove had informed him that the treasure was the actual Ten Commandments . . . the very ones God had given to Moses on Mt. Sinai. Inwardly DJ was surprised that such an artifact existed, and had been found, but he didn't show it. He maintained cold objectivity. The briefing had taken place one week ago and, up to now, his instructions had been simple. Keep the archeologist under surveillance. Don't lose contact with him. Don't move in on him. Just observe and keep detailed records, until the President granted permission to confiscate the treasure.

Other than a demand that the case be resolved successfully, the only other requirement was that he keep the assignment strictly confidential. He would have every government resource and asset at his disposal, but no one must know what they were trying to locate, and eventually take.

DJ had taken it all in stride. He didn't let Hargrove's desperate behavior penetrate his thick reserve of confidence. He was a problem solver. Hargrove had a problem. He would solve it. That was his job. Selfishly, he was excited. It was sheer luck to have such an easy assignment so late in his career. This was a true plum. He'd retire after this one.

At the time of the briefing, DJ didn't know much about the Ark of the Covenant or the Ten Commandments. Hargrove had briefly explained why their discovery by an American citizen could have such an extreme negative affect on world politics and economy. It had all sounded terrible, but it was peripheral, outside the shell of DJ's assignment. Besides, he planned to be successful, so consequences of failure didn't matter.

In the days after the initial meeting with Hargrove, DJ had learned all he needed to know about the Bible, the Ten Commandments, and the Ark that held them. His knowledge was utilitarian, useful facts that would help engineer success. He'd learned its dimensions, which told him how big a vehicle he would need. He'd learned its weight, which told him how many men to have ready to carry it once he confiscated it.

Never in his career had DJ observed so much interest in a single man. And now, at the worst possible time, it looked as though McAlister had escaped. Later that very day Hargrove was briefing the President for the first time. Hargrove was not aware that McAlister might have escaped. It was too late to inform Hargrove; he would already be at the White House waiting to see the President. Even if DJ could get through to him, in his boss's current weak mental state, this type of news would demolish him. There was only one solution. If McAlister had, in fact, gotten away, DJ needed to find him immediately.

He called his team leader, who was in the surveillance van outside McAlister's house. "Anything yet, Scott?"

"Nothing, sir. It's been two hours, fifty minutes."

DJ knew exactly how long it had been. To the second.

He thought for a moment, then said, "Have you heard the scratching?" Early on in the assignment, the listening devices in the house had picked up odd scratching noises coming from the living room, even when McAlister wasn't home. One day, after McAlister had left the house, DJ had sent one of his agents into the house to find out what it was. The scratching was coming from a three-inch-long, jumbo scarab beetle that

McAlister had brought back from one of his Egyptian campaigns. Beetles were considered sacred in ancient Egypt. McAlister's was iridescent green, and he kept it in a large aquarium on the mantle above his fireplace.

DJ could hear Scott's muffled voice as he covered the phone and asked the technician listening to McAlister's house if he had heard the scratching noise. Scott came back on the line. He paused. "No, DJ. He hasn't heard any scratching at all."

"Damn it! Damn it, Scott. I don't like this. McAlister's out. I can feel it. I want you in there right now. Do you hear me? Right now!"

"There's no way he could've gotten out, sir. We've been here all . . . ."

"I said *now*, agent!"

"Yes, sir. But what do we do if he's home?"

DJ hated agents who couldn't improvise. "Go up to the door alone. Knock first. If he's home, tell him you're selling newspaper subscriptions or something and then leave. But if he doesn't answer I want you and your team in there immediately. I want the door down and all of you through every inch of that house. Search the whole place. Use the thermal imagers. He may be in there hiding. Got it?"

"Ten-four. Out."

DJ slammed the phone down and shook his head. "He'd better be there. Damn it, he'd better be there."

Of all the days to lose McAlister, this was the worst. It was simply unacceptable. Any minute Chief Hargrove would be briefing the President on the catastrophic danger of not confiscating the Ten Commandments *before* McAlister made their discovery public. Hargrove was going to describe the mission as a slam dunk. He was going to gloat about how they had already had McAlister under twenty-four hour surveillance. And why not? They had every government resource at their disposal. But now it looked like McAlister might have escaped the surveillance. DJ shook his head. Unacceptable.

He wadded up his paper coffee cup, threw it forcefully into the trash can, kicked the can across his hotel room and started for the door. He needed to get over to McAlister's house. What worried him most was that the beetle was gone. He knew from experience that people who are leaving, and not planning on coming back, always take their pets.

CHAPTER 2

Washington D.C. The Oval Office

FBI Director Hargrove sat in the Oval Office wishing the President would meet with him in more relaxed surroundings, like he did with the other advisors with whom he had weekly updates. Why does the President always keep it so formal with me? he wondered. He longed for the early days of his job, when he and the President were more friends than co-workers, when they shared a relaxed jocularity. But after Ruby Ridge, Waco, and the series of increasingly more devastating terrorist bomb-ings, their meetings had become more formal, and more difficult. During his weekly updates, they seemed to review the same crises over and over again. They were still focused like a laser beam on tracking terrorists around the world, still working on child porn and organized crime, but the low-hanging fruit was gone and progress had become slow, and methodical, and the President had become impatient.

Hargrove's area of responsibility was without a doubt the one that had suffered most during the President's term. At least the economic advisors, who met with the President in a less formal conference room, were able to get the Fed to lower interest rates, and push through tax cuts, and economic stimulus packages. Even when things were bleak, they normally left their meetings laughing, patting each other on the back, while he got to meet with the President alone, in the Oval Office.

Hargrove fidgeted with his pen, as he waited. This was not a regu-larly scheduled meeting but, rather a preliminary briefing on yet another potential crisis. Everyone on the President's staff had been asked to watch out for anything that could further destabilize the country's already fragile foreign relations. Issues that might adversely affect Israel, Palestine, or any Arab or Muslim State were of particular interest since the relationships were already strained to the breaking point.

Unfortunately, the issue that Hargrove needed to discuss with the President could impact both Israel and the Palestinians. The NSA had picked it up out of the blue, as part of routine surveillance, and Hargrove needed to move quickly. If it got too far along it could be disastrous not only for relations between the U.S., Israel and the Arabs, but also to the economy. In short, it could derail the four areas the President currently held sacred above all others; relations with Israel, relations with Muslim allies, the United States economy, and crime.

Finally, the door between the Oval Office and the briefing room next door opened and the President of the United States strode briskly in, only casting a cursory glance at Hargrove. Behind the President came the perpetually stoic Secretary of State, Dick Almond, and absentmindedly following Almond was Rashid Dahlan, advisor to the President on Arab affairs. Rashid walked slowly, obviously still thinking about the meeting from which they'd just emerged.

Secretary of State Almond took his usual chair in front of, and to the left, of the President's desk. He wore his trademark dark gray suit and red tie. He was bald but had thinning white hair on the sides of his head which he combed straight back. He looked pale, his skin papery.

In contrast, Rashid's suit was a ridiculous light gray pinstripe, unseen in the White House since the seventies. He had a dark complexion and wore the unshaven beard of his homeland. He wasn't much to look at, but he knew Arabic custom, culture, and political philosophy better than anyone else alive.

The President moved quickly behind his desk, sat down, and started to write on one of the documents he'd been carrying. He wore a dark gray suit with a light blue silk tie. His black shoes were the shiniest Hargrove had ever seen. Sweat dotted Hargrove's forehead and he felt his nervousness double. He hated himself for it. *He's just a man*, he told himself.

Without looking up, the President said, "Well, Hargrove, what's this emergency all about?"

Hargrove could tell the President was in no mood for idle chat. "Mr. President, there is something I wanted to bring to your attention without delay. An archeologist—an Egyptologist, to be exact—is getting very close to finding one of the most famous lost treasures of all time." He paused for dramatic effect, but the President continued to write.

After a few seconds, the President said, "Good. Something to celebrate for a change. Is that all? Is that why you needed to see me, Hargrove? To tell me about the success of a treasure hunting archeologist?"

Hargrove didn't like the inference he was wasting the President's time with little more than a news story, so he decided not to hold back. "There's more, sir. A lot more. The treasure that he's after, and that we believe he's close to finding, is the original Ten Commandments. The ones Moses received from God on Mt. Sinai."

The President paused. He looked up for the first time and put down his pen. He was a smart man and Hargrove could tell he was synthesizing the information, linking the past and present, digesting the implications.

"Tell me you're kidding."

"No, sir, I'm not. I wish I was. I don't need to tell you that the United States finding of a biblical icon that is tied to both the Jewish and Muslim religions, an icon that they would both claim ownership of, is the last thing we need right now, in fact, it . . . . "

"Wait!" The President interrupted. "What? What's that you said? Tied to the Arab world? I don't understand. I get the tie to Israel, Moses is the great Jewish prophet, his story—the first five chapters of the Bible, or the Pentateuch, is the Jewish Torah, but how are the Ten Commandments tied to Arabs, to Muslims?"

Hargrove continued. "Oh sir, Moses is not only . . . ."

Suddenly Rashid thrust a resolute index finger in the air. He spoke with the confidence that had evolved from advising people with little institutional, and no innate, knowledge of his subject of expertise. "Moses is one of the *great* prophets of Islam."

The President looked at Rashid, bewildered. "What? Muhammad is the prophet of Islam!"

"Allah rewarded Islam with many prophets. Moses was given the Law, the Ten Commandments; David was given the Psalms; Jesus was given the Gospel. Yes, Muhammad, revealer of the Qur'an, is the most revered prophet, but of the lesser prophets, gentlemen, Moses is the most important. Both Moses and Muhammad are direct descendants of Abraham's two sons, Isaac and Ishmael. They are inextricably linked. They're blood brothers. All Muslims know this."

Rashid had stolen Hargrove's thunder by delivering the news that Moses and Muhammad were linked. Hargrove said, "It's true, Mr. President. Unfortunately, here again, we have something that both Israel and Palestine, and therefore all Muslims, will lay claim to. If the Ten Commandments are found, both cultures will demand we hand them over."

The President looked at Rashid. "Is this true?"

"If you find the Commandments, and the revered Ark that holds them, the Arabs will lay claim, as will the Jews. They consider it their duty to strive for possession of all significant religious icons. Moses is the supreme figure in Israel, he is to the Jews what Jesus is to Christians. Moses is also a central Muslim prophet with direct links to Muhammad."

"Israel and Palestine have a long history of bloody fighting over religious objects and holy sites. As you all know, the most contentious battles have been over the hill in Jerusalem called Temple Mount by the Jews, and Haram al-Sharif by the Muslims. Both consider it an extremely holy location and time and time again it has caused peace negotiations to break down. Yes, Mr. Hargrove is correct. They will fight over this too. If an American finds it, both will demand that it be handed over to them. Of course there is only one Ark, only one set of Commandments."

Rashid reflected for a moment and then smiled. "Actually, they might view this as the perfect way to make the U.S. chose between Israel and

Palestine: between Jew and Muslim. A very dangerous situation, similar to playing against the fork move in chess. No matter what move you make, you lose."

The President grimaced. He couldn't afford to jeopardize relations with Israel, they were a key ally and gave the United States a reliable military presence in the incredibly volatile Middle East. Israel had been at war for much of the last fifty years with Palestine, a country that was 97 percent Muslim. The war had effectively pitted Israel against all Muslims. And, since the United States had always supported Israel, Muslims worldwide resented the United States. Because of that, the President needed to continue to walk the tightrope to maintain the limited support from Muslims that he currently had. It was the only way he'd be able to continue the campaign against terrorism without serious world-wide dissension. Choosing between the two was something that he couldn't do. No President had ever chosen between Israel and Palestine, between Muslim and Jew, and if at all possible, they never would. It could spark World War III.

"Then we just won't give it to either of them." Almond spoke up.

"Then both will be angry," said Rashid.

"Why do we have to announce this at all? For Christ's sake this is going to be more trouble than it's worth." The President looked at Hargrove.

"I have a plan, sir. I'd like to review it with you in a minute. But first I'd like to call your attention to two more potential risks. Both domestic."

"*More?*"

"Yes, two more. One could effect the economy, the other our crime rates. The one that could effect the economy is called the Jesus-Mary Effect. I'm sure you've heard of people who find these figures of Mary that cry or statues of Jesus that bleed? Or of the occasional images of Mary that mysteriously show up on buildings?"

The President nodded, he had heard of such things.

Hargrove continued, "People flock to these locations in droves. The media moves in and then there's a snowball effect. Before you know it, there are pilgrimages, tours, vendors hawking plastic crosses . . . you name it."

The President nodded again and Hargrove leaned forward. "I had someone on my staff look into this phenomenon, sir. A great deal of research has focused on the economies of the cities where these events occur. Studies show, overwhelmingly and conclusively, that overall spending in these cities drops by 20 to 30 percent. The economies tank. People stop buying durable goods and start buying candles and Bibles and rosaries. An economic disaster occurs every time one of these weird things show up. We already have serious economic concerns in this country. The last thing we need is for some guy to unearth the Ten Commandments, which have been missing for a few thousand years, and to have everybody in the country suddenly find religion and stop spending. Finding the Ten Commandments is big. Thousands of times bigger than a shadow on a wall that looks like Mary. Our economy could really be impacted, GDP growth could further deflate. We'd have an economic disaster on our hands. As you know, sir, it only takes a small percent decrease in growth for people to start screaming about the economy worsening, recession, and depression."

Hargrove paused. The President looked reflective. He leaned back in his chair and focused on the ceiling. "'It's easier for a rich man to fit through the eye of a needle than through the gates of heaven.' Or something like that. You're right. This could be a nightmare. It could erase everything we've implemented to get things going again. Religion and the economy don't mix. You said there was another concern?"

"Yes, sir. The other issue was brought to my attention by the biblical expert who advised me on this. It's a little known fact that the Ten Commandments, which we commonly accept today, are not the real Commandments."

"What kind of statement is that? Sure they are. I've been hearing the same Ten Commandments preached at me my whole life!" The President reached for the seldom-used Bible he kept in his desk drawer.

"I've got them right here, sir." Hargrove held up his briefing sheet. "These are the accepted Commandments." He read them aloud. "One: You shall have no other Gods before me. Two: You shall worship no idols or graven images. Three: You shall not take the Lord's name in vain. Four: You shall keep the Sabbath day holy. Five: honor thy father and mother. Six: You shall not murder. Seven: You shall not commit adultery. Eight: You shall not steal. Nine: You shall not bear false witness. Ten: Do not covet thy neighbor's house or wife."

When Hargrove had finished reading them, he rose from his chair and moved to the window. "But, Mr. President, these are not God's Commandments. Yes, they are ones Moses recited *verbally* in Exodus 20 all right, but . . . *Moses made a few of them up*. No one ever saw the original commandments because Moses broke them. After Moses broke the first set of tablets, God put His Commandments on a second set of stone tablets. The Commandments on the second set were the same as the ones on the first set. They are reviewed in Exodus 34. They are very *very* different from Moses' version, the Commandments I just read to you. This . . . discrepancy . . . is evidently one of the reasons Moses broke the initial set of tablets. He *had* to break them! They would have proven that he lied to his followers."

"You're saying Moses . . . lied?"

"I'm saying that when he came down off that mountain and saw his people worshiping golden idols, he was so mad and disgusted, he came up with some commandments that would put them on the straight and narrow again. Call it a lie, call it a fib, I don't know. All I do know is he didn't recite the same ten that God had written in stone. The bottom line is that Moses' version was more strict than God's. Wait until I tell you which four he added. They are more strict than anything else on the list."

The President said, "You know, all I can think about is how Charleton Heston broke the tablets in that movie where he played Moses. It never occurred to me that once they were broken, a second set would be made."

"Yes, sir, and the second set has never been found."

"So, what is the issue?"

"Sir, the real Commandments, God's version, do *not* include the following rules: You shall not kill. You shall not lie. You shall not steal. You shall not commit adultery." Hargrove paused, to let them sink in. "These Commandments are the cornerstone of our criminal justice system and the basis of our entire moral structure. Think of it. They are *not* included in the real Commandments. You can check for yourself in Exodus 34." He paused again and then repeated, "They are simply not included in God's version. It's pretty scary, when you think about it. The most stringent rules we have, the ones that govern our country and have historically kept our people from becoming uncivilized heathens, are null and void. Not real. If this archeologist, McAlister, is successful in finding them and the media gets a hold of this . . . they'll have a field day."

The President was speechless. He knew Hargrove well enough to know he'd done his research. He could be confident the information was accurate. He ran his fingers through his hair. The implications were clear. An escalation of the tension with Israel. A possible fatal blow to the fragile Arab alliance, the implications of which were too numerous to contemplate. Negative impact on the economy. As for the effect on crime; killing, stealing, lying, and committing adultery were fundamentally accepted as some of the worst crimes any American could commit. Staples of hard crime. Since the terrorist attacks the American people were already spooked. They were dangerously nervous. Everyone had been given a lesson in how fragile the system was. He'd heard briefing after briefing on how if consumer spending were to get any lower the country could enter an economic chasm the likes of which had not been seen since the Great Depression. *It could be the beginning of the end. How could this be? How in the world could this be? He'd been through so much. He wasn't sure he could deal with another big crisis.*

The other men sensed his panic. Almond, who knew him best, could see that he was nearing his breaking point. Could this be the straw? he wondered. He was ready to suggest a solution when the President looked up.

"Recommendations, gentlemen?"

Hargrove jumped in, "Sir, my best agent recently concluded a case. He's retiring soon, but he has time for one last assignment. He's already got the archeologist under surveillance. I recommend as soon as the archeologist locates the Commandments, we move in and grab them. Total surprise. No one gets hurt. No one knows it was us. In and out, and we've got the Commandments."

The President thought it over. He was looking up at the ceiling and without moving his head he looked at Almond and raised his eyebrows.

"If we ask him, would the archeologist just give them to us?" Almond asked Hargrove.

"Never. It's the find of a lifetime. For an archeologist, it's bigger than finding King Tut's tomb. It means he'd be rich and famous. A legend. We're asking the public to go on normally with their lives. To turn around and ask this man to give away the biggest archeological find of all time would not work. Plus, we have a profile on him. Apparently he's . . . stubborn."

Almond looked at the President, "Then it's simple. We take it from him. We take it, stash it away, and the whole issue is averted. We simply cannot allow anything to happen that would piss off the worldwide Muslim community even more. Hell, the people running those governments are itching for us to screw up so that they can pull back their support."

Silence.

Inwardly Hargrove prayed the President would approve his plan. This was an assignment he knew he could complete successfully. And he so desperately needed a success.

"What's his name? The archeologist?" The President asked.

"Thomas McAlister, sir."

"Poor bastard. We're going to take one of the greatest treasures ever known to mankind right out from under his nose. After we've got it, if he talks, even to the media, they'll think he's lost his marbles. Do it, Hargrove. Keep it tight. No leaks. I don't want to hear about it again until it's done."

Hargrove nodded, thanked the President, and quickly left the room.

Finally, a slam dunk. This was what he needed. A project with a beginning and an end. One that would give him something to hang his hat on, when some of the others went wrong—which they inevitably would. He smiled on the way back to his office. "McAlister, you'll never know what hit you."

CHAPTER 3

Special Agent DJ Warrant methodically wove through traffic on his way to the McAlister house. Not being present when the surveillance team broke in had been a rare mistake. It was minor, but he'd wanted his people inside McAlister's house as soon as possible, and he hadn't wanted them to wait for him to get there.

DJ was the FBI's number one field agent, but many high-level FBI employees were at a loss as to why. He had been extensively profiled— more than once and without his knowledge. They'd found that he had very few of the traits that the most successful agents typically possessed. Yet, he was the FBI's *most* successful.

But DJ's key success factors were difficult to measure and even when identified, did not fall within the standard definition of the superlative agent. He was disproportionately stubborn and dogged. He owed much of it to his father, who had been a bronco rider in a West Texas rodeo. DJ's father's often repeated motto, "Once you get on, don't ever let 'em buck you off," was exactly how DJ approached each case. True, there were other agents who were stubborn and had plenty of perseverance. The difference was that DJ applied these qualities to a greater degree than anyone else. He had long since separated from his family, and he had long since given up every hobby and bad habit that he'd ever had. As a result, his stubbornness and his ability to tirelessly pursue his prey knew no bounds. When most agents were heading home for dinner with their families, DJ was passionately beginning the second half of his day. This made him twice as productive as other agents.

He also had a unique ability to be his own profiler. Through experience, and a sort of osmosis, DJ was often able to understand the thoughts, and predict the actions, of his prey. He understood the criminal mind, its fears and motivations, and could save time by not bringing in professional profilers.

His best quality, however, was one he never, ever, talked about it. In fact, he rarely allowed himself to even think about it, for fear of jinxing himself and losing it. DJ was not clairvoyant, but once he understood all the aspects of a given case—the players, their backgrounds, their motivations, the crimes they'd committed, what time they woke up and went to sleep, what they ate, and wore—he often got "feelings" that would help him solve the case. He thought of these feelings as a high-grade intuition, but people at the Bureau called him "The Witch." They said he cast spells on criminals, causing them to fall into his hands. Yet it was these premonitions, combined with his stubbornness and his free-ranging ability to endlessly pursue his prey, that had given him the highest percentage of solved cases in the history of the agency.

He was sorry he'd missed busting into McAlister's house. The break-in would have been the only fun—the only spark—in what had been a boring last assignment. Surveillance in Phoenix. Hargrove had put him on this project for two reasons. The first was because he was retiring in three months and didn't have time for a long-term assignment. The second reason was as a thank you for the job he had done on his last case.

DJ was in the FBI's Special Projects group. They were given assignments that were either too confidential to run mainstream or that simply didn't fit under any other department. He'd just been given a commendation for breaking up a cult ensconced in a farm house in Western Kansas. They had four semi-automatic weapons per person and enough dynamite to fill the back of a pickup truck. The real problem was the kiddy-porn they'd been using to fund the purchase of all the guns and dynamite. He put all of that in the search warrant and one night, at 3 a.m., he and his team tore that farmhouse apart. He shook his head as he thought about it. A religious group selling kiddy-porn to buy weapons to kill people. It made him happy to be retiring soon.

At least it had been a challenging assignment! Moving on to this one had been like going from Vietnam to Disney World. But now things had changed. This assignment had become a real problem. If McAlister had gotten out of their surveillance net it meant that DJ had been outsmarted. It meant that McAlister had not only figured out that he was being watched, but that he was crafty enough to escape.

DJ dreaded having to tell Hargrove that the archeologist had escaped and that they might never find the treasure. But McAlister couldn't have gone far, and there was the slight chance that DJ could find him again before his next update to Hargrove. In a rote motion, he rubbed the handle of his gun, similar to the way a devout person might pray for divine intervention when faced with a crisis.

For the tenth time in an hour he tried to figure out how McAlister could've gotten through the curtain of surveillance that he and Scott, his surveillance team leader, had custom designed. Where had the weak point been? Finally, he said, "*Forget it!*".

"Forget what?" Elmo asked.

DJ had forgotten that Elmo was sitting next to him. Elmo was his case partner. They were polar opposites and worked together perfectly. Elmo was short, had pasty white skin and black oily hair. He wore black-framed glasses and always seemed to be wearing a light blue, short-sleeved polyester shirt. He was also beginning to go bald on both forehead and crown. His entire wardrobe looked like it had cost less than twenty dollars. But Elmo's defining feature, his emblem, was the Phillips 66 pocket protector that he'd gotten for free from the gas station where he gassed up his seldom used Honda Civic. Sometimes DJ chided Elmo about the pocket protector, but it never bothered Elmo. It had saved far, far too many shirts when one of the green, black, blue, or red felt-tip pens that he carried had broken open.

DJ took Elmo everywhere. He didn't like Elmo and he didn't dislike him. He didn't really even know him, despite having worked with him for ten years. He did, however, respect Elmo's special talents. Elmo was a computer geek and an information horse. He knew how to get at any piece of information available for the getting. Elmo understood the Internet, all the government data bases—both public and classified—all public records, and virtually any others. With a computer, a modem and ten minutes time, Elmo could tell you anything about anybody who had ever been put into a database. And these days, most everything and everyone was entered somewhere.

DJ worked on instinct; he hated computers. He had spent the first three-quarters of his career in a computer-free environment. Typewriters and carbon paper he knew; computers he did not. But DJ was smart, and he understood the value of computers and the information they could access. He marveled at the information Elmo could extract. And the speed! Information that would have taken a team of five men at least a week to gather ten years ago could now be on the screen in minutes. Elmo was great, and the government had supplied him with the fastest computer and modem available. Stuff that wasn't available to civilians yet. DJ always joked that his weapon was his Colt .45 and Elmo's was his laptop. They made a perfect team. DJ protected Elmo and kept him happy. Elmo remained DJ's loyal partner, providing him with the information he asked for, and needed, to solve his cases.

DJ remembered Elmo's question. "Forget nothing, Elmo. I was just thinking out loud."

DJ saw the sign for McAlister's street. He flicked on his blinker and slowed to make the right turn onto Nightingale. An Army green Land Rover Discovery was waiting at Nightingale, to make a left turn onto the street DJ was turning off of. When the driver of the Discovery saw that DJ was turning, he began pulling out and turning left. As DJ turned right, and the Discovery turned left, DJ was thinking about what he expected to find at the McAlister house. For a split second, he saw the silhouette of the driver of the Discovery through its tinted windows. Immediately, an inner bell sounded, deep within his subconscious.

DJ felt a tingling below his solar plexus. It was happening. The old, welcome feeling that meant a clue was not far away. Somewhere, lodged in the gray area between knowledge and intuition, a clue was developing. If he could only figure out what it was! What had triggered it? From experience, DJ knew he needed to playback mentally the preceding two minutes. But he had to hurry, this one was fading fast, leaving him. He needed to grasp it soon. Come on, DJ, just play it back. He slowed the car. Elmo looked over at him, but remained silent; he knew what was going on.

DJ replayed everything, quickly, like Elmo's computer, but his mind was even more agile, faster. He'd been driving, thinking about the house ahead. He'd turned on his blinker, hit the brake, and seen the Land Rover. He remembered thinking the Discovery was good in foul weather and that he liked the Army green color. Then, briefly, he'd seen the silhouette. The profile of a man through tinted windows. The driver's profile. Hmmm. What about it? *Could it possibly have been . . . ?* DJ peered into the rearview mirror. The Discovery was gone. Without warning Elmo, he immediately whipped into the nearest driveway and jerked the car to a stop.

He had it now. The profile of the driver of the Discovery reminded him of the archeologist! No. Impossible. Driving down his own street in the middle of the day? Right past the surveillance van? Come on, he told himself, get to the house and look for clues. Don't waste time with your little mental games.

Despite already being late to the scene, DJ knew himself too well. He would never change. He had to follow the man in that Discovery, until he was sure it either was or was not Thomas McAlister. He rolled his eyes at himself as he shoved the car into reverse.

Elmo also knew what was happening. In his ten years with DJ, he had seen him do a great many unpredictable things. Things that Elmo would never have thought of doing. He had seen DJ link seemingly unrelated information, synthesize it, and use it to solve unsolvable mysteries. DJ sometimes had "feelings" about things, and Elmo could tell he'd had one of his feelings about the SUV they'd just passed. For DJ, solving crimes was an art but for Elmo, it was a science. Together, they had solved more crimes than any other team in the history of the Bureau. It was a record they took pride in, though they never discussed it.

DJ pulled out of the driveway and sped back to the stop sign. "Pull up a picture of the archeologist!"

Elmo began typing, accessing the case files that he'd downloaded to his laptop computer.

DJ wanted to get to the McAlister house and this was probably going to be a huge waste of time, but he had to do it. Christ, he thought, I wasn't even *looking* at the guy behind the wheel of that car. What the hell am I doing following him? Wasting time. I'm two blocks from the goddamn house! DJ knew that ninety-nine times out of a hundred these hunches led nowhere, but he lived with the memory, of the ecstatic feeling he got, when, one time in a hundred, they solved cases. He always followed them and Elmo never doubted him.

He could see the Discovery about a mile up the road. He floored the Taurus and was a car behind the Discovery in seconds. Elmo turned his laptop toward DJ. It showed both a head shot and a profile of Thomas McAlister, taken at an annual anthropological meeting of Egyptian specialists. He was at a podium, giving a speech on early Egyptian architecture. It showed a youngish face, sun-bleached blond hair, and blue eyes alive and excited with the thought that an ancient Egyptian civilization might have shared architectural concepts with other early cultures.

DJ looked at the picture. He needed to see the driver again. The Discovery pulled into the parking lot of a drugstore. DJ pulled into the lot, but kept his distance. The man got out and walked into the drugstore. DJ didn't see his face. After ten minutes of waiting, DJ called the McAlister house and told his team to sit tight, he'd be there soon.

The man came out of the drugstore with two heavy-looking plastic bags. At forty yards, DJ was almost positive it was McAlister. But what the hell was the man doing driving down his own street in the middle of the day? Especially if he was trying to escape from under their surveillance? Moreover, how the hell did he get out from under their blanket of surveillance? DJ had put his best team on McAlister. He followed the Discovery back down the same road, four miles past Nightingale, to a five-star resort called the Camelback Inn. DJ followed McAlister down a narrow winding asphalt paths, until McAlister pulled into the driveway of a detached cabana. Cabana Nine. McAlister got out and went inside.

DJ was furious with the surveillance team, but euphoric at his luck. He drove past Cabana Nine and left Elmo in the car while he walked to the front desk. He showed his FBI badge, and asked who was staying in Cabana Nine.

"That would be Miss Havenport, sir."

"Do you know the man staying with her?"

"We don't inquire, sir."

"She paid cash?"

"She hasn't paid yet, sir. She'll pay when she checks out."

"And when is Miss Havenport scheduled to check out?"

"Tomorrow morning, sir."

"Thanks." DJ smiled as he walked out. He had the bastard. Smart guy, this archeologist. But he had him! Now that McAlister thought he was safe, his guard would be down. His mistake would make it even easier for DJ to move in and steal the treasure. It almost assured him of a successful final case before retiring, and because of its importance, and its ties to the White House, it probably meant a high-level commendation as well. Things couldn't have worked out better.

CHAPTER **4**

The leader of the on-site surveillance team, Scott Caffrey, watched from inside the house as two men got out of the Ford Taurus and began walking to the front door. He knew them both well. DJ, with his white-gray hair and knowing eyes, wore a silver Rolex on his left wrist that accentuated his rough, deeply tanned skin. Scott could see the Colt .45 automatic that he wore on his belt. And Scott could tell by the pinched look on DJ's face and his brisk pace that he was not happy.

Close behind, taking hurried steps, was Elmo. Short and thin with greasy hair and Woody Allen glasses, Elmo carried a small black case. His black hair was parted on the side and his clothes were simple. Scott already knew that Elmo wouldn't say a word to anyone the entire time he was in the house. The other commandos had already learned to ignore him. They knew he would come in a nervous wreck and wouldn't relax until he had his computer plugged into an electrical outlet and his modem into a phone line.

DJ came in and sat on one of the large leather chairs in the living room. He could tell that McAlister was gone by the way the men were scurrying around the house. The team was already looking for clues as to how he got out and where he may have gone: maps, scraps of paper with phone numbers, creases in phone books, etc. There would be hundreds of things to check.

DJ let out a deep breath. He examined his fingers, pursed his lips, and shook his head. He closed his eyes, rested his head against the back of the chair, and said, "Scott, give me the report. Here's the order I want it in: estimate of when he left, how he got out, and clues as to where he's headed. Go." DJ kept his eyes closed as he listened.

"We still don't know when he got out, sir. We're checking everything, current water temperature at all the faucets, temperature of the mattress springs, humidity levels in the bedroom and bathroom, trash bins, everything. Nothing yet. He definitely went out one of the basement windows. It's open, the screen is off and he didn't bother to close it behind him. As for where he's headed? No clue yet. At this point that's all . . . ."

DJ opened his eyes, leveled an obsidian stare, and held up his hand, stopping Scott cold. He said, "Scott, the open window, it's in back right?"

"Yes, sir."

"Here's what happened. McAlister went out the back basement window very early this morning, while it was raining. Your man in back didn't pick him up because looking through night vision binoculars when the rain is warm is like shining a flashlight on a green blanket in the dark. If McAlister crawled slowly he would've been impossible to see. Have someone look around the yard, we should be able to find out which direction he went."

Scott yelled to one of his team to begin looking for clues starting outside the basement window and working out towards the perimeter.

"The motion detectors didn't work, because he was moving so slowly. I should've put in perimeter weight sensors, Scott," DJ said. "I won't make that mistake again, and neither will you."

He walked over to the aquarium. Scott followed him. It was empty. DJ wanted to lift it up and slam it down onto the floor, but instead he took a deep breath. White anger rose within him, but he pushed it back down. He'd give Scott one more chance.

He lowered his voice and whispered tersely, "Scott, I couldn't be more displeased about the sloppiness of your operation. Your team let McAlister slip away. This will go into your file. Now listen to me, and listen good. McAlister is over at the Camelback, in Cabana Nine, registered under the name of Havenport. Get a full surveillance team over there by five o'clock. He's checking out tomorrow. This is your last chance."

Scott was dumfounded. He had heard DJ was good, but this was beyond good. The information DJ had was eerie, almost as if the man were some kind of seer. His crack team of experts had had the McAlister house under full surveillance, video and sound and motion, using the most modern equipment, for an entire week, and by all accounts, Thomas McAlister had not left this house today.

"You sure, Chief? I mean, how could you know that? You weren't even here with us last night."

"Scott, I don't think you're in a position to question me. Be goddamn careful with McAlister. He's slipped by us once. We cannot afford to let it happen again."

"Yes, sir."

DJ started to walk out of the room. He wanted to check McAlister's closet to see what kind of clothes he'd left behind. Before he left the room he turned and said, "Oh, and by the way, that man you have checking outside."

"Yes, sir?"

"Have him check the sewer cover in the corner of the back yard. All the houses around here have them. I'll bet you a six-pack McAlister pried it off and crawled away through the sewer." DJ turned and walked out. Scott would later find that DJ was right about that too.

CHAPTER 5

Thomas McAlister drove by his house, saw the smashed front door, and knew that the people watching him, the ones in the white van, had broken in. He was taking the chance of driving by in broad daylight because it was important for him to know who was watching him. He'd hoped to see men in blue jackets with oversized yellow letters on the back that said FBI, forensic workers in orange suits, or possibly even a competing archeologist. Instead he only saw one man in plain clothes, on the side of the house, bent over examining something on the ground.

Somehow, someone had learned he was close to discovering an archeological treasure of monumental importance. He hoped they didn't know what it was. They must have some idea of its value, though, or they wouldn't have set up such an elaborate and costly surveillance effort. It hadn't taken long for him to realize someone was following him, bugging his home and office, and monitoring his mail and e-mail. All this effort, and he didn't even have the treasure in his possession yet. But he would . . . soon.

Regardless of who was doing the spying, the most important thing was that he'd finally gotten out from under the surveillance. He never would have driven down Nightingale in the middle of the day, but the Discovery he was driving wasn't his, and it had tinted windows. That's how suspicious and nervous he'd become over the past few weeks. But now, after successfully escaping, he was free to go after the treasure without being followed.

His discovery would send a disabling shock through both the religious and economic worlds. He had tried his best to keep it totally secret but, already, someone was following him, trying to determine what it was, and more importantly, where it was.

Thomas couldn't help smiling. *His escape had worked!* He was free to slip back down to Mexico to dig up his unimaginable treasure, confident that it would not be stolen from him the minute he brought it up out of its three-thousand year old hiding place.

Rather than turning right off Nightingale to return to the Camelback Inn, Thomas decided to make a left, to stop at a nearby drugstore. He needed bottled water and food for the long drive to Mexico. As he waited at the intersection, a blue Taurus approached from the left. It signaled to turn onto his street, so he made his left hand turn. At the drugstore, he picked up eight bottles of water and a case of Snickers bars, a favorite of many archeologists. The peanuts provided quick protein, and the chocolate both sugar and caffeine for energy.

After returning to the Inn, Thomas immediately turned on the weather channel. Although he wanted, and needed, a quick nap, he pulled out his duffel bag and began repacking.

He'd arrived last night, after crawling through a basement window into his backyard while it was raining. Slowly, so as not to set off any motion detectors, he had inched his way on his stomach around the periphery of his yard to a manhole cover in the back corner. After three minutes with a crowbar, he had lowered himself into the sickening wetness of the sewer and crawled north, to the end of the block, where he had been picked up by his accomplice. They had returned to the Camelback, where he already had personal belongings smuggled out of his house days earlier, in his briefcase.

Suddenly, Thomas froze. *Had that been a noise in the other room?* Was someone trying the door knob? Quickly, he grabbed the small .32 Beretta from his dop-kit and cautiously peered around the doorway of the bathroom. Someone *was* trying to enter. He couldn't believe the events of the last seven weeks had led to this. Only one day before leaving to unearth one of the greatest treasures known to man, he was standing in a hotel bathroom in Phoenix, a few miles from his house, with a gun drawn, round chambered, ready to shoot whoever was coming through the door.

Seven Weeks Earlier

The call from Dean Washington's secretary, Carol, came on a perfect, 85° F afternoon in May. Coincidentally, Thomas had recently reminded himself how well things had been going lately. Though not a superstitious man, he'd knocked on wood after having the thought. It wouldn't help.

Thomas was being summoned to the dean's office. The dean of faculty, not the dean of students. For a professor, a summons to the dean's office could be just as bad, if not worse, as receiving one as a student. Thomas's mood changed instantly. The day took on an entirely different feel. The sun was still shining but the tint had changed, it seemed darker, as if the tone were one octave lower. He was pretty sure he knew what the dean wanted to talk about, and it wasn't going to be career enhancing.

Dean Washington had hired Thomas six years ago. Thomas had been a first-round draft choice, with a sterling pedigree—an undergraduate degree from Harvard, Magna Cum Laude; a Ph.D. from Harvard; and two years working in Egypt as an associate under Karl Johnson, where he had led the team that found the tomb of Amenophis III.

What was rare, and impressive the Dean most, about Thomas was his extensive fieldwork in Egypt. Although Thomas had not led the expedition, he had led the sub-team that had actually "discovered" the tomb of Amenophis. He did it by developing a technique that injected ultrasonic waves into the ground to locate air pockets beneath the earth's surface. One of the pockets turned out to be the tomb. Johnson was so happy with his young assistant that he had urged him to stay on for the first round of excavations, which took a year and a half. That, coupled with his excellent educational background, made him an attractive recruit for all the top schools. Most students had one or the other: an education but no significant field work or reams of field work but a less than savory transcript.

Armed with both, Thomas had shunned lucrative offers of a professorship from Harvard, Stanford, Yale, and other top universities. All of those schools were already leaders in the field of archeology. Instead, he had chosen Arizona State because, although it had a good archeological department, he felt that with a strong, innovative department head, it could quickly become one of the best. The Harvard of the twenty-first century. Currently, Arizona's department lacked vision and leadership. He could provide both. He could lead the department to fame. It would be the Harvard of the West.

Dean Washington had been refreshed by Thomas's attitude. He marveled at his qualifications and had hired him as the clear successor to Professor Brown, current Dean of Archeology, who was scheduled to retire in a year. The stage was set for Thomas to build his own archeology department—his legacy. He would renew the focus on primary research with well-funded expeditions. He'd add important curricula and hire top professors. He'd set up new fund-raising, and build a new state-of-the-art archeological library that would rival Harvard's Tozzler. The old, undersized archeological building would be renovated, to provide the new professors with enticing offices. The plan was set. But then something unexpected had happened.

In the winter of Thomas's first year at Arizona, Professor Brown's wife had fallen and broken her hip. During her recovery in the hospital, she had contracted pneumonia and, four weeks later, she had died. The entire staff had mourned her death and, when spring came, Professor Brown had made an announcement. He would not retire. He had sold the retirement home that he and his wife had planned to use and was determined to stay. Thomas's promotion would have to wait.

One year turned into two, two into three. Brown didn't want to reform the department. He had made it what it was. And Brown had, in fact, built a strong department. In other circumstances, Thomas and Brown would have been much closer, but whenever they were alone, there was a tension between them. The ruling lion, cognizant of his young challenger, unwilling to secede.

Thomas still argued for his ideas, but Brown and his contingent of old guard professors always shot him down. While he waited, Thomas tried to push the department in other ways. He invited interesting guest speakers from other schools. He chaired departmental fund-raisers geared towards expanding the department. And, whenever possible, he tried to introduce new ideas and new ways of thinking about archeology. It was exactly that—the introduction of a new idea—that had resulted in the dean requesting a meeting with him. But this wasn't the first time.

A year ago, Thomas had invited an amateur "pop" archeologist, named Grady Dillinger, to speak at the university. Not fully adhering to the university's bureaucratic guidelines, he had arranged for the hall and scheduled the visit himself. When the Board of the University found out about it, they tried to cancel the appearance. But Dillinger had already been paid half his fee and, under the contract, the university would be liable for a huge penalty if the lecture weren't allowed to take place.

Grady Dillinger believed an ancient *un*recorded culture that existed eight to ten thousand years ago had profound influence on the earliest cultures in "recorded" history (such as the Sumarians, the Egyptians, and the Olmec of Mexico). He argued that these seafaring people were incredibly adept at mathematics and astronomy and that their original homeland was either destroyed or was currently lying under water, due to a cataclysmic earthly event. Somewhat like the theory of the Lost City of Atlantis.

Thomas had always found this theory interesting and, if nothing else, excellent food for thought. Scientific archeologists hated the theory, because it couldn't be proved. But thinking archeologists—what Thomas called romantic archeologists—loved the idea. More importantly, this was exactly the type of unencumbered thinking Thomas wanted his students exposed to. Thomas was always willing to listen to new ideas. It kept his job interesting, his mind sharp, and his knowledge of current events in his field unsurpassed. Unfortunately, Professor Brown and the Board at the university favored the scientific point of view. *If you can't prove it, we won't teach it.*

Dillinger's lecture had been the best attended historical lecture ever given at the university. The audience had so many questions that Dillinger had to stay an hour after the allotted time for the question and answer session. The university Board had been furious. They considered this type of historical "rabble rousing" dangerous, and they focused their anger on Thomas. Washington had given him an official demerit in his record. Thomas had appealed the action, but could do nothing. Such things were not contestable.

When Dean Washington's secretary phoned, and said the dean wanted to see him as soon as possible, Thomas was pretty sure he knew why, but he had no idea of the profound impact the meeting would have on his life. Since he didn't have morning classes on Thursday, he made plans to meet with the dean at nine o'clock sharp.

The door to the dean's office opened at one end of a large rectangular room. Mahogany bookcases ran the length of both walls. The absurdly high ceiling was grounded by plush hunter green carpet. Dark cherry furniture twinkled in the morning sunlight that flooded through the crescent-shaped window behind Washington's desk.

The secretary announced his presence. "Professor McAlister to see you, sir." She backed out, quickly shutting the door behind her.

Thomas strode across the office to the desk, his eyes on the dean, who stood staring out the window at the students below. Thomas waited for the him to turn around. When he did, his face was stern, and Thomas knew what kind of meeting it was going to be.

"Morning, Thomas." The dean motioned to the chair in front of his desk that Thomas always sat in . . . a very old Chippendale, with a pink silk cushion.

"Good morning, Francis."

"How are you?

"OK, thanks. You want to have this talk over a cup of coffee?"

"Not this morning, Thomas." That's when Thomas knew he was in more trouble than usual.

"Thomas, this isn't easy for me. Do you recognize this?" He held up an article that Thomas had recently handed out to his students entitled, "Similarities across Antediluvian Cultures—Math to Mythology."

"Of course I recognize it, Francis. I handed it out in my 400-level Egypt class."

Washington said, "Thomas, what is the policy on new material at Arizona State?"

"This is an article from an academic magazine, Francis. I have the necessary copyright disclaimer on it."

"This isn't about copyright, Thomas! *What is the policy on new material?*"

In a rote, unenthusiastic voice, Thomas recited, "It has to be reviewed and then voted on by the Curriculum Review Board in order to be entered into the official university teaching material archive."

"Right! So what the hell are you doing handing this out to your students?"

"Francis, that is an article published two weeks ago. I saw it, I obtained permission to copy it, and I handed it out. It's new . . . it's fresh. The kids love it. The goddamn Curriculum Review Board only meets *once a quarter*! I needed this *now*!"

"Once a quarter is good enough for all the other professors, Thomas."

"This is the information age. We need to be able to disseminate information quickly. Real time. I know of other professors who don't like waiting a quarter, who don't like letting good educational material rot on the vine!"

"Wait, wait, *wait*! Let's not get off track here. You know our policy, Thomas, and until it changes, it's *still* our policy. *Everything has to be approved.* Did you not go through the process with this because you knew it *wouldn't* be approved?"

"I got that article out of *The Journal* two weeks ago. The Curriculum Review Board is not due to meet again for two and a half *months!* My class will be over by then. I've got a great group of kids this term. I wanted them to see the damn article!"

"Why not simply tell them where to find it in the Library?"

"Come on, Francis, you used to teach. I wanted them *all* to see it. Not just the one or two brown-nosers that would actually trudge over to the library to read it."

Dean Washington lowered his voice. "Look, Thomas, this isn't the first time. You were warned over the Dillinger incident, and then again three months ago when you showed that ridiculous video about where the lost city of Atlantis might be. That makes this your third infraction. The third time, it goes to the council."

Thomas rolled his eyes. "Okay, when does the Disciplinary Council meet? I'll go explain it to them myself."

Washington hesitated, took a deep breath and exhaled slowly. In a voice of consolation he said, "This thing just isn't working out."

Thomas started to reply and then stopped. The words echoed in his head. "What do you mean 'this thing?' You mean *me*? What do you mean, this *thing*, Francis?"

Washington sighed again. "The Disciplinary Council had an emergency meeting last night. They voted to suspend you indefinitely. They just . . . they're just tired of the *constant battle*. You're suspended immediately, under Article 252, of the School Board Provision: failure to get all classroom materials approved by the Curriculum Review Board, prior to distribution to the student body."

"The constant battle? *The constant battle*? You mean the constant battle to *teach*? To get kids interested and to get them to *learn*?" Thomas had risen from his chair to stand over the Dean's desk.

"Call it what you want. Every professor here knows that if you break the rules three times in a row, you can be voted out. You've had fair warning, Thomas." Washington shuffled papers on his desk.

Thomas fell back into his chair, flabbergasted at the extent the Council would go to uphold such a ridiculous rule. "Francis, come on. You know if I'm suspended indefinitely I'm as good as fired. Hell, I am fired. That goes in my permanent record. Why not ask me to resign?"

"They want to make a point with you. They don't think what you're doing is right. You're breaking rules. They think a lesson early in your career will do you good in your next job. You cannot go on breaking rules."

"These are rules that are meant to be broken! What I'm doing separates great universities from mediocre ones!"

Washington leaned forward, meeting Thomas's glare. "Look, Thomas, things weren't working out for you here anyway. When Brown delayed his retirement, that was only the beginning. We're small here. Not used to bigger ideas. I think you'd be happier somewhere else."

And that was when Thomas knew it was over. Washington had brought him in, believed in him, backed him. Washington had been his ally, but no longer. They'd gotten to him. Washington had become one of them.

Thomas stood, slightly dazed, and then turned and started to leave. He wanted to get out before he did something he'd later regret. He wouldn't fully understand the impact of this crushing blow for days, but he understood enough for now.

When he was halfway to the door, he turned. "You sold me out, Francis. You let them railroad me. Didn't you? You son of a bitch."

"I'm in trouble, too, Thomas. I let this happen. Some say I let it go too far . . . that I should've had a better handle on what was being distributed to my student body."

"It was a historical article related to archeology, Francis! Not *The Communist Manifesto*!"

"The *Communist Manifesto* is *approved* reading, Thomas."

"God help you all." Thomas muttered as he slammed the door to the Dean's office.

His eyes welled with tears as he walked down the stairs of the administration building to his car. His dream was over. It would never be. He got into his car and started to drive. It was ten o'clock in the morning. An hour later, he was on a dirt road a mile from Highway 89, just south of Florence, with no recollection of how he'd gotten there.

He pulled over and put his head on the steering wheel. Archeology was his life. Teaching had been his passion; his dream, to become head of the department. Because of his driving ambition, he'd put everything else on hold. Now the Board was going to teach him a lesson? It was like living in a nightmare where everything was reversed, where those who tried the hardest, and cared the most, were punished. He was more dedicated, more passionate about teaching students, about expanding their minds, than any member of the Board. And what had it gotten him? Fired.

Thomas felt shattered. His life, its structure, what psychologists would call his "world view," was toppled. Every decision he had made in the last six years had been filtered by the knowledge that someday soon, he'd be head of the archeology department. But now everything had changed. He was a different person entirely, yet still surrounded by things he'd purchased as part of his old life. He was living in a stranger's world. A silent tear careened off the steering wheel, then made a dark circle that widened as it spread on his pant leg.

CHAPTER 6

When Thomas was treasure hunting as a boy, he had always felt that whatever he was looking for was just under the next rock or only one more scoop of dirt away. He had loved the thrill and the excitement of the chase, and he still did. "Never give up," had been his slogan, and it still was. Keep searching. Never give up. The treasure will be there, just as it was left thousands of years ago. The adrenaline rush of always being on the verge of finding a treasure had always been with him . . . even in his day-to-day life.

This perpetual excitement, this eternal optimism, pervaded everything he did. People sometimes wondered why he was always in a good mood, always ready with a kind word. Occasionally, he wondered if he were too nice. Too happy. But he always shrugged off that notion. No such thing. It was his nature. He'd found what he was passionate about at a young age. Archeology.

An archeologist has two career options. Really only one, but the romantic side of Thomas, and the adventurous side, liked to believe there were two. The first, and more conservative of the two, was to teach. That was what 99 percent of all archeologists did. They taught, wrote and did field work during summer breaks or on a sabbatical. That was the road Thomas had chosen. He had decided to teach and his legacy would be the fine department he would build at Arizona State. He would be Head of the Department, possibly become Dean of Faculty, then retire and spend winters in Egypt, exploring and writing. His course was set.

To that end, Thomas had spent the first six years of his career, the critical building years, working towards that goal. Investing in it. He could have been out in the field searching for treasure, looking for undiscovered tombs of Egyptian pharaohs, but he hadn't done it that way. He had chosen to contribute to what he thought was a greater good.

Now that dream was gone. With this suspension on his record, he would never chair a department. He couldn't go out and demand a job at a Harvard or Yale or Stanford, like before. He'd be lucky to get a regular teaching job at an average school.

The second, more romantic pursuit for an archeologist, was fieldwork, but field work was expensive. The 1 percent of all archeologists who dedicated 100 percent of their time to fieldwork were either independently wealthy or so well-known from their university work that they could gather the financial support necessary to sustain a long series of field projects. It was that kind of notoriety that Thomas had hoped to build, so that someday he would be able to lead fully funded expeditions. Now . . . this option was also closed to him. With the death of both his dreams—the only two things he had ever been passionate about—he fell into a deep depression.

He tried not to ask himself how much of this he had brought on himself. Yes, others were to blame too, but his own actions demanded scrutiny. Hadn't he relished being the young maverick? When Brown decided not to retire, hadn't he played the renegade, pushing the administration, the faculty, and the students? Had he tried *too* hard to show them all how good a university could be, if only they all would try as hard as he did? Hadn't that invited jealously? Antagonism?

Wallowing in his self-made stew of perfectionist's self-pity, he came to realize that regardless of what happened in the future, his life would never, *ever*, be as he had planned. Or hoped. This realization was unlike any he'd experienced before. And at an adult level, he felt an innocence slip away, to be replaced by a feeling that it was too early to accurately identify, but that felt a hell of a lot like cynicism.

The next day, he was in his basement, listening to the best version of "Stormy Monday" that he owned, the one by Muddy Waters, drinking Boodles Gin at one o'clock in the afternoon, when the phone rang. Since he'd quit working, it had rung a lot. People were calling to find out what had happened and to see how he was holding up.

A half-full highball glass in his left hand, Thomas would never have answered the phone if he still had one of the Marlboro cigarettes he'd been smoking in his right, but he'd just put it out. His brain told him to reach for the lighter but his hand reached for the portable phone and he picked it up and hit TALK before his brain could exert control over his motor functions.

He glared at the red light on the phone. What a sick little social norm. Ring a bell and sit and wait for someone to answer you. "Hello?"

"Thomas McAlister, please." It was a man.

Thomas put the phone down and took his time lighting a Marlboro Light. He never smoked and he'd bought the Lights because they were longer. It took him a long time to light it. Finally, he picked up the phone again and said, "Hello?"

"Thomas? Is that you?"

Thomas rolled his eyes. Who the fuck else would it be, he thought. "Yeah."

"Thomas, it's Gene. Gene Smith. How are you?"

Thomas had gone to graduate school with Gene. Now, he was a professor at Dartmouth. They had kept in touch over the years, each calling the other for an occasional favor. Gene was always interested in research. He loved libraries, and was always finding old forgotten books and manuscripts. He had recently found some forgotten Egyptian papyrus in the Belgium National Museum in Brussels. Thomas took a sip of his drink, remembering what Gene's face looked like. He had always liked Gene. He decided not to hang up on him.

"Washington fired me, Gene."

"*What*? You're all they had going over there! Shit, Thomas, you're one of the ten best archeologists alive!"

"Well, you can tell it to Washington, but it still won't pay the bills . They fired me for teaching the Atlantis Theory."

"Those close minded SOBs! I'm going to send the whole goddamn

Board of Directors a copy of *Inherit the Wind.*"

Thomas smiled. He'd forgotten about that. He decided to rent *Inherit the Wind* soon. His life story. "I didn't even get a trial."

"Well, if you want a referral at Dart, let me know. Foster, the Dean over here, is good. Not progressive, but fair."

"Thanks. I'll pass for now, but thanks. What's up, you old pedantophile?"

"Do you still have that rare version of the *Amenophis Builders Notes* that you used to keep for the Library of Cairo? The one with the complete Book III?"

Thomas smiled and looked over at his bookcase. There, in a climate-controlled case, lay the *Amenophis Builders Notes*. One of only three in existence. Thomas's version was the only one with a complete Volume II, Book III. Technically, it was the property of the Egyptian government but, since he had uncovered it in Room Four of the Amenophis III tomb, he was entrusted with it, with the caveat that he make it available to other researchers. It was worth three-quarters of a million dollars, maybe a million at the right auction. *More than enough to fund a yearlong expedition in the Valley of the Kings.*

"Yes, I've got it right here, Geno. What do you need?"

"Well, I've got a translation here—Morgan's first edition—but in the middle of Volume II, Book III, Morgan skips five pages. Skips them cold. He notes it with an asterisk, saying that these pages were unreadable at the source. But his translation is off of Carter's version, not yours. I was wondering, old buddy old pal, if you could copy those pages for me and fax them over. What do you say?"

Thomas smiled. This was exactly why he liked Gene. Ever the sleuth.

"Sure, I'll fax them to you. I don't have a copier here, though. I'll have to take it over to the university." He caught himself and a wave of dread poured over him. "I mean, I'll take it to Kinko's."

"Thanks, Thomas. It's Volume II, Book III, pages four through nine. Front and back. I really appreciate it. It's for a class I'm putting together on Egyptian building techniques."

"No problem. I'll do it tomorrow. Is that all right, time wise?"

"Sure, that's perfect, no rush. Hey, you ever read that thing cover to cover? The *Builders Notes*?"

"You know, Gene, I never have. But, if I don't rent *Inherit the Wind*, I just might do it tonight. It's still early here."

Gene gave Thomas his fax number and apologized again about the job, reminding Thomas to call if he wanted a referral, and they hung up.

He liked old Gene the Pedantophile. Tomorrow he'd like Gene a whole lot more.

CHAPTER 7

Gene had made him feel slightly guilty for being entrusted with such an important document and not having taken the time to read it: history of the building of the tomb of Amenophis III, combined with notes on the restoration of temples at the Necropolis of Saqqara. Thomas had read about half of it. Like the notes on the building of any large structure, it was tedious and, after a while, repetitive.

An Egyptologist could not possibly read every document written by the ancients. Most of them were records of economic transactions. The *Amenophis Notes* would be interesting to a student doing a dissertation on the detailed construction of an Egyptian tomb, or to someone wanting to learn about ancient restoration projects, but not to a seasoned Egyptologist. That would be like a World War II expert reading not only the plans for the buildings that Hitler's architect Albert Speer built, but actually reading the construction notes taken as the building went up. Too much detail.

But Thomas was drunk, too drunk to drive to the video store to rent a movie. So he started to read the *Builders Notes*. There were two volumes, each containing three ten-page books. He had read Volume I years ago, so he started with Volume II.

The notes were written in hieroglyphics, and although Thomas was fluent, it was slow going. Especially when drunk. To make matters worse, Thomas continued to drink as he read. He was into Book Two when he finished the gin and discovered he was low on cigarettes. Instead of going out for replenishments he kept reading. His eyes became heavy, yet he plodded on. It was 4:00 a.m. when he turned from the second book to the third. In a mental fog, he was having trouble interpreting the symbols. The normal process of understanding each symbol, sentence, paragraph, and page became laborious. He read on, however, determined to finish.

There were times when he thought he might be asleep, but the reading had become more vivid and then, suddenly, it was in the first person. Someone was writing about strange visitors, guarded treasures, and time spent—days spent—by a stranger with a long silver beard in the old temple at Saqqara. But soon Thomas got lost, had trouble following a line, trouble defining basic words. He wondered why the Notes had changed so much. Why they'd gone from basic restoration description to the story of a man with a long silver beard, who traveled with guarded treasure, and then on to a story about a fair-haired maiden, so beautiful, so vulnerable, yet so full of veiled deceit, and he could see the veil but he couldn't see through it, no matter how hard he tried, until finally she became the incredible, perfect-woman in Turgenev's *Torrents of Spring*. The girl who opens her window to the street, to her young lover, bosom exposed, sweet wind blowing beautifully through her immaculate hair, and Thomas ran to her, and she embraced him with all her might, pulling him close, against her bosom, in a move that was all at once so taboo, innocent and sensual that for the first time since his firing Thomas became happy, truly happy. But, then, the footsteps behind him, always the inevitable footsteps. And there was Sir Thomas Moore. Approaching. Not with his rose, the famous last rose of summer, but rather a gun. And Thomas remembered that every season ends, and all roses die, and he remembered the lines to Moore's incredibly sad poem about the rose, lying senseless and dead, soon to be followed, by friendship, love, gems, hearts, and all fond ones that have flown, and then amazingly, shockingly, there in the Notes, Moore asks, in all his crotchety genius, how the hell could anyone live in this bleak world alone?

At seven in the morning, Thomas woke up. He was beginning to feel the effects of a serious hangover when adrenaline shot through his body. He knew, instinctively, that something had happened the night before. With difficulty, he took himself chronologically through the previous

night. Something had excited him while he was reading the Amenophis
Notes. He couldn't immediately remember what it was, but he knew one
thing. He was on to something . . . and it was big.

Thomas' mouth felt as if it were stuffed with cotton as he walked up
the stairs to the kitchen. The pain in his head reverberated with each
step. He had never before consumed so much alcohol. Normally a very
light social drinker, his tolerance was low. And he never smoked. It was
a habit he abhorred. He took the empty pack of Marlboros from his
pocket and flipped it into the trash can.

He opened the refrigerator door, not knowing what he'd find.
Thankfully, there was half a pitcher of orange juice. He filled a glass,
quickly took two small sips, and immediately felt better. It would be
hours before he would feel normal again. In fact, if it weren't for the
miniscule shots of adrenaline he kept getting, he would've been really
sick. He took another sip of orange juice and headed back down to the
basement to find out what the hell he had read that had gotten him so
excited. Whatever it was, it was thankfully proving much stronger than
his hangover.

When he reached his desk, he eased himself into his chair and picked
up the *Amenophis Notes*. After Gene had called, he'd read some or all
of Volume II. Somewhere, in one of the three books, he'd hit on something. But he had no idea what.

He perused Book I and didn't see anything but standard builders
notes. After he almost threw up from moving his eyes back and forth
across the pages too quickly, he took a short walk around the basement.
When he returned he finished Book II. Still nothing. With only one book
left, he was becoming convinced that it must have been a dream that
had gotten him so excited.

He opened Book III and after reading two pages it all came rushing
back to him. It was widely thought that slaves had built all of the pyramids and temples in Egypt, and it was true, slaves had performed much
of the unskilled labor. However, a large contingent of highly skilled artists
and craftsmen, most of whom lived in a village called Deir el-Medina,

made the biggest contribution.

Abubaker, the author of the *Amenophis Notes*, who chronicled the building and restoration of the temples, had been one of these skilled artisans. His job had been to paint temple interiors. When he wasn't working, or waiting for a project to begin, he wrote in his journal. Book III of the Abubaker journal documented a restoration ordered by the Pharaoh Thutmosis III. It described general repair work on certain deteriorating areas of the Pyramid of Zozer, a pyramid located at the Necropolis. But this was not what caught Thomas's eye. Pyramids were often repaired; the Zozer pyramid was already a thousand years old in the time of Thutmosis III so its restoration was completely normal. What caught Thomas's eye was something else.

One day, while Abubaker was making routine observations, he wrote that around twelve o'clock noon, a tall man with a long silver beard arrived at Saqqara, accompanied by twenty guards. They were on foot and, as they walked, the guards surrounded a wagon pulled by oxen. Abubaker couldn't tell what they were transporting, because it was covered with hide. He assumed that the load was valuable, because the men were heavily armed. He noted that ten warriors walked in front of the wagon and nine warriors walked behind it. One rode atop the wagon. At that time, in Egypt, it constituted a very well-funded group of soldiers. The bearded man walked in front of the short caravan, and was clearly the leader.

Thomas read faster. Abubaker wrote that the bearded man entered the ancient pyramid of Unas, where there were extensive texts written on the walls, and had not come out for two days. He described the man as a tall Egyptian, with a mane of silver hair and a prodigious silver beard. Abubaker called him Son of Reuel, Priest of Midian.

When Thomas read this, his heart skipped a beat. He read the passage a second time and again the translation was the same. This was definitely the passage that had excited him the night before. His pulse quickened, dampening his hangover. *Could it be true? Could this be what it looked like it was?* It must! After all, the Builders Notes was a primary historical document of the best kind: written first hand, from direct observation.

Thomas stood up, then sat down again, unsure what his next move should be. He had to learn more. *If what he read were true, then he had stumbled upon one of the most significant pieces of new biblical information since the Dead Sea Scrolls were discovered!* He read it again, and again, arriving at the same conclusion each time. He shook his head, feeling completely bewildered. Amazed. There was only *one* Son of Reuel, Priest of Midian . . . and that person was . . . *Moses!*

This was possibly the most incredible piece of evidence Thomas had ever uncovered. Here, in a primary source document, was an original account of a sighting of Moses that had gone completely undiscovered. For that alone it was significant, because after the Exodus, Moses was not known to have ever returned to Egypt. But what mattered to Thomas, what he *had* to answer was: *what did Moses do in the temple of Unas for forty-eight hours? And what was in the heavily guarded box on the ox-drawn wagon?*

First, Thomas had to be sure. He would have to scour the Pentateuch— the first five books of the Old Testament—to be sure that Moses' return to Egypt was, in fact, not documented. He would also have to study every line in the *Builders Notes* to see if there were any more clues confirming that the man was Moses. If he couldn't disprove his theory, there would be only one more move to make. He would go to Egypt, to the temple Unas, to try to find what Moses had done in there for two days and two nights.

Thomas tried to recall all he knew about Moses. He knew Moses wasn't Reuel's real son. The Bible clearly stated that Moses was found floating in the Nile, and that no one ever knew the identity of his birth father. Moses was thought to have been from the House of Levi, but even that was suspect. After fleeing from Pharaoh, Moses had married a woman named Zipporah, who was daughter of Reuel, Priest of Midian. Even though he would have only been Reuel's son-in-law, Thomas was sure that Abubaker was referring to Moses, when he wrote "Son of

Reuel." He was sure, because Reuel didn't have any sons, only daughters . . . seven of them!

Many Christians, and people in general, forgot that Moses was raised in Egypt and schooled in Egyptian ways. They remembered him as the Charlton Heston figure who fought the Egyptians, parted the Red Sea, and descended Mount Sinai with the Ten Commandments.

In fact, Moses was schooled in Heliopolis, an ancient city outside Cairo known for its immense sanctity and religious significance, and only a few miles from Saqqara. Given his knowledge of Egyptian ways, it would not have been hard for Moses to reenter Egypt after the Exodus. He knew the landscape and he understood Egyptian culture. The fact that the diarist, Abubaker, thought that Moses was an Egyptian was very plausible. The only unanswered questions were what had Moses done for two days in the temple of Unas—the oldest pyramid in Egypt, the one that held the famous Pyramid texts—and what was the heavily guarded treasure on the ox-drawn cart? A treasure hunter by nature, Thomas felt the latter question gnawing at him, and he knew he wouldn't be able to relax again until he had the answer.

When in Egypt as a student, Thomas had been inside Unas. In fact, he'd been in it several times, not so much to study it as to simply see it. The Saqqara necropolis was the most ancient of all Egyptian sites and was one of, if not the, earliest massive stone structures man ever attempted to build. Recorded man, that is. The writings on the walls, or pyramid texts as they were called, were the oldest in all of Egypt, dating to before 2700 BC. Saqqara was built by the great Egyptian architect Imhotep, and was located about thirty minutes outside of Cairo.

Inside the temple of Unas was an amazing room, with ancient hieroglyphic writing covering every inch of the walls. There were stars on the ceiling and it was believed that the walls represented the earth and the ceiling the heavens. Therefore, many scholars thought the writings were an attempt by this earlier civilization to pass along the secret worldly knowledge that they possessed. The hieroglyphics were thought to be written by extremely early priests from Heliopolis but, truthfully, no one really knew who carved them. They seemed to have been written at different times rather than all at once and, amazingly, because they were so old, they were still undeciphered. Over the years there had been many different interpretations but, to this day, no one was sure of their meaning. All that was known was that the early Egyptians carved them, in the most permanent place they knew, in an attempt to communicate with future generations about their world. If Moses had wanted to get a message to future generations, there would be no better place to do it than inside Unas.

Over the next two days, Thomas poured over everything he could get his hands on regarding Moses and his life. He started with the Pentateuch and ended with the renowned book *The Life of Moses*. There was absolutely nothing that told of Moses returning to Egypt after the Exodus. Therefore, if the man described in *the Builders Notes* was Moses, and Thomas had a strong intuitive feeling that it was, then the trip must've been a secret one. That meant that whatever he had with him on that trip was valuable.

From Thomas's perspective as an archeologist, anything worth guarding was worth finding. There were so many treasures commissioned by God in the first five chapters of the Bible that it was hard to believe that God hadn't encouraged idol worship. Thomas closed his eyes and treasures paraded by, as if he were a child on the night before Christmas. There was the golden bell, the gleaming engraved onyx stones, and the bejeweled breastplate. He saw the Staff of Aaron, used to intimidate Pharaoh and, ultimately, to bring about the plagues. He saw the Jar of Manna, that perplexing life-force mentioned only briefly in the Bible, but with utmost reverence. There were many shapes and forms fashioned from silk, gold, glass and jewels. After the parade was over Thomas opened his eyes. W*ait! There was something else.* Thomas closed his eyes again. It was the grand finale, the greatest of all the Biblical treasures. The last treasure in the parade was the golden Ark of the Covenant, proudly moving by with two unearthly cherubs riding on top.

Thomas crinkled his nose. Yes, movies and books had raised it to another level, making it king of all treasures. But, in the process, the Ark had been overdone. Commercialized, then over-marketed. Like a once beautiful prostitute who lowers her price as her looks diminish, the Ark had been overexposed, over sold. In the minds of many it had already been found, many times over, in toys stores around the world, with the words "Made in China" or "Hecho en Mexico" printed on the bottom. It was now a glossy golden rectangle, invented by Steven Spielberg. But something about the original story of the Ark pulled at Thomas's memory. Something he'd read long ago. He opened a file deep in the recesses of his mind, one of the dusty ones labeled *Ark of the Covenant: Ten Commandments*. Seldom used. He could not grasp the fact eluding him so he put a little yellow post-it note on the mental file. It would eat at him all day.

The past week had been like a ride on a rickety roller coaster. Now this. Thomas leaned back in his chair and reviewed the choices he'd made in his lifetime. Really, there were a few key choices that one made in life, sometimes just two or three, that determined a whole life's outcome. One of Thomas's choices had been to focus on his career with such determination that no relationship he'd been in had ever flowered, or matured. It hadn't been a conscience decision. On the contrary, if he'd ever really given it any thought, he might be married by now.

After choosing to teach, he knew the path he was on would not be one of glory. There would be no more lost tombs. No more hidden treasures. Instead, student by student, one by one, he would try to transfer some of his passion about archeology. He had swept personal fame and gratification aside to focus on a greater good.

Now, freed from the encumbrances of the university, the system, he imagined himself standing in front of Saqqara. He felt the sweet flood of adrenaline, the feeling of hope and wild anticipation. He'd felt it before, when he was searching for Amenophis. The tedious, expectant waiting, while the stairway, flooded with sand, had been cleared, and then, when the thick slab of door had been lifted away, success. Personal, self-fulfilling, greedy success. He imagined his name on front pages of newspapers worldwide: *"Thomas McAlister discovers the greatest lost treasure of all time."* He envisioned his face on television, heard his voice on talk radio, discussing how challenging it had been to find something that had been hidden for more than three thousand years. Personal gratification.

He also imagined Dean Washington sitting in front of his television, watching the interview, shaking his head at what a fool he'd been for letting Thomas go. Professional redemption. He would still use the experience to teach others. There was nothing like a big treasure find to encourage children, and archeology students, all over the world to begin their own mini-campaigns. He couldn't teach in a classroom, but he could still lead by example. Lead by success. This would be his new purpose, his new charge . . . his real destiny. It galvanized him.

Thomas smiled for the first time in days. It was time to go to Egypt.

CHAPTER **8**

Like other times when he needed grounding or purpose, Thomas ran to the thing that had always been there for him, the only thing that had ever been faithful. Egypt. Like a good dog, Egypt had never let him down. She had given him notoriety and a career . . . a purpose for living. He hoped she wouldn't let him down now, when he needed her most. He purchased a ticket on a flight leaving that evening.

An Egyptologist, schooled at Harvard and trained in Egypt, Thomas was notably accomplished. But after he accepted the job at Arizona University, what set Thomas apart from other Egyptologists was that he did not blindly follow already accepted ideas, or academic precedent. He felt blind acceptance was dangerous and narrow-minded. He respected his elders, but he didn't necessarily believe them. This was contrary to the existing system

Questioning current theories seemed natural, even logical. But in the world of archeology, especially Egyptology, it was radical. Once anointed into the select, insular society of Egyptologists it was expected that an archeologist believe everything that his peers had written. Their theories could not be changed or questioned, only, occasionally, politely debated. Fervent challenge of existing beliefs was heresy. Punishable by banishment.

When an archeologist discovered something significant, Egyptologists, more than any other anthropological discipline, put faith in the views of the founder. The founder became the expert, his view dogma, and new learning was stifled. These original theories were rarely challenged or improved upon, even when new evidence was introduced.

Thomas's refusal to automatically accept existing theories had made him a maverick, and a bit of an outsider. It ultimately got him fired. But he wouldn't change. He simply wanted old ways of thinking proved, just like new theories had to be. He wasn't being disagreeable; he was after historical truth, at any price. Plus, suppressing the truth would hamper some of the theories he planned to put forth and support in the future.

When he graduated and claimed that he believed there was still a major undiscovered tomb in the Valley of the Kings, the reigning Egyptologists called him not a rebel, but a fool. He spoke so firmly on the issue he would have been ostracized if he had kept it up, but luckily there was an equally foolish professor planning an expedition and Thomas was able to join as assistant. This got him out of the controversial lime-light before he had caused irreparable damage to his image, and it got him the field experience that would subsequently make him so marketable.

Later, after he and his team had found the Tomb of Amenophis III, Pharaoh of Egypt for an incredible thirty-seven years, right in the Valley of the Kings, Thomas became semi-famous for leading the sub-team that made the actual discovery. It also shortened the memory of those who had opposed his earlier radical approach. He was transformed from rebel to prophetic darling. And he was welcomed back to the States with open arms by the best schools in the country.

After accepting the position at Arizona State, Thomas toned down his attack on existing theory. He was still interested in supplementing existing information but he began to focus more on new exploration and discovery. It was a bit of compromise, but this new attitude, combined with his newfound fame, quickly won him academic praise. He was then credited with igniting an Egyptian renaissance, unlike any since Howard Carter made Egyptian Pharaohs famous in the early 1900s. Thomas, with Dean Washington's support, planned to create a department that would rival Harvard's.

Now, as he packed, Thomas swore there would be no more compro-mise. His original fury had subsided, he had learned his lesson. It was every man for himself. He would never rely on another man to determine his fate, as he had relied on Washington. It was an opportunity that he looked upon with relish, and reservation.

Teaching at a university had been similar to playing a team sport, like baseball or soccer. Success was often determined by the other members of the team, and often the weakest link decided the fate of all. Fieldwork, and treasure hunting, were akin to golf, or even bowling. The individual alone decided his or her own fate. Thomas was finished with the team concept. His experience was proof that the lowest common denominator ruled, and that new ways of thinking were criticized. He'd always known that most original thinking, most work that challenged convention, had come from independent, entrepreneurial, enterprising minds. He vowed never again to let weak, sterile, conservative minds play a role in shaping his future.

He would not give his next six years to building a new reputation at another university. He would strike out on his own. Now, he would go the other route . . . living and working in the field, dedicated to finding the treasures that would rewrite history.

He would start this new life with the incredible clue he'd discovered in the *Amenophis Builders Notes*. There had to be a lead hidden somewhere in the temple of Unas, and he would find it. He hoped it would tell him where to find the oxen-drawn treasure that had been so heavily guarded by Moses' men.

Thomas's immediate problem was money. Exploration trips were expensive. Although he was only at Stage I, if he found any clue at all it could easily turn into a costly minor expedition. He had not exactly been frugal over the past six years. He had traveled extensively, often purchasing expensive artifacts for his collection.

Because of that, and the fact that he lived a comfortable life, he had only saved about $300,000. A hundred thousand of that was invested in stocks and another $100,000 was in a 401K account. He had $100,000 cash in a money market account. He would leave half in the money market account and he would take $50,000, open another bank account, and use that to fund his search. Hopefully, he would find something valuable to sell to recoup his expenses. Maybe he'd even generate some income. But archeological treasure hunting is extremely risky at best, and he knew he could not rely on it for any kind of monetary gain. For now, the benefit was psychological, and the trip was part of his healing process. It felt good to turn the key to his front door, solidly locking the deadbolt in place. It was comforting to see the cab waiting in the drive-way.

So he set forth, his war chest looking more like a petty cash drawer, free from his former life, fired from his job and, if not on the verge of a great discovery, at least armed with a great clue. Thomas flew towards Cairo and with every mile he thought more and more about finding treasure in Egypt and less and less about the burning in his stomach, the burning that had been there ever since he'd walked out of Dean Washington's office.

CHAPTER **9**

Thomas arrived in Egypt ready to solve the mystery of the bearded man at the temple of Unas. He checked into his hotel and called his close Egyptian colleague, Martha Stevens. Martha and Thomas had been graduate students together at Harvard. Martha, born in Cairo, had returned to Egypt after graduate school to practice her true love, looking for undiscovered tombs in the Valley of the Kings. She had assisted Thomas on the Amenophis dig and had been only feet away when Thomas, paint brush in hand, had dusted the sand off of the first step leading down to the tomb. They had discussed that moment many times, both agreeing that nothing they had done since equaled the excitement of that first day, working with the knowledge they'd found the tomb of a great Pharaoh, knowing the days that followed would be filled with suspense, adventure, and discovery.

Martha was currently working with a group excavating the tomb of Senneferi, a noble whose tomb was located on the west bank of Luxor. The tomb had been discovered in 1895, but Martha and her team had re-opened it in 1992. She was one of the brightest and most dedicated people Thomas had ever met, and he always called her when he was in Egypt. Usually it was a social. This time, he needed her help.

Martha, for her part, was ecstatic when Thomas called. A smile formed on her latte-colored Egyptian face when he said he was on his way to Egypt. His call had come at a perfect time, allowing her a much needed guiltless break from the tedious mapping of Senneferi. She immediately agreed to help him regardless of the task. He hadn't even hinted at what they'd be doing; in fact she had detected a slight evasiveness, but she was deeply intrigued that it would involve Saqqara. She knew her friend wasn't flying in for a sightseeing trip. Thomas was a shrewd, analytical archeologist, with an extreme amount of focus and perseverance. If he wanted to visit Saqqara it meant he was up to something.

While listening to Thomas on the phone Martha reviewed what she knew about Saqqara. It remained a mystery to all Egyptologists, because it was so old. Experts agreed Saqqara was the true link to earlier, ancient Egyptian cultures. At the necropolis of Saqqara, one of the most ancient burial chambers was the pyramid of Unas. In it, the walls were covered with ancient Egyptian writings. Renowned Egyptologists, such as R. O. Faulkner and others, had tried to decipher the writing, but there were so many archaic phrases that no one had ever been completely successful. The issue with the texts at Unas and with Egyptian history in general— and the real reason that Saqqara was so revered, so special—was that Egyptian writing, and early Egyptian culture in general, seemed to have just sprung up from nothing. There was no history of development. No gradual ramp of learning. No simple architecture that gradually got better and more complex. No language, mathematics or astronomy that predated the very advanced systems that the early Egyptians had used. It was as if they were all simply placed there, fully developed.

Contrary to the way modern cultures developed, older Egyptian civilizations were better at building, better at mathematics, and better at astronomy than later Egyptian cultures. It was as if someone who was very intelligent had come to Egypt, taught the Egyptians, and then abruptly left. Certainly the Egyptians evolved and developed over time but, in most areas, their knowledge and skills actually decreased. As time passed, some of their former learning and skills were forgotten. The sphinx, for example, was so old, no one knew when it was built. But no later culture ever bested it.

Egyptologists felt that if anyone could fully decipher the Pyramid texts at Saqqara, they might shed some light on these earlier cultures, and where the advanced knowledge had come from. But to date, no one had been able to do it. All of this ran through Martha's head, like a familiar song, as she nodded into the phone and agreed to pick Thomas up early the next morning for their 30-minute drive to Saqqara.

Martha arrived in her black Mercedes station wagon at 5 a.m. Thomas went around to embrace her before getting into the passenger side. Her first impression was that he looked thinner than last time they were together. She offered him still warm Egyptian Om Ali bread and a cup of aromatic Egyptian coffee that she had purchased in the old quarter on her way over. She secretly watched his face as he sat in the car, opening the bread. The lines around his eyes and forehead were deeper than last time, and she detected a look of deep concern, unnatural on his normally good-natured face. But they'd been apart a long time and rather than pry, Martha decided to wait and see if Thomas would volunteer the reasons behind his worried look.

While they drove across the barren, sandy-tan desert outside of Cairo, Thomas recounted the events of the past weeks and Martha's eyes welled with tears at her good friend's loss of job. Thomas had seemed to have the perfect career. *Bright, young successful archeology professor to become next Dean of the Archeology Department.*

On the phone, and again this morning, he seemed a little harder, or more direct, than he had in the past. Was life taking its toll on him? Had he lost some of that youthful exuberance? "You're always welcome here, Thomas. We could use you in the Valley. Just say the word. There aren't many people who have been intimately involved with discovering a Pharaoh's tomb. Field experience may not matter on certain college campuses these days, but it certainly matters in the Valley."

Thomas appreciated her sympathy but wanted her to know that he didn't want to dwell on it. He didn't want to slip back to the place he'd just emerged from. He changed the subject. "Martha, I think I'm on to something. Maybe . . . something big." He told her about the odd entry by Abubaker in the *Amenophis Notes*. He told her his Moses hypothesis and Abubaker's comment about the man being Reuel's son. She knew that Reuel had fathered only daughters, but reminded Thomas that it would be a stretch for the man who had arrived at Unas to actually be

Moses. "It may have just looked like him. There may be another Reuel, Priest of Median," she said.

She was playing devil's advocate so that her friend wouldn't be let down if they didn't find anything. But she did concede that it was odd that someone, no matter who it was, had spent so much time inside the temple. And she agreed that they must've been traveling with something that was valuable if there were that many armed guards. Back then, most people owned only what they could carry, so the presence of an armed escort was a telltale sign something valuable was nearby. But Martha, like Thomas, was a scientist, and it was going to take a lot more than one entry in an ancient diary to convince her that Moses had visited Saqqara.

They arrived at the necropolis at sunrise. It was quiet, except for the barking howls of a few coyotes. They sat on the warm hood of the car and watched the sun come up, absorbed in their own thoughts. Sunrise at the ancient pyramids in Egypt could be a mystical, almost religious experience. When the globe began to turn from orange to yellow, Thomas broke the silence. "Did you remember to bring the battery-operated light? I saw the ladder, in the back of the station wagon, but not the light."

"Yes, it's under that tarp, with the cooler. How about you get the ladder, I take the light?" The light was a commercial grade, 10,000-watt portable lamp used by construction companies for night jobs. Many of the tools archeologists used, like lighting, vehicles, and digging implements, had to be construction grade because of the harsh working conditions.

As they approached Unas, Thomas said, "It's bigger than I remember."

"I always think that about the pyramids, in the morning." Martha smiled, unusually happy to be back in the field with Thomas again.

They were ninety feet from the pyramid when a figure, shrouded in shadow, emerged from the still dark west side of the temple. Thomas slowed his pace and whispered to Martha. "Do you see that?"

In Egypt, like in other countries, bandits tended to frequent places where tourists gathered. Thomas was also conscious of the fact that

Saqqara, being a necropolis, or city of the dead, was also haunted.

They continued to walk, but more slowly. The figure approached them. After twenty more paces, they could see that it was only one of the security guards hired by the government to keep vandals away. Martha knew many of the guards, but not this one. They showed him their National Institute of Archeology identification cards, which allowed them to conduct research at any site, anytime. This was one of the highest forms of identification in Egypt, and they were allowed to pass. Martha offered the guard a cup of coffee from their thermos and the man graciously accepted, agreeing in return to carry the light and its heavy battery into the temple.

Once inside, the man asked, out of curiosity, what they were doing. Martha smiled. "We're going to take some pictures, to be studied at the University." The answer was sufficiently boring and the guard left, to continue watching the grounds.

Martha and Thomas set up shop in no time, agreeing to start at one end of the room and work, one wall at a time, until they had scoured every inch of the rectangle. They would shine the light on one wall and inspect it closely, inch by inch, Thomas at the top on the ladder, Martha standing below, until they met in the middle. They would look for anything out of the ordinary, such as writing that did not fit the existing hieroglyphic pattern, or text that looked new or altered. Thomas had a theory that Moses might have hidden his work by writing very small, or by integrating it into existing text. He told Martha to look for letters or images that may have been added or altered to create a code, cipher, or hybrid language.

The hieroglyphics used in the temple of Saqqara were not merely painted on the wall. They were carved, or etched, into the walls by skilled artisans, using tools very much like the modern-day hammer and chisel. The resulting grooves in the stone were then washed and painted.

Since the chamber was rectangular, Thomas and Martha started their search with the north wall, where the doorway was. For an hour, they examined every inch of it but found nothing out of the ordinary. They broke for another cup of coffee, moved the light to the east wall, and began the same examination process. This wall was about twice as long as the one they had just completed. It took them over two hours to examine it. Again, they found nothing out of the ordinary.

At lunch time, instead of having another cup of coffee and one of the Snickers that Thomas had brought, they purchased falafel from a vendor. They sat in the shade of one of the temples, on some of the scattered ruins, and talked. They ate hot falafel and wondered aloud what had happened to old Mustafa. Once a chef at a five-star hotel, he had left his job to become their cook on the Amenophis expedition. They had never eaten better, ever, on any expedition. Neither had heard from him since. They laughed, remembering the night Mustafa had put a rubber scorpion in Thomas's soup. But Thomas wasn't completely in it. He knew that they only had two walls to go, and he was worried. Actually, he was scared. If nothing materialized, he was done. Out of ideas. Back to having no purpose, and no plans. He wasn't ready to go back home empty-handed.

They finished lunch and started the third wall, another short one. They finished in forty-five minutes. Again, nothing. Thomas's heart sank. It looked as if he wasn't going to find anything. He started to wonder if this had been a ridiculous wild goose chase. Had he been so eager to leave home that he had flown all the way to Egypt for nothing? Was his judgment impaired? Was Martha humoring him, because he'd lost his job? She had said it was a long shot. Was that her way of saving him from further humiliation?

He shrugged and started to move the light so that it pointed to the last wall, the west side. He had just set the light back down when suddenly Martha screamed. "Oh my God! Don't move that light, Thomas!"

"What? What do you see, Martha?" Thomas asked, expecting to see her frozen in place, looking down at a scorpion or a snake. But rather than looking downward, she was looking past him, at the west wall. Thomas's gaze followed hers. But he saw nothing out of the ordinary.

"What? I don't see it."

"*Up there!*" Her eyes didn't move from the wall. She was pointing to the corner, where the wall met the vaulted ceiling. "Up there, Thomas. Do you see where the hieroglyphics have crumbled away? Look there, below the ceiling. The wall has started to crumble and deteriorate. Do you see it? There's something there! It's . . . well, maybe it's nothing. I can't see it now, but when you were moving the light it was there. There was something up there that didn't belong. It looked like . . . ."

Thomas located the place where the veneer of smooth plaster had crumpled away from a large section, just below the ceiling. But he was disappointed. He'd noticed that same section earlier that morning.

"Yeah, so?"

"I saw something that looked like the bottom half of a letter. It was curved, not straight like most hieroglyphics. Move the light back to the south side of the room. I saw the shadow when you were moving the light."

Thomas moved the light until it shone on the south wall, but at an angle. Sure enough, emerging from the crumbled section was the shape of a letter that did not seem to be part of a hieroglyphic symbol. "I see it now!" He tried to dampen his excitement. "Slide the ladder over here, will you?"

This crumbled away portion of the wall, slightly south of the center, had been noted in many research studies on Unas. No one knew what was written underneath the missing section and people had given up trying to find out. Since no one understood the writing in the temple, it had been impossible to deduce from context what the missing section might have said. And, since experts could not fully decipher the writing on the ninety-eight percent of the wall that had not crumbled away, they had not spent much time trying to find out what was written on the part that *had* crumbled away.

Thomas climbed the ladder, took out his flashlight, and focused on the faint curved line. After hours of studying the other walls in the pyramid, it was crystal clear to him that this particular line hadn't been carved by a professional craftsman. It had been done by an amateur. The groove was not as deep or as smooth. The professionals carved with eerie exactitude.

"What do you see?" Martha's voice reflected her impatience.

Thomas turned towards her. He was beaming. "I think we've found it!"

Martha held her tongue. The entire message had deteriorated and fallen away. It had become dust on the floor of the temple, ferried away on the shoes of countless thousands of tourists. All they could see was the very last letter that had been written. And only half of that. But she kept quiet. Thomas needed a win, if only temporarily.

"This line is definitely not hieroglyphic, Martha. No way. And it wasn't carved by an expert either. From what I can see, existing hieroglyphic writing was chipped away and this writing was carved over it, rather crudely. That's probably what caused the whole message to disintegrate. Too much stress and activity. The smooth layer of plaster that the original builders spread over these walls to carve into has completely eroded. Whoever made these marks was trying to go too deep, at a time when the plaster was too old, too dry. The vibration made small fractures, eventually causing all of this to crumble away. Did you bring any paper, Martha?"

"A small note pad."

"Spell Moses in Hebrew for me." Martha wrote as instructed and held the pad of paper up so that Thomas could see it. Thomas smiled as he read it. "See the last S?"

"Yes," she said.

"Look at this." Thomas pointed to the tail of a letter that extended downward from the broken section. "It matches, Martha. Do you see it?" Thomas couldn't contain his excitement now. "It's the lower half of a Hebrew S. If I'm right, it could very well be Moses' signature! Jesus, Martha, we may have just found Moses' autograph!"

"But Thomas, how will we ever find out? The entire signature and the message that was above it is gone . . . forever. It's the dust we're walking on."

"Maybe not, Martha. Maybe not."

CHAPTER 10

With trance-like focus, Thomas transported himself back to ancient Egypt. It had always been easy for him to do. While he stared at the missing section on the wall he completely opened his mind. He let all of his experience and knowledge as an archeologist and Egyptologist seep out into the open and he combined that with the millions of bits of information about how it must have been, back in Egypt, 3000 years ago.

Moses had chosen the inside of a temple, the most permanent place he knew, which meant it was an important message. He entered the room, and selected a place that was high, near the ceiling, so that people wouldn't be able to vandalize and erase his message. He then chipped away the original text, until he had a clean slate. Then he added his own message. The problem for Moses was that he was not a skilled engraver. With the smooth veneer of plaster nearly gone, Moses would've had to etch with a heavy hand, not possessing the finesse it takes to carve into a limestone wall and make it last for centuries. In addition, Moses' inscription would not have been painted or coated with the proper preservative. So, over time, Moses' text had eroded, his message destroyed, undiscovered . . . until now.

Thomas had to squeeze the message out of this wall, somehow. But how? Martha was right. It was gone. It had become dust. Thomas closed his eyes and put his forehead against the wall. What did he know about the ancient scribes, about carving, about geology, limestone, and pressure?

Limestone was literally compacted sand, sand that had gotten hot enough, at one time, to compact but not to fuse completely. So, what happened to sand when pressure was applied? Thomas pictured himself driving across the desert, leaving imprints in the sand. He thought of the ski trips he'd taken to Aspen, the tire imprints on the snow-packed roads. In both cases, the weight of the vehicles left compacted material below the surface. As Moses chiseled and banged letters into the stone, the layers of limestone underneath should've become compacted. Even if the writing was gone, the limestone underneath, where the chisel head hit the wall, should still be compacted. There had to be a way to read the compacted rock debris on the wall where the writing had once been. But that would require looking at the wall three-dimensionally, which was impossible. Or was it—

"Martha!" he exclaimed, startling her, "Do you know any pediatricians?"

"No, I've never needed one. I have friends with kids, though. Why?"

"The sediment behind Moses' message may have become compacted while he was chiseling it on the surface." He pointed to the spot on the wall where the message had been. "I think the message might still be here? If we can get some kind of portable ultrasound machine, we might be able to read it. The compacted sediment will be thicker where his chisel hit the wall. A machine might pick that up."

Martha cocked her head, thinking. "Hmmm, you might be right. Damn it, Thomas, I *know* you're right! You can be so creative sometimes, Dr. McAlister. I knew there was a reason I liked having you around. Here I was ready to give up . . . and you know, I think it just might work. Come on, let's get back to Cairo. Let's go find that ultrasound machine."

At sunrise the next morning, Martha picked Thomas up again outside his hotel. After swearing up and down she was not pregnant, and that she was not going to use it on herself, she had gotten a portable ultrasound machine from a doctor recommended by her sister. It was in the back seat of her car, beside an old, tan, dot matrix printer. As they drove, the sun evaporated the coolness of the night, and the trip passed more quickly this time.

Saqqara was exactly as they'd left it, only there was no guard in front of the Unas pyramid this time. Martha erected her sign outside the temple:

"CLOSED: RESEARCH BEING CONDUCTED." Thomas entered with a flashlight and began to set up the lighting. Once the room was fully illuminated, he put the small step ladder under the eroded section of wall.

Martha had received brief instructions on how to use the ultra-sound machine from the doctor. After connecting it to the portable battery and the printer, she showed Thomas how she planned to run the sensor across the wall, so he would know the sequence of what was being printed.

Although this had been his idea, Thomas had become more and more skeptical, in the last twelve hours. If the sediment had originally been compacted, it could've easily loosened over the course of the last three thousand years. Limestone was a rock made of compacted, not melted, sand and there was a chance that the small earthquakes and tremors that are constantly reverberating through the earth's core could have loosened the sand.

Martha said, "I hope this works. I know some other applications in the Valley of the Kings, where looters or the floods have ruined carved text. I've spent hours wondering what was written on those walls."

Thomas nodded. He was too focused on his work to discuss future uses of the technology. When Martha flipped a switch, a red light appeared and the machine started to hum. An ink nozzle on the printer began its snappy "self test" start-up procedure.

Martha climbed the ladder and placed the hand sensor at the top of the wall, where it met the ceiling. She very slowly moved it from left to right, allowing time for the sound waves to pass through the wall then bounce back into the receiver. Immediately, the printer began to crankily spit out the results. The cursor went back and forth, furiously spraying ink on the paper.

Thomas's eyes were glued to the paper. Up to this point, all the ultra-sound images he'd ever seen had been stuck on friends' refrigerators. Those curious, two-dimensional cone shaped figures that, through the use of shading, produced pictures of fetuses that always reminded him of new-born kangaroos. Rarely had he ever been able to discern the shape of a baby from those images, let alone its gender.

At first there was no image at all, only light gray shading. Then, as more paper emerged, Thomas saw faint forms of Hebrew letters cutting through in a darker shade of gray. His heart leapt as paper continued to pour from the machine.

"I don't believe this," he whispered.

Suddenly, the machine stopped and he panicked. He glanced up at Martha and saw that she had taken the sensor off the wall and was moving it down one row. The printer started up again, as soon as she started the left to right movement.

"Anything?" Martha asked. "I just moved the sensor down a row."

"Yes, it's working, Martha! It's perfect. *Perfect*! Keep going. Make sure you get the entire area where the text was destroyed! Don't worry if you overlap rows a little, I'll cut that away later."

"What are you getting? Ancient hieroglyphics, or something else?"

Thomas's voice was full of youthful exuberance, "No, no, Martha, not hieroglyphics. It's ancient Hebrew. It's what *Moses* would have used."

Martha grinned at him. He'd done it.

As the paper streamed out of the printer, the letters remained clear. Looking at them, Thomas knew he would be able to read them. He couldn't wait to see what they said, but there wasn't time to read them now. He needed to get the message and then get out of the pyramid, before someone wanted to know more about what they were doing there. He wanted to get back to his hotel, to a safe, controlled environment.

The paper formed one long continuous sheet, and Thomas gently folded it along the perforation lines, making sure that it was not damaged or wrinkled. The printing had stopped, and Thomas was aware of Martha by his side. He stood up and gave her a hug. "I couldn't have done this without your help. I owe you a big one."

"No need to say any of that, Thomas. These past two days have been therapeutic. I needed to get away from Senneferi. But listen, that ancient Hebrew can be rough. If there are any words you can't decipher, let me know. I have a friend who specializes in ancient Hebrew. Dr. Sinistar is his name. I can give you his phone number if you want."

"Thanks, Martha. I'll call you if I need his help. Right now I want to get off the grounds and get back to my hotel room."

They quickly gathered their gear and left the site. Martha dropped Thomas off at his hotel. "If you need anything call. You know I'd love to have dinner, but I can tell you can't think of anything except the message. Good luck with it."

Thomas was shaking by the time he reached his room. He forced himself to suppress his euphoria by countering it with the knowledge that a thousand things could go wrong. He considered what to do next. He knew he should eat, even though he didn't feel hungry, but instead decided to begin deciphering the text. With shaking hands he removed the ultra-sound paper from his field pack and laid it out on the table.

After arranging the sheets, Thomas cut the paper with the scissors on his Swiss Army knife to remove overlapping lines. He then taped it so it was in paragraph form, with all sentences and lines matching. Then, he immediately began to decipher it. The script was definitely ancient Hebrew, proving that it had been added at least a thousand years after the hieroglyphics on the pyramid walls. This was good. Thomas was fluent in Hebrew, so he didn't need a translator. Despite that, he did check his translated passages against his Hebrew dictionary, just to be sure.

He worked for two hours, uninterrupted, even by thoughts of Dean Washington and his old job. He translated most of the message fairly quickly and then went over it more carefully to see if he could pick up any of the words he didn't get the first time through. Finally, only five words remained a mystery. He used X's as placeholders for the five words he could not get. Thomas was now ready to read the message. Since he had translated the message in fragments, he had no idea what the text said.

He was getting ready to read it when he stopped, got up, and took a beer out of the refrigerator beside the sink. He twisted off the top, walked back over to the table and wrote in black pen, at the top of the document: THE MOSES RIDDLE. This is what he read:

Moses Riddle

I, son of Egypt, Father of Hebrews, never good with tongue or pen, am challenged to create a message that will at once conceal what I must hide while, at the same time, reveal what I must make known. I do it for you, because future, less destructive generations, must be allowed a window to eternity.

Thomas couldn't suppress his smile. He stopped and took a long drink of his beer. It was cold and good, but it didn't slow the rapid beating of his heart. He continued reading.

Broken once, it must be preserved for future civilizations to experience. It cannot be left here to the thieves and robbers, or worse. Here is my riddle, my challenge, to whomever considers himself worthy of revealing that which God has made.

Thomas stopped reading, momentarily wondering if he was worthy of this incredible find. Then he realized that not only was he worthy, but that this was his destiny. This was why everything in his life had happened the way it did. Every event, every choice, had led him to being the one man who was worthy of Moses' challenge. He continued.

Like Egypt, it appears as one. Like Egypt, if you know her, it is two. This is not my original, but my only one. To the parched man; water. To he who is lost; bearings. To the godless; XXXXX. I take it west, to a place where the XXXXX XXXX rules, where XXXXX visited long ago, where it will be well maintained. It will be at an accouterment, worn by that great hunter in the sky, the same as the great complex at Giza. You will find it, in the middle of the eastern middle, marked by a circle in a square.

If you can determine the XXXXXXX, and have the vision to

know where it lies, then you have a great responsibility. Greater than many before you, and most after, for you will be keeper of the window to eternity. In the wrong hands, the window may be forever broken, stranding all who come after it to eternal wandering. Moses

"Jesus, Mary and Joseph," Thomas said aloud. *This is incredible.* What in God's name do I have here? He stared at the riddle and finally read it two more times, committing it to memory. A message from Moses. *Moses!* Extraordinary. *Mind-boggling.* In all likelihood, he was the first person who'd read these words since they were carved into the wall three thousand years ago. It was a rare and lucky occurrence, in the world of academia, to actually be the first to read a historical document. What made this nothing short of miraculous was that it was written and signed by . . . *the* Moses. Since the riddle had deteriorated, and become unreadable except by x-ray, it was as if Moses had written this note specifically to him.

Reading the riddle for a fourth time, Thomas realized he had a new problem. He was not an expert at solving riddles. He didn't know anyone who was, either. He was, however, a logical man. He would approach solving the riddle in a logical way, sentence by sentence. The first two paragraphs seemed to be informational, Moses was explaining what he was doing and why. It seemed logical to focus efforts on the three primary questions: Who, What and Where.

Trying to solve the riddle without the missing five words might lead him down the wrong path, though.

Thomas called Martha and got her friend's phone number.

"Dr. Sinistar, my name is Thomas McAlister. I'm a professor of Egyptology and a friend of Martha Stevens. I have some ancient Hebrew text Martha says you may be able to help me decipher." Thomas intentionally didn't use the word "interpret." That would have implied he needed help understanding the meaning of what was written.

" Yes, yes, Thomas. Martha called to say you might contact me."

The man sounded agreeable.

"I'm working on a text written in ancient Hebrew. I'm fluent, but there are five words that I cannot decipher. I've never seen them before, and they are not in any translation dictionaries. The context doesn't help. I was wondering if you might translate them for me? Do you have a little time tonight?"

"I'd be happy to. It would be best if you read me the entire text. The context is very important and will surely help me. Some words have more than one meaning, as you know, and that way we don't just get the word, but also what it means as part of the sentence."

Thomas cringed. He chose his next words carefully. There was no way he was going to share the riddle with anybody. "Dr. Sinistar, at this point of my study, I'd rather not share the whole thing, if that's all right with you. I'd like to get the five words defined, generally, and then I'll put them in context myself."

Dr. Sinistar's pause lasted longer than it should have. Thomas wondered if he was trying to show his disapproval. "All right, of course. Why don't you spell them over the phone, rather than faxing them to me. I'll call you back later this evening, with the translation. Will that meet your needs?"

"That will be perfect. Thank you so much. I greatly appreciate this." Thomas read the letters of the words and Dr. Sinistar repeated that he'd be in touch later that evening. Thomas was left with an uncomfortable feeling. Something about his rapport with Sinistar had changed after he'd declined to read the whole message. As if Sinistar was offended, or extremely disappointed. Thomas wondered if Martha had told Sinistar where they'd obtained the text. No, he comforted himself, she wouldn't do that.

Although Thomas knew he shouldn't try solving the riddle without the missing words, he couldn't resist the temptation. He made notes as he read, already feeling confident about certain parts of it.

The first paragraph was an introduction. Its intent was to identify the writer and to explain why he was writing. The fact that the writer called himself "Father of Hebrews," proved that it was Moses. No one else could have used that terminology. In addition, Moses had added that he was not good with tongue or pen. This made sense. In Chapter Four of Exodus, Moses had expressed that he was insecure about his ability to speak or write. This handicap is what drove him to ask Aaron to travel with him on his journeys to talk with the Pharaoh.

In the second paragraph, Moses wrote that his subject had religious significance. He called it a "window into eternity" for future, less destructive generations. He was anxious about the object's safety and wanted to ensure its future.

Thomas was not a biblical scholar, but he could think of many objects that Moses might want to preserve. They had all been part of his earlier treasure parade: the Staff of Aaron, the Ark of the Covenant, the Jar of Manna. There were other possibilities, too.

The second paragraph held a more specific clue. Moses wrote that "it" had already been broken once, and he didn't want it to be broken— or stolen—again. The Ten Commandments came to mind, except they had not been merely broken when Moses threw them off the face of Mount Sinai, they had been obliterated.

In the third paragraph, Moses got into the meat of the riddle. Thomas decided to take this paragraph sentence by sentence. There were Egyptologists more knowledgeable about Egypt, but he had something working in his favor. This was not a standardized intelligence test, or a classroom. This was the field, where intelligence had to be combined with experience, quick thinking, and craftiness. Those qualities, when combined with his persistence, provided a fertile platform for solving the riddle. He closed his eyes, took a deep breath, and cleared his mind.

He reread the third paragraph and determined the first four sentences dealt with *what* Moses was hiding. The last three sentences dealt with *Where* Moses was hiding it.

Like Egypt, it appears as one. Like Egypt if you know her, it is two. Thomas fully understood these first two sentences. Egypt, although one country, had always had a deep divide between north and south. The divide still existed. There were even pharaohs who changed the seat of the throne from Cairo, in the north, to Luxor, in the south, in an effort to bridge the gap. It was rarely talked about, outside of Egypt. Despite outwardly appearing as one country, Egypt was really two distinct regions. Thomas took this inference to mean that Moses' treasure was commonly viewed as one, but, in actuality, was one of two.

The third sentence read, *This is not my original, but my only one.* Maybe there were originally two of them, Thomas thought, but the object in his possession was the only one in existence at that time. The line was intriguing to Thomas. He had no idea what to make of it. He would have to learn more, to figure it out.

In the fourth sentence, Moses spoke of the importance of the object, and how it related to mankind. *To the parched man; water. To he who is lost; bearings. To the godless; XXXXX.*

Unfortunately, Thomas could not define the last word. He assumed, from context, that the word was *hope, deliverance,* or *salvation.*

After examining the first four sentences, Thomas knew that, at some point, there had been two of the object and only one remained. He understood Moses was hiding the second one, and that mankind needed the object, because it would provide some sort of fulfillment, guidance, or help.

The last three sentences covered *where* Moses was taking the treasure. *I take it west, to a place where the XXXXX rules, where XXXXX visited long ago, where it will be well maintained.* Without the help of Dr. Sinistar, Thomas was stymied. Moses was taking the treasure west, which could literally mean anywhere. Thomas prayed that the words Dr. Sinistar came back with were definite places and not words that were riddles in themselves. He would have to wait.

The next part of the riddle involved the constellations. *It will be at an accouterment worn by that great hunter in the sky, the same as the great complex at Giza.* Thomas smiled. Anyone who knew constellations and the secret behind the Great Pyramid complex at Giza would be able to interpret this line. Thomas had studied both.

There was only one great hunter in the sky. Orion. The constellation of Orion. Before he continued, Thomas checked the English definition of *accouterment*, to make sure he was correctly interpreting the ancient Hebrew symbol. He was. It meant jewelry, or a garment, worn in addition to one's regular clothing. The accouterment in the constellation of Orion was famous. Orion's belt.

Thomas had once studied Orion, in an advanced class on ancient Egypt, in college. The Orion constellation was very significant to the ancient Egyptians. Years earlier, a construction engineer, Robert Bauval, had noticed that the three pyramids at Giza, including the great pyramid, were aligned in a fashion that looked similar to the way that the three stars of Orion's belt were aligned. Thomas and a few of his classmates had been given the task of checking the relative position of the three stars and comparing it mathematically to Giza, to see if the relationship matched. By working with the Director of the Adler Planetarium in Chicago, they found that Orion's belt stars did have an uncanny alignment to the layout of the pyramids and that the Egyptians had been more astronomically advanced than anyone had ever imagined. In addition it was proven that Orion had been a major factor in their belief system.

It was a fluke that Thomas knew this. He might have eventually figured it out, but thanks to professor D. H. Smith back at Harvard, he knew it already. He was getting closer. The treasure would be hidden somewhere in the West and in or around a pyramid formation that matched Giza. Therein lay the problem. There was a hell of a lot of land west of Saqqara.

Finally, Thomas came to the last sentence in the third paragraph. *You will find it, in the middle of the middle, marked by a circle in a square.* This clue sounded like specific instructions on where the treasure was located within the site. He wouldn't need to solve this part until he had located the specific pyramid structure.

Thomas placed his pen on the table and finished his beer. The first round was complete and he felt pretty good. He still had no idea as to *what* the treasure was. As for w*here*, he knew that the treasure was west of Saqqara and that it was hidden somewhere in or near a pyramid formation like those at Giza. Now, he needed help.

Thomas jumped to his feet and paced the room. He had made a serious mistake. He should not have been so quick to seek assistance. He had been too eager. It would've been far better to keep the project self-contained, to have taken the time to go to the University of Cairo tomorrow to complete the translation himself. Or, since there were a limited number of people in the world who were expert at deciphering ancient Hebrew, he could've asked each of them for one word apiece. He didn't even know Sinistar. *Stop it, McAlister! Stop second-guessing yourself. Martha recommended Sinistar.*

What about Martha? Should he have involved her? From the outset, he had known he'd need the help of others. Martha had been the perfect choice. But how long had she been working at Senneferi? Cataloguing was tedious, boring work. Years, decades, spent with a horsehair paint brush in one hand and a pencil in the other, delicately moving sand around, intricately reconstructing history. Could she have hit the proverbial wall?

She knew everything, except the translation of the message. At anytime, she could return to Unas with an ultrasound machine and make a copy of the riddle. Sinistar could translate it for her. Maybe he should destroy that section of the wall. No, that would be stupid. His whole train of thought was ridiculous. Martha would never betray him. She was incapable of such an act.

Thomas had been in Egypt many times and knew many of Martha's friends and colleagues. He'd also worked with numerous other Egyptian specialists . . . but he had never heard of Sinistar. Of course, that could be because he didn't work with linguists that often. Still, it was odd. But, again, he needed Sinistar. He couldn't solve the riddle without a linguist. It was too late now anyway.

The phone rang and Thomas snatched it off the hook on the first ring. The following conversation was burned into Thomas's memory. Sinistar had said, "I have the information you wanted, Dr. McAlister."

He read him the five words and biblical history as Christians and Jews had always known it was forever changed. It came like a tidal wave and hit Thomas like a physical blow.

"Are you there, Dr. McAlister? Dr. McAlister . . . sir . . . are you there?"

The implications were so enormous, it took a full minute for Thomas to get back to the present. "Yes, I'm sorry, doctor. I-I dropped my pen and had to pick it up. Dr. Sinistar, if I reread the words I provided for you, could you repeat the meaning for me? I want to be crystal clear, so that there's no misunderstanding so I won't have to bother you again. Now let's start. I'm reading Hebrew concurrent to Late Classic."

Thomas waited for Sinistar's answer. The linguist sighed impatiently and said, "Yes, yes, Dr. McAlister. I know."

Thomas's pulse was racing, as he carefully spelled the words. "The first word is *chabar*, spelled: C-H-A-B-A-R. It means?"

Dr. Sinistar, resigned to doing this Thomas's way said, "*Chabar* means *salvation* or *deliverance*."

Thomas smiled. "Good! That was my guess." He wrote the word down. "Let's go to the next words, *kanaph* and *nachash*, spelled: K-A-N-A-P-H and N-A-C-H-A-S-H. What do they mean?"

"These were harder. I have never in all my life seen these words written in Hebrew. The word *kanaph* means *feathered* or *plumed*. The word *nachash* means *dragon* or *serpent*. It's very, very odd, especially when I tell you the meaning of the final word."

Thomas shook his head. He thought his heart might leap out his chest. The implications were staggering. Almost incomprehensible. He spelled the next word for Dr. Sinistar.

"I could find no reference for this word, Dr. McAlister. None at all. None. And that is a first for me. So, I did a letter for letter translation, Hebrew to English."

Thomas waited. "And . . . what did it spell?"

"The letters spelled the following word: V-I-R-R-A-C-H-O-C-A." Then Sinistar quickly added, "This is all very strange, Dr. McAlister.

Very strange, indeed. That the word *Virrachoca* would be present, with words referencing the Mayan Plumed Serpent . . . all written in ancient Hebrew. I'm sure you're aware of these words, Doctor. And their Mayan origins?"

Thomas stared at the three words he'd written, and slowly under his breath whispered, "Jesus Christ!" They were ancient Mayan, purely Central American words, yet gleaned from an ancient Egyptian text.

Thomas ignored Sinistar's inquiries. He had to end this conversation immediately. He didn't want to give Sinistar a chance to become even more suspicious. If this turned out to be an actual Mayan reference in an ancient Hebrew text, it would be a career defining find. This was the stuff legends were made of. "One last word, Doctor. "*Cagullah*, spelled: C-A-G-U-L-L-A-H." He spoke slowly, as if speaking to a child.

"*Cagullah* is the Hebrew word for '*treasure* or *valuable gift*.' It refers to something considered priceless or beyond monetary value."

Thomas wondrously murmured the words to himself.

"What was that?" Dr. Sinistar asked.

Thomas didn't hear him. His mind was racing ahead. He was no expert in Mayan history, but he knew the Plumed Serpent was the ultimate Mayan god. He also remembered that Virrachocas were the ancient men who "came from the east" to teach the Maya all they knew about organized society, farming, math and astronomy. *If the riddle was, in fact, written by Moses . . . it was a direct link between ancient Eastern cultures and the West! It would prove one of the biggest and most hotly debated historical theories! It would be a bombshell.* Thomas regained his composure.

"Nothing, Dr. Sinistar. I was just mumbling, a bad practice." The riddle was starting to make sense to him now and he wanted to explode with joy. But he needed to finish this phone call, without arousing even more suspicion.

"This was a fascinating exercise, Dr. McAlister. You did say these words were from the same ancient text, didn't you?"

Thomas sensed where Sinistar was going. He'd already indicated that he knew the words referred to the pre-Columbian, ancient Maya civilization. He had quickly put two and two together. *It should've been impossible for any reference to pre-Columbian Mexico . . . to be written in ancient Hebrew.*

Thomas had to quickly produce a lie to deflect attention from his startling discovery. "No, I didn't say that. You must have misunderstood me. How could they be? We have pre-Columbian Mayan references *and* ancient Hebrew."

Dr. Sinistar continued. "That is what is so fascinating about these words. What on earth would an ancient Hebrew be doing talking about the Mayan Plumed Serpent or the ancient Virrachocas? This is all very odd, if you don't mind me saying so, Doctor. Where, may I ask, did you get the piece that you're translating? Martha did mention that the two of you were out at Saqqara today. Was it there?"

Damn it! Why had Martha told him they'd gone to Saqqara? There was so much text at Saqqara that was still not deciphered, anything was possible there. Thomas did not like Dr. Sinistar's level of interest, and the man was continuing to assume the words were from the same text, even after Thomas had told him they weren't. "I'm sorry, Doctor, but I cannot discuss the work any further, other than to reinforce that these words were not taken from the same text. I thank you heartily for your work, Dr. Sinistar. It was a tremendous help!"

"My pleasure, Thomas, my pleasure. Did you and Martha enjoy your trip to Saqqara today?"

Thomas wondered if Dr. Sinistar had already been looking into his whereabouts, to find out where he'd gotten the passage. He hoped it was not too late.

"Yes, we took a sight seeing trip, for old-time sake. I hadn't been there in years and longed to see it again. It was just as I had remembered."

"Do you plan to go back?" Dr. Sinistar asked. "Or is your work complete?"

"As I said, I'm on a pleasure trip, Doctor. I don't plan to return to

Saqqara, but I may tour some other sites."

"A pleasure trip, so soon after what happened at Arizona State? You must have been a wise investor, Doctor. That American bull market must have been good to you."

Dr. Sinistar was mocking him now, trying to draw him out. Sinistar knew he was on to something. He had either figured it out from the translation, or Martha had told him something about their discovery. Surely she would not do that! Thomas decided to check back with her anyway.

"I've been able to put away some travel funds. I needed a little break, before I start the job search again, and Egypt was a logical place. I hope you will excuse me, Dr. Sinistar. I really must be going now. Again, I appreciate the help. Good-bye."

"Au revoir, Dr. McAlister."

Thomas thought nothing of the fact that au revoir didn't really mean good-bye. But rather, we'll meet again.

CHAPTER 11

Thomas filled in the new words and read the riddle again.

Moses Riddle

I, son of Egypt, Father of Hebrews, never good with tongue or pen, am challenged to create a message that will at once conceal what I must hide while, at the same time, reveal what I must make known. I do it for you, because future, less destructive generations, must be allowed a window to eternity.

Broken once, it must be preserved for future civilizations to experience. It cannot be left here to the thieves and robbers, or worse. Here is my riddle, my challenge, to whomever considers himself worthy of revealing that which God has made

Like Egypt, it appears as one. Like Egypt, if you know her, it is two. This is not my original, but my only one. To the parched man; water. To he who is lost; bearings. To the godless; salvation. I take it west, to a place where the Plumed Serpent rules, where Virrachoca visited long ago, where it will be well maintained. It will be at an accouterment, worn by that great hunter in the sky, the same as the great complex at Giza. You will find it, in the middle of the eastern middle, marked by a circle on a square.

If you can determine the treasure, and have the vision to

know where it lies, then you have a great responsibility. Greater than many before you, and most after, for you will be keeper of the window to eternity. In the wrong hands, the window may be forever broken, stranding all who come after it to eternal wandering. Moses.

To expedite his research, Thomas assumed two things: that the riddle was written by Moses and that Moses had hidden something of great value. Assuming these things would allow him to devote his time to uncovering the most critical piece of the riddle, which had become figuring out *where* it was. Treasure was treasure, and with no job and no family, he had become a treasure hunter. Whether it was Aaron's staff, the Ark of the Covenant, or the Jar of Manna or something else entirely, he wanted it.

He focused on the last three sentences of the third paragraph. When he had first read the riddle, without filling in the missing words he had thought the word *West* referred to western Egyptian cities like Marsa Matruh or As Sallum. He reminded himself not to exclude far western Libyan cities, like Tripoli. But now, with Sinistar's translation, entirely new ideas emerged. The portals of the past opened and, through them, he found himself looking across the Atlantic. He forced himself to relax and think clearly. It was all very far-fetched, and he needed to be sure.

The two words that made Thomas forget about the Egyptian cities and focus on much more exotic, western lands were Plumed Serpent and Virrachoca. Although Thomas was not an expert on any country but Egypt, he did have working knowledge of the history of several other ancient cultures. He knew there was only one ancient group that could be associated with both Plumed Serpents *and* Virrachocas. The Olmec of Mexico. The Olmec, who preceded the Maya, were the dominant culture in Mexico during the time frame in which Moses had lived.

Thomas slowed the frenetic pace of his thoughts. Did he really have a riddle, written on the wall of a temple in Egypt, by Moses, that referenced the Olmec culture? If he did, if Moses had referenced the Olmec, he—Thomas McAlister, fired professor of archeology—had discovered an extraordinary piece of history. The message from Moses would be heralded as one of the greatest discoveries of all time. Thomas smiled and said aloud, "This alone is treasure."

After studying the riddle again, Thomas concluded that Moses had, in fact, referenced a continent believed undiscovered until Columbus. The Spanish had coined it the New World. Now, the modern world would learn that Moses had known about the continent almost 2500 years before Columbus was *born*!

Most archeologists would have dismissed his hypothesis immediately; for many others, it wouldn't even have flowered in their minds. Thomas was one of the few Egyptologists who had always believed that there was a link between pre-Mayan and other far eastern cultures, including the Egyptians, Africans, and Chinese. Many books and theories had been put forth on the subject, some good, but only loosely based on fact, some bad—so extreme as to suggest that aliens were the link. Thomas stuck to rational arguments. Arguments that may not have been scientifically proven, but that made perfect sense.

Even expert Mayanologists, like Michael Coe, admitted there were similarities between eastern and western cultures and that there could be a link. Thomas fully understood that without proof, without hard data, conservative academics would never endorse the theory. The difference between himself and these other professors was that he was able to use his imagination. He was able to look at history as one might look at an impressionist painting. Up close, objects were barely discernable, often nothing more than lone, harsh brush strokes, but at a distance the brush strokes and colors blended and the subjects became clear. He didn't need proof beyond a reasonable doubt. This wasn't a court case. The circumstantial evidence was simply indisputable.

Children were still taught that Columbus discovered the "New" World. Some teachers added that Vikings may have beaten him to it. Others, who liked to be historically accurate, reminded kids that the Indians were already there. When the really bright kids asked where the

Indians came from, the teachers usually said that they had trekked across North Eastern Russia to Alaska, thousands of years ago, when the Bering Strait was frozen. If it were a college class, the professor might add that maybe, just maybe, someone got in a boat on the western coast of Africa and paddled out to sea and the naturally occurring currents carried them to America. Which of course is exactly what Thor Heyerdahl did, and documented, in his famous book *Con Tiki.*

What the professors usually didn't mention was that as far back as 2000 BC, both ancient Egyptian and ancient Chinese cultures were very accomplished mariners, and that it would have been quite easy for them to cross either the Atlantic or the Pacific oceans. If you took a northern route from England to America, across the Atlantic, there were so many islands you rarely lost sight of land. The ancient Egyptians buried a 141-foot ocean-going vessel right next to the great pyramid at Giza, as if to challenge future generations. It is still on display at Giza.

Thomas had always known and accepted that if Thor Heyerdahl could cross the Atlantic, the most violent of all oceans, on little more than a raft, the ancient Egyptians could surely have made it across in a 141-foot ship.

The problem for historians had always been that there was not one shred of physical evidence that anyone from the Old World had ever set foot in the new one before Columbus, except for a few Vikings. That wasn't to say that there was no evidence at all. On the contrary, there were some very compelling arguments to be made for the mixing of cultures and sharing of information. The twenty named days of the Mayan 260-day calendar were almost identical to the names of the days in Eastern Asian civilizations. The quadripartite universe of the Maya, color, plants, animals and gods, were amazingly close to Asian ones. From a mathematical and astronomical perspective, the incredibly complex calculations that the Mayans used to predict lunar and solar eclipses were also similar to those of other cultures. The process for making their paper, called Amote, was also not unlike that used in other cultures.

There were many other less scientific similarities, like the Chinescolook of some Mayan pottery, and the Egyptian appearance of many Mayan statues, like the Chacmool idol at the Temple of the Warriors at the popular Mexican tourist destination Chichen Itza.

Thomas had always believed that, at some point in the very distant past, ancient cultures across continents had mixed. The idea fascinated and motivated him and he'd been teaching the theory for years. Standard course reading for his 400-level World Survey class in each of the last ten semesters had included Nelson's *The History of Civilization*, Stevens' *Comparative Ancient Cultures,* and Jerrod's *Through the Past Darkly.* These books had been approved by the Curriculum Review Board years ago. When the article, "Similarities across Antediluvian Cultures—Math to Mythology" was published, Thomas had to get it to his students despite the fact that it had been published immediately after the quarterly Curriculum Review Board meeting. It was his sharing of this idea with his students that had contributed to his being fired.

By not accepting the widely believed theory that the cultures on the two continents had evolved separately, he could believe that when Moses referenced the Plumed Serpent he was referring to the well-known Mayan god and when he used the term Virrachocas, he meant the ancient visitors to the Olmec and Peruvians. Thomas was able to conclude that Moses had taken the treasure across the Atlantic to what is now Mexico. What better place to hide a valuable treasure than a place where crime was punishable by death?

Thomas leaned back in his chair and lifted his shoulders several times to relieve his aching neck. Moses may have had difficulties giving speeches, but he had created a brilliant riddle that the people of his day couldn't have solved. The people of Moses' day did not know that another continent existed across the Atlantic Ocean. If mariners had known, they had never put their knowledge in writing. But somehow Moses had known about it. He had assumed that future cultures would have the wherewithal and means to locate the western continent after finding and accurately solving his riddle. *You were right, Moses.*

If Moses had taken the treasure across the Atlantic, then the three

pyramids, laid out like the stars forming Orion's belt, must be somewhere in Mexico, Guatemala, or Belize. But, by God, how would he ever
find them? Despite his limited knowledge of pre-Columbian Aztec and
Maya, he did know that there were thousands of mounds and pyramids
in Mexico. Looking for three arranged in a specific pattern could take a
lifetime.

Happy with the progress he'd made, Thomas decided to stop for the
night. His sub-conscious mind needed to work on the riddle. It needed
to ferment. He had narrowed the *where* in the riddle to Mexico, at least
for the time being. He had further to go on the *what* part, but at least
he had a good list of possibilities.

The next day, Thomas called his colleague, Don Ozgood, who specialized in Mayan studies at Arizona State. "Don, Thomas McAlister here.
How are you?"

"Why, I'm fine, Thomas. How are you? I hope you're not spending
time dwelling on the Board's decision. A right bad decision. They keep
that up and they're going to have faculty recruiting problems. You're
sorely missed, you know."

"Thanks for the kind words, Don. Appreciate them. I'm not dwelling
on the firing too much. Listen, I'm doing a favor for a friend and it
involves pre-Columbian Maya. You know lay folks, they think we archeologists are specialists on the whole globe."

"I hear yuh."

Thomas continued, "She's looking to find some old pyramid or
mounds that her father took her to as a child. They're somewhere in
Central America. She said there were three of them in a row. Since I have
nothing better to do, I agreed to help her find them. What I'm wondering is . . . are there any site maps, maps of any kind actually, that would
show me all the known pyramids in Mexico? Is there such a thing? It
didn't exist for Egypt until the seventies."

"Hmmm, let me think about that for a minute. It's going to be tougher
than you think. There are hundreds of pyramids down there. No, more
like thousands, most of them unexcavated and not mapped. Ever since

the technology to do a good mapping has been around, the Mexican government has put tight controls on site hunting. I'll tell you how I'd approach it, which wouldn't be the only way."

"If it's what you'd do, Don, it's good enough for me."

"There were two people who did a pretty good job of site mapping before the Mexican government took control. One was Karl Ruppert, way back in 1934. He mapped around thirty sites. He took readings by sextant. Ruppert's stuff is pretty close to accurate. The map is hard to get hold of, check the Tozzler Library at Harvard. They should be able to produce it for an old alum."

"Sounds good, Don."

"The next decent attempt was made by Rod Frates, a rich guy from Oklahoma. I think it was 1983 that he mapped about 110 sites, with an early global positioning system. He found more pyramids than Rupert and was more accurate, but he won't share the maps with anyone."

"Just my luck. My friend will be disappointed. Her quest might end before it even begins. Know of any way I could get a copy?"

"It just so happens I have a copy. I got it from a very good Mexican friend, who is employed by Instituto Nacional de Antropologia e Historia in Mexico. I could loan you a copy, but I'd have to ask you not to show it to another soul. I'm not supposed to have it. If this ever got into the hands of looters, it would spell disaster for the sites. Like I said, most of them are unexcavated and only show up on this one map. The Mexican government has become very secretive in recent years, so much has already been taken from that country.

Thomas worked to hold back his excitement. "If you send me a copy, you have my word I'll show it to no one. When I'm through with it, I'll either send it back to you or destroy it, whichever you prefer, Don."

"OK, good enough. I'll have to make a copy first. Where do you want me to send it?"

"Well, I'm in Egypt right now. If you could send it next day air, to my hotel, that would be great. Send it COD, of course. Thomas McAlister c/o The Four Seasons. Cairo."

"Simple enough. By the way, if the site she's looking for is well known, it might be on a public map. There are four maps you should probably have anyway: *Guia Roji* is published annually by the Mexican Government; the second is the standard topographical map published by the Mexican Insituto Nacional de Estadistica, *Geografia e Informatica*; the third is a *National Geographic* map, 1989 version; and last one is a Pemex's road atlas. Try them, you might get lucky."

"That's what I'll do, Don. I appreciate this, I really do. Have you got any idea where I could get copies of these four other maps?"

From experience, he knew that each map would show significant differences in everything from topography and form to distances. He wasn't looking for a challenge. He wanted the path of least resistance. Plus, every day equaled money, and money had become a finite resource.

Don audibly sighed. "Well, I wouldn't do this for just anyone, Tommy, but listen . . . I don't plan to return to Mexico for another six months. If you want, I can send you mine, but promise me you'll return them."

"Don, you have my word. I swear it. I can't tell you how much I appreciate this."

"You're onto something, Thomas. I can hear it in your voice. Listen, this may not matter to you but I thought you'd like to know. Washington's up for a seat on the University Board next month. We all think it played into his decision about you. A few of the current Board members are in with Brown. You weren't their favorite person. The whole stinking mess is costing Washington big-time credibility with the professorial body."

At Arizona State, a department dean's salary was doubled while serving on the Board. He would also receive other executive privileges, like a car allowance and country club membership.

"Thanks for letting me know, Don. That makes some things a little clearer."

"No problem. I thought you should know. Good luck with whatever you're after. Hope you find it."

Next, Thomas placed a call to his old friend, Dick Hightower, Director of Celestial programs at the Adler Planetarium in Chicago. Dick could provide data on Orion: statistics, angles, and other pertinent information.

A new discipline had recently emerged in anthropology, called astro-archeology. It combined the discipline of archeology with astronomy. Thomas liked the concept, but he was no expert in the field. What he did know about Orion was that it was a constellation in the northern sky representing a hunter, and that the three stars that comprised the hunter's belt were called Orion's Belt. The three pyramids, at Giza, had been erected to mirror it.

Luckily, Dick provided all the information Thomas needed off the top of his head. Actually, he knew far more than Thomas needed. He explained to Thomas how to draw Orion's Belt to scale, with a ruler. The angle was obtuse, 175 degrees, almost a straight line.

Thomas stayed in Egypt two more days. He received and studied the maps from Don on the first day. After an entire day spent leaning over them, he was unable to find three pyramids that matched the structure of the stars in Orion's Belt. There were many pyramids that came close, since ancient Mexican cultures built more than one pyramid in a complex, but none that matched.

The second day, he took Martha to lunch. Afterward, she drove him to the airport. He let her know that Dr. Sinistar had seemed overly curious.

"He was extremely helpful to me, but he was too curious and inquisitive. Wanting to see the whole text, first saying he needed it for the translations, then later asking out of sheer nosiness. He grilled me about what I was going to do next in Egypt, where I was going, who I'd be seeing. It was like he knew I'd found something. Do you know what I mean? Should I worry about him?"

Martha nodded. "He hates it when he thinks someone might know something about Egypt that he doesn't know. It's like a competition with him. I should've warned you. You don't need to be concerned, though. I've never known him to be unethical. And he doesn't get around that much anymore, since he lost the use of both of his legs." Thomas felt better, but only slightly.

Disappointingly, he was leaving Egypt with no idea of what the treasure was. He'd told himself he didn't care, that the important thing was *where* it was, but inwardly he did care. He did not relish the idea of going on a wild goose chase. He felt he should have been able to figure it out by now. He had a riddle that had been carved into an ancient Egyptian temple, by a man who was born in Egypt, in a language that he was fluent in, in a time period he was expert in. The missing ingredient had to be the religious aspect. It was impairing his ability to solve the riddle. Thomas was not a biblical scholar but he'd have to become one fast.

Martha dropped him at the airport and kissed him good-bye. She hadn't asked what he was looking for, or where he was going next. Questions like that were taboo among archeologists. She'd seemed content with his pledge to call her to explain everything when it was all over. He checked his bags and boarded the plane. He carried on all of Don's maps and the other Riddle material. He wanted to do two things on the plane: learn more about Moses' life from the Bible, and sleep. He removed the Bible from his Filson bag. He'd planned to sleep until lunch and spend the afternoon studying, but, after reading a few pages of the Bible, he couldn't put it down.

One of the greatest mysteries of all time is who wrote the Pentateuch, the first five books of the Bible. One of the most widely believed theories was that Moses wrote some, or all, of them. Of the five books— Genesis, Exodus, Leviticus, Numbers, and Deuteronomy—scholars believed that if Moses only wrote one of them, it was most likely Deuteronomy. Deuteronomy was a summary of Moses' exploits and, in a way, a summary of the other four books. It was written in the first person, by someone who was very close to what had taken place. Because Deuteronomy mirrored the other books so closely, and because the author was so well informed, scholars believed it might have been written before the other four books.

Thomas decided to read all five books, front to back. He had read the Bible in the past, and had often referred to it as an historical document, but had never focused on Moses. He was an hour into the flight when he read the first few lines of *Exodus*. What he read startled him. *Exodus* was all about Moses' life, his relationship with God, and with Egypt. But, there was an unexpected contradiction in the account . . . and a surprise.

Thomas reread *Exodus*, Chapter 20, several times. After returning from Mount Sinai and a conversation with God, Moses had proclaimed, *from memory*, the Ten Commandments to his followers, who had assembled before him. The ten he recited were those that are well known to every Jew and Christian today.

1. You shall have no other Gods before me.
2. You shall worship no idols or graven images.
3. You shall not take the Lord's name in vain.
4. You shall keep the Sabbath Day holy.
5. You shall honor your father and mother.
6. You shall not murder.
7. You shall not commit adultery.
8. You shall not steal.
9. You shall not bear false witness.
10. You shall not covet your neighbor's house, or spouse.

Later, in Chapter 32, Moses *returned* to Mount Sinai. This time God wrote the Commandments on two stone tablets and gave Moses specific instructions on how to build a special chest, called an ark, in which to carry them. He also gave Moses instructions on how to make other sacred objects, such as a bejeweled gold breastplate, two onyx balls inscribed with the names of the twelve tribes, and a golden crown.

Thomas recognized the movie scene that Charlton Heston had made famous, in Chapter 32, verse 19. Moses had come down from Mt. Sinai with the tablets, to find his people worshipping a golden calf and involved in licentious behavior. In his anger, he had thrown the two stone tablets to the ground, destroying them. Immediately after the tablets were broken,

Moses and Aaron, and those faithful to God, had slaughtered thousands of their former followers.

It was here that Thomas realized something new about the story. Up to this point, Moses had only verbally communicated the Ten Commandments to his people. No one had actually seen them, because the tablets had been smashed. Thomas had been taught that the Ark of the Covenant contained the tablets. But, if Moses had shattered them . . . how could they be in the Ark? Maybe only the fragments were inside? Gripped by the story, Thomas read on.

Suddenly, he discovered a passage that he didn't remember ever having read before. It contained a wholly different message, which astounded him. He wiped his forehead and looked furtively around the First Class cabin. The other passengers were diligently reading novels and business periodicals. No one was paying attention to him.

In Chapter 34, verse 1, God had told Moses, "Cut two tablets of stone, like the first two, and I will write upon the tablets the words that were on the first tablets, which you broke." God went on to tell Moses to make a second Ark, but not like the first golden one. This one was to be a simple wooden box, made from acacia wood.

Thomas reached into his bag and pulled out the Moses riddle. The words echoed in his mind, but he carefully reread the lines. *"Broken once, my treasure must be preserved for future civilizations to experience."* And then, *"Like Egypt, it appears as one. Like Egypt if you know her, it is two. This is not my original, but my only one."*

That was it! Moses was telling him that the object was the second set of Commandments contained in the second Ark, the simple wooden one.

"Yes!" he said, softly, but with passion to himself.

The woman in the seat next to his looked over. "Sorry," he said, "I just solved a very difficult riddle."

She smiled, mouthing the words, "No problem," before returning to her reading.

He had solved the riddle. He didn't know where the treasure was but he did know what it was. Now if he could locate it, he could, with one find, prove that both pre-Columbian cross-Atlantic communication took place *and* uncover one of, if not *the*, greatest lost treasure that mankind had ever known. It would also redeem him professionally. But there was more.

Thomas kept reading and two significant questions arose.

Later in Exodus, after the new tablets were made, Moses had gone ahead with the construction of the ornamental golden Ark. So there are two Arks . . . the ornamental one and the simple one, but only one set of tablets. I wonder which one Moses was referring to in the riddle, the gold one or the plain one? He re-read the riddle but it gave him no clue.

The second astonishing fact he found was that after Moses returned from Mt. Sinai the second time, with the new set of tablets God had given him, he had summoned all of Israel and read them the Commandments as written by God. This was the first time he had read the text *as written*. In the two earlier references to the Commandments they had either been recited from memory, Exodus 20, or broken and not recited at all, Exodus 32. So that passage—Exodus 34—recounted the first time his people had heard God's real and intended Commandments. *And . . they were not the same as before. They were very different!*

Thomas read and reread the passages. Each time, he came to the same conclusion. The real Ten Commandments, as written by God on the second set of tablets, mentioned nothing about killing, committing adultery, stealing or spreading lies about others. Not a word! *Can this possibly be true? If so, why haven't scholars ever made light of this important contradiction? It's right here in the Bible.*

Thomas quickly sorted through the implications. What might happen if he found the real tablets and made public that the four most strict Commandments people live by are not those that God intended? But, rather, those that Moses made up to keep his rowdy followers in line?

First, of course, no one would believe him. But once the tablets were dated, and verified by comparing Exodus 20 to Exodus 34, it would be obvious. A perfect fit. He would have proof that Moses lied, and it would reveal to the world that the Ten Commandments of today, those that our legal system are based on, are false. It would demonstrate that the real Commandments are much more lenient. But would this be a good thing? Did he want to discredit the major Jewish prophet, and a minor Islamic one, while showing that the rules God intended us to live by were more lenient than originally thought?

He continued that line of thinking. People are strange. If the public found out that the real Ten Commandments do not match the accepted ones, certain parts of society might come apart at the seams. Religion might be discredited and crime could skyrocket. Historically speaking, the Commandments were the foundation of the judicial system. They drove order and discipline into law making. What might happen to those same laws, that same peaceful order, if it was shown that the basis for which they were formed was a lie? If it were shown that a prophet who had a key relationship with God, the major prophet of the Jewish faith, had lied? Thomas could see it on the cover of every newspaper in every city in the world: Moses Lied—thou shall not kill, lie, steal, or commit adultery not true Commandments! Let the murderous orgy begin.

But that was only half of it. Next would come any archeologist's worst nightmare: a dispute over ownership. It wouldn't just be the Pope, the Jews, and the Christians. Oh no. The entire Middle East, the Arab epicenter, would demand the Commandments be given to them. Each religion, each culture, was in its own way iconolatristic. Each was willing to change laws, impose sanctions, reverse promises, and shed blood for possession of certain artifacts. They had proven it many times. Government involvement in any archeological find always signaled trouble. Having a treasure impounded for two years while bureaucrats lazily debated provenance took all the fun out of the job.

Thomas reigned in his imagination. There was no guarantee he would find anything. Still, he was happy with his progress. He now felt reasonably sure that he knew what the treasure was. He still didn't know where to look for it. There was a lot of land in between Texas and South America, but he was excited about the search.

"I can get you a blanket if you're cold, Mr. McAlister." The stewardess had noticed the goose bumps on Thomas's arm.

"Thanks for asking, but how about a glass of celebratory champagne?"

"What are you celebrating?" Expectantly.

"Moses."

"Well, that's a first." She paused. "I'll be right back." She saw his Bible as she turned away. *Damn*, she thought, *he's a priest. I keep telling mother all the good ones are taken.*

A short time later, he had his champagne.

CHAPTER **12**

Thomas, for all of his training and semi-academic fame, was not a well-rounded archeologist. Egypt was his domain. He knew Egypt intimately and was well aware of her place in history, but he did not know any other culture quite as well. He would need help, if he were going to travel into Mayan country.

Before leaving Egypt, he'd called the university to talk to Don Ozgood again. He'd told him he was looking for a Mexican archeologist who specialized in the Maya, to serve as a consultant and guide for a short trip he was taking to Mexico. Ozgood recommended a man named Arturo Bandera. Ozgood's friend, and occasional guest speaker, Bandera was a Mayan expert living in the state of Oaxaca. Thomas had gotten the address, thanked Ozgood, and immediately called Bandera.

Bandera was home on sabbatical and there was enough good chemistry on the phone, that after a short introduction and phone interview, Thomas agreed to fly down and meet with him in person. That way, if Bandera were the right man to help him, they could start right away. If, for some reason, he and Bandera didn't click, he'd already be in Mexico and could interview other potential candidates.

The cab that brought him home from the airport was backing out of his driveway, and Thomas was in the process of unlocking his door and thinking about what to pack for a hot Mexican trip, when someone walked up behind him.

"Your friends from the university were here while you were away."

"*What?*"

"Your friends from the university came by while you were away."

Mrs. Wallace, the neighbor who always watered his plants and fed his beetle when he was away, was scurrying up the driveway. She lived alone and was a terrible snoop, but Thomas didn't mind. He had nothing to hide and she was extremely reliable.

She had her knotted her brown hair into a tight bun that accentuated her shrew-like face. Her drab-green knee-length dress was covered with one of the two aprons she rotated daily. Today, it was the aqua one.

"What friends, Mrs. Wallace? I wasn't expecting anyone. Are you sure it was someone from the university?" Thomas waited for her to reach him and then invited her into the house. He threw his briefcase onto the couch and removed his suit jacket, draping it carelessly over the arm of the chair while he listened.

"Yes. Two very nice men. They knocked at the door while I was feeding Howard. They said they were colleagues of yours at the university. They said they needed to talk with you about your current research project. I told them you were away for a few days. They asked if I knew where you were."

"What did you tell them?"

"I told them you'd gone to Egypt. You told me that's where you were going. You didn't say I shouldn't tell anyone."

"Did they ask any more questions?"

"Yes, they certainly did. They wanted to know if you'd left the university before or after you started your current project. Shouldn't they have known that? I told them I hadn't the slightest idea and that it wasn't my business. But . . . ." Mrs. Wallace's mouth closed and she seemed to be thinking about the conversation.

"But, what?"

"Well, it was the way they looked at each other. They seemed to think you purposely quit your job to work on some new project."

Thomas's mind raced through a series of possibilities. Who would know that he was working on something? Martha, Don Ozgood, and . . . Dr. Sinistar.

"Was one of the men in a wheelchair?"

"No, they both walked fine. I did notice that someone waited in the car for them."

"What else did these colleagues of mine ask?"

"Nothing. Once I told them I didn't know anything, they stopped asking me questions. They could tell I didn't like their nosiness." Mrs. Wallace patted her bun. "Besides, I didn't particularly like the way they looked."

"What did they look like?"

"Well, one had very dark skin, but he wasn't black, mind you. He looked Middle Eastern, and, well, since you're an Egyptologist, I just figured that he was Egyptian. He was short and kind of heavy. He had a little mustache. Too little for the shape of his face. The other man was like a thin version of Al Gore. Basic looking."

Thomas couldn't think of a single Egyptian acquaintance who matched Mrs. Wallace's descriptions. He wondered what Dr. Sinistar looked like. But it couldn't have been Sinistar, since he didn't have the use of his legs. He had no idea who the other person could've been.

"If it's something important, they'll call or come by again. Don't worry about it, you did fine."

Mrs. Wallace smoothed the front of her apron. "I didn't particularly care for these men. I won't judge them, though. Goodness know, I'm no beauty and I'm not perfect, and they were actually . . . very nice."

Thomas was about to leave the room. "Mrs. Wallace, I have to go on another trip. This one may take longer. Can you feed Howard for me until I return?"

He didn't wait for her to reply, but took the stairs two at a time, to get to his bedroom. He pulled the largest duffel bag out of the closet and tossed it onto the bed. He located his Kabar survival knife on the shelf above his clothing and threw it into the bag.

"Of course, Thomas." Mrs. Wallace appeared in the doorway. She was wringing her hands. Suddenly she'd become very nervous.

"Mrs. Wallace? What's wrong?"

"Well . . . I was hoping you knew those men and were expecting them."

He stopped packing, realizing something was seriously wrong.

"Why, Mrs. Wallace? Do you have something else to tell me?"

"They asked me if you'd been working here, at home, before you went to Egypt."

"Yes?" A slow steady stream of dread came over Thomas.

"I told them I didn't know. You know, that we weren't so close that I would know something like that. I told them that it was certainly possible because you do keep a home office in the basement."

"That's okay, Mrs. Wallace. That's no big deal."

She continued, sheepishly. "They . . . asked if they could see your office. They said they needed to get in touch with you, and that maybe something down there would help them figure out where you were."

Thomas's pulse quickened. "Yes?"

"They had said they were colleagues of yours, and there was something that you might have that could help them. Something that you wouldn't need, but that could really help them." Her eyes began to flood with unshed tears.

"Mrs. Wallace, it's okay. You didn't do anything wrong. Don't worry about a thing. I don't keep anything of value here at the house." He lied. "Can you tell me what happened next."

She continued, seemingly relieved. "I went downstairs with them. As I said, they were very nice people, Thomas. Not suspicious at all. It's a good thing I let them go down there, because when we got down to your office, we noticed that you'd left a very valuable Egyptian book, sitting right outside of its special humidifier case."

The book, *The Amenophis Notes*, didn't have to be in the case all the time. But he didn't tell her that, she was already too worried. "Did you put it back in the humidifier?"

"Well, first they looked at everything you had out on your desk, including the book and then they . . . they . . . said that, that book, *The Builder's Notes*, they called it, was what they were looking for."

Thomas was fuming inside. They'd looked through his private research!

Mrs. Wallace must have seen it on his face because she immediately said, "Thomas, it was really no big deal. They didn't care that you'd forgotten to put it back in the case. They said they wanted to borrow the book. They said it wasn't yours, that it was on loan to you, and they even had a letter confirming everything, that you had signed, with a picture of the book. They said they would return it in a few days. I figured you wouldn't miss it, since you were in Egypt."

"Mrs. Wallace, I don't want you to worry about it. I'm sure I'll get a phone call soon. I may have a message on my machine right now. You said you didn't get their names or phone numbers, didn't you?

"They did show me their credentials, but I didn't think . . . oh, it all happened so fast. One minute I was feeding little Howard and the next minute, the men were in the basement telling me they needed to borrow the book. They flashed me their cards again and told me the book wasn't really yours and that they'd bring it back anyway and . . . ."

She kept talking but Thomas tuned her out. He sat on the edge of the bed, evaluating options. His whole plan was in jeopardy. Whoever had taken the book could discover the same clue he had found. They could travel to Saqqara and search for the Moses Riddle, exactly as he had done. Hopefully it wasn't too late. Quick, decisive action was the only way to prevent disaster. He would have to destroy the riddle. In archeology, there is only one time when it is okay to destroy an historical artifact, and that is when it is done to preserve something of even greater value. The treasure mentioned in the riddle was far more important than the riddle itself. He must save Moses' carefully hidden artifact from getting into the wrong hands at all costs. He found it difficult to even think of ordering the defacement of the pyramid, but it had to be done. He needed to call Martha immediately. She would have to return to Saqqara, and scrape off the layer of limestone where Moses had carved the riddle.

Thomas grabbed his address book and dashed to the phone, with Mrs. Wallace close behind.

He dialed Martha's number in Egypt.

"Thomas, please forgive me if I've done something wrong! You know I didn't mean any harm. I hope you'll still let me come over and feed Howard. If you decide not to, I will completely understand."

"Mrs. Wallace, please, believe me, this is not your fault. Those men would've gotten in here, whether you let them in or not. Don't you worry about it for a second."

Martha wasn't home, and he got her answering machine. "Martha, it's Thomas. I just got home and discovered someone has stolen the *Amenophis Builders Notes*. I need you to go to the temple and destroy the riddle. A chisel and a hammer should do it. Make sure no one can do what we did. Call me on my voice mail to let me know that you got this message. It needs to be done immediately, Martha. I'll owe you one." He started to replace the receiver, but added, "And Martha, be careful."

Thomas rushed past Mrs. Wallace to the bedroom. He had to move. Whoever was smart to enough to find the riddle would be smart enough to solve it.

"I don't know when I'm coming back, Mrs. Wallace. You've got the key to my house. Please water and feed Howard. And this time, nobody gets in okay? And the conversation I had on the phone is not to be repeated."

"Okay! Don't worry about a thing. I've learned my lesson. Nobody gets into this house."

» » « «

Thomas met Arturo at the airport in Oaxaca and they drove north to his ranch, where he lived with his wife, son, and daughter. He liked Arturo the minute he laid eyes on him, and his feelings were confirmed when he accepted a warm handshake and peered into dark brown, friendly eyes.

Arturo was clearly of Mayan decent, with little, if any, Spanish blood. He was short, no more that 5'3", had straight shiny black hair, and a typically round Mayan face. He wore Wrangler blue jeans, with a large oval belt buckle made of silver with a gold appliqué lining, a light blue short sleeved shirt and a straw cowboy hat. He dressed like a lot of good field archeologists Thomas had worked with. He spoke excellent English and had an honest smile. The few times Thomas had worked with Hispanic colleagues he'd found them to be innately nice people but sometimes they were so amiable, it had disconcerted him. He'd found himself wondering what they were really thinking behind their smiling eyes. He didn't get that feeling with Arturo.

Thomas didn't say so but he also liked Arturo's faded, red Ford F150 pickup. It was exactly what he would've driven if he lived on a ranch outside of Oaxaca. In the field, the more primitive the vehicle, the closer you were to finding something.

They arrived at the ranch as the sun was setting over the western mountains. Before they even reached the house Thomas smelled onions, garlic and the unmistakable scent of fresh cilantro.

They were greeted by Arturo's two small children, George and Sophie, who introduced themselves to Thomas while tugging and pulling Arturo toward the house. Arturo's wife, Maria, had put dinner out as soon as she heard the truck coming up the driveway. The minute they walked into the house, she ushered them into the dining room for chicken enchiladas smothered in chiwauwau cheese, Spanish rice, and refried beans.

It was a wonderful dinner, followed by good conversation. Despite his anxiety about the project, Thomas let the conversation unfold naturally. He and Arturo got to know each other, and Thomas came to understand why Don Ozgood had recommended Arturo. He was a first-rate archeologist, in a country with a deep archeological history. He had worked at the top-level sites, meaning he was routinely entrusted with Mexico's most valuable artifacts. Thomas learned that Arturo had recently been involved in a major find at Copan. As it turned out, Arturo was home for a year, on a sabbatical, writing a book about the recent Copan expedition.

At one point, long after dinner was over, after they had retired to the beautiful patio that Arturo had built, there was a lull in the conversation. Thomas had already decided that Arturo was perfect for his mission. In fact, he found himself hoping that Arturo wouldn't turn him down. He refilled his wine glass with the smooth Mexican Merlot from the Sierra Madres, and passed the bottle to his new friend. "Arturo, as you know I'm pure Egyptologist. I don't know much at all about the pre-Columbian history of your country. Or post-Colombian, for that matter." Thomas paused. "Though I know Benito Juarez was a very great man."

Arturo raised his glass and they both drank to Juarez.

Thomas continued. "I am involved with a very important, private project. I am funding it myself. I have no sponsor. No one else has the information I posses. I have narrowed my search to Mexico, and I need help. I need someone who knows Mexico inside and out. I was hoping you might be that person. If you have time, and the interest . . . ." In America, Thomas would have added that he would compensate Arturo, but he knew a little about the Hispanic culture and it was much, much too early to discuss that type of thing.

Arturo hesitated, and Thomas saw his face harden. Thomas wondered if he'd said something wrong, something offensive.

"Thomas, is your hidden object Olmec or Mayan in origin? Or was it crafted by another Central American culture? With all due respect, sir, all digs inside Mexico must be sanctioned by the Instituto Nacionale de Antropologia e Historia, of which I am a member."

Thomas immediately understood the reason for Arturo's concern. Many an honest archeologist had been lured into corruption through the quest for hidden treasure in Mexico. Arturo didn't know Thomas well enough to know that he wasn't just a greedy looter looking for gold wherever he could find it. "No, no, Arturo. What I am looking for was made elsewhere, in the Middle East, actually, and is only being *stored* in Mexico. I assure you it is not of Mexican origin. If it were, I would certainly go through proper channels."

Arturo looked relieved. "I had to make sure. Ever since those Spaniards showed up a few hundred years ago, we've been a little wary of foreigners wanting to look for treasure in our country. We can continue."

"If you feel you can trust me, and if you're interested in participating in something of great historical significance, I will explain the entire thing to you. What I can tell you now is that I would need your help locating the object. I have a few clues as to where it is, but nothing exact. Once we find the object, we'll need to excavate and remove it. Quickly, if possible. I don't think I'm the only person looking for it. Some of my research was recently stolen from me and I've got a bad feeling about it."

"It's that valuable."

"If it's what I think it is, yes."

"I am on sabbatical. How long do you think it will take?"

"It's hard to say. I don't know enough at this point. I'd guess as little as one week. If I need to return to Arizona for equipment to extract it, that might draw it out to a month. But I want you to know, Arturo, this won't be a normal archeological dig. I have to move very fast. As I said, my source document has been stolen. It contained my initial clue. There are several steps in between my source document and the treasure, but if I've gotten this close, someone else could, too."

Thomas stopped and thought about the long, sickening gouges Martha's chisel would make on the soft limestone interior of the temple at Saqarra. "There'll be no procedure. No real mapping, no offsetting or surveying. We get the treasure and get out. Then, when it's safe, we can go back and study the site. Obviously I'm generalizing. If you agree to help me, I'll tell you everything."

Arturo nodded. "Well, it's late. Let's go to bed. We can talk about it more in the morning. Is that all right with you?"

"Of course. You need time to think about this. Talk it over with Maria. It wasn't in your plans for a sabbatical."

» » « «

Martha reached Saqqara about ten o'clock that evening. She'd gotten home from work at half past eight and showered, before checking her messages. There had been an edge in Thomas's voice that she hadn't heard before. She had immediately dressed and driven to Saqqara. She had a hammer and chisel in the tool box in the back of the Mercedes. She was planning to deface a national treasure . . . but it was to save a priceless world icon.

Subconscious alarms sounded when she noticed a van parked in the visitor's lot. The grounds had been closed for over two hours. It could be parked here for a million reasons: maintenance personnel, guards, tourists with a broken down car.

She hurried the hundred yards to the temple Unas, which contained the pyramid texts, but she froze as she approached the entrance. A light was shining out of the doorway of the temple. She advanced cautiously. She could hear voices inside. It sounded like they were arguing about something. She inched her way along the wall of the temple, trying to stay as inconspicuous as possible. When she reached the entrance, she peeked through the partially open door. There, in his wheelchair, pointing up at the portion of the wall that contained the Moses Riddle, was *Dr. Sinistar*.

Martha hugged the side of the door and slowly took another look. Sinistar wasn't alone. He was at the base of a ladder barking commands to someone who was working near the location of the riddle. He was holding something in his hand, pointing.

Thomas's message had said that someone had stolen *The Amenophis Builders Notes*. The theft must have been arranged by Dr. Sinistar. Inwardly, Martha cursed herself for giving Dr. Sinistar so many details of Thomas's visit. She had to get a message to Thomas to tell him that not only had she not been able to destroy the riddle, but that Dr. Sinistar was trying to find and decipher it.

She inched backward, into the darkness of the Egyptian desert. With no moon, it was pitch black. She spun, ran to her car, and raced back to her apartment. She was still breathing hard when she left the phone message for Thomas.

» » « «

The next day, Thomas met Arturo on the same patio. Arturo told Thomas about the various microclimates around Oaxaca over a breakfast of true Mexican omelets. Thomas took it as a good sign that they were eating alone. After breakfast they took a walk around the ranch and Arturo, with still no agreement to help, asked questions about the clues that had led Thomas to believe the treasure was in Mexico.

Despite misgivings about sharing information before he had Arturo's agreement to assist, Thomas took him through the events of the last two weeks, explaining how he'd found the clue in the *Builder's Notes*, found the riddle in Egypt, and gone on to solve it. He told him that he was now looking for a formation of pyramids that were laid out like the stars in Orion's belt, like those at Giza, which Thomas demonstrated by arranging rocks on the ground. After their walk, Arturo took Thomas to his home office, a comfortable room off the living room, with a Satillo tile floor and a beamed ceiling of thick Mexican oak. Thomas showed Arturo the exact arrangement of the stars that Dick Hightower had given him for Orion's Belt.

"The pyramids must have this same formation. Don Ozgood loaned me these maps. Hopefully they will be familiar to you. Don said these are the best available."

Arturo smiled as each of the maps was rolled out on the library table.

"You're smiling. Why?"

"I've used each of these many times. They are as familiar to me as my wife's face. For a long time these *were* the best maps of Mexico. And to many people they still are. However . . . ."

Arturo strode to the custom-built wall unit that covered the entire east wall of his office. He reached to locate a key, hidden behind a vase on one of the shelves, and used it to unlock the doors that enclosed the middle shelf. There was a dowel in the middle of the shelf, holding about ten rolled maps in place. He reached in, slid one of the maps out, and brought it over to the desk. Thomas moved his maps out of the way.

As Arturo unrolled his map, from right to left, Thomas first saw the Atlantic, then a small bump about the size of the head of a nickel, which was Cozumel, after which came the Yucatan Peninsula, and then all of Mexico.

"This is a recent satellite photo, commissioned by the INAH."

Thomas nodded. He owned similar photos of Egypt.

Arturo continued. "I worked on this project. These are the first results and they've come directly to me from Washington. I haven't even registered them with my government yet."

"What are these clusters of dots that are all over that place?" Thomas pointed to only a few, of the hundreds of places, where there were small groups of three or four dots.

Arturo smiled. "Those, my friend, are the genius of this map. Many regions of Mexico, to this day, remain unexplored. Consequently, many of our oldest sites remain unfound. We know of some, but we needed a way to be able to find them all. A cost analysis showed that the expense of sending expeditions out to look for them was prohibitive. We needed a means, like your depth charge technique in the Valley of the Kings, that would enable us to know where all the ruins lay, without having to travel there."

Thomas had used sonar images, retrieved from planting small explosives underground, to lead him to hollow areas in the Valley of the Kings. The process had been ground-breaking, literally, and had been well chronicled in archeological journals.

Arturo continued, "Unlike the Valley of the Kings, where the ruins are relatively close together, the ruins in Mexico are spread out over thousands of square miles."

"The situation sounds inordinately challenging."

Arturo smiled with pride. Thomas could tell he was leading up to something, savoring his coup de grace. Arturo pointed to the map. "What I did, you see, was to tell the people in Washington who run this satellite to have it move across this area just as the sun was rising. Every mound, every ancient pyramid, even the old cenotes, would cast a shadow. I had them take pictures, wide, nonstop pictures. They sent them all to me. This one is the best. Every pyramid in Mexico can be found by its shadow. Every mound is here. We picked up naturally occurring hills and mountains, but we overlaid a topographical map and erased them. Thus, we were left with only our pyramids, and we are a whole lot smarter than we were before. Nice, huh?"

"Ingenious, Arturo!" Thomas exclaimed. "Pure genius. I may try something like this in Egypt!" He caught himself. "After you've published your paper, of course."

"Good luck, amigo, these satellite companies are real snobs. It was like, how do you say, 'pulling teeth,' to get them to do what we wanted."

Thomas took out the drawing he had made of the Orion constellation and placed it next to Arturo's satellite photo. "Let's see if your map can help us find our destination. You take the western half of the map, and I'll take the eastern. Okay?"

The two men scanned the map, inch by inch, looking for a cluster of dots that might represent Orion's belt. They weren't more than ten minutes into the examination when Thomas hastily reached for the paper on which he'd drawn the stars. Using his mechanical pencil he connected the dots, then laid the paper over the map. The pyramid shadows were visible under the paper, and Thomas had found a cluster that lay directly on the path of the lines he had drawn. *"I've got it!"*

"Let me see." Arturo moved over to take a look. "Yes, that's it. That's a match."

"I can't believe it. We've got it! The accouterment to Orion, in the land of the West."

CHAPTER 13

The pyramid formation was in the state of Veracruz, where the oldest ruins in all of Mexico were located. Olmec territory. The formation was known as El Manati. It was a small site that had never been excavated, located about five miles outside a small town called Mercado. Arturo had heard of it, but had never been there. They could only find a few general references to it in the books in Arturo's library. It was approximately 150 miles, or a three hour drive from Arturo's house. They made plans to leave at four-thirty the next morning, in order to reach the jungle before the high heat. That gave them the rest of the day to load Arturo's pickup with supplies. There was no question of Arturo's involvement. He was hooked, and Thomas wanted him. Maria had seen the gleam in her husband's eyes and was happy that he would have an exciting break in his year long sabbatical.

Thomas accepted Arturo's voluntary, solemn promise that he would not tell another soul about the project. There was no need for a confidentiality agreement. It would have been an insult. As they packed, he filled Arturo in on the details of the Moses Riddle. He told him everything hoping that Arturo might help with some of the still missing facts.

Thomas told Arturo about the Amenophis notes, and read Arturo the exact translation of the Riddle the next day while they were driving. Occasionally, Arturo asked him questions, but mostly Arturo stared at the road, occasionally crossing himself. He didn't say so but he was shocked at what he was hearing. Shocked, at the sad sequence of events that had led up to Thomas finding the Riddle. Shocked, that the man beside him had put so much information together in such a short period of time. He was also worried about the theft of the *Builders Notes*. He didn't share any of these thoughts with Thomas. Nor did he tell him that he had a .357 Magnum, seven shot revolver hidden under the front seat of the truck.

Arturo's map indicated there was a road from Mercado to El Manati, but recommended they stay away from the town so as not to arouse suspicion. "I think we should park the truck in an inconspicuous spot a few miles outside of Mercado. We can cut our way through the jungle from there. It will take a couple of hours, and it will be slow going, but no one will know we are there."

Thomas had seen Arturo loading Bushmaster machetes into the back of the pickup, and nodded his agreement.

El Manati had remained a small dejected site buried deep in the jungle, while the huge sprawling ruins of nearby La Venta and Palenque attracted the academic attention and the tourist dollars. The jungle surrounding El Manati was thick, hot, humid, insect-filled. Thomas was accustomed to the desert, where he could walk right up to his target needing only a hat to shield him from the sun, and good boots to keep the sand out.

They had driven three hours when Arturo suddenly pulled off the dirt road onto a sandy median. Thomas's pulse quickened. The old feeling, the excitement, of being close to lost treasure returned. They gathered their supplies and started their trek inward. Arturo left a note on the windshield explaining that he was a government employee conducting official survey-ing work so that his pickup wouldn't get stripped while they were gone.

The going was tough from the beginning. The network of thick, wiry jungle grew right up to the shoulder of the road. Every step had to be earned by chopping or cutting. There was constant stopping to re-chop a stubborn branch or to re-apply the super-strength military mosquito repellent. As the early morning hours passed, Thomas grew to respect Arturo's resilient and tenacious leadership style. It became clear that from an anthropological perspective Arturo, and his ancestral Maya, were perfectly suited for this terrain. Short, stocky legs and arms perfectly evolved for chopping vines and bending and ducking under branches. It was no wonder the Maya had flourished here.

Arturo doggedly cut and wove, always maintaining the same consistent pace. He was at one with the land. Thomas, much taller, often had to stop to chop away the higher plant growth. This meant raising the machete above his head, causing him to use more calories and different muscle groups. Thomas stopped to swing and cut, Arturo glided over, under, and through. After only ten minutes Thomas's shoulder was burning, and he often had to hurry to catch up, never able to fall into that mind numbing, steady-smooth chopping pace that would have helped make the trek more bearable.

It was close to noon when they reached their destination. Thomas was instantly disappointed when he saw what was left of the pyramids. Accustomed to the huge, overbearing structures that pocked the Egyptian horizon, it was hard to believe that the three hills before him had ever been pyramids. At best, they were mounds, covered with brush and small trees. No rock formations, or any formal man made structures, were even visible.

"Are you sure this is El Manati?"

"Yes, yes, this is El Manati. These pyramids are known, but appear on few maps. In their day, they were probably twice as tall as they are now. Yes, Thomas, this is your site."

Thomas thought of the last verse of the Moses riddle. *You will find it in the middle of the eastern middle, marked by a circle on a square.* Thomas took this to mean that he needed to excavate the easternmost pyramid, in the middle of its east side. He needed to find the middle of the eastern pyramid but these pyramids were badly eroded and were shorter than they would've been in Moses' time. Thomas considered how he might find the middle as he helped Arturo set up camp near the base of the pyramid. He determined the only way to find the true middle was to try to use the angles of the pyramid's sides to calculate its original height. After they'd set up camp he began to climb to the top of the eastern pyramid, counting paces as he went.

It was not high when compared with most well-known pyramids in Mexico, but it did get Thomas above the tree line, and the view was magnificent. He gazed across an endless green sea, in all directions. So different from the dry Egyptian desert. Far off to the west he could see a few two-story buildings in what must've been the little town of Mercado.

The riddle had directed him to find the spot halfway up the eastern side. He counted the paces down. Forty. He then walked back up twenty paces and drove a stick into the mound next to his foot, to mark the halfway point. Before he and Arturo started digging, he would use the lightweight surveying camera to pinpoint the true middle. But neither of those points would be where they would start digging.

Since the apex of the pyramid had eroded, Thomas would input the slope of the sides of the pyramid into a trigonometric formula to determine how high the pyramid had been 3000 years ago. They would then start digging at the real halfway point. If all went well, when they hit the side, there would be a mark, hopefully a circle in a square. And, that would be how he would know he was in the right spot.

They had tortillas, Snickers, and water and then started to dig. It was tough going. They were in direct sunlight all afternoon. As the day progressed, so did the heat and humidity. The earth was hard and dry, and fine dust drifted up into their eyes and collected on their sweat-soaked skin. Digging together, continuously, it was three hours before their shovels struck the hard surface of pyramid rock.

His heart skipped a beat when he felt the vibration of solid rock through the shovel. Arturo's next try struck home, too. Hard digging so close to a find was normally taboo, but they were not excavating like true archeologists. They were treasure hunting and Thomas had made it clear to Arturo that there was no time for traditional charting, stratiography, or trowels or brushes to whisk away the dirt. This find was much too important to do the job right. That would have taken months, or in bureaucratic Mexico, maybe even years, even with Arturo's influence. No, in this case, hard-core shovel digging was the only option.

Normally, Thomas followed governmental procedure, but even Arturo agreed that had they waited, it would've given whomever had stolen the *Builders Notes* time to solve the riddle and claim the site as their own. Plus the process would've locked Thomas in a bureaucratic battle for years. Worse, competition might show up at the sight, outnumber him, and take the treasure by brute force. Even if they posted guards, which inevitably had to be done during long digs, it was like advertising. Plus, guards couldn't always be trusted.

Despite the desire to be quick, they soon agreed that it would take a minimum of three days to get all the soil cleared, identify the right panel, move it, and excavate the contents. At seven o'clock, after a full day of travel and digging, they were exhausted. They retreated down the hill to their camp, and started a dinner fire. Thomas left Arturo for a few minutes to climb back up the mound, and take a look at the surrounding country at night.

He climbed to the crest of the middle pyramid, passing the hole they'd dug on the way. What he saw when he got to the top stopped him dead. They weren't alone! There was light coming from the far side of the next pyramid.

Thomas crouched and watched the pattern of the light. He saw a shadow moving steadily, rhythmically. Someone was working. This was the worst possible scenario. Someone was already here, and it looked as if they were digging. Could they be working on the same project? Had someone already interpreted the texts? Or had he misinterpreted the texts? Was he digging on the wrong pyramid?

He crept down the middle pyramid, towards its twin to the west. He reached the base and worked his way halfway up and then horizontally around its circumference to get a closer look at whoever was working over there. He considered going to get Arturo. Site robbers were notoriously mean, hardened and unforgiving, willing to commit crimes and take any measures to keep from getting caught.

Halfway to his target, he angled right and crept low, forcing himself to go slowly, listening for the ka-chunk of the shovel after each step. The hood of a green sport utility vehicle came into view, the word DISCOV-

ERY written in white across the hood. It was parked near the base of the mound, and although the passenger door was open, the interior light was not on. A cord ran from the back of the truck up to the base of the mountain, providing energy for a powerful flood light that illuminated that side of the pyramid.

The ka-chunk was much louder now. He prayed he wasn't too late. He crouched, and wove his way closer through the thorny vines and dried brush. He barely noticed the burning in his thighs and back as he became increasingly more obsessed with learning who was under the light and what they were searching for.

A few more feet.

Finally he could see the pale yellow of a straw hat. It looked like it was only one person. That was good. Not a major expedition. But were there other people here, guarding the site from a distance? My God, he's digging intently, Thomas thought. He crept forward to get a better look. As he did, he set off one of the oldest and most primitive alarm systems ever invented. He tripped a wire that was attached to a pole holding a few tin cans. They fell rattling to the ground, piercing what had been, aside from the sound the shovel made, an amazingly peaceful evening.

Thomas dove headfirst to his right, hoping he could scramble away from the source of the noise to hide. He sailed through the air for a much longer period than he felt he should have. He realized his dive was toward the downward angle of the pyramid and he readied for a hard landing.

The landing knocked the air out of his lungs, but it was something else that set off internal alarms. Something was terribly wrong. Something underneath him was stabbing, stinging, trying to get out from underneath him. A burning sensation shot into his stomach. He immediately thought of a scorpion or snake. The pain was excruciating. He saw light come toward him and he stifled a moan. Carried by someone who was running toward the sound of the cans, the light swung quickly back and forth like a pendulum. Before he could move, a long shadow stretched over him.

"Roll over! I've got a gun!" The voice was female, and it was fierce.

But Thomas couldn't move. The slightest twitch sent cords of unbearable pain rippling through his midsection.

"*Roll over, damn it*!"

Thomas managed one word. "Can't."

His captor came closer and leaned over. He saw yellow hair fall from beneath her wide-brimmed hat.

All he could see of her face was an intent, angry expression. She deserved to be angry. Someone had been spying on her out here in the middle of nowhere – where she was vulnerable. But Thomas detected no fear in her voice, only fury. "Try anything and I'll shoot you. This gun is fully loaded. Roll over so I can see your face."

"Can't. Pain. No joke." Thomas tried to move, but gave up.

"If this is a trick I'll shoot you in the back of the head, I swear it." She put the flashlight on the ground, but kept the gun focused on him as she adeptly rolled him over with her free hand.

She picked the flashlight up and pointed it toward his stomach. "My god!"

Staring up at the stars Thomas said, "Scorpion? Snake?"

"You should be so lucky. *Echinocactus grusonii*, more commonly known as the Golden Barrel cactus. It's a small stem cactus, known for it's very hard, very sharp spines."

"Feels like I hit a den of scorpions."

She slid the deadly little .38 in her belt, removed a Swiss Army knife from her pocket, found the tweezers, and kneeled next to Thomas. "Here, hold the flashlight so that it focuses on your stomach." She began plucking needles.

"Name is . . . Thomas." He winced and closed his eyes.

"Ann."

The indirect light from the flashlight shown dimly on half her face. Despite being half blinded by pain, he could still see that she was young, tan, and determined. She concentrated on her work with objectivity. Efficiency. Like a good surgeon.

She would've had to have been in the field quite awhile to get a tan like that. He wondered what she was doing, who she was, but mostly what she was looking for. She wasn't volunteering anything.

"What are you doing out here in the middle of the Mexican desert, Thomas?"

He was ready for her question, "My friend and I are hunting puma."

Her work suddenly became less gentle. Thomas clenched the flashlight and bit his bottom lip until it bled. "We haven't found any though. In fact, we're thinking of . . . giving up and . . . going fishing."

It had the desired effect and her plucking softened.

He continued his story. "We're camped on the other side of that big hill." Thomas saw her smile, presumably at his reference to the "big hill."

"Camped?"

They were both walking an information tightrope. Archeologists in the field were always guarded, never divulging information to strangers. Often they tried to lead each other astray by deflecting interest, twisting facts, or, when called for, bold-faced lying. Each would show as little interest in the other as possible and they would go to any length to try to deceive, in an attempt to get the other person to believe that their reason for being there was trivial, or even a mistake. Thomas continued his improvised ruse.

"Yes, camped. Our tents are already up. Why the skepticism?"

"I just wondered why you would camp out here, when we're so close to Mercado."

Thomas knew Mercado was only five miles away down a passable road, but he and Arturo had wanted to stay out of the little town at all costs, to keep from arousing interest. "I didn't know there was a road to Mercado, or we probably would be there tonight. Is it passable?"

"Yes, *and* there is a nice little hotel in town."

Was she trying to get rid of him? "Are you at the hotel, or are you camping?"

"I'm at the hotel."

Thomas didn't want her to think that he was interested in staying at the site when there was a hotel so near. Going with her would give him an opportunity to learn about the purpose of her exploration. There was a chance she would even volunteer the information.

Her plucking had become less frequent and less painful. "I'm going to unbutton your shirt, to see if I got all the spines. It may hurt."

"It's okay. I'm think I'm officially in shock."

She quickly unbuttoned his shirt and pulled up his T-shirt. "I don't see any more, but you've got a nice raw spot right down the middle of your abdomen. You should put some antiseptic on it, when you get back to your . . . campsite."

"Would you mind if my friend and I hitched a ride with you to Mercado?

"I guess that would be all right. I was getting ready to call it a day when you stumbled over my early warning system. Give me a few minutes to pack up my gear."

"Great, that will give me time to get back to my friend and tell him we'll be sleeping in a real bed tonight. Thanks for the first aid."

As he scrambled to his feet, Thomas saw the small .38 automatic pistol. This Ann was a tough one, and smart. Any woman who worked alone in central Mexico would be a fool not to carry a gun.

He took two steps up and reached down to pick up the tin can contraption. "What's this for? Why do you need a warning system? Digging for treasure?"

In the night, he still hadn't seen her face, but now jaw muscles bulged, as she glared at him, "I like to know when someone is spying on me! And as for what I'm doing over there . . . it is absolutely none of your goddamn business." She turned and walked back to her site.

Thomas wondered, as he hurried back to collect Arturo and the equipment, what he would tell her tomorrow when she saw them back out here, and found out they were not hunters at all, but archeologists, come to dig at her site.

CHAPTER 14

The sole hotel in Mercado was a shrimp-colored, two-story Spanish mission made of mud and straw bricks and reinforced with logs. It had been refurbished and converted into a ten-room hotel. The owners, a Mexican couple, ran the hotel themselves, making it a cross between a real hotel and a bed and breakfast. Ann was their only guest. Thomas and Arturo took the two rooms at the end of the upstairs hallway, put their bags inside the doorways, and immediately headed to the small, dark dining room. Ann was already there, drinking a Carta Blanca and eating grilled shrimp at the bar.

Thomas and Arturo took a table by the entrance. A few dimly lit chandeliers—formerly iron wagon wheels—dangled haphazardly from the ceiling. The tables were wooden and square. On the opposite wall, where Ann was sitting, was a long, dark, mahogany bar with a huge mirror behind it. The bar was nice. Much too nice compared to the strictly functional dining room. The owners had obviously imported it from somewhere in the States, or Europe, and it made for a memorable cross between rustic and cosmopolitan. Thomas relaxed. He liked the place. It felt more homey than his house in Arizona had these past few weeks.

Thomas had a Carta Blanca, Arturo, a glass of El Presidente brandy. After the drinks came, they ordered dinner.

"What do you think of her, Arturo? Have you heard of anyone who is supposed to be working El Manati?"

Arturo sipped the brandy, scrunched his face at the first taste, and said, "I honestly don't keep track of what goes on here. Ask me what's going on at Copan, and I can tell you anything. But El Manati? No idea, amigo."

"Before I set off that damn can alarm of hers, I got a look at what she was doing. She was digging furiously out there. Just like we had been. She's looking for something, and she's in a hurry."

"I've been an archeologist a long time, Thomas, longer than you. I can see the excitement of yesterday is gone. You're worried. We're the same, you and me. We believe that nothing is safe until it is home, under lock and key. And I know that having someone already working your site is killing you. But don't jump to conclusions. Right now we don't know anything about her. Except that she's cute." He smiled and winked. "She might even be a looter, you know."

When Thomas didn't comment, Arturo continued. "Then again, could she be looking for the same thing you are, Thomas? Could there have . . . been . . . any leaks?"

"It's possible. But I doubt it. Aside from the *Builders Notes* being stolen, I've kept this close to the vest. And I can't believe anyone could've figured out the clue in the *Notes* already. Maybe she found it through other means. I've talked to quite a few people about different pieces. Martha. Sinistar. Don Ozgood. Dick Hightower. I guess it's possible someone could have pieced it together. My activities may have aroused suspicion. Thank God Martha is destroying the riddle. I don't think I could take it if one more person shows up out here."

Thomas took a long drink of his beer, content for the moment with the knowledge that, by now, Martha would have already been to Saqqara to chisel away the sediment that held the riddle. Somewhere just above his subconscious and below his conscious mind, he noted that Ann had great calves.

Their dinners came, green peppers stuffed with corn and shrimp served with rice and beans, and they ate quietly and quickly. It had been a long and challenging day.

Occasionally, Thomas glanced over at Ann. She was eating slowly, while reading from a journal. Her sun bleached hair was pulled back from her face in a ponytail. She had removed the safari hat and he could see strong lines of jaw and neck.

She wore standard khaki shorts with wool socks and heavy Vasque boots that jungle archeologists often use. Thomas, a sand dweller, preferred expedition Filsons, but knew a lot of good field people who wore Vasque because of the Gortex. She didn't wear jewelry or makeup and would have looked ridiculous if she had. It would have been like putting a bow on a lion. Thomas saw the owner, Jose, clear Ann's plate and bring her another beer.

Arturo finished his after-dinner drink and excused himself. "That's it for me. I've got to call home. I'll meet you at breakfast. Have a good sleep."

Thomas watched Arturo as he waved at Jose and walked out of the room. He wondered if he had decided too quickly about Arturo. He had come highly recommended, but he'd never had a major find of his own. Might this be his chance? How easy it would be, to get rid of Thomas out in the middle of nowhere after they'd unearthed the treasure. Thomas had seen treasure do amazing things to people. He'd seen it turn good, honest people against each other, exactly like Bogart and his buddies in the great study on greed, *Treasure of the Sierra Madres*.

But, at this point, he had to trust Arturo. He couldn't do this on his own, and that was the bottom line. He hoped Arturo was really going up to his room, and not back out to the site, to work all night with friends who had followed them in, and who would help him extract the treasure, leaving Thomas with a hole in the ground where his treasure- his future-had once been.

Quickly, before he could give in to his negativity, he pushed back his chair and, sore from the day's workout, sauntered over to the bar. He chose a stool at the opposite end from Ann. He ordered a Carta Blanca, and then another. Occasionally, he glanced down at her, but she didn't look up. She was still reading the journal, still drinking beer. She had long, honey blond hair, tied back with a light blue ribbon. She had a certain feline quality that he hadn't observed in a woman in a long time. Narrow, smiling eyes, full lips, sureness of foot. And that supreme cat-quality, equally proportioned contentedness and confidence, mixed with an air of authoritarian control.

He wanted to talk to her, but he didn't want it to come off like he was pumping her for information. Even more, he didn't want it to seem like he was coming on to her.

Jose appeared, busily writing on his order pad. "Mr. McAlister, would you like to pay for dinner now, or would you rather I add the bill to your room?"

"Add it to my room bill, Jose. I may stay for another couple of days." Thomas watched Ann from the corner of his eyes. Had she heard Jose use his last name?

At first nothing happened. And then he saw it come over her. Her posture changed. She became more erect. She looked up from her book and her head whirled, until she was looking straight at Thomas. He met her gaze.

"Did he say *McAlister*?" .

Oh man, he thought. She's already getting pissed. "Yes."

"And your *first* name is Thomas?"

"Yes."

"You bastard!"

"Pardon me?"

"*The* Thomas McAlister?"

Thomas looked back over each shoulder, as if she were talking about someone else. "You've heard of me?

"You pretentious son-of-a-bitch. You're asking me if I've ever heard of the man who made the most significant Egyptian find in the last fifty years? The man who pioneered the archeological use of sound wave analysis to determine density? Um . . . let me think of an appropriately sarcastic answer to that question."

"I think you just did." To archeologists engaged in their trade, Thomas was well known. But he never knew how far that limited celebrity went outside of his University. "How did you know all of that?"

"Don't patronize me. I have my doctorate in archeology. That stuff about you is taught in Archeology 101."

"I taught some lower level classes and the subject rarely came up," he replied.

"Well, your classes were always full, weren't they?"

Thomas shrugged and took a drink of his beer. "Packed."

"See."

There was a pause, she shook her head and said. "Hunting! Hunting mountain lions! No. No. Puma! Oh that's rich, Thomas. Is that what you always do? Show up at a site and lie? Is that why you're so renowned?"

"So, you're an archeologist?" He changed the subject. Jose brought another beer without being asked.

"Yes, I am, but only a humble female Mayanologist. Nothing to compare with the great Thomas McPharaoh, Prince of Egyptology! But then, why do you care? You probably don't want to talk shop. You're on a hunting expedition with your buddy. Is that your guide?"

"That's Arturo Bandera."

"Jesus H. Christ! Is the Convention of Famous Archeologists in town or something? Arturo's a legend. I read he was at Copan right now."

Thomas sipped his beer and waited. Maybe this hothead would understand that she was attacking him for no reason. It was common to try to deceive others around a site, if you were in danger of jeopardizing your find.

They sat in silence. Thomas drinking, Ann feigning reading.

It struck him that she might not know the rules. He watched her take a drink in the mirror behind the bar. She was younger than he . . . quite a bit younger. She might even be fresh out of graduate school. She had probably worked sites on commercial digs, but never her own. That was it, of course. She had probably never discovered anything herself, never known the thrill and the fear; never had to lie, to protect her goal.

He would have to treat her as he would treat some of his best students, if they had just graduated and were out to make a name for themselves. He remembered when he was in her shoes. He had been a cocky hothead.

"Listen, Ann, I'm sorry I lied about hunting. I'm here on business."

He carried his beer to her end of the bar. Jose moved to the other end, to give them privacy.

Ann shoved the chair out for him with her foot. "So Thomas, I guess the ten thousand dollar question is, what the hell is an Egyptologist doing in Mexico?" It's worth more than ten thousand, Thomas thought.

"You're asking me to lie to you again, Ann."

"No, you do that on your own, without being asked."

"How did you get interested in the Maya?"

She paused, obviously considering whether or not she wanted to share it with him, then said, "I was interested in math. I was going to major in finance my freshman year at Stanford. I took an anthropology course as an elective: Introduction to Central American Cultures. I learned that the Maya had an elaborate, extremely advanced arithmetic system that was more complicated but better thought out than the calculus course I was taking, not to mention their astronomy. That was it. I was hooked."

"Did you do your graduate work at Stanford?"

"Yes, I stayed there. I loved it. I finished at the end of last year. Three years for my doctorate."

"That's impressive. Now let me ask you. What are *you* doing out here?"

"Unlike you, I can tell. I'm trying to find information on the origin of the Maya counting system. I want to take it back even further. Try to find out where they got it. The locals say they've seen Olmec carvings on the sides of the El Manati pyramids."

Thomas sighed inwardly. He believed her. He finished his beer and ordered another. He wasn't sure how many he'd had. He fleetingly thought about slowing down.

Ann said, "Jose, two shots of tequila, salt and lime. On me."

Thomas could feel himself getting numb. He protested, but couldn't really say no. When they finished, Ann ordered two more. When they toasted the Maya, Thomas let Ann drink her tequila and he drank beer.

Suddenly she slid off the bar stool, walked over to the old dusty juke box, and dropped a few coins into the slot. Thomas wondered what she would play. Probably something by the Smashing Pumpkins or Pearl Jam, if they had any of that stuff. He prayed it wouldn't be anything by Garth Brooks. He heard the needle strike the record and skip once. It made him smile. That was a good sound he didn't hear much anymore. The familiar beat of "Under My Thumb" rolled out of the huge speakers in the bottom of the juke box. Maybe it was the tequila. Maybe the dark cantina with the Manhattan style bar, or the music, or Ann . . . but Thomas began to feel very good, and he knew he would remember this night for a long time.

Ann returned to her bar stool. He saw that she had sharp blue eyes. "Good selection."

"Yeah, I played it twice. They have Hot Rocks on that old thing."

As the music played they talked about archeology, how they had gotten into it, and the things they wanted to accomplish. Ann asked Thomas about Egypt and what it was like to find such a major treasure.

They laughed a lot, but when he asked about her family, she became oddly quiet. Her eyes pooled and she looked close to crying. She said her father had left home when she was very young, and the only thing her mother had ever said about it was that it was for the good of the family. Obviously it was a wound that had not yet healed.

Slowly, imperceptibly, Thomas led the conversation to topics he knew would make her happy. Though it seemed like minutes, they actually talked for several hours, casually drinking the entire time.

At midnight, Thomas realized he was very drunk. It came over him suddenly. One minute he was fine and the next, he was wasted. He watched Ann's lips move, but he couldn't understand what she was saying. The words were familiar, but he couldn't get them to make sense.

Could she tell? Was she drunk too? Hadn't she had more to drink than he? He had been the one refusing shots earlier in the night. In the back of his soused mind, he knew that if she was drunk, he might not appear as drunk as he was. Suddenly, he noticed he had a shot glass and a beer sitting in front of him, but she had only beer. For the last hour, he had taken a tequila shot with almost every beer. Ann had insisted he try one of the true Mexican tequilas. He'd conceded only after Jose had reaffirmed its quality.

Had she lost some of that athletic posture? She was talking about the Maya, their ability to count, their understanding of zero before the Romans . . . she was going and on and on and on. He found it all inordinately interesting, and he wanted to tell her about the incredibly advanced systems the Egyptians used but he couldn't get a good coherent sentence together. Suddenly, she turned to the bartender, and told him they'd had enough. Then, seemingly in the middle of the conversation, they got up to leave.

"Where are the rooms?" he asked, to no one in particular. He swayed. She helped. "Wha's my room number? Where is the key? Oh, you have it. Tha's good! Don' lose it! Might need it. If we ever find the damn rooms."

They walked up the stairs with arms draped around each other for support. It was difficult for either to tell who was supporting who. It was very dark. Thomas could feel Ann's ribs through the firm veneer of skin and muscle. He was having trouble keeping his eyes open.

She was asking him something. Her first question didn't make it through the fog, but he comprehended the second.

"Why would an Egyptologist be in Mexico?" He repeated. "Why? Hmmm, I think you shouldn't be asking me that . . . but it's a good question. Why would I want to be here? Let's sing and maybe it'll come to us." Thomas started singing.

The whole thing was clear in his mind's eye, through the fog of the tequila, it was so simple, if he could just say it. Just tell beautiful Ann that the Egyptians and ancient Mexicans were linked because Moses had ordered the Ark be buried here . . . for all time . . . until someone solved the Moses riddle which, Ann, no one would have ever done if I hadn't thought to use an ultrasound which was so important because the wall had crumbled away . . .

"*Oh, here we are! My room!*" They jostled through the doorway,

Thomas talking on and on. It felt good to explain, to share freely . . . finally someone he could talk to . . . and then the lips, the soft lips, and then down, down . . . into the black velvety darkness of sleep.

CHAPTER **15**

A shaft of Mexican sunlight found the small hole in the window shade, and hit the wall a few inches above Thomas McAlister's face. With each minute, the beam of light got closer and closer to Thomas's eyelids.

The sun rises quickly, and the time from when the light grazed his eyelid until it was wholly focused on them was short. In his dream there was a blow torch emitting a hot blue flame onto his exposed eyeballs, melting them like wax.

He wakened with the worst headache he'd ever had. Where was he? What was this place with these rustic adobe walls? He looked around the sparsely furnished room until he saw something that brought most everything back. It was the shiny light blue ribbon Ann had used to tie her hair back into a pony tail. It was sitting on the table beside the bed. What had he done? He chronologically traced the events of yesterday to the bar at the hotel. He remembered being there, talking to Ann, listening to music but at a certain point, he could remember no more. He couldn't even remember leaving the bar.

A shot of adrenaline was all that enabled him to get out of bed. He slowly turned his head. The other side of the bed had been slept in, but Ann was gone. He was in his boxer shorts. Christ almighty! What had happened here last night? *What had he told her?* He threw on his clothes, his wallet still in his jeans, and bolted from the room.

There were stairs to his right. As he headed toward them, he fought nausea. He went back to the room, fearful that he might throw up, but the door was locked. He thrust his hand into his front pockets, searching for keys. Nothing. He made his way down the hall to the stairs and took them two at a time. No one was at the front desk. He had to find a bathroom fast. He remembered where the bar was located and hurried to it. The first thing he saw was Ann and Arturo having a full Mexican breakfast.

At first they smiled to welcome him but, as they saw him run forward, shirt untucked, unshaven, hair askew, with a wild look on his face, their smiles disappeared. They both pointed toward the men's room.

By the time he was there, he had controlled his nausea. Seeing Ann and Arturo happily breakfasting together had sobered him. He cupped cold water on his face, which helped further calm his stomach.

He returned to the dining room, color better, and slumped into the extra chair at the table. Ann was shaking hot sauce on the last of her scrambled eggs. He reached for Arturo's water and slowly sipped a few drops, unable to look at their plates. Staring at the floor, head in hands, he asked Ann, "What's that you're putting on your eggs?"

"This, my hung-over friend, is the single best hot sauce ever made. This is only the second place I've ever found it. The first place was in Arizona. I bought a bottle and then, when I ran out, I started ordering it by the case from the distributor. I keep a bottle in my purse. Try a few drops on a piece of toast. It's great for hangovers."

Arturo looked sympathetically at Thomas. "You look a little pale, amigo."

"I feel like I was drugged. I've never had such a headache. I *never* drink like that. Well, almost never." He looked at Ann. "You don't really keep that in your purse, do you?"

Ann reached for her canvas backpack and pulled out a bottle of the deep, red colored sauce. "I can't live without the stuff. Come on, try some it'll help your hangover."

"All right, give it to me." Thomas took the bottle, shook some on a piece of toast and took a bite. It cut the taste of stale tequila and had good flavor. And it did seem to settle his stomach. "Not bad," he said. "Lesson number one for graduate students on a dig. A dig is not a vacation. It's not a party! It's work. Business. *Despite* what you witnessed last night."

Ann and Arturo looked at each other and winked.

Arturo said, "We've all had nights like yours last night. They are cleansing, every so often. And, from what you tell me, you've been through a lot lately."

Thomas didn't like being placated or lectured, especially in front of Ann, but everything Arturo said was true. "Will someone tell me what the hell happened last night?"

"Ann will have to tell you that. I retired early."

Ann smiled deviously. "What part don't you remember?"

"I remember talking with you, here at the bar. I remember you . . . forcing me to try that Commerativo tequila, but I don't know how I got upstairs." He paused, trying to think of anything else. "Or . . . how I got to my room, or anything after that." The feeling of hot, soft lips and . . . thoughts of treasure danced through his mind, and he had the grave feeling that something regretful had happened last night. Something that shouldn't have, and that couldn't be taken back. Suddenly, he remembered the ribbon in his room. Had she taken him upstairs and—

Ann smiled and started to speak, but Arturo interrupted, "First things first, Ann. Thomas?"

"Yes?"

"There's one thing you need to know, as a professional."

"All right, Arturo. What do I need to know?"

"Last night . . . you told her."

"*What*!"

Arturo nodded.

"Told her what . . . *exactly*?" Thomas already knew the answer. He was furious with himself.

Ann saw a cold look come over him. It was a look she wouldn't have thought his friendly eyes capable of. She nodded gravely. "Yes, Thomas, you told me."

"I told you why . . . Arturo and I are here?"

Ann nodded.

Thomas gazed at the floor. Talk about unprofessional. Had he lost his mind, as well as his job? *I told her. What do I do now? How do I get rid of her?*

"She wants to help us, Thomas."

"Out of the question! We don't need any help!"

"She says we're digging in the wrong place." Arturo continued, his voice measured and calm. His eyes watched Thomas's face, waiting for a reaction. "I think she's right."

"*What?*"

"Yes, you told her that the riddle said that the treasure could be found 'in the middle.' And that is why we were going to dig in the middle of the pyramid. But Ann says that the Mayans would have been the ones who actually buried the treasure, since they would have had thousands of laborers at their disposal and the Egyptians would have had only the men who had come over on their boat."

"So?" Thomas said flatly.

"She says if the Mayans buried the treasure, they never would have interpreted the middle of the pyramid as being height divided by two, as we did."

Thomas looked perplexed. "Why not?"

"Because the Maya viewed the size of the pyramid not by its outer structure, but by its volume. If the pyramid was a cup, they would not think about the cup in terms of its surface area, how high and wide it was. They would think of it in terms of how much it could hold? So if you want to know where the middle is, you must measure the volume, *not* the distance, and divide *it* by half."

Thomas began the calculations in his head, "OK, we can do that. That would mean that the middle is going to be lower, since pyramids get smaller and lose mass as they go higher. Yes. Since we know the measurements of the original pyramid, it can be done. *It can be done!*"

Ann shoved a napkin toward Thomas. "I've already done the calculations."

He saw the pyramid, nicely drawn with the corresponding metrics.

He saw the original middle, then the new one, farther down the slope, now that Ann had calculated the middle based on area and not height. The mathematical calculations were neatly written off to the sides. The new middle was significantly lower.

Thomas looked at Ann. He was a proud archeologist, but he could also acknowledge good work, even when it replaced work that he'd done and that he'd previously thought correct. He knew the danger of not being able to admit when you were wrong.

Suddenly Ann said, "Well, I'm through with my breakfast. I'm going to go up and get ready for today. We've got to measure the pyramid and start digging." Her look of assumed confidence said that she was now a member of the team. Payback for helping them understand where the Maya would have most likely buried the treasure.

Thomas looked at Arturo. Arturo shrugged. It was Thomas's call. He looked at Ann and an abrupt memory of hot, soft lips flew through his mind. He pushed it out, wishing that he had more time to find out about her background before making such an important decision. They needed her expertise but, damn it, they'd just met her. Finally, he thanked her for her contribution by saying, "Great! Meet you at the truck in fifteen minutes."

CHAPTER 16

With the calculations already done, it only took a few minutes to locate the site of the dig. They dug in shifts. Arturo and Thomas started. Thomas wanted to work off his hangover before it got really hot. After an hour, he stopped and Ann took his place. An hour later, he replaced Arturo. They rotated until lunchtime.

When he was finished eating, Arturo headed for the truck and Thomas used the opportunity to speak privately with Ann. "What happened in my room last night?"

"Why do you ask?"

"Were you . . . drunk?"

"I was tipsy, but not wasted. You were singing. It was hilarious. You even sang, 'I'm tired and I want to go home.'"

Thomas grimaced. "That's it? I was singing and . . . and you helped me to my room? Did we . . . kiss . . . or anything?"

With a deep throaty southern accent she said, "Why, Thomas McAlister, I believe you honestly don't remember. That's a shame, because I believed you when you said I was the absolute *best* kisser!"

» » « «

They worked all afternoon, rotating every thirty minutes because of the steadily increasing heat. By dinnertime, they had a hole five feet deep and about six feet wide. They knew they should hit the outside of the pyramid soon. In preparation, they switched to smaller shovels and worked with greater care, more like the well-trained archeologists that they were. This felt more natural to Thomas and helped him relax a little. The earlier pace had made him feel like a grave robber.

After dinner, they resumed digging. The pit was so deep now that only one person could dig at a time. It was on Ann's shift, at the edge of darkness, that her shovel hit something solid.

Ann stood straight up, with a huge smile on her face and looked at Thomas and Arturo, who were sitting over by the fire. The reflection of fire made her eyes look red, like the Devil's.

"I hit something!"

She was wearing a white tank top, soaked through with sweat, smudged with dirt. The sweat on her chest and arms glistened, and her tan was the color of dark honey, a shade or two darker than her hair.

Thomas walked over, remembering all the times that he had hit something solid, only to find that it was a stray rock. "Don't get too excited yet."

Like a boxer who had knocked his opponent down, Ann stood in the corner farthest from where the shovel had made contact. Thomas jumped into the pit with her and examined the exposed area with a flashlight and horsehair brush. He could feel the heat radiating off her body as he worked.

"Hey, Arturo! No loose rock. We've hit the side of the pyramid! Good work, Ann. We'll stop now and continue tomorrow morning. We might do more harm than good, if we continue tonight."

Driving back to Mercado that night was one of the hardest things Thomas had ever done. He wanted to stay at the site and work all night to find Moses' treasure, but patience would be their best tool during the next several hours of excavation.

All three stopped for a quick meal in the hotel dining room-bar, and Arturo excused himself first again. He wanted to get a chance to talk to his kids before they went to bed. Thomas and Ann were alone at the table.

"Tequila?" Ann asked.

"Sure, I'll have Jose bring a bottle over. Only kidding. Actually, this beer is hitting the spot."

"Any thoughts on what we'll find tomorrow?"

"I've had two concerns all along. One is that someone deciphered the pyramid text long ago and that they are the ones who destroyed the wall at Saqqara. We've assumed that it crumbled away naturally, but I'm not so sure. My second concern is that grave robbers may have seen the markings on the stones of this pyramid, the circle on the square, and taken whatever was hidden here."

"What are the odds it will be there?"

"I don't know. Long probably, but there's no way to tell. This site is not far from Mercado. At any time during the past 3000 years someone could have come over here and started digging around. My instinct though. My instinct tells me it's here."

Ann's eyes lit up. Thomas loved seeing the excitement on her face. It was how he had felt on his first trip to Egypt.

The sounds of "Under My Thumb" suddenly filled in the quiet that had followed his expression of hope. They both turned toward the juke box. Jose waved at them. He had remembered their selection from the evening before. Ann searched Thomas's face. "Want to dance?"

He almost said no, but he was having such a good time, and there was something about this woman he really liked.

"Sure."

Thomas led her around the floor at a slow pace. Halfway through the song, he gathered enough nerve to try to finish the conversation he'd started earlier in the day. "Ann, I hope I wasn't too . . . last night, I-I hope I didn't do anything that offended you."

Her head was against his chest so he couldn't see her smile. "You weren't obnoxious. And you didn't offend me. I'd had a few drinks myself."

"I don't remember much."

"Really?"

"I think I remember one thing, but . . . I'm not sure."

"Yes. What was that?"

"I think I remember kissing you."

"Did I kiss you back?"

"What do you mean?"

"You said you kissed me. Did I kiss you back?"

"Listen, you should probably know something about me. I . . . don't date much. I mean I get setup a lot, but nothing has ever come of it. I guess you could say I'm . . . out of practice. In the condition I was in last night . . . and being with such a . . . well, with you, I thought maybe I'd made an improper advance."

"Let's just say that the feelings expressed were mutual. Ever since I was a little girl, I've always wanted to kiss a famous archeologist!"

He laughed and unconsciously pulled her closer. She closed her eyes and her mouth went slack as she let out a deep breath. He loved the feel of her warmth against him. It had been a long time, too long, since he'd felt that kind of closeness.

"What exactly did happen anyway? I remember a kiss."

"That's what happened. We kissed. It wasn't very long."

Not long enough? Or too long? he wondered.

Jose had played four songs off of Hot Rocks, in the order that they appeared on the album. When "Under My Thumb" ended, "Ruby Tuesday" started.

Thomas said, "You know, I love the Stones, but I never liked this song"

"Come on, let's sit."

They went back to their table. Jose had brought them a fresh round of Carta Blancas. Thomas took a drink of the cold beer and glanced at Ann. He found her staring at him, and she smiled, almost apologetically.

He was generally considered good-looking. He'd been popular with girls in both high school and college but had never let it go to his head. Good looks could get him a date, but they didn't guarantee that it would be fun, or that the girl would be interesting. But his dedication to archeology hadn't left much time for dating, and he'd never gone out with anyone exclusively for more than a year.

The most serious relationship he'd had, with a girl named Jill, had ended when he left for Egypt with Karl Johnson on the Amenophis campaign. As a single professor at Arizona his peers had often tried to set him up, and occasionally there had been the flirtatious student, but Thomas was never serious enough about any of them to sustain longer term involvement.

Now, sitting with Ann, Thomas felt nervous. It had been years since he'd been genuinely interested in someone, since a date hadn't been contrived, planned, and at some level, rehearsed. He felt teenage angst, that even mix of nervousness and excitement. It constricted his chest and throat. What was happening with Ann was natural, and it felt good. She was spirited, energetic, and challenging. And so passionate and forward looking.

They sat in comfortable silence and listened to "Ruby Tuesday." The next song on Hot Rocks was "Let's Spend the Night Together." Like the evening before, the beer was affecting him, so Thomas ordered water. The song reached the chorus and Mick sang, in his most convincing tone, "Let's spend the night together. Now I need you more than ever. Let's spend the night together now". Synchronicity. The song, at that very moment, was verbalizing the exact words that Thomas had been thinking. But it was wrong somehow. Not only was it too early, since they'd only just met, but he shouldn't be thinking of women at all. He was on a dig. The most important dig of his life.

Ann was making him lose focus. Images of her at the site stirred warm memories. Her hat cocked, strands of blond hair dangling around her face, which glistened in the sunlight. Sweat dripping from her chin, as she forced the shovel into the hard Mexican earth with surprising strength. Well-toned thighs and calves flexing, chest heaving, as she shucked her shirt to dig only in the sleeveless T-shirt.

But Thomas's feelings for Ann were not one sided. He had a special place in the hearts of younger archeologists. In the Internet age, when most young people were chasing dollars, he'd given hope to those who were truly passionate about archeology. His finds had revitalized the profession. He was proof that there was more to be learned, that there were significant artifacts still to be found. He was proof that it was okay to challenge old ways of thinking. When they said the Valley of the Kings would bear him no fruit . . . he had proved them wrong. All of them.

It had given students like Ann reason to sit through the tedious introductory classes. When mothers, fathers, grandparents, and in-laws asked about their major, becoming an archeologist was a point of pride. Ann was one of the new breed of questioning archeologists who looked at Thomas as a mentor. Other professors at Arizona somewhat jealously called them McGroupies. People, primarily women, who took Thomas's class because of the academic stardom created by him being featured in the textbook, and because of his good looks. But that label had been misguided. Sure some of the students registered for those reasons, but the vast majority did so because they wanted to learn from someone who was as fervent and excited about the prospect of adding to historical knowledge as they were. And many of his students went on to do so by becoming world-class archeologists.

"Tomorrow will be a long day," he said, abruptly. "We should turn in."

Ann looked slightly disappointed, but agreed. "You're the boss."

They climbed the stairs together and he continued past his room to hers.

"Here I am," she said.

"All right, well, get some sleep. I'll see you tomorrow, early."

She stopped him with a light touch on his forearm. "Thomas?"

He turned. She rose on tiptoes to kiss him. A long, soft, warm, full-lipped kiss. And that confirmed it. It was the same kiss as last night. The one that had, subconsciously, competed all day with the image of the treasure. The kiss had shared equal time, which was not a good thing. Or was it.

She lowered herself, turned, slid through the door and was gone. Back in his room, Thomas grinned as he remembered the old joke about boxers, *no sex before a fight*, and Woody Allen's jazz spiff, *no sax before a fight*. Before nodding off to sleep, he mumbled aloud, *"No sex the night before the biggest archeological find of the new millennium either!"*

CHAPTER 17

When Thomas entered the dining room early in the morning, he was surprised to find both Ann and Arturo halfway through their breakfast. He quickly sat down and ordered. Ann thought he seemed more serious this morning. And remote.

"How are you two this morning?"

"Very well, thank you, Tom." Arturo eyed him over the rim of his coffee cup.

"Make sure you both get enough to eat. If the stone we hit yesterday doesn't have the correct markings, we could be in for a long day."

Arturo nodded agreement. Ann wanted more information. "What if the inscription *is* there? What do we do then?"

Thomas paused to enjoy his first taste of the strong Mexican coffee, hoping that Ann didn't see the concern he felt over her question. It wasn't only that he didn't like the question. Though not a superstitious man, he never like talking as though the mission were already complete and successful. It was also that the he didn't like her level of interest. He knew it was avid curiosity, but he would rather she let things play out naturally.

His eyes met Ann's. He couldn't quite read her. She looked a little afraid and a little too curious. Which was it? Maybe she wasn't ready for such a big find. "If we find it," he said, silently knocking on the underside of the table, "then we'll cover it up and leave it where it is."

"What?" Ann looked horrified. "What do you mean, we'll leave it? We can't *leave* it!"

Arturo folded his napkin into a square and leaned forward to peer at Ann with widened eyes. "If we do find the inscription, Ann, how do you propose we move such a stone? Do you know how much each one of those stones weighs?"

Ann was visibly shaken by the news that they would not be able to excavate immediately. "Why, we'll rig a pulley and pull the stone out with my truck! We'll get a pulley and . . . we'll—" She threw her hand up into the air in exasperation. "Oh, come *on*, guys, there has to be a way!"

Arturo laughed, "That is one of the mysteries of these pyramids, Ann. As you undoubtedly know, we still can't figure out how the Mayans cut and moved these 4000-ton stones in the first place. There is no way the three of us are going to move one of them an inch without a heavy-duty commercial winch and without anchoring your truck. If we tried to do it today, the tires would simply spin in place."

"Arturo's right, Ann. If we find the inscription, we'll cover it up and leave. I will go back to the States for a winch and all the other supplies we'll need for excavation and transport. We've got to do this right."

"But . . . who will guard the find?" Ann asked.

Why would her first question be about guarding the find, Thomas thought. It's been sitting out here unguarded for over three thousand years.

"I'm not sure we need a guard, but Arturo and I have already worked that out. He will stay here."

Ann put her fork down and took a drink of water. She realized that the plans had been determined before she had entered the picture. She wondered what, if any, her role would be. Would they include her? Would they let her help out? The last two days, since she'd found out who Thomas was, had been two of the most exciting of her life. Yes, she had acted mad when she learned his true identity, but in reality she'd been excited, and things had only gotten better. Not only was she spending time with a handsome mentor, but they were hunting treasure, her lifelong dream. She didn't want it to end.

Thomas glanced at her from the corner of his eyes. He scraped his plate clean, drained his water, pushed his chair back and said, "Okay, let's hit it." He'd wait until they had located the inscribed stone before making a decision on what to do about Ann.

They drove to the site in Ann's Range Rover Discovery.

It was just as they had left it. They quickly removed the loose dirt they had used to cover the previous day's work and Thomas took first shift. He began the tedious work of clearing the area with a paint brush, gently moving the dirt away, layer after layer.

Ann peered into the pit, asking questions. Like artists, archeologists each have their own technique, their own preferences as how to best go about clearing a site without disturbing it. Thomas worked expertly, with both hands, usually his small trowel in one hand and a stiff, horse-hair brush in the other. Over the years, he had become ambidextrous, the result of countless hours of toiling in the Egyptian desert.

"I think the stone we're looking for will have three lines on each side, near a corner, that meet at each crease. If the square stone could be flattened, like a map, the lines would form a circle, like a two-thousand year old bulls-eye. At least that's my theory. So, I'm looking for corners." Once he reached the bottom edge of the first stone, he started to dig horizontally. An hour later, he saw the distinct line of a seam, where the next block began.

Thomas slid the trowel in his back pocket and switched brushes, using one with stiffer hair to whisk away the hardened earth from the original rock. The stone he'd been working on did not contain the inscription. He paused to wipe sweat from his forehead with the sleeve of his shirt. Ann and Arturo were both sitting on the mounds of soil at the mouth of the hole, watching him intently. This was Thomas's project, and they knew not to interfere. It was widely known that few people were better at tactical digging than Thomas. If he determined this was not the correct location, they would be ready to assist him in moving on to try a new one.

They were now looking at two stones, side by side, midway up the pyramid. Thomas squinted up at his companions. "We have a couple of options. We could clear the area to the left, or keep moving to the right to find the next seam."

Ann said, "Should we flip a coin?"

Thomas effortlessly pulled himself out of the pit, like a gymnast on the parallel bars, and searched in his field bag for his surveying equipment. He stuck an orange flag in the ground above the seam, and strode down the pyramid. He quickly set up a tripod one hundred feet from the base of the pyramid. He was so familiar with the equipment that one task flowed into the next, each movement liquid. Economical.

He was on the verge of finding something. He could feel it. The heavy telescope slid onto the tripod with a reassuring click, and he was pointing the view finder at the pyramid seconds later. This was his world, his tried and true equipment, and it was totally familiar to him. He worked in a trance-like state, totally comfortable with everything around him. His initial insecurity about this being Mexico and not Egypt that had been secretly gnawing at him for days evaporated. All his senses, at every level, were tuned to the work at hand. He was, as they said in sports, *in the zone*.

He lined up the vertical crosshair with the center of the rounded peak of the pyramid. He peered through the scope for several minutes without speaking. Then, he hiked back to the excavation site and jumped into the pit.

"Arturo, toss me the #5 trowel, will you?" This was like a small digging tool, like a gardening shovel, but wider. Digging hard to the right, he cleared dirt quickly, letting chunks fall to the bottom of the pit. Then, using a small trowel and a digging method called planning, he cleared debris away from the side of the stone, coming within millimeters of actually scraping the stone.

Then, never looking away from his work he said, "Arturo, I need the hearth brush." This was a rough brush made of longer horse hair. He used this to whisk away large amounts of dirt and debris without scratching the stone. He brushed quickly, in a meditative state, totally absorbed in his work, until finally the upper corner of the stone appeared. He took an old toothbrush from his shirt pocket and moved it back and forth across the area, removing microscopic amounts of dirt at a time.

"What do you see, Thomas? Anything?" Ann hadn't moved from the edge of the cavity.

"Nothing yet, Annie." he said, so absorbed in his work he didn't realize he'd used a pet name for her. It was the first time he'd ever called her Annie, and she liked it. She took her eyes off the stone, and looked at his back, amazed at how much she liked hearing him use the personal form of her name.

Suddenly, Arturo's voice boomed, "*Yes*, senor, *yes!*"

Startled, Ann spun to see what he was screaming about, but he was already running down the hill toward the truck, shouting unintelligible Spanish and waving his hat in the air.

She turned back to Thomas.

"What is it, Thomas? Did you find something?"

Thomas was using the handle end of the toothbrush to pry dirt out of a circular crevice, close to the corner of the stone. He had already cleared two lines and was finishing the third. "*I've found the marker!*"

In a lightning fast motion, he moved the brush up, whisking away the last remnants of debris. Lines, cut near the corner of the stone, met at the edge of the rock to form . . . a circle. A circle on a square.

"Ann, get Arturo. I want you to both come down and see this!" She turned, and ran down to the Rover, where Arturo was still hooting and hollering.

Alone in the pit, Thomas took a deep breath. This meant so much more to him than the fact that there might be treasure behind this stone. The latest series of events in his life had made him question himself as a professor and archeologist. Doubts had begun to creep in. Had the Amenophis find been a fluke? Should he have asked the Curriculum Review Board for approval? The questions fed on themselves, buttressed themselves, until they became firmly supported, rational arguments that diluted reality. Years ago, back in Egypt, hadn't he questioned his decision to dig where he had at the Amenophis site? He had known the

Curriculum Review Board's rules, so hadn't he, in a way, engineered his own firing? In the days past, cons had begun to stack up against the pros, making him scrutinize the one thing he'd always held sacred: his talent as an Egyptologist.

The finding of the marker was the last critical dependency. Up until now, if he had failed, he would be going home with his lingering doubts confirmed, essentially a failure. But here it was. He'd found it.

Yet, underlying every thought, never far from the surface, was the knowledge, the black, nightmarish fear, that maybe, quite possibly . . . there was nothing behind this stone.

CHAPTER 18

Present Day

Thomas stopped working to listen. There it was again! *Someone was trying to open the door to his cabana.* In a fluid motion, he grabbed the Beretta Tomcat from his dop-kit, crouched, and inched his way to the doorway of the bathroom. Gun steady, his index finger on the trigger, he peered around the corner just far enough to see the entrance to the room.

How the hell had things come to this? Had he really reached the point of being willing to shoot an intruder in order to get back down to Mexico? And where was Ann? She had said she had a couple of errands and would be back in an hour. It had been two already. A recurring fear reminded him that he'd decided rather quickly to bring her to Arizona with him.

The door swung open and a blond pony tail whipped around as Ann stepped into the room and shut the door. Thomas let out a breath and stood up. He was too skittish. Of course it was Ann. He replaced the gun and walked into the room. She saw him and smiled. Without saying a word she put her bag down, walked over, and kissed him fully on the lips.

"So, Doctor, who is it that wants to know what you know so damn badly? Did you find out?" She pressed herself against him and nuzzled her face in his neck.

"No, I still don't know. The front door was smashed and there was someone in the yard, probably trying to figure out how I escaped. That white van was in the driveway, but no clue as to who they were." Thomas felt himself responding to her hug when the phone rang. He pushed Ann away, instantly concerned. Who could possibly be calling? No one knew they were here.

"I'll get it," Ann said. "My name's on the room registry." She picked up the receiver, and held it slightly away from her ear so he could listen at the same time. "Hello?"

"Miss Havenport?" The voice was Hispanic.

"Yes, this is she."

"Miss Havenport, it is Hector, the valet. I helped you with your baggage."

"Yes, Hector? Did we forget something?"

"No, senorita, but . . . I need to talk to you. Quickly."

"You need to talk with me?" Ann repeated Hector's words to buy time. She covered the receiver with her hand. "What should I do? Invite him here?"

"It could be a trick. If someone followed me, this could be a way to get us to open the door."

"I remember Hector. I tipped him well because he helped me load the winch into the back of the Rover. He may really be trying to help us."

"All right, invite him over." Thomas headed to the bathroom for his gun.

"When can you come, Hector?"

"It must be now!"

"Come along then. Knock three times, pause, then three times again."

With the gun in his hand, Thomas flattened himself against the wall of the bathroom. Within seconds, there were three quick raps on the door, a pause, and then three more. Ann unlatched the lock and opened the door. Hector slipped into the room and she quickly closed and re-locked the door behind him. Thomas came around the corner, the gun tucked in his jeans at the small of his back.

Hector's eyes darted from Ann to Thomas and back to Ann. "I'm sorry to disturb you." He was clearly nervous with Thomas in the room.

Ann calmed him. "This gentleman is with me, Hector. You can speak freely. What is this about?"

"I am in the office and I begin to walk out, but I hear a man say he is FBI. So I listen. My friends . . . many are . . . illegals, but this man, he is not looking for illegals. He ask who is in Cabana Nine. I remember nine, because you give me big tip, senorita. The clerk, she give him your name, tell him you check out tomorrow morning."

"When was this, Hector?"

"Maybe ten minutes ago, senorita. And he ask who the man staying with is."

"How did he know about the man?"

"I do not know, senorita."

Ann glanced at Thomas as he moved to the window and peered out through the curtain. "There still could be time."

"Thank you so much, Hector!" She reached for her purse and removed a one-hundred dollar bill. "Can you remember anything else?"

Hector's eyes widened. "Muchas gratias, senorita! The man, he drive a blue Taurus. He leave hotel, after he know this room number."

Blue Taurus? *Blue Taurus?* Thomas wondered why that would seem so familiar to him, but he couldn't recall.

Ann walked Hector to the door. "Thank you again, Hector. Please, tell no one about this. Okay?" He nodded and was gone.

"Stupid of me to drive down my own street in broad daylight! I think I remember seeing a blue Taurus as I turned off Nightingale. The driver must have recognized me through the window. FBI? Why the hell would *they* be following me? I should've sent *you!*"

Ann rubbed his back. "It's a chance you needed to take, Thomas. We've got some time. The clerk told him I was checking out tomorrow. The man left after finding out about us. He either has to come back alone or send a team. If we move quickly, we can still get out of here without them knowing we've gone."

"They know your car now, Ann. We've got to get another. If we leave yours here, and sneak out, they'll think we're staying all night. That'll give us a good lead."

"We can't do that, Thomas! You know I worked long and hard for

Lucille and there is no way I'm going to desert her. Plus, we need her. We've mounted the winch and modified the gas tank."

Lucille was Ann's Land Rover Discovery. Thomas knew Lucille was a matter of pride for her. She'd worked hard for the car and it was a symbol of her independence. And she was right about all of the modifications they'd made. Replacing the winch and redoing the work they had done on the gas tank would delay the trip considerably.

"Annie, what's more important here, Lucille or what's waiting for us in Mexico?"

"Thomas, I can't do it. I can't leave her here to be impounded, torn apart, or sold off at auction."

"Wait a minute. I know exactly what we'll do!"

A forest green Discovery, an exact replica of Lucille, pulled in front of Cabana Nine thirty minutes after Ann placed the call to Off Road Rental Company. She had told them it was urgent and must be delivered immediately. They could pick it up by noon the next day.

By the time it arrived, they had loaded their gear into Lucille and Thomas was lying on the floor in back, waiting for Ann. She wanted to be outside when the rental vehicle arrived, so she could direct it to the right parking spot. She had moved Lucille, to make room for it.

Ann paid the delivery kid with travelers checks and sent him away with his ride. She tucked the keys to the rented vehicle under the driver's seat floor mat and hustled toward the oleander hedge that separated the Camelback Inn from the adjoining property. She had barely passed through the hedge and was about to get into the driver's side of her car, when two FBI vans pulled into the Camelback parking lot, ready to set up surveillance on Cabana Nine.

To exit the adjacent property, Ann had to use a driveway near the entrance to the Inn. She crept forward, keeping an eye out for government vehicles, the blue Taurus in particular. Traffic cleared and she pulled out, turning left, feeling relieved that there was no Taurus in sight. She turned right on Scottsdale Road and took it all the way to 360, Superstition Highway, then turned onto 10 South. Staying on 10 would have been faster, but she took Exit 162 to the two-lane highway 347. It would take them through various back roads, to the border town of Lukeville, then to Sonoyta, Mexico. From there, they could cross the Mexican border and head south/southeast into the state of Veracruz.

As they passed Firebird Lake, Ann smiled, remembering their trip north three weeks ago. They had taken back roads, and though they were hurrying, they were also exploring. They were exploring each other. Filled with the curiosity and hope that comes with a new relationship. Long rambling conversations. A sensual excitement. It felt good to give herself to someone again, to trust and share. Everyday she'd let herself go a little more. She understood why they called it "falling." She had fallen, and fallen hard, for Thomas McAlister.

Sitting in the passenger seat, Thomas, too, had a small smile on his face. He hoped Ann didn't see it, and he looked at her out of the corner of his eye. She was smiling too. He was tempted to ask why but thought better of it. He would never know that she was smiling for the exact same reason he was.

It had happened quickly for him too. He had immersed himself in Ann, knowingly. Willingly. The excitement of being newly in love had rejuvenated him and he understood how some people could marry so many times. They had fallen in love with falling in love. There had been only one drawback the entire time. It was the gnawing sensation that someone was getting closer and closer to figuring out where the treasure was, and that they were readying an attempt steal it from him. First, the Amenophis notes were stolen. Next he'd gotten the voice mail message from Martha telling him that she had seen Dr. Sinistar working inside the temple of Saqqara. Now, he knew the FBI had him under continuous surveillance.

Thomas knew he had to take whatever measures were necessary to get back to Mexico unnoticed. If he weren't successful, if he got caught, it was likely the treasure would be taken from him. That thought had been enough to motivate him as he had crawled through the repugnant, claustrophobic Scottsdale sewer one night earlier.

Thomas reclined his seat a little. Enjoying the calm after the storm.

All his plans were made. All the contingencies in place. He'd done all the planning he could do. Some he had told Ann about, some he hadn't.

CHAPTER 19

At the border, Thomas took over at the wheel. "Why don't you take a nap, Ann," he said. "It'll take us a few more hours to get to Cidudad Obregon, near the coast. Then we'll be on the edge of the Sierra Madres, and we can find a place to stay."

Ann reclined the passenger seat and tried to sleep, but her gyrating thoughts wouldn't let her. So she laid back and rested her road-weary eyes, thinking about the decisions she would have to make.

Thomas kept his eye on the rearview mirror, searching for a blue Taurus or anything that looked like a government vehicle. Arturo had remained in Mercado to guard the site and the treasure. He had trusted Arturo, a man he hardly knew, with the most important treasure he'd ever found. He had no other choice. Early on he'd convinced himself that Arturo was trustworthy. He reminded himself to trust his instinct.

Thomas envisioned driving into Mercado and learning that Arturo had checked out of the hotel. He imagined driving up to the pyramid, seeing the huge rock behind which the treasure had been hidden dragged from its place, hiding place exposed: treasure gone. Nonsense, of course. Everything would be fine. He'd learned long ago, even at archeological sites that you know contain treasure, you have to trust people. You simply cannot be there all the time. He had to trust Arturo. Thomas had given him permission to call in his brother if he needed any help. Hopefully that need hadn't arisen.

Thomas stole a glance at Ann. Never having had anything stolen from her, she was more worried about the extraction. They had affixed a huge commercial winch to the front of her Rover, but the stone they were intending to pull was three to four times as heavy as her truck. She didn't think they'd be able to move the stone. She had also been particularly worried about how they would smuggle the treasure out of Mexico.

Mexican law stated that if a Mexican historical artifact were unearthed, the government had to be notified. The treasure automatically became the property of the government, even if it hadn't originated in Mexico.

Unfortunately, new Mexican legislation had been passed, creating huge amounts of bureaucracy which made it difficult to get a permit to excavate and impossible to lay claim to anything found. Thomas's view was that the early Mayans clearly played a role in the preservation of the treasure, but they did not, and should not, own it. The Ten Commandments were not Mayan. For that reason, he would not notify the government but, rather, smuggle the tablets out of the country.

With the help of a friend who was an amateur race car driver, he had removed the gas tank on Ann's Discovery and run the line to an auxiliary tank mounted on the bottom of the truck, where the spare tire was usually kept. They had mounted the spare on the rear door. The Ark would be placed in a box disguised as the gas tank. Ann voiced her concern about cases of Mexican border patrol guards disassembling entire cars in their search for drugs. It would take a lot less than full disassembly for them to find the fake gas tank, since a false tank was often one of the first things border officials checked for. But she was willing to take the chance. Luckily, she and Thomas were exactly what they said they were, archeologists with permission and credentials provided by the Mexican government—Arturo actually—to conduct preliminary excavations at sites in both Oaxaca and Veracruz. They were hoping these credentials would earn them a quick pass across the border.

So Thomas drove south and became more relaxed with every mile. He was in love and completely unaware that at that exact same time tomorrow DJ Warrant, special agent for the FBI, would be three miles behind him in a military helicopter, following his every move.

» » « «

DJ, in his twenty years with the Bureau, had rarely been as angry as when he had burst into Cabana Nine and found it had been vacated. Once again, he'd been outsmarted by a couple of amateurs and he was furious.

The one good thing that had come from the incident was that DJ had learned something about the professor and his accomplice. He learned they were not to be underestimated. As Elmo's computer profile had stated, they were not only highly intelligent, they were highly motivated. DJ knew it would be a heightened state of motivation, because he knew they were onto something big. He'd talked to people at the university and found out that if the project involved archeology and Thomas McAlister, it was important.

After DJ had recovered from the initial shock and embarrassment of losing his two civilians for a second time, he went to work. He told Elmo what he wanted and, within thirty minutes, he had a border crossing report stating that a green Land Rover Discovery had crossed yesterday, at Lukeville.

An hour after that, DJ was in a government helicopter, in Mexican airspace, three miles behind Ann's Discovery, watching them through high-powered binoculars as they drove south. He had ordered, received, and was in the process of deploying a full surveillance team in Mexico, to ensure that he did not lose them again.

Even if Thomas had been facing in the other direction he would have needed binoculars to see the helicopter. As DJ watched the blob of green on the horizon, he swore that Thomas McAlister was not going to elude him again.

"What are we going to do down here in Mexico, DJ? What's the plan?" Elmo stunned DJ with his questions. He rarely asked any.

"The plan, Elmo?" DJ slapped him hard on the knee. "The plan is to take custody of the artifact." And then, more to himself than to Elmo, he added,. "Yep, we're going to let genius boy down there find it for us

. . . and then we're going to *snatch it,* before he knows what hit him. And as for his girlfriend, I've got plans for her, too."

CHAPTER 20

When Ann and Thomas reached the Hotel Mercado, things were exactly as they had left them. The heat had not relented, the unpaved road running through town was still dusty, and the skinny shorthaired dogs still lazed in whatever shade they could find. It felt good to be back. They told Jose they would be sharing a room this time.

"Jose, will you and Maria join us for a margarita on the rooftop before dinner? Ann and I would like to enjoy a sunset tonight. It was a long drive."

"We'd be honored, senor," Jose replied.

"Excellent, seven o'clock then?"

"Seven o'clock it is, senor. I'll tell Maria."

"By the way, have you seen Arturo?"

"Yes, yes, every day. He is over at El Manati now."

Thomas relaxed, "Good. Well, it's been a long trip. I think we might rest for a while before dinner."

Jose smiled. It was clear that Thomas and Ann had fallen deeply in love. He could sense that they were having a hard time staying away from each other.

Once they were in the room, Ann rushed into Thomas's arms. He pulled her close, feeling the breath go out of her. He buried his face in her clean citrus-smelling hair and then they kissed, and continued kissing, finally collapsing on the bed, removing each other's clothes, without pausing for a breath.

» » « «

A few hours later they were greeting Arturo and sharing the news of their budding relationship. They drank margaritas with Jose, Maria, and Arturo, and Maria served cabrito, rice, black beans, and warm corn tortillas. As they talked, Arturo mentioned things were good at the site, which was his way of informing Thomas, in front of Jose and Maria, that everything was fine.

Maria had strung white Christmas lights on poles over the dining section of the hotel roof and Jose had installed an outdoor speaker, through which he played slow Mexican guitar music. There was a lively discussion ranging from Mexican winters to what foolish bastards the Spaniards had been as they conquered Mexico, burning codexes, instilling Christianity; essentially destroying a culture.

After dinner, Jose and Maria excused themselves. Arturo stayed long enough to tell Thomas that while he was in the States, he'd only seen one young couple at the site. They wanted to see an unexplored Mexican site. Arturo told them this one was off limits to the public, due to some indigenous Indian burial concerns, which sent them scurrying off with a story to tell back home.

"I must leave you now. I'm embroiled in a 'hoop' tournament at the local tavern."

"Basketball?" Ann asked.

"No, no. Hoop, not hoops. To play hoop, you screw a hook into the wall at about eye level. Then, you tie a string to a metal ring, a hoop. You put the hoop on the hook and fasten the other end of the string to the ceiling. Then you take the ring off the hook and let it dangle from the ceiling. To play, you take the hoop, move away from the wall, get behind a line, and then let the hoop swing toward the hook. The object of the game is to get the hoop to land on the hook."

"Sounds difficult."

"It is. And a lot of fun. I am a finalist in the tournament. I am playing against a local man. The whole town is rooting against me. It has really united them. Tonight is the final round. So I must go and warm up. What time do we start tomorrow? I assume you got everything we need?" He looked directly at Thomas.

"Yes, everything. We'll meet for breakfast at six and get to the site by seven."

"See you then. Wish me luck!"

Thomas refilled Ann's margarita glass from the pitcher Maria had left behind for them. They walked to the edge of the roof near the foot-wide wall. Thomas stood behind her, with his arms around her, hands resting on her abdomen, as they watched the sun setting in the west; a huge, solid orange globe, the sky a beautiful rose-colored backdrop.

Finally, she turned to face him. He cupped her face with his hands and softly kissed her lips, tasting margarita.

They kissed for a long time and, suddenly, Thomas heard her breathing change. When he felt a tear drop on his wrist, he squeezed her more tightly.

"What are the tears for, Annie?"

She shook her head. "I don't know. What will happen to us after this is all over?"

He hadn't thought much about the future. "We'll go on. Maybe become professional treasure hunters. Focusing on the biggest, most important treasures."

He felt her tremble. "I don't know, Thomas. I-I don't feel . . . good about this." She was crying harder now. "I-I never expected to . . . to fall in love. I feel like somehow this can't last. Like everything is going to end. I don't want anything to ever happen to us."

"Annie, why would anything happen to us? Everything is fine."

"That's the p-problem. Everything is too fine. I have this feeling of dread, when I think about what's going to happen."

"What do you mean?"

"I don't know how to explain it," she paused, "Did you ever see the movie *Raising Arizona*?"

"A long time ago."

"Remember the family, you know, Holly Hunter and Nicholas Cage? All they'd ever wanted was a baby, but they couldn't have one naturally.

So they steal one, and they're having a great life, you know. But every once in a while the movie cuts to this really determined, mean-looking man driving down the highway on a motorcycle. He's pure evil. And you just know he's driving towards their house. Into their lives. You know he's going to take away their happiness."

"I remember it, vaguely. He comes and steals the baby."

"Right."

"So what does that have to do with us?"

"All I've ever wanted is someone like you. And I have this overwhelming feeling that something bad is coming toward us, moving quickly. I'm scared." Ann put her arms around him and squeezed as hard as she could, trying to get under his skin.

Her tears were like a hot branding iron on his shoulder. Ann was a strong independent woman, and he'd never seen her act like this before. He wondered what had triggered it.

"Nothing's going to happen, Annie, I promise. I won't let it. I love you. You love me. I'll always protect you." At this, she held him even tighter. He continued, "I've got everything worked out. Planned. We're going to find Moses' treasure and then go away together. We'll make love all day, every day, and dream up our next archeological project."

He brought her face up to his and he kissed her while she cried. The warm night breeze caressed their skin. He brought a chair over to the wall and pulled her onto his lap. With only the Christmas lights and a canopy of twinkling stars for light, she unbuttoned the top of her dress, allowing his hands easier access to her full breasts. Soon he lifted her sun dress and she straddled him. As they made love, she cried silent tears, and they whispered promises to each other.

The only other sounds that could be heard came from the small tavern, two blocks away, where from the volume of the cheers, it sounded like Arturo was losing.

CHAPTER 21

The next day, Thomas, Arturo and Ann drove to the site in silence, each thinking about the job at hand and their individual assignments. They had risen early, eaten a large breakfast, and now, as they drove, each held a cup of the steaming-hot Mexican coffee that Jose ground special for them every morning.

Ann drove Lucille as close to the pyramid as possible, so that they could unload equipment. Thomas had come to breakfast with the site drawn on graph paper.

"At this stage, the planning is more essential than the actual work. If something goes wrong due to lack of planning, it could take us months to recover."

He had taken Ann and Arturo through the extraction plan and now, in the morning heat, he went over it again. Ann saw why he was so good at what he did. He had everything planned, contingencies for every situation. He had ranked every conceivable method they could use for each task by the time it would take, and by risk to the Ark. They were to begin with a low risk, moderately paced plan. If the first way didn't work, they would try the second, then the third.

As Thomas spoke, Ann realized that while they had driven to Arizona and back, Thomas had been hard at work the whole time. Planning, readying, scheming. She should've known it all along. He was one of the best, and this treasure would be the biggest find of his life—and he'd had some pretty big finds. But she'd never known that he'd done all of this preparation. Just like his plan to escape the surveillance, this was creative, yet logical and simple.

Now, she felt embarrassed. Driving back and forth to Arizona, she had slept when it was his turn to drive. But he always remained awake during her turn driving, to write, or gaze out the passenger window. When she asked him what he was writing, he would say, "Oh, just notes." But here they were, in the middle of Mexico, about to make the most significant archeological find of all time, surely the most religiously and politically sensitive, and Thomas had the whole damn thing planned out to the last detail.

Plan A was simple. They would use an auger with a masonry bit to drill horizontally into the large, square stone that concealed the treasure. They would insert a large camelot, a tool used by rock climbers to gain secure attachments quickly, into the resulting hole, to get a firm grasp on the stone. After insertion, camelots expand, so pulling would only grind one deeper into the rock.

Thomas explained that he would fasten the camelot to the cable, which would be attached to the Ramsey RE series winch that he had mounted to her Discovery. It would pull up to 10,000 pounds dead weight. The back of the truck would be anchored to an outcropping of rock that was bigger than the stone they were extracting from the pyramid. If all went well, the stone would slowly slide out of place, just as it had slid into place, over three thousand years ago. As the stone moved, Thomas and Arturo would slip steel trusses in the cavity, to brace the rocks above it.

"I had the girders cut to the exact length of the stones we're removing."

"When did you do that?" Ann asked. "I didn't even know you had measured."

Arturo laughed. "Nothing escapes this man, Ann. He is very thorough. He thinks of everything. Everything."

After they had unloaded the equipment and reviewed the plan a third time, Thomas turned to Ann. "Move the truck directly in front of the stone, about midway between the pyramid and the outcropping we're going to tie on to. While you do that Arturo and I will use the auger to drill the hole for the camelot."

"All right. Are you sure you guys don't need my help in the pit?"

"We can handle it, and there isn't room down there anyway. Don't worry, Arturo says these old pyramid stones cut like butter. You stay up there and get the truck perfectly aligned. If it's not, we may bend the frame. When you're done, run the cable from the hitch around that large boulder, and then back onto itself so it will tighten as it's pulled. When you're finished, we should be ready for you."

Several minutes later, Ann appeared at the mouth of the cavity. To her complete surprise, almost disbelief, the hole was already drilled. "You're done! That's amazing. How in the heck could you drill through two feet of solid rock so fast?"

Thomas laughed. "You're working with two professionals, my dear."

Ann was still surprised, but noticed the little pyramid of rock powder that had collected on the ground, below the hole.

"You guys are good," she said.

"Did you get Lucille fastened to that boulder?"

"Sure did. We're ready if you're ready."

Thomas selected the largest camelot and slid it into the drilled hole. He flicked the switch that activated it and they heard it click as it opened inside the hole. He jerked the cable several times. It held firmly.

Ann hauled the twenty-ton capacity cable from her winch to the edge of the pit and eased it over to Thomas, who used a heavy duty carabiner to connect the Rover to the cable.

"Shall I get the braces?" Arturo asked.

"I think it's time," Thomas said.

The moment of truth. Arturo smiled at his cohort and slapped him on the back. He positioned the braces on either side of the stone, leaving only enough room for it to slide out cleanly.

"Okay, Annie, get in the truck and very slowly activate the winch. Give it five seconds on the first try. Watch my hand for the signal to cut it early. Do you understand?"

Ann got into the truck. "Got it!"

"Arturo, you stay over here with me. We'll watch the stone for movement. I'll also be keeping my eye on the cable, to make sure the connections stay secure."

"With you, amigo!"

Thomas felt ready. This was it.

He gave Ann the signal to start the winch. He heard it whine as the cable tightened, and then screech. For a moment, everything remained at a standstill, cable taut, winch screeching, and he felt the huge rock move, ever so slightly. But it was not enough. At this rate he'd burn out the winch. He gave Ann the signal to cut power.

Ann left the truck and jogged over. "Is everything okay? What happened?"

Arturo said, "It moved. Did you feel it, Thomas?"

"Yes, but not enough. There was too much strain on the winch. We'll blow the motor at this pace. Annie, come here."

When she was by his side, he pulled a leather pouch from his pocket. "This is it. We're going to go for it on this next try. These are low grade industrial diamonds cut into little round balls. Like marbles, but smaller. As long as the stone is in motion, it will roll on these diamonds and not crush them. As soon as all motion stops, it will crush them. You're looking at my entire supply. This is all I could afford. So, this time, we will not stop until the stone is out."

He poured about fifty diamonds from the bag and strategically scattered them in the stone's pathway. "That should do it."

"Where did you get the diamonds, Thomas?"

"Later, Annie. It's an old trick. Greasing the skids. Now listen you two. Our stone has already moved. Once it hits these, it should really start to roll. Be ready. Watch me for directions."

Arturo nodded his approval. This was a surprise, even to him.

"Annie, aim for twenty seconds this time, or until I tell you to stop. If it's slow going, I may give you the thumbs up, meaning keep going even after the twenty seconds are up."

In the rush of excitement, she said, "Roger that." It occurred to

Thomas that Ann had used a pilot's acknowledgment. He made a mental note to ask her if she'd ever done any flying.

"When we get the stone out, our treasure will either be in a cavity within the rock we're moving, or behind it. I don't know which. The riddle is not clear on that point. If it's in a cavity, we'll have to pull it out. What do we do, once the rock is out of the way, Arturo?"

"We quickly determine where the treasure is located and, depending on its weight, use one of three methods to move it to the back of the truck. Then we drive to the garage behind our motel."

"Right! And why do we do that, Ann?"

"Because we want to secure the treasure by getting it to a pre-determined safe place. Then we come back here to see if there is anything else of importance. Then, using the overhead pulley, we push the stone back into place."

"Good. Now let's get this damn treasure!"

Ann ran back to the truck and Arturo moved his brace as close as he could get it to the stone without blocking its path. The diamond balls had convinced him that the stone would slide out this time.

Thomas gave the sign to Ann, and she started the winch. The cable tightened and all slack disappeared. It began to whine, then screech, but the huge stone didn't budge. Then the winch began to emit an incredibly loud shriek. Thomas was about to signal Ann to cut power, when slowly, almost imperceptibly, the stone started to move. Suddenly, its edge found a few of the diamond balls and it began to roll smoothly, much faster than Thomas had anticipated.

Thomas heard and felt the whoosh of air, as it was drawn into the cavern created by the extracted stone. Then, a cool exhale, in which he thought he smelled both wood . . . and metal. He suppressed his excitement.

When there was four feet between the stone and the pyramid he gave Ann the signal to halt. The winch stopped. He and Arturo quickly slid the braces into place. "Thank God!" he said, sighing with relief. "I don't think the stones above shifted at all."

He ran his hand along the entire back of the stone. "No cutaway, Arturo."

He reached into his back pocket and grabbed the small Maglight flashlight. He twisted it on, and directed the narrow beam into the dark hole, and waited for the dust to clear.

"Jesus."

In the middle of the cavity, Thomas saw a wooden crate, looking as though it had been placed there only a week before.

"Can you see this, Arturo? Am I seeing things?"

"No, amigo, what you see is real."

Thomas moved closer, but didn't touch it. He saw inlaid clay stamps, with hieroglyphic writing and other symbols he recognized as Egyptian. Speechless, he sat on his heels and stared into Arturo's olive-black eyes. He shook his head. "Moses' treasure, my friend. Moses' treasure."

Leaping to his feet, he grabbed Arturo and lifted him off his feet. "*Annie!*" he shouted. "Come see this!" He and Arturo reached up for her and pulled her into the pit, jumping up and down with her, in a celebratory dance. She pulled herself away from them and knelt by the crate.

"Hieroglyphics!" she said, more to herself than to them. "It's real, then. Moses really did come to Mexico to bury his treasure. I'm . . . speechless! Thomas . . . Thomas, do you honestly believe this is the Ark of the Covenant and the Ten Commandments?"

"I'm sure of it. I'd stake my reputation on it. Either way, we'll find out tonight."

And then, as Ann raised her arms and screamed the word, "Yes!" into the air, a helicopter swooped nimbly in over the pyramid, blowing sand in every direction, and the celebration abruptly ended.

CHAPTER 22

Coming out of nowhere, the helicopter flew in low, over the pyramid. Sand was blowing hard, in no discernable pattern, making it hard to shield eyes.

Arturo and Ann stood frozen in disbelief. Over the roar of the blades, Thomas yelled to Arturo. "Get the truck! Get the truck!"

Arturo scrambled out of the pit and ran for Ann's truck, while Thomas threw a rope around the crate. Using the pulley system they had set up for a fast extraction, Ann helped him drag the box out of the cavity and onto the wheeled miner's cart. While they dragged, Thomas glanced over his shoulder at Arturo. Behind the truck, he could see several cars coming up the dirt road from Mercado, lights flashing, a huge curtain of dust behind them.

"Pull, Ann!" Then to himself, *Christ, who are these people? They're coming out of the woodwork like rats on a sinking ship!*

As Ann pushed the box down the hill, the words of Hebrews 9:16 rang in her mind, about how all those who touched the Ark would perish.

Arturo had turned the truck around and the backend was now about twenty feet from the box. Then he was out, opening the back hatch with his face down, eyes shielded from the sand.

The helicopter was directly overhead. Sand whipped all around them. Ann and Thomas desperately pushed the trolley cart with the box on top over to the truck and, with Arturo's help, heaved the box up onto the back gate.

Arturo slammed the hatch. Thomas yelled, "Let's get the hell out of here. I'll drive!"

The helicopter moved lower. Thomas saw two men. Suddenly a deep voice thundered through a loud speaker, *"Do not move! Face down on the ground. Face down on the ground, now!"*

Ann yanked Thomas's arm. She was yelling, but he could barely hear her words. "When we pulled the box out, I saw something behind it. There was something behind the box. I'm going back for it!"

Sand pelted both their faces and Thomas yelled. *"There's no time! Get in the truck. That's an order!"*

A pellet of sand flew into his left eye. Instinctively, both eyes shut. He reached up to rub them and when he opened them again, he saw Ann running back toward the pyramid. He stole a quick look at the road. The vehicles were much closer, their flashing lights clear through the swirling sand and dirt.

Arturo honked the horn of the truck and motioned for Thomas to hurry. Thomas ran to the passenger window. "Ann saw something. She went back. I couldn't stop her!"

When Thomas turned back toward the pyramid a lightening bolt of panic struck him. A team of four men, dressed in black assault uniforms, were moving quickly over the side of the pyramid, much the same way he'd approached the first night he'd met Ann, only they were carrying machine guns.

Thomas realized he had two choices. Let them have her, hope they wouldn't hurt her, jump in the truck, and get the hell out of there, or leave Arturo with the truck and attempt to rescue Ann. In the first scenario, he might lose Ann, in the second, they might all get caught and lose the treasure.

He ran after Ann. He had covered ten feet when the soldiers saw him. They began sprinting towards Ann. They reached the base of the pyramid before Thomas did and trained their short barreled close-combat machine guns on him from twenty feet . . . pointblank range. One of the black marauders roughly pulled Ann from the pit and held her tightly, pinning one arm behind her back.

Once Ann was detained, the helicopter made another pass, this time focusing on Thomas. Everyone raised their hands to shield their eyes and Thomas used the diversion to make a dash for the truck. He zigzagged as he ran, like he'd seen people do in the movies. Any second, he expected to hear gunfire, or at least see sand kicking up next to his feet, but nothing happened.

Thomas jerked open the driver's side door and slid onto the seat. "They got her. Let's go!"

He slammed the accelerator, the wheels spun, caught, and they sped down the dirt road toward Mercado. Within thirty seconds of driving, they could see the helicopter directly above them through the sunroof. They could also clearly see two military SUV's driving toward them from Mercado.

Arturo glanced over his shoulder. "The soldiers are handcuffing Ann." They faded out of sight as dust flew up from the back of the vehicle.

The two camouflage vehicles, which looked like Ford Broncos, had stopped and were turning perpendicular to the road, lights still flashing.

"Who the hell are these people?" Arturo yelled.

Thomas rolled it over in his mind. "I have no idea. It's got to be whoever was watching me. FBI." He swerved to avoid a mammoth pothole.

"You think they could have picked you up again?"

"We'll see who it is soon enough, we can't outrun these guys. They've got a whole goddamn platoon after us out here."

Whoever had planned the attack had waited until the exact moment he'd extracted the treasure from the pyramid. They knew what they were doing, and were well-equipped.

Thomas cycled back through the timeline. The only other people who had complete knowledge about the treasure were Martha, Arturo, and Ann. In that order. He doubted Martha would ever double cross him. Even if she had, she wouldn't have had the time or resources to mount this kind of campaign against him. Arturo had been left alone with the treasure for four weeks, ample time to steal it.

He had trusted Ann as much as he had Arturo. Possibly more. He had fallen deeply in love with her. She would have nothing to gain by stealing from him. Anyway, they had spent almost every waking hour together since they'd met. She wouldn't have had time to plan something like this.

He had been hit at the time when the treasure hunter was most exposed—the moment the treasure was unearthed. Unfortunately most archaeologists and treasure hunters didn't have contingency plans in case they came under attack. The most they typically had was a gun.

Thomas glanced at Arturo, who was gripping the handle on the dashboard. "The letters on the helicopter are English and those soldiers were not Mexican. Did you get a look at them?"

"Yes. They looked American, or maybe European. Did they say anything?"

"One of them told me to get down on the ground. He sounded American."

"Looks like they've got a roadblock up ahead."

"The soldiers are positioned behind the trucks. They've got guns ready."

"Take out the binoculars and see if you can get a look."

Thomas slowed slightly and Arturo took a minute to assess the situation. "Yeah, they're back there with guns. Think they'll shoot?"

Thomas looked grave. "If they wanted us dead, they would have shot us back at the pyramid. They had us cold." Thomas down shifted and the Rover jerked forward. "I'll reduce speed. When we're within a hundred feet, I'll veer to the right, hit that gully over there, and swing around them. We'll make this look good. Okay?"

"Watch the sand on the median, it's thicker than on the road. It may grab the tires."

"Okay, thanks. Once we're past them, I'll pull back onto the road. I'll try my best not to roll it. God, Ann would kill me if she heard me say that." But Arturo was too nervous to smile.

Two hundred feet from the blockade, Thomas let up on the gas and the Land Rover began to coast. At the point of no return, he briskly downshifted and whipped the car into the gully that ran beside the road. The angle was much steeper than he'd anticipated. They were approaching rollover angle and Thomas felt the left tires come up just as they hit the bottom. He jerked the wheel to the right, then back again. They leveled out and the tires settled onto the dry creek bed.

Thomas could see the soldiers scrambling to get back into their SUV's. No shots had been fired. Half a mile later, Thomas slowed again and turned back up the escarpment onto the road.

They were fast approaching the town of Mercado. The Broncos were in pursuit and the helicopter was still directly overhead. The road improved as they neared town and Thomas estimated they could hit Mercado doing about seventy miles per hour.

Helicopters were rare in Mercado, as were camouflage Broncos. The villagers lined the street as if there were a parade. As Thomas approached the town he flashed his bright lights and honked his horn, hoping to get people clear of the street.

They flew into town at 75 miles an hour. People on both sides clapped and cheered, grateful for the unexpected diversion.

In less than a minute, they were out of the town and into a dry expansive desert.

The helicopter shot ahead of them. Thomas glanced in the rearview mirror. The Broncos were gaining.

Nose tipping up, the helicopter made a smooth turn, then set down in the middle of the road a quarter of a mile ahead. Thomas instinctively slowed.

"What do we do? Go around them again?"

Thomas considered options. They would gain nothing by going around again. They'd only get sandwiched again five minutes later. Looking back, the Broncos were so close he could see the earnest faces of the two men in the front seats.

think they've got us, friend. Let's find out who the hell's so interested in our treasure." He looked back at the crate sitting in the rear of the truck and shook his head. "They sure are serious, and well funded, for Christ's sake! Helicopters and all."

CHAPTER 23

Thomas slowed and finally came to a stop about a hundred feet from the helicopter, well out of range of the wash from its mammoth propeller. The Broncos stopped behind the Discovery and the occupants expertly positioned themselves with rifles behind open doors.

The door of the helicopter slid open and a man stepped out. Holding his hat against the gusts created by the propeller, he walked toward Thomas and Arturo until he was clear of the helicopter, and then stopped to assess the situation. He looked beyond the Land Rover at the Broncos, checking their position. He turned back to the helicopter to make sure the road was fully blocked and that the sniper who had been riding with him was out, rifle ready. He did all this as if he owned everything; the vehicles, the helicopter, Mexico, all of it. Only when he felt he had the situation fully under control, just as they'd drawn it on the white-board earlier that day, did he turn his attention back to the Land Rover Discovery.

Silver hair protruded from under his cowboy hat. He wore a tan camel hair blazer over a white oxford cloth shirt, and jeans. He had on cowboy boots and a belt with a slightly oversized belt buckle. He came toward them, but he didn't walk. He sauntered. He was DJ Warrant, and he knew he'd just stopped a car on a highway in Mexico that contained the most important artifact ever found on the face of the earth. He'd stopped a car that contained the Ark of the Covenant and the Ten Commandments.

He walked right down the center of the road. Beyond him, in the helicopter, Thomas could see a small bald man sitting, typing at a laptop.

The cowboy stopped about 20 feet from the Discovery, looked directly at Thomas, and waved him out.

Thomas nodded at Arturo, opened his door and got out. They were in flat desert now, and a hot wind blew across the highway. Thomas stopped five feet in front of the man. Just out of striking distance.

DJ looked at Thomas, smiled, reached into the inside pocket of his blazer, took out a pack of Marlboros and in one blurred motion that Thomas didn't even completely see he had a cigarette in his mouth and a shiny zippo lighter out to light it.

He looked Thomas in the eye as he lit the cigarette, and said, "You're bigger, up close. Taller."

"I'd like to say you look bigger, too, but I've never seen a picture of you before, never had you under surveillance, Mr.?"

"You don't need to know who I am, Thomas McAlister. After today, you'll never see me again. Nor any of these other men."

"Disappointing, you're all so nice. Pleasant. With all your guns and equipment. So I don't get to know your name. Can I ask what you want with my friend and me?"

"You mean Arturo Bandera? We actually don't want anything with either of you. We want what you've got in the back of that truck, Mr. McAlister."

"Do you know what I have back there?"

"Sure do. And I'm gonna take it off your hands right now."

"If you want to take what I have back there, there is nothing I can do to stop you. You've got seven men, eight, counting the computer geek with the laptop, and all of them are carrying weapons. I'm curious, though. Do you know the power it possesses? Have you done any reading or research about what it can do?"

"Wives' tales."

"No. Biblical tales. Ever read Hebrews? Revelations? Heavy-duty Bible stuff, Tex. The Bible, believe in Christ or not, is a fairly accurate historical document. Do me this favor. Leave it in its box. Don't touch it! And don't let any of your men touch it, okay?"

DJ pulled a flat World War II issue Colt .45 automatic from his holster and pointed it at Thomas. He motioned toward the helicopter and four men got out. Two of them carried rope. One carried a crow bar.

"Enough chatter, Professor. Open the back of the vehicle."

Thomas walked slowly to the rear of the Discovery and opened the hatchback. DJ took a look at the box and motioned to someone in the helicopter.

As if choreographed, Elmo jumped down and came running, his laptop open.

DJ pried open the lid of the crate and peered inside, using a short black flashlight for light. Elmo held up the computer so DJ could see it. DJ looked back and forth from the box to the computer a few times, nodded, and then closed the box.

"Okay, boys, take her away."

They firmly closed the lid to the box, wrapped it tightly with the rope, and then carried it to the helicopter, one man per corner.

DJ followed them. Thomas walked beside him. "That box is heavy. How did you know that the four of them would be able to carry it?"

DJ threw his cigarette on the highway and paused to grind the heel of his boot on it. "It was made by master craftsman Bezalel, of acacia wood. Two and a half cubits long, one and half cubits wide, one and a half cubits tall. The acacia is overlaid with pure gold inside and out. Four rings, one on each corner, cast from gold for the acacia poles used to carry it. Exodus, Chapter 37, verse 1. Four rings, two poles equals four men, Professor." DJ continued walking.

Thomas followed. "I need to find Ann. Is she back at the pyramid?"

"I don't know where she is. Why don't you go back there and see?"

Thomas grabbed his arm, spun him, and said, "Listen, I need to know where she is! Do your men have her or not?"

DJ smoothed the crease on his jacket. "Thomas, relax now. Let's not get all excited here. You've been so good up until now. I'm telling you I don't know where she is. Why don't you go back to the pyramid and see if she's there, okay?"

"Goddamn it, you know exactly where she is! I don't know who you are, but you're not the kind of man to leave things to chance. Now I'm asking you where she is, so I can go get her."

DJ stepped backward and ran his hand over his forehead. As he did, he looked up for a while, and then, in a completely changed tone, said, "Well, I'll be. I've been down here for days and that's the first Mexican eagle I've seen!"

It was an old trick, maybe the oldest. Distraction. But it worked. Thomas looked up and as he did DJ hit him hard in the stomach. He fell to the ground, gasping.

Then DJ boarded the helicopter. Thomas could hear the blades beginning to pick up speed. Between clenched eyelids he could see DJ standing on the platform looking down at him, intense satisfaction on his face, even a little smirk. This case was turning out to be far better than DJ ever would have predicted.

Thomas was still gasping when Arturo reached his side. The helicopter blades were kicking up a blinding gale. Sand pelted them. It felt like hundreds of little bee stings. Just before it got too loud to hear, DJ yelled down at them, "Hey McAlister, I'll save you some time. Don't bother looking for Ann at the pyramid. She won't be there!"

CHAPTER **24**

Washington D.C.

The National Museum of Art is located in Washington D.C., less than a mile from both the White House and the Pentagon. Founded in 1937 by a joint resolution of Congress, it was completed in 1941 during the presidency of Franklin D. Roosevelt. Most of its initial art was from the personal collection of Andrew W. Melon, who donated it upon his death, in 1937.

When the United States government acquires a valuable artifact, the National Museum of Art is the first place it goes, especially if it is a secret treasure. This was true for three reasons; first, the government owns and operates the museum and, therefore, can maintain secrecy. Second, the museum is close to the Pentagon and convenient to visit and watch; and third, and most importantly, the NMA only hires people who are tops in their field. And, unlike other government agencies, they pay well.

George Valmer, who had been Chief Director of the Museum for fifteen years, could not recall ever having such a powerful group of Washington insiders at the museum to discuss a single artifact. Then again, he had never had such a valuable treasure. Over the course of his long career, he had seen most of the thousands of secret treasures that the government had acquired, from masterpieces stolen by the Nazis to the best fakes ever made . . . but *never* anything of this magnitude. The Ark of the Covenant and the Ten Commandments! It was beyond comprehension.

The Deputy Director of the CIA, Charles Hargrove, had called him on the phone only yesterday and told him, on a secure line, that he had come into possession of the Ark of the Covenant. If anyone else had called, and said they had the Ark, George would have chuckled and gone along with the joke. But he knew Hargrove, and Hargrove didn't joke. Ever. So George had believed him.

The Deputy Director said that they were bringing the Ark to the NMA under armed guard. They wanted its condition evaluated and contents analyzed before showing it to the President. He said they hadn't touched it, other than to open the crate it was in to do a visual identification. George was thankful to hear this. He had seen many priceless relics defaced at the hands of non-trained, overzealous field agents.

George had immediately asked Hargrove's level of comfort on its authenticity and the Deputy's response had reassured him. "FBI personal watched while the Ark was taken directly from its three thousand year old resting place in a pyramid, and at no time has it left the sight of my most trustworthy agent, the agent that found it, DJ Warrant." George knew, even as the Deputy Chief spoke, he would date the artifact anyway.

George hung up the phone, pulse pounding, with images of the famous golden Ark running through his head. That was yesterday. Since then he had not slept. He had prepared his formal conference room in the basement of the NMA for the arrival. The government had spared no expense on the conference room, it was the best the Museum had to offer. George had personally overseen its construction several years ago. Mahogany walls, plush carpeting, huge conference table, and audio and video conference technology. But what really made the room perfect was the freight elevator that led directly from the receiving dock to the conference room. It had been built for just such occasions.

At nine o'clock sharp, the group assembled. DJ had been with the Ark since taking it from McAlister on the dusty Mexican road. He had ridden with it in the helicopter, then on the C-120 transport back to D.C., and last night he used it as a foot rest in a top-secret Pentagon warehouse in Virginia, at the edge of the Virginia, D.C. border.

DJ, at George's direction, had his men position the crate on a heavy-duty cart, in the center of the room, as close to the conference table as possible. The crate, dry, dusty and dilapidated, was a sharp contrast to the glossy mahogany table. George dialed up the surgical lights over the table, fully illuminating the crate that held the Ark. It was like a rock star, alone on stage: famous, yet enigmatic.

"Any coffee?" DJ asked.

George had a buffet set up on the side of the room, but only about half the guests were using it. No one said so, but they were too nervous to drink or eat.

"Of course, sir. You'll find everything over here." George spun DJ around and graciously steered him to the coffee.

They chatted superficially, everyone's thoughts on the Ark, until ten minutes after nine, when the energy in the room was too great to wait any longer. Deputy Chief Hargrove sat at the end of the table, with George on his right.

"Gentlemen," Hargrove said, "I want to do quick introductions and then get about the business of looking at what we've got here and, of course, preparing it for the President tomorrow."

Complete silence.

He paused and looked around the table, getting a few nods. Mainly he saw the eyes of nervous, expectant people, trying to look assured. "I, as you all know, am Deputy Chief Hargrove of the FBI. Our agenda this morning is as follows. I will introduce the government personnel, George Valmer will introduce his museum experts, and we will then open this crate and examine the Ark of the Covenant." He looked around at mortally serious faces. Complete silence again.

"Our objective is to determine the condition of the Ark and its contents for the President of the United States. If everything goes smoothly this morning, I can tell you with certainty that the President himself will be in this very room tomorrow at 9:00 a.m. to view the Ark."

Hargrove let the gravity of that statement sink in. Basically the President didn't go anywhere if it wasn't either a fantastic PR move, a fund raiser, or a matter of national security. In this case, it was the latter.

George spoke up with a question. "Chief Hargrove, has the President been notified that the Ark has been . . . found?"

"Yes. I briefed him yesterday, immediately after receiving DJ's verbal report." He smiled at DJ, the hero of the day.

"Do you know whether he plans to make any sort of *public* announcement regarding the fact that it's been found?" He said the word public with singular disdain.

Hargrove smiled at the question, clearly understanding why George was a museum director and not a politician. "George, the unearthing of the Ark is a true national security emergency. If we announce to the public that we've found it, two very troublesome things would likely happen immediately. First, the economy would shut down because everyone would be in church. We've done studies on what happens to local economies when these images of Mary turn up. You remember, like the one in Florida a few years ago. Spending is cut by half. Economies tank."

Hargrove looked around the room then continued, "Secondly, we'd have World War Three on our hands. Both Jews and Muslims would claim ownership and our entire foreign policy would be in jeopardy. If you hadn't noticed, neither culture is fond of anyone else possessing one of their religious icons. They've waged wars over much, much less. No sir, that's not what the President needs right now. He needs allies, not enemies. We have to keep a lid on this gentlemen. *A tight lid*! I hope that answers your question, George. We *cannot* make an announcement in the near term. This is the kind of thing you have to build the public up to slowly. A story has to be built around it, with heroes and villains. The public, and the world, must be told exactly what to think. They cannot be left to their own devices."

Hargrove did not mention the fact that Moses had lied and that it was likely that the Hebrew words on these tablets would not match the widely accepted Ten Commandments. There was no reason to tell everyone in the room. His argument for keeping them secure was strong enough without disclosing that fact, plus there was always the inherent danger of a leak.

"Now, let's roll through introductions." Hargrove went on to introduce two of the most powerful men in the country. "On my left, you all know the Secretary of State, Dick Almond. On his left, the Secretary of Defense, John Churchill. Next to John there is DJ Warrant, our top field man. The man who found the Ark for us. DJ will retire on this one. Right, Deej?"

DJ nodded, now sure that his retirement lay in the box next to the table. When the attention shifted, he could be seen smiling a little, thinking about his full pension, including the sizable retirement bonus promised at the successful conclusion of this case.

"Dick, John, DJ, this is Director George Valmer. He runs the NMA, and George, why don't you introduce the two gentleman you've invited today?"

George nodded at the members of the Cabinet. "Pleasure to meet you. On my right here is Dr. Mark Nelson. Mark is one of the foremost Egyptologists in the world." But he didn't find the Ark, DJ thought to himself. McAlister did.

"And next to Dr. Nelson is Dr. Carl Stevens. Dr. Stevens is an expert in Biblical Historical studies. There is no one who knows more about biblical history, and the field of biblical artifacts, than Dr. Stevens. I am honored to have them both here today. Together, they create the perfect team for the analysis you have requested. You can be assured that their analysis of the artifact will be irreproachable."

Finally, with introductions complete, Hargrove said, "All right, then, let's get to it. Let's open the box!"

DJ was sweating now. He wished he'd taken a better look at the contents. He'd been instructed not to touch or tamper with what he found. True, it would have been difficult to disassemble the massive, 3000-year old wooden crate, but it would have saved him the terrible heartburn he was experiencing as the two archeologists stood up to begin their work. He told himself to stop worrying! He had been there when Thomas extracted it.

First Dr. Nelson and Dr. Stevens rolled the cart away from the table a few feet so they could stand on either side of it and work. The Ark was in a crate made of old timbers that looked as though they could easily be pulled off with use of the special tools the two men had laid out on the conference table. With rubber gloves on, the two experts began to gently pry the top off the crate. After five minutes of slow, even, deliberate prying, the top was ready to lift off.

The two men were visibly excited. Dr. Nelson paused to clear his throat. "We are going to place each piece we remove on the artifact table we've set up in the corner of the room. Later today, we will begin the dating process."

George threw a questioning glance at Hargrove, who nodded his approval.

The two experts then slowly, ever so gently, removed the lid of the crate, carried it over to the table in the corner, and set it down. They hurriedly returned to the box and, both, for the first time, looked down into the crate.

Immediately, Dr. Stevens passed out. DJ and Dr. Nelson caught him before he hit the floor and laid him gently on the soft wool carpet. No one attended to him and both Dr. Nelson and DJ went back to the table to look inside at the Ark. The others watched as the two men peered down into the crate.

The color of gold reflected off their faces. Dr. Nelson's face lit up with excitement, like a ten-year old who had been given a pocket knife.

"My God! It's marvelous! It looks just as the Bible says it should!" He started to reach down into the crate to touch it.

"Don't touch!" Nelson quickly pulled his hand back as Deputy Chief Hargrove sprang up from the end of the table and pushed him away from the crate.

"I didn't mean to startle you, Doctor, but please do not touch anything until we have all seen it. I don't need to remind you that it is the property of the United States government."

Dr. Nelson looked up at him, still in a trance-like state. It was unfathomable to him that he was seeing the biblical icon he had studied so extensively.

Hargrove patted his back. "You're doing fine. Please continue with the crate. You were going to remove the sides next?"

Dr. Stevens was coming to. DJ threw some water on him.

After Stevens fully recovered, the two historians worked together and, in twenty minutes, they had the top half of the crate dismantled. The top half of the Ark was visible and everyone could see the lid of the Ark with its two golden cherubs facing each other. Now, able to see the treasure, the normally reserved government officials became excited and occasionally nodded or smiled at Valmer. He felt his personal stock rise each time they did so.

The experts continued dismantling the dusty crate, plank by plank, until the entire Ark of the Covenant was exposed. Everyone was transfixed. Ever the observer, DJ looked around. The full view of the Ark had everyone paralyzed. Hargrove, Almond, Churchill, Valmer: all of them catatonic. He wanted to retire. Now. And he wanted a cold beer, but it was too early in the morning.

Dr. Nelson and Dr. Stevens stepped away from the Ark. "Take a closer look," Stevens said to George Valmer. He rubbed his hands together. "It looks exactly like what is described in the Bible, Exodus 37. Down to the rings on the corners for the carrying poles."

Dr. Nelson had made a trip to the artifact table and come back with some sort of chemical testing kit. He looked at Deputy Chief Hargrove. "At this time, we need to conduct a simple test, to authenticate the gold. Okay?"

"Open it first." Hargrove replied.

Dr. Stevens objected. "Deputy Hargrove, there are standards . . . tests that only take . . . ."

"*Open it now*!" Hargrove demanded, his face red, final. "Open it, let us see what's inside, then do your test as we examine the contents. If it's the tablets, put them over on the artifact table. That way we can look at them while you run your tests."

The professors shrugged, then nodded. They first tried to lift the lid by hand, but they were unable to budge it. They examined every inch of the lid with their eyes and gloved fingers, looking for a hidden latch. Next they picked up their prying tools and nervously, gently, positioned them in between the lid of the Ark and the body.

Hargrove settled down and observed their work. Clearly they were experienced. They worked well together, slowly sliding the prying tools around the lid to ensure it was loose before trying to pry it up.

Finally, they were ready to pry the first corner up, but Dr. Stevens paused. "I have been thinking, these last few minutes, of a verse of Scripture—"

"Oh, don't tell me it's First Samuel 6:19!" DJ barked the reference, before the scholar could quote it. "I certainly hope you're not going to try to scare everyone into thinking we can't open it, Doctor."

"What are you talking about?" Dick Almond asked.

"The Bible says God killed seventy men for daring to look into the Ark. Doctor Stevens is about to say that he thinks we could all be in danger if we open the Ark."

Almond adjusted his glasses with nervous fingers. He wished he hadn't asked. "Hmm. That was then, of course. This is now. Don't you think, John?" The Secretary of Defense nodded. He wasn't religious.

"History is history." Hargrove said. "Let's move forward, gentlemen."

George Valmer had been whispering with his two experts and they returned to the work of getting the lid off. Dr. Stevens placed the sharp edge of a small pry bar under the lip of the lid and began to slowly lower the handle, forcing the lid up. He moved to another area and then to another. He was careful to apply only slight pressure to each area. Since the box was covered in gold, as the Bible described, there was the distinct danger of causing indentations. Gold is a soft metal, which is why craftsmen use only a ten or fourteen carat gold mixture for objects that receive daily use. Hargrove had not let them test this gold, so they did not know whether it was hard or soft.

As Stevens went around, he became more confident. The gold was holding up well, and seemed to be hard enough for him to begin to pry a little harder. He began his second round, and then it happened!

Crack!

Everyone jumped. The perfect silence was interrupted. A two inch long chunk of the Ark flew up into the air and landed on the table, bouncing once before it skittered another couple of inches.

No one moved. People sucked in their breath. *Had they broken the Ark? Was God warning them? Was the Ark a time bomb getting ready to blow them all up?* They looked at the gold piece, then at Dr. Stevens. The tool in his left hand was shaking. In silence, he slowly reached for the piece of the Ark sitting on the table. Everyone watched, frozen.

With a rubber gloved hand he picked it up, looked at it and smiled. "It's just a small broken piece of wood. Easily restored." Tension evaporated. Smiles were exchanged.

As Hargrove was saying something to George about myths and magic, DJ watched Dr. Stevens' face as he further examined the piece that had come off of the Ark.

First his face was inquisitive. Then it changed. He began to look worried. As the volume of chatter in the room rose to a new height, DJ became aware that there was something terribly wrong. Dr. Stevens' face registered terror.

Someone was starting to tell a joke when DJ said, "Doctor, what's wrong?"

No one had heard him, including the doctor who was now pale and shaking visibly.

DJ said it much louder, too loud. "Doctor. What is wrong with you?" Everyone stopped. They looked at DJ, then at the Doctor.

He was turning the piece over and then back, over and then back, looking at both sides. Then he looked at the Ark itself.

They all saw it at the same time. The area where the piece had been was bright yellow. The real Ark had been made of acacia wood, a dark wood, that would have gotten even darker with the passage of time. But this wood was yellow. *New. New wood!*

DJ grew purple with rage. He instantly knew that he was looking at newly milled *pine*. There was no wood in the world that looked quite as bright, quite as yellow, as newly milled pine. And there was not a person in the room who didn't know what that meant. This Ark was a fake.

Dr. Stevens said, "It's a fake!" and handed the piece of wood to Dr. Nelson. "Paint! Gold paint! This isn't the Ark of the Covenant. It's only a decent copy. Designed to fool the unknowing." His eyes came to rest on DJ.

All eyes, Hargrove's in particular, were on DJ.

DJ felt guilty without knowing why. He said, "I saw Thomas McAlister take this Ark out of that pyramid! I saw it with my own two goddamn eyes, I tell you. I've been with this box since we took it from him!"

"You took this from *Thomas McAlister*? The *Egyptologist*?" Mark Nelson's mouth dropped open.

George Valmer asked, "Could McAlister have faked it?"

Then, importantly, Deputy Chief Hargrove asked, "DJ, can any of your men verify that this is the same box you took from McAlister?"

DJ was stunned. "Are you accusing me of pulling a switch, sir?"

"You've been on this case long enough to have had a double made. You retire soon. Your pension is good, DJ, but not that good. It wouldn't be the first time an agent went for the big payday before retirement."

DJ was shocked. He had a perfect record. Unblemished. Highly decorated. And now his whole career was being questioned? He was on trial and the only way to get off the hook was to produce the real Ark. The problem was he had no idea where the real Ark was.

He was so furious he couldn't speak. He stomped over to the imitation Ark. In an animalistic rage, he grabbed hold of the lid and ripped it off, throwing it across the room.

"Careful, that's evidence!" Hargrove raged.

All eyes were on DJ as he peered down into the box. They waited as he reached down and closed his hand around something. He brought his hand up and held it high over the box and then sand began running through his fingers.

"Sand," DJ said. "Fucking Mexican sand."

When the sand had passed through his fingers there remained, to his complete surprise, a small piece of paper resting in his palm.

"What's this?" he said, startled, looking at the paper. The room was quiet.

The paper was the same size as those found in fortune cookies.

"Well, what does it say?" Hargrove asked.

"It's an Internet address."

"Which one?"

DJ shook his head. He knew instantly what it meant. He'd been had. DJ shook his head and read it: "www dot Yahoo dot chat dot biblical archeology dot com."

He looked up. "Thomas McAlister masterminded this entire hoax."

CHAPTER 25

Washington D.C. The Oval Office

When FBI Director Hargrove convinced the President to take a personal interest in the hunt for the Ten Commandments, he had no idea it would be anything more than an open and shut case. While gigantic in proportion, the case itself had seemed very simple. Follow the archeologist and take the treasure from him. Instead, he had thrown up his breakfast this morning, something that had never happened before, and he sat shivering convulsively, waiting for the President to enter. He had brought DJ Warrant with him, to lend credibility to his explanation.

Hargrove looked over at DJ. He was gazing into space, stoically, hard faced and stone jawed. DJ had never visited the President before and Hargrove hoped he would act appropriately. The Oval Office was not a place for emotions or maverick-like tantrums, and DJ was capable of both.

The President was fifteen minutes late for their briefing. Hargrove could tell from the look on his face that he was coming from a bad meeting. His stomach clenched and he felt bile stinging his esophagus. He and DJ stood.

"Mr. President, thank you for meeting with us. I've brought Agent DJ Warrant with me. DJ, I'd like to introduce you to the President. Mr. President, DJ Warrant, the agent assigned to the Ten Commandments case."

The President said, "Nice to meet you, DJ. Please sit down."

DJ said, "Likewise, sir." And sat.

"Gentleman, you have my full attention for fifteen minutes. I'm running late. I apologize. I hope you have good news for me."

Hargrove felt dizzy and disoriented, but he started right in, eager to get the briefing over with. "Actually, sir, we have a serious complication. We feel it's only temporary and, in a matter of days, possibly weeks, we will have the situation rectified. It was something that no one could have possibly predicted. DJ is our most experienced field agent and with him involved you can—"

"Hargrove, stop right there!" the President snapped. Hargrove stopped and stared blankly at the President.

"I don't have time for the approach you're taking, Hargrove. Give me the facts. Am I to understand you don't have the Commandments?"

Without waiting for Hargrove to collect himself DJ spoke up. He sensed his direct style was exactly what the President needed right now. "Sir, the archeologist, Thomas McAlister, outwitted us." He clenched his jaw and his teeth ground together. It had hurt his whole person to admit that.

"He must have gone in the night before the scheduled extraction and replaced the original Ark with a fake. We didn't think he could or would do it at night, in the dark, so our surveillance was down. The next day, when he pulled the treasure out of the ground, he pulled out the fake. And that's what our team went in and confiscated. A fake. Well-made. Well-planted."

The President had a blank look on his face. It was almost comical, DJ thought, but he snapped back to the present when the President said, "Are you fucking kidding me? You're supposed to be our best agent. You follow this guy for months. You go down to Mexico with a highly trained Special Forces team that it cost me *ten million dollars* to train, and an Apache assault helicopter, and you get hood-winked by some goddamn *academic*? Some f'ing *professor*?"

"He's no normal professor sir, he's very wily, I wouldn't be surprised to learn that he had been in the mili—"

"I don't care if he's the goddamn roadrunner and you're wily coyote!

I want those Commandments. Now, you get them. Where is McAlister?"

Hargrove had recovered and decided to give DJ a break, "He disappeared after we took the Ark, sir, but—"

"The *fake* Ark. Let's not forget that small difference, Hargrove."

"Yes, sir. The fake Ark. We left with the fake and McAlister melted into the desert. We didn't think we had reason to continue surveillance."

"Great," the President said sarcastically.

"We have a lead. Inside the fake Ark there was a web address. It's the address to an internet chat room. We feel he'll show up there soon."

"Your plan is to find him in an Internet *chat room?*"

"Yes, sir. That's the plan."

"I don't want to know anymore." The President said. "Hargrove, I don't have time to get involved and do your job for you. I *cannot* micromanage this! I'll remind you of all the technology and resources you have at your disposal. Use them. These are resources the archeologist doesn't have. We've got an election year coming up and the three things I will not allow are a down-tick in any of the key economic indicators, an up-tick in crime, or anything that creates more tension than already exists in the Middle East. That's what makes this project so important. That's why I had hoped and prayed for a positive briefing here today. Jesus, one man is causing all of this? Hard to believe. Maybe we should hire him and plant him in Iraq." The President relaxed a little. Hargrove could tell the worst was over.

He spoke up, "Actually, sir, the archeologist McAlister is something we wanted to discuss with you."

"Yes?"

"As DJ said, McAlister has proven quite a challenge. He's very shrewd, an immaculate planner. DJ and I have talked this over at length, and with McAlister around we may continue to have these complications. There may be a need to . . . remove him . . . permanently. You know, in order to guarantee that we get the Commandments. We think we can use the woman we seized at the dig site as . . . bait."

DJ stared intently at the President. This was a key moment. He'd always wondered how the decision was made to assassinate someone.

"Do whatever you need to do to get the Commandments. I consider this a threat to national security. Whatever it takes." He looked sternly at Hargrove. "Are we clear?"

Hargrove nodded. His request to kill McAlister had been understood, and granted. The President would now distance himself.

"Clear, sir."

"This briefing will now be removed from my official calendar. There will be no record that the three of us ever met today and no notes of our conversation. You are both to remove this meeting from any record you keep of your activities. DJ?"

"Yes, sir. Clear, sir."

"Have a good day, Gentlemen. Next time I'll expect a more positive briefing."

So that's how wet work is ordered, DJ thought. Be vague, but use key phrases like "whatever it takes" to convey meaning, then distance yourself by removing the meeting from the official record in case there is ever an inquiry. Jesus, DJ thought, I could never be a politician.

CHAPTER 26

Thomas McAlister was smiling as the warm Mexican night wind swung his hammock gently back and forth. He was imagining what DJ's face would look like when he discovered the Ark was a fake, when he saw the fortune cookie size piece of paper with the Internet address on it. He hoped there were a lot of people present when it happened. He considered it direct payback for the sucker punch.

Schooled in Krav-Maga, an aggressive hybrid martial art developed by the Israeli military, he normally would have swept DJ's feet out from under him, rolled and struck him while he was bewildered. He hadn't retaliated, because he wanted Ann back, but also for a more obvious reason. Thomas had known that as that helicopter took off, it was taking DJ to the most embarrassing, most humiliating moment of his entire career. When the lid was removed from the Ark and it was found to be a fake, it would be worse than any blow Thomas could've bodily inflicted.

Arturo's wife, Maria, had left the white Christmas lights strung over their patio turned on, and in a move full of understanding, she'd moved a small table close, so he could reach his iced tea without getting up. Also sitting on the table, in his aquarium, was Howard, Thomas's pet scarab beetle, that he'd given to Arturo's children. Last time he left Arizona he'd had a feeling that he wouldn't be returning anytime soon.

As it turned out, the Ark the Moses Riddle had led them to was indeed the second Ark that God had ordered Moses to make, as described in the tenth chapter of Deuteronomy. He'd thought it would be. The gold one had probably been melted down centuries ago. Because of the warnings in the Bible, he and Arturo had been equally nervous about opening the crate that held the Ark. But once they had removed the crate, and taken off part of the ancient clay casing, they were thrilled to see the simple wooden box, darkened with age, but wonderfully preserved. The lid had lifted readily off, and inside was the most incredible thing Thomas had ever seen: two very rough-cut stone tablets, deeply engraved with ancient Hebrew. Holding one and then the other, he had read the script to Arturo. Thomas was the first person to handle the tablets since Moses had placed them in the Ark over 3000 years ago.

They were, almost word for word, the rules outlined in Exodus 34. One: you shall have no other gods before ME. Two: you shall make for yourself no molten gods. Three: you shall observe the Feast of Unleavened Bread. Four: you shall work for six days, but on the seventh day you shall rest. Five: you shall celebrate the Feast of Weeks, and the Feast of Ingathering at the turn of the year. Six: three times a year you shall bring all your male children before the Lord God. Seven: you shall not offer the blood of My sacrifice with leavened bread. Eight: the sacrifice of the Feast of the Passover is not to be left over until morning. Nine: you shall bring the very first of the first fruits of your soil into the house of the Lord your God. Ten: you shall not boil a kid in its mothers milk.

After replacing them, Thomas was again struck by the power the tablets possessed. Their ability to create worldwide pandemonium. If made public, their unearthing would be the media event of the century. Their image would be plastered on the front pages of every newspaper and magazine in the world. Moses would be Time Magazine, Man of the Year. The fact that the four strictest Commandments were not included would create public uproar. The potential moral shift that resulted would fall squarely on Thomas's shoulders. As would any economic deterioration or escalation of tension in the Middle East.

Yet he would become rich and famous. And any shadow that hung over his career as a result of the firing would be gone. The dilemma was simple. Should he place personal comfort and professional success first and risk unknown economic and religious stability? Or let the world rest, and sacrifice his financial and professional future?

At least Thomas was still in a position to be able to ask such questions. He had outsmarted his pursuers for a second time. It had required an immense amount of planning, but the execution of the plan had not been difficult. It had actually gone better than expected.

When he had returned to the states with Ann, to procure the necessary provisions to extract the Ark, he'd had a fake Ark custom made and shipped to Arturo. At the time, he hadn't known which version of the real Ark would be in the pyramid. So, he had instructed his artist to make it look like the first one that God asked Moses to make. The popular golden one.

Then, the night before the planned excavation, he and Arturo had gone out to the site, used the winch on the Discovery to move the pyramid stone, unearthed the genuine Ark, and replaced it with the fake. It had taken them all night. He had barely pulled the blanket over himself before Ann woke up, totally unaware that he had left. That day, in full daylight, they had unearthed the fake. Which was stolen from them the minute it was out of the ground.

Thomas tried to remember when he had decided to substitute a fake for the real thing. He couldn't remember exactly when he'd conceived the idea. Maybe never. Maybe he'd always just assumed that he would, starting back when Dr. Sinistar was overly curious. It was the only way to ensure the real one wasn't taken from him. Caution, planning, and deciding outcomes had always been hallmarks of his life and work. He was an excellent chess player. He would have been a good courtroom lawyer.

Thomas swung out of the hammock and stood at the edge of the patio, gazing up at the sky. *Where in the world was Ann? Who had her? What was she doing that very minute?* Thomas had become so accustomed to her presence that he often subconsciously assumed she was in the next room. Sometimes, during the past few days, he even thought he heard her voice, but a split second later the painful realization that she was gone would return. But she was not simply gone. She'd been taken. He was angry with himself for not protecting her. But there was also a tinge of guilt.

He should have told her about the switch. Arturo had questioned him about her exclusion from their plans. His reason had been simple. They didn't need her help, so why bother including her? Why trouble her with the knowledge? But they both knew it was something else. He'd always had a deep inability to fully trust even those closest to him. He was aware of it, and planned to work on becoming more trusting. But not yet. Although he loved Ann, he hadn't been able to make her privy to everything. Like Arturo.

During this entire campaign Thomas had only left one thing to chance. It was when he had left Arturo alone, to guard the Ark, while he went back to the states to get supplies. Arturo could have called friends, removed the Ark, and disappeared a rich man. But he hadn't. Now Thomas would trust Arturo with his life. Why hadn't he given Ann the same break? What quirky, dysfunctional quality made him so damn distrusting? He swore he would change. When he got her back, he would make himself trust her! He would test *himself* . . . not her.

The one benefit now was that Ann was unable to tell her kidnappers where the real Ark was located. As it turned out, the location of the real Ark was Thomas's only bargaining chip, his only way to get Ann back. That was why he'd left them the Internet address, so he could communicate . . . and bargain. He had the advantage. And it wasn't his only advantage. Thomas knew a lot more.

He knew who had stolen the Ark, because he knew where it had been taken. Thomas and Arturo had placed a GPS tracking device, the kind sold at Radio Shack, into a small compartment in the body of the crate that held the fake Ark. They had tracked it directly from Mexico to Virginia for the night and then to Washington D.C. It had been in Washington all day at a location that matched the address of the National Museum of Art. Thomas knew the director there, George Valmer, and he now knew that the United States Government had tried to steal the Ark from him.

Since the Ark had not moved from the Museum all day, he figured they had probably opened it by now. Thomas smiled. Valmer had probably called in that old-school buffoon Mark Nelson, to examine the Ark and its contents. With Nelson on the case, there was a good chance they would not have discovered it was a fake yet. Nelson was probably still amazed the tablets had turned to sand. He was probably trying to tell Valmer the fact that Moses put an e-mail address in the Ark was a futuristic prophesy. Thomas finished his drink and reached for his laptop. Time to check the biblical archeology chat room.

He set the IBM Thinkpad in his lap. After plugging it in to his cellular phone, he logged on, went to Bookmarks in his browser, scrolled down the list of sites and clicked on the Biblical Archeology chat room. The screen's pop-up box asked him to type his user name, then he proceeded to the chat room. He typed in *Moses* and clicked the ENTER button.

The colorful chat room Home Page bounced up on screen. Thomas surveyed the people already in the room: *jasper, mary, sexpert, jade, redtrouble, texastwat, divadreversed, hal,* and other similarly innocuous names. Thomas figured the government would make direct contact using a name he'd recognize, but also probably indirectly through someone who would act as though they were unrelated to the discussion about the Ark.

Thomas posed his question, and clicked SEND.

Moses 10:01 p.m.
Any Egyptians out there tonight?

Blackjack replied in the public forum.

Blackjack 10:02 p.m.
Moses, nice to meet you. I'm African, but not Egyptian. Same continent, different country.

Thomas nodded. Blackjack could be a person assigned to chat with him. Another public message appeared for him from Blackjack.

Blackjack 10:03 p.m.
Moses, you ever been to Africa, or Egypt?
Moses 10:04 p.m.
Yes, I have, both. Tell me what country in Africa are you from?
Blackjack 10:05 p.m.
I grew up in Ethiopia. Ever been there? Did you like Africa? What state are you from?

Moses 10:06 p.m.
Blackjack, I never said I was from the States. Yes, I liked Africa. It is a beautiful continent. What city in Ethiopia?

Blackjack 10:07 p.m.
I just figured you were from the US, most people here are. I'm from Adis Abeda.

Then, suddenly, someone named GOD entered the room. Thomas knew this was his contact. It was confirmed when a private message appeared on his screen.

Private Message
GOD 10:08 p.m.
Hello, Moses. Good to see you again. Wish you were here.

Thomas's heart jumped.

Moses 10:09 p.m.
Hello, God. Glad I'm not. How are you this fine evening?
GOD 10:10 p.m.
I'm not doing well, thanks to you. Something that belongs to me is lost.

Moses 10:10 p.m.
Interesting. I thought you were omniscient. But then, if you were, you could find what you don't have. Ironically, I've lost something, too. Go to the private room RUSE. We can talk it over.

GOD 10:11 p.m.
Seek and you shall find, Thomas. See you in Ruse.

Private Room Ruse
Moses 10:12 p.m.
I don't like the way you've handled this, God. You're sloppy. Hitting me was a mistake. You've tried to steal what is not yours and you've taken Ann. If you've hurt her, in any way, we're through.

DJ squirmed in his chair. It infuriated him to be called sloppy by a civilian. What made him even angrier was that Thomas was right.

GOD 10:14 p.m.
YOU don't like the way this has been handled? I've got a pine box, spray painted gold, full of fucking beach sand!

Thomas smiled

Moses 10:14 p.m.
Good. It's all you deserve. I did the research, solved the riddle, found the treasure . . not you. You're lucky to get sand. Have you hurt her?

GOD 10:15 p.m.
The Angel has not been hurt. So far. Only slightly scuffed. Currently, she is very comfortable. But that can change, quickly. You tell us where you are. We'll bring her to you. You don't have to tell us where the Ark is, until you see her.

Moses 10:16 p.m.

You'd better be telling the truth. And, you aren't in a position to dictate!

GOD 10:17 p.m.

We will make a trade. The angel for the Ark. You'll tell us where you are. We'll bring her. You don't have to tell us where the Ark is until you see her.

Moses 10:18 p.m.

Feeling a little powerful, aren't we God, considering I've got what you want.

GOD 10:19 p.m.

NO! I've got what YOU want! If you want to see her again, you'll tell me where you are right now, without any more games! We'll bring her with us. You have my word.

Thomas knew the government had a dirty past, and had probably killed many innocent people, but he didn't think they would kill Ann over this. Not as long as he had possession of the Ten Commandments.

Moses 10:20 p.m.

Your word means nothing to me. I'll agree to exchange the Ark for her, but it will be on my terms. If you kill or hurt her, you'll get nothing. I've got the Ark, witnesses, and access to the press. If we don't do it my way, I'll release it to the press. The country will be screwed. Best of all, you'll be screwed.

GOD 10:21 p.m.

It will be on my terms, it has to be, or it won't work. Now tell me your location!!!

Moses 10:22 p.m.

God, you've gotten too pushy for me. We do it my way. Since you're not ready to accept that right now, I'm leaving. See you here tomor-row, same time. And don't bother trying to trace this call, I have a cellular modem. Bye.

GOD 10:22 p.m.
Don't you fucking leave, Thomas!!

Moses logged out 10:23

Thomas turned off his computer. It was time for one of Maria's fabulous dinners.

In Washington D.C., in the basement of the Pentagon, DJ slammed his fist against the wooden table. "*Damn-son-of-a-bitch*!"

He sat next to Elmo, who had been typing for him, playing GOD. DJ glared at a man working at an electronics board on the far side of the room. The man was listening. Waiting. He was a government call-tracing expert. Currently, he was on the phone with the administrator of the Yahoo chat room, waiting to get the URL of the person who had dialed in using the name Moses.

Finally the man took off his headset.

"Well, what'd you get? Where the fuck is he?

The man shrugged. "Untraceable. He used a cellular modem."

The next day, Thomas logged on at ten o'clock at night. He and Arturo had just returned from taking the Commandments to a superb hiding place. Again, he used the name Moses.

During the time Ann was gone Thomas had been very busy. It had helped take his mind off her. But, frequently, her face would puncture his thoughts and he would have to push her from his mind. Not only was there the guilt from not trusting her, but he also missed her intensely. More than he had ever missed anyone before. He dreamt of her every night. He smelled her hair, heard her voice, felt her softness.

He would agree to a trade if it would give him the chance to get Ann back. At least that's what he would tell them for the time being. Stalling a little would give him time, to devise a plan both to get Ann and hold onto the Commandments. Maybe he'd give them another fake.

Tonight Thomas was not in the hammock. He was at the table in Arturo's kitchen. Arturo was next to him. The rest of the family was in bed.

"Here we are, Arturo. This is the Yahoo, Biblical Archeology Chat Room. Wait until you see all the lonely souls chatting in here tonight." Thomas logged in and scrolled through the list of participants.

"Our man isn't here yet. Watch for God to enter. I'll try to draw them out."

Moses 10:01 p.m.
Anyone from Egypt here?
Blackjack 10:01 p.m.
I'm here, Moses. How you doin tonight, brother?

Moses 10:02 p.m.
I'm fine tonight, Blackjack. How're you?
Blackjack 10:03 p.m.
Just arguing with a friend right now. Hey, how old are you and where you from?

Moses 10:04 p.m.
I'm from the midwest, and I'm 28.

"Here we go, Arturo! Our man has entered the room. See this entry?" Thomas pointed to the message at the top of the screen. **GOD has entered the room.** "I'll wait for him to make the first move. Don't want to appear too eager."

Arturo had never seen a chat room before. "I don't think I'd be too good at this," he said.

Private Message
Blackjack 10:05 p.m.
So, Moses, do you go both ways? Want to get it on, brother?
GOD 10:06 p.m.
Moses, are you there?
Moses 10:06 p.m.
No, but thanks for asking, Blackjack. I've gotta go, God is here. GOD, see you in the same room we used last night.

Private Room Ruse
Moses 10:07 p.m.
Yes, I'm here. Have you reconsidered?
GOD 10:08 p.m.
OK, we do it your way. So how do you want it to happen?
Moses 10:08 p.m.
Next Friday at one o'clock in the afternoon, I will be in a room in a building in Manhattan. I will only tell you the address of the build-

ing one hour before you are to bring Ann there. Once you have brought her, I will call you and tell you where the Ark is. You'll need to have a helicopter, with a 100-mile range, standing by at Mexico City Airport. You will call the chopper; they will need to verify that it's the real thing. On board the chopper you'll need a 1000-pound winch, a trained biblical scholar, an archeologist, a bible, and two scuba divers with enough air for an hour at fifty feet. Make sure the archeologist has "instant" carbon dating technology. It's new, but you can get it.

GOD 10:11 p.m.
You've got it under water?
Moses 10:12 p.m.
Yes. Wax sealed. Safe and dry.
GOD 10:12 p.m.
I'd like our man to stay in the room with you two, until we have word that we've got the real thing.

Moses 10:13 p.m.
That's acceptable. You'll get the real thing. You have my word. Taped to the top of the crate the Ark is in will be a small black case. Inside is a small piece of wood that I shaved off the Ark. Use it for dating the Ark. It's the piece that I used.

GOD 10:14 p.m.
If you lead us to another fake, I'll have you shot and dumped in the East River. Don't think I can't.

Moses 10:15 p.m.
I didn't lead you to the first fake, you presumptuous asshole! You followed me! You bring me the real thing, you get the real thing.

GOD 10:17 p.m.

Let me give you a number to call to reach me. 303.446.1000. Don't bother trying to trace it, you can't.

Moses 10:18 p.m.
If I see any sign that you aren't going to let her stay with me I'll give you the wrong location. One that is booby trapped. Once your team verifies authenticity, she and I walk. Clear?

GOD 10:20 p.m.
Roger. All we want is the box. Not Ann, despite her splendid qualities. You said a room in Manhattan and we'll have an hour to get her there. What part of the city should we have her in? I want her there in time. You know how midday Manhattan traffic can be. Just get me close, Professor.

"Can you believe this guy, Arturo? He never stops. And it's so like a government official to call the Ark of the Covenant a box."

Moses 10:21 p.m.
At 11:00 EST, have her near PJ Clark's. Know where that is?
GOD 10:22 p.m.
Best hamburgers in midtown.
Moses 10:23 p.m.
Yeah, yeah, and Bass Ale, on tap.
GOD 10:24 p.m.
We might get along, in other circumstances, Professor.
Moses 10:25 p.m.
Doubtful.
GOD 10:26 p.m.
So where are you right now anyway? We tried to trace you last time, couldn't of course. You still down south? We haven't seen you come across the border.

Moses 10:27 p.m.
I'll call you at noon next Friday.
Moses logged off.

CHAPTER 28

The next day, Arturo's brother Esteban, who ran the family farm, flew
Thomas across the border in his Cessna 206 to a small town in west
Texas called Dryden, in Terrell County.

Arturo and Thomas had talked about the future before he left. They
had become close friends during the past few months. They had agreed
once this was all over with they would document their find in the major
academic journals. At least then, people would know the truth about
the Ark and the connections between the ancient Egyptian and Olmec
cultures. It would be the next Roswell, except with factual data, and
believable witnesses.

Thomas's plan, which he began to finalize on the drive from Texas
to Manhattan, was to trade the Commandments for Ann, then return to
Mexico to properly document the site where they'd found the Ark. The
extraction had happened so fast, he'd hadn't been able to do further
exploration. Ann had said she thought she saw something behind the
Ark, and Thomas felt there could be other important artifacts in the
same chamber as the Ark or in adjoining chambers.

Though he hadn't had too much time to dwell on it, this find would
have a huge impact on the world's understanding of history and the way
cultures had evolved. He could show conclusively that not only was there
contact between Eastern and Western cultures, but there was contact of
the most significant kind. Even a deep relationship.

Archeologists had never come up with satisfactory explanations for
the Olmec glyphs dating to pre 3000 BC depicting Euro-people with
facial hair. Or the statues with Negroid features. Or the advanced agri-

cultural and astronomical state. This will move them, Thomas thought, as he sped over Route 349 in his rental car. Yes. This will move them.

The only problem was that he was going to lose his biggest piece of evidence. Frustrated at the coming need to prove he had possessed something that was currently in his possession, he plotted ways to keep the Ark and still get Ann back. He couldn't risk trying to give them a fake again. There had to be a another way.

When Thomas reached Odessa he turned east and headed for Abilene. His trip would take him through Ft. Worth and Dallas, through Little Rock, Arkansas, then up to Lexington. He would turn north at Lexington, taking I-75, in order to steer clear of D.C. Then he would slice eastward again on I-70, to Philadelphia, then right into New York, where he would reclaim Ann.

He stopped at a Sonic in Odessa and had a double cheeseburger, fries and a shake. He liked not having to get out of the car. He thought of Ann as he ate. They would move her to Manhattan soon. He wanted to get there quickly, if only to be closer to her.

He didn't like to use the overused, ill defined phrase "soul mate" but he couldn't think of a better way to describe how he felt about her. He'd never felt this way about a woman before. Their common interests were strong and did not dissolve as the demands of everyday life together increased. The strong bond of archeology and his strong physical attraction ran parallel to this deeper, core emotional tie. It all seemed perfect. Predestined. Written in the books of their lives.

God, he missed her! Hair smelling of citrus. Puffy, pouty lips. Deep laugh, which once unleashed could go on and on. He missed discussing archeology with her. She was a very talented Mayanologist and he had come to respect the way her mind worked . . . the way she walked around a problem or question. She had the potential to be one of the best in what was a young field of study. His chest tightened.

Odessa was Texas' version of any-town USA, and he moved through it quickly, cruising steadily across the stark west Texas landscape on his way to Ft. Worth/Dallas, glad the car had air conditioning.

His mind didn't stop reviewing his plan. He needed to get in touch with two people. A professor and friend at Arizona State, John Randle, and a close college buddy, Drew Montgomery, who lived in New York and traded on Wall Street.

He planned to call John to get his credit card number, in order to anonymously book a hotel reservation in Manhattan. He and John were good enough friends that John would give it to him, no questions asked.

He needed to call Drew for help with finding a safe place for the exchange, and because he needed money. He had been paying cash for everything. Plane tickets to Egypt and Mexico, hotels in Egypt, Arturo's expenses in Mexico, and Ann's in Phoenix at the Camelback. He had also paid cash for all the expensive equipment he'd needed for the extraction, as well as for the custom made fake Ark. He was running low, at a crucial time.

So he drove on and on. Reviewing his plan, using an iterative process that had always worked for him. He broke the plan into piece parts, tactics, then examined each one, each piece, to see if it held up. Turning it over in his mind, looking at it from different directions. Assessing how it could be improved, strengthened, shortened, or streamlined. Once he understood the weaknesses, the risks, he could begin to build contingencies. Alternate plans that would allow him to succeed despite unforeseen obstacles. One of his concerns was that the government had already bugged his friends' phones. He didn't know who they'd pick. Close friends? People in certain geographies? He felt this time they would spread the net even wider.

His central idea was to get to Manhattan, stay in an out-of-the-way hotel under an assumed name, and prepare for the trade. If this didn't work, he had a backup plan, but he didn't want to use it.

That evening, Thomas spent the night outside of Dallas in a Marriott Courtyard. He liked Courtyards because they were set up for business people. He could have driven hours longer, but he wanted to sit at a desk and outline his plan.

He checked in, using cash and a fake name, ordered a Domino's pizza, and called John Randle on his cell phone. He knew John would be home. John was always home. Unlike many of his peers at the university, who might be anywhere at anytime, John did not travel. He published good books through the use of secondary research. Thomas liked hands-on primary research, but John had told him many times, sometimes in heated discussions, that rediscovering writings that had been lost for hundreds of years or drawing fresh conclusions was just as valuable as actually making a find. Regardless, John was living the American dream. A wife, two kids, solid job, nice house, and predictable future, right down to having 28 percent income tax built into his retirement plan.

John Randle answered on the first ring. Thomas intentionally did not give his name. He knew John would recognize his voice. "Johnny, how's my favorite home-body?"

"Well, well, well, if it isn't my favorite Egyptologist gone AWOL. Where are you, buddy?"

"Hey, John. You know that nice cellular phone your wife gave you for your last birthday?"

"Yeah, what about it?"

"Do me a favor and turn it on. Okay?"

"Give me five minutes."

"Talk to you in five."

John answered in half a ring. "What the hell are you up to, buddy? The FBI has been at the university, interviewing all of us. They're trying to find you."

"You're kidding. I didn't know how bad they wanted me. I guess it's bad."

"Bad? Oh, it's bad! They've talked to *everyone*. They even came here, when I was in class, and talked to Sue. They told her that if I was hiding you, I could get in big trouble. Jail even. Harboring, they called it. For a while they were on campus every day, watching."

"This is amazing. Are they hiding or out in the open?"

"Hiding?" John blurted. "Thomas, they subpoenaed all the documents in your office. They took it *all*. There's police tape across your door! I thought you'd at least know that much!"

"They've been in my office? They've taken my files?"

"They had a warrant. Washington was present. It was all legal. They said it was part of the discovery process or something. What the *hell* are you involved in?"

Thomas was thinking, trying to remember if he had any documents relating to the Ark in his office. Had he ever taken anything there? He hadn't. He was sure of it. He hadn't been back since he'd gotten fired. None of it mattered now anyway.

"Thomas? You there, buddy?"

"Yes, here. What did you ask?"

"I asked, what are you involved in? People are starting to talk. You know. Make things up."

It's always more interesting to make things up, to fill in gaps, than to know the truth, Thomas thought. The guessing game would keep the social scene busy for weeks. "I can't say, John, but it's big. It's nothing criminal. Listen, I was going to ask you for a favor, but I'm not sure that I should, after hearing all of this. I don't want to get you in trouble . . . and I especially don't want them to know where I am yet. The whole University is too hot . . . you're too hot."

"Hold on a minute, Tom, Sue is saying something. What honey? Sue says . . . *what?* Thomas, they're in the *driveway.*"

"*Who's* there, John? *The FBI guys?*"

"Yes, listen . . . they're knocking on the door. Sue says it's the same car that was here the other day. A Taurus. They . . . hey just a second there—" Thomas could hear men's voices and footsteps on John's tile entryway floor.

"John, they must've been listening when I called you on the land line number! I've gotta go, buddy! Be honest with them, don't try to be a hero. Okay?"

"Tell them I'm coming, Sue! Sure, Tom, no problem. You be careful!"

Thomas hit the end button on his cell phone. He was shocked. Even though he'd agreed to make the trade, they were still after him. Instead of laying low and waiting for him in Manhattan, they were actively pursuing him. Something about that didn't add up. Why not wait for him? They must really want me, he thought. They must be more pissed off about the fake than I thought. If they found him, they'd probably beat him or drug him to get the location of the Ark. Obviously the Cowboy was willing to go to any extreme to ensure that he wasn't outsmarted again.

This meant trouble. He'd have to continue using cash for everything, which was both suspicious and difficult. He found the phone book, looked at the map on the inside page, then looked up Western Union. He located one near his hotel, then called Drew Montgomery.

He didn't get Drew the first time, so he waited an hour and tried again.

Drew answered this time.

"Drew, it's Thomas."

"Hey, what's up, Pal? How's it going?"

"Drew, has anyone called you about me . . . asking questions?"

"What do you mean, *questions*? Where are you, Tommy? You sound a little tense."

"Listen up, Drew. I need your help. Do you have a cell phone?"

"Yes." Drew's voice grew serious. He gave the number to Thomas.

"I'll call you back." Thomas hung up as Drew was asking why the switch of phones.

After calling him back, Drew immediately asked. "Why the switch? Are you in trouble?"

"In a way. Most of my friends' phones are bugged. I called someone I'd worked with at Arizona State at home a few minutes ago and there were people at his door within five minutes. I think cell phones are okay, but I'm not even sure about that. Can people trace cell phone calls these days?"

"I don't think so. Too many cell towers. Well, I did see a movie recently where they tried. Who's after you?"

"I've found something really big and the government wants it. Bad."

"What did you find? I didn't think you'd been on any big digs lately."

"I can't say right now, Drew."

"Come on, it's me, who would I tell?"

"I'll tell you soon. For now, trust me. It's big. So big that I need some help from you."

"Can I get in trouble from it? I mean, I'll do whatever you need. I'd just like to know if it's legal first."

"It's legal. I'm not a fugitive or criminal. I need a loan and I need you to set something up for me."

"The loan's no problem. What do you need set up?"

"First, let's talk about the money. I need you to send about $20,000 to a Western Union outlet in Dallas, Texas. Can you do that?"

"Within an hour."

"Don't send it in your name. I'll be in Manhattan soon and once they figure out you're a friend of mine, they'll trace all your financial activities. Have Tracey do it. Are you still seeing her?"

Drew's voice lowered to a whisper. "No, I'm not seeing her anymore, but I do have someone else who can do it."

"She's there now?"

"Yes."

"Okay . . . that's good. Send it as soon as you can." Thomas gave him the address of the Western Union by the hotel. Then he explained the other favor he needed. "I need a private room in a public building, like a hotel room, but more public. In a hotel, the government could shut off a whole floor and make the place a whole lot less public than it's supposed to be. Know what I mean?"

"How big does the room need to be?"

"Big enough for three or four people to have a meeting. It would be nice if there were two doors, one on either side of the room."

"I don't even need to think about this. I've got the perfect place."

"Where?"

"My new club. I'd been on the waiting list for the Harvard Club for five years. Six months ago I got in. Members and guests can use conference rooms. Most have two doors, one for members and another for the help to come through. Sound like it would work?"

"Sounds perfect, Drew. Can you book one for me? I'd need it for two hours on Friday. It needs to have a phone."

"What time on Friday?"

"From about twelve thirty to three o'clock."

"I'm sure I can get one then."

"Two things, Drew, and write all this down, okay? First, you cannot be there. Tell the front desk, or whatever they have there, to reserve it in my name and that I'll have two or three guests. Secondly, the fewer calls and contact between us the better. Sorry to be so secretive. I'll explain everything later. I'll call you tomorrow sometime, to confirm the room. Okay?"

"I understand. Consider it all taken care of. Sounds serious, Tom. Be careful and let me know if you need any more help. I've gotten to know quite a few people around this town, not all Ivy League types either, if you know what I mean."

"Thanks, Drew. What happened to Tracey?" Thomas always made a point to remember the name of Drew's last girlfriend, as a joke, because the names changed so frequently.

He lowered his voice again, "Uh, I'll tell you when I see you. I've met someone new."

Thomas smiled. "Name?"

"Jennifer. Not the same Jennifer as last time though."

"Good. Okay, do you have all the information you need?"

"Yes. I'm going to get this set up. Harvard Club, Friday, conference room with two doors and a phone, from twelve to two. Oh, yeah, and twenty-thousand dollars. Need more?"

"No, that's enough for now, thanks. I'm good for it. I'll get it back to you in a few weeks or so. You'll still have enough to trade with tomorrow, won't you?"

"Ha! Take care, pal."

Thomas and Drew had become close in college. Thomas had always preferred to know a few people deeply, rather than a lot of people in a shallow sort of way. He and his group of five friends had named themselves The Inner Circle. It was a diverse group and in an odd way, Thomas identified differently with each member. Both he and Drew had fathers who had left home. They had confided in each other, and it had led to a close friendship.

Since college, Drew had become a successful trader on Wall Street. He had dated scores of women and was apparently still cycling through them. Thomas liked Drew, and appreciated his thirst for life. He just wasn't sure when Drew had last read a book.

» » « «

In a rare moment of calm, DJ glanced up at the picture that was tacked to the wall of his cubicle. It had been carefully cut from a magazine. It was of a lake, somewhere in the hills of northern New Mexico. On the far side of the lake were cabins, rustic looking, but new. They were spread apart, with trees between them for privacy. Some had small docks in front, with boats, and some did not. Merely looking at this image immediately dropped DJ's diastolic and systolic blood pressure five points apiece. The picture represented his retirement. It represented his dream. Everything he'd ever wanted: peace and tranquility, on a beautiful lake. With a boat at his disposal, for those days when he felt like eating fish for dinner. His plan was to retire and to find this dream cabin, where he would live out the rest of his days. Happy and content. Payment for the hectic, frenetic years with the FBI.

Just as he started to drift back to that familiar question, the welcome question, of whether he would buy a Boston Whaler, a Cobalt, or a Sea Ray, Elmo walked by and handed him a fistful of papers.

"Here are the border crossing reports you asked for. Alphabetized by city and cross referenced by geographic location."

DJ stared at him, images of gurgling motor boats still floated through his head. "Thanks. Good work." He put them on his desk and wondered what Elmo's retirement plans were. They had never talked about them.

He shook himself back to the present and the search for the ever frustrating archeologist, Thomas McAlister.

This had become one of the most stressful assignments he'd ever had. He remembered thinking what an easy, almost laughable, assignment it originally appeared to be. Watching a man go about finding a treasure. An easy surveillance. But that was before he'd gotten fooled. Thrice.

First McAlister had disappeared right under the watchful eye of his best surveillance team. Then, after finding McAlister at the Camelback Inn, he disappeared again, only to be caught when he was halfway to Mexico. But then came the big blunder. The worst embarrassment of DJ's career. McAlister had somehow extracted the real Ark, and planted a fake one. Bringing the fake one back to some of the most powerful people in Washington and telling them it was the real thing made him look like an incompetent fool.

No. This was no longer an easy case. Nor would he approach it as one. McAlister was smart and tricky. Wily might be a better word. He was better prepared than most of the adversaries DJ had ever come up against. Sure he was a civilian, but he was smart. Most criminals got a gun and then thought they could do whatever they wanted. They got cocky. Not McAlister. He was too smart for violence. He was a planner. He was the worst kind of adversary. An intellectual one. DJ hated him. Not because he couldn't keep up with him, but because, with most criminals, he could rely on them to act on a base, primeval level. DJ was in touch with that level and could easily replicate it, which usually helped him predict his opponent's next move. With McAlister, it wasn't about emotion or testosterone; it was about brains. Advance planning. Contingencies. Out thinking and out maneuvering his opponent.

McAlister was not to be trifled with any longer. DJ needed to make the upcoming trade cleanly. Then, and only then, would he get his revenge. He had a special surprise in store for Thomas McAlister. A dirty, dark, forever surprise, that would take care of him for once and for all.

DJ looked again at the serene picture of the lake and the cabins and, for a second, by some odd visual aphorism, he could have sworn he saw wind blowing across the water, making little ripples and small waves. *A tempest in his paradise.* He closed his eyes and shook his head, and the image was normal again. The way he liked it. Serene.

CHAPTER 29

The trip from Dallas to Lexington was uneventful, miles and miles of freeway, with endless hours to work through various options for the exchange.

After a night outside of Lexington, Thomas started the twelve-hour drive that would put him within a two to three hour striking distance of Manhattan. He wanted to arrive early on Thursday, to scout the city and work out escape routes. They had told him that after the trade they'd leave him alone, but he no longer believed them. He reasoned that if the government wanted the Ark, they would also want every picture, note, and map of its unearthing.

In order to adequately plan, Thomas needed to move around the city inconspicuously. He didn't need a full disguise, just enough to throw off anyone who was scanning crowds and passersby.

He stopped at a Wal-Mart outside of Lexington city limits and bought what he thought a person from Kentucky might buy, if they were going on vacation to New York. He tried for tourist mixed with serious Nascar fan. His crowning purchase was a pair of brown polyester socks that he wore with white Nikes and a University of Kentucky baseball cap. He added some cheap sunglasses that he grabbed off a rack by the check out counter. He would look nothing like Thomas McAlister. It would be fun playing someone else for a few days.

He got on I-75, which would take him up to Cincinnati. It was a nice drive through a lot of country that he'd never seen before. He was left with two overriding impressions. One was that this part of the country, including the Adirondacks, was one of the most beautiful, underrated parts of the country. The other was that the divisions between social classes was getting wider everyday.

Despite America's first world economy, despite all the technical progress and productivity increases, there were still large numbers of people living well below the poverty line. The government had forced it. Low income citizens were addicted to minimum wage, welfare and Medicare, and it was impossible to wean them off. The secret effect was the creation of a slave class. Low level healthcare, food and shelter were provided, but what Thomas saw as he drove were people living lives worse than that of the average institutionalized prisoner.

That night, Thomas stayed in a bed and breakfast. The government would be expecting him in the area tonight, or tomorrow, and would be monitoring the major hotels for people named McAlister and single men paying cash. He didn't think there was any way they could monitor every small independent. He paid cash anyway.

Early Thursday morning, he drove the final three hours to Manhattan. He crossed through the Holland Tunnel and arrived exactly where he wanted to be: Canal Street. He didn't know where he'd stay. He'd know it when he saw it. He could have asked Drew for a good inconspicuous place but there was a chance they could get to Drew. Anyone would talk, if threatened the right way. At times Thomas thought he was being too cautious, but he had nothing to lose by being overly cautious, and there was Ann to lose if he got caught.

He drove a few blocks on Canal and came to the edge of Chinatown. Street vendors lined the sidewalk selling Dooney & Burke's knockoffs and $5 sunglasses with Gucci labels.

As he drove, Thomas became instinctively paranoid. Every parked van could be an observation team. He was also suspicious of anyone who looked directly at him. Then, one block later, he saw it. The Hotel Tokyo. Perfect. He passed the hotel, took the first right and was lucky enough to catch someone leaving a parallel parking space. He waited, parked, and was pleasantly surprised to see that the head of the meter had been knocked off by vandals. He grabbed his bags and strode around the corner to check into the hotel. The rooms, utilitarian ten by twelve, white square boxes, were not as inexpensive as they should have been.

He immediately changed into his tourist outfit, then left to run some errands. He picked up a detailed map of Manhattan and a Kodak Polaroid camera and film. Then he looked for a parking garage about five blocks from the Harvard Club. He'd put the rental car there.

Once that was settled, he walked over to forty-fourth Street and took a look around the Harvard Club. He took pictures of both sides of the street, the alleys behind, and the surrounding blocks, so that he could study escape routes later. He wasn't sure if he'd need to escape from anything, but if he did, he would be ready.

On the way back to the Hotel Tokyo, he stopped to have a beer at the Lion's Head Tavern, his second favorite saloon in Manhattan. After two, instead of one, he picked up carryout in Little Italy, and then a *New Yorker* at a small corner market. It would list any conventions or other activities that might affect traffic.

In his room, after dinner, he used the Polaroids with the street map to determine routes that would get him away from the Harvard Club quickly. After an hour, he called Arturo. He felt guilty about his decision and needed Arturo's reassurance.

Arturo picked up after three rings.

"Arturo, it's Thomas. Everything all right down there?"

"We're doing well here. How about you?"

"I've made it to Manhattan. The meeting is tomorrow."

"Have you decided what you are going to do?"

Thomas had left Mexico with the question unanswered. Would he trade fairly for Ann? Or would he try to trick them again? Since Ann was gone he'd been deeply troubled. He'd missed her. But there was more. A feeling he couldn't remember ever having in any great quantity before. It was fear. He was scared of losing Ann. The prospect of not having Ann made him realize how much he'd factored her into the rest of his life. Despite the historical value of the Ark, the short answer to Arturo's question was . . . yes.

There was a thick suspense on the line as Arturo waited for Thomas's answer.

"Yes. I'm going to give them the real thing. That's why I called. I wanted you to know. You've been with me almost the whole way. I hope you understand. I have to give it to them. No tricks this time. A straight-up trade. I need her. I need her healthy and with no strings attached. I love her, my friend. I hope you understand."

"What do they say? You can't put a price on love? You just proved it. I understand. If it were my Maria or the treasure, I'd do the same."

Thomas let out a long-held breath. "Thanks for understanding, and for the vote of confidence. I go back and forth, but I know I'm doing the right thing."

"She's a treasure. Get her back and bring her back down to Mexico. We'll excavate the site. We'll do it right this time, and we'll take long siestas in-between."

"Are we all set for tomorrow?"

"Yes, we are ready. It'll be there."

"Be careful. Stay back."

"Don't worry, these guys scare me. We'll make the drop and then we're out."

"Good. I'll call you afterward."

"Of course. I'll be waiting. Good luck. Tell Ann I miss her."

A nervous twinge shot through Thomas. He'd be seeing Ann tomorrow. "OK. Bye."

He hung up and shook his head. *God, I'm getting soft!* Then he reminded himself that trading an object, however valuable, for a person was not soft. It was compassionate. Humane.

Maybe I'm getting old. The thought made him shudder. *Why couldn't they have kidnapped someone else! Anyone else! Then I could tell them to keep her.* But somewhere, deep, deep inside, he knew he would've traded it for anyone, because it was the right thing to do.

CHAPTER 30

Car horns awakened Thomas at five in the morning, two hours before the wake-up call he'd asked for. Amazingly, the hotel did have room service. He ordered a full breakfast, but even after eating and reading the *New York Times*, it was still earlier than he had originally planned to wake up.

There was no longer any reason for the tourist garb. The government needed him, he was in the city, and if they saw him now, so what? He was going to tell them where the Ark was at one o'clock anyway. Maybe they could coerce him into telling them a few hours early, but why?

Since he was going to the Harvard Club, he dressed somewhat formally. But also made sure they were comfortable clothes that he could move quickly in if he had to. Khakis, a white oxford, a loose navy blazer, and a pair of brown Cole Haan loafers. As he dressed, he pondered how to spend the next five hours.

He didn't have to dwell on the problem long. He'd visit his old haunt, The Met. The Metropolitan Museum of Art, in Central Park, north of the Plaza Hotel. The minute it occurred to him, he hurried so that he could get there sooner. It was the perfect distraction. He had made plans and been over them numerous times and now he needed a good, solid distraction so that his unconscious mind could work: review, check and re-check.

At twelve sharp, Thomas was sitting on the bench in front of Jules Bastien-Lepage's masterpiece, *Joan of Arc*. He had given up trying to figure out how many shades of green the painting contained. It was his favorite in the Metropolitan, and as he looked at it, three thoughts entered his mind simultaneously. One was that counting shades of color would be pointless, because the green was blended so masterfully. The second was that if this painting were even close to portraying the real woman, then Joan of Arc must've had strikingly beautiful eyes. The third was that it was almost time to go get Ann.

He checked his watch for the tenth time and sprang up, heading toward the cafeteria, where he knew there was a bank of phones. He dialed the number the cowboy had given him and someone answered on the first ring. It was not his tormenter. This man was younger and more tense.

"Harvard Club. Third floor. Conference room 222. One o'clock sharp. Got it?"

"Yes, but—"

Thomas hung up the phone. He walked briskly out of the Metropolitan, past the lions, past the hot dog vendor, going south toward the Plaza, wondering if, at that moment, government men were scrambling to surround the Harvard Club.

The Plaza Hotel sat at the first intersection south of the museum. Thomas casually walked in and booked a room for two nights. He used a fake name and paid cash. The FBI would expect him to leave New York immediately after the trade, so he'd decided to stay.

He pocketed his key and kept walking south, block by block, until he reached forty-fourth Street and the Harvard Club. It was exactly 12:45. His palms were sweating and he had butterflies in his stomach. Worse, he was early. He decided to go in anyway.

He crossed forty-fourth and walked towards the club. It was in the middle of the block. He scanned the street and noticed two plain white vans that could potentially be filled with agents. He seriously doubted they were. Too obvious. No big antennas or one-way mirrors, just ordinary vans. The street was empty. Thomas assumed it was always that way after the noon rush. He glanced back at one of the vans, and because of the way the light fell on the window, he thought he detected movement, but he couldn't be sure. He turned to face the club, then quickly swung around for a quick look, but he was too late to see the arm of the agent who had been reaching to the dash to grab his cell phone.

Thomas walked deliberately down the street. When he was adjacent to the door, he turned abruptly and pulled open the heavy door. He found himself in a luxurious foyer. It was very old, very Eastern. The foyer smelled like money, not metaphorically, but like actual dollars mixed with wood polish. The walls were dark mahogany, the floor marble. The familiar Harvard coat of arms hung behind the receiving desk.

Generally, it was what he expected, but it made him realize he should've done more than take pictures outside yesterday. He should've come in, learned the exact layout, been more prepared. On a day like today, there should be no surprises. Luckily he was early and had a few minutes to look around. A few minutes to make up for his lapse.

He told the severely beautiful blonde behind the desk that he was a guest of Drew Montgomery and that he would be using room 222 for a two hour meeting beginning at one o'clock. Before he could tell her his name, she said, "Certainly, Mr. McAlister. Please be seated and an escort will be here shortly."

Before Thomas had time to cross his legs, a man in a black business suit entered from a side door. "Please come with me, Mr. McAlister."

Thomas followed through two doors into an even larger receiving room. They moved on toward a huge wooden spiral staircase. The wall along the staircase was lined with oil paintings of stern-faced old men. Probably past club presidents. It seemed working at the Harvard Club was very serious business. At the top of the staircase, his escort turned left down a long, wide, deserted hallway carpeted in plush ruby red. They stopped outside Room 222.

The man turned the heavy, well-oiled brass handle and said, "Here you are, Mr. McAlister."

"Thank you." The room, a rectangular conference room, was decorated as beautifully as the rest of the building. The walls were the same dark wood, only instead of paintings of proud old men, they held wonderful impressionist renderings of flowers and meadows. The carpet was the green of freshly minted dollars.

There was a small mahogany buffet with coffee, soft drinks, and cookies at the far end of the room. The man walked over to the food table and showed Thomas a button to push if he needed to order more refreshments.

Thomas noticed another door, opposite the one they had entered through.

"Where does that door lead?"

"It opens to a back hallway. One we use to deliver food and drinks to the rooms. So that waiters don't upset members by traipsing through the main corridors with food carts and drink trays."

"Is the door left unlocked at all times?"

"Yes, sir, unless someone asks that it be locked . . . which has happened a few times." The man smiled awkwardly.

"Thank you. I'm going to wait here for my guests. Please remind the woman at the front desk that they will use my name and not Mr. Montgomery's."

"Very good, sir."

The minute the man left, Thomas opened the door to the back hallway. No one. The hallway, with its tile floor and tan walls, was stark in comparison to the public routes. One end held more doors leading to other conference rooms, the other a stairway.

He returned to his conference room and poured a glass of Evian. He had finished half the glass, when there was a knock at the door. He stood at the head of the long conference table. "Come in."

The door opened and a man in a mildly wrinkled blue suit walked in. He quickly, expertly, glanced around the room then turned around and said, "Okay," to someone outside the room. Then, Ann stepped into the room.

She looked full of life, so much more substantial and so much more beautiful than he remembered! "*Ann!*" He rushed to her. She held out her arms and smiled with tired, sympathetic eyes. For a fleeting moment,

Thomas noticed it: was it sadness? Regret? Something else? But it was so short, gone so quickly, that even the lingering memory of it was quickly over-ridden by all his other emotions.

He lifted her off the ground, burying his head in her soft, citrus-smelling hair. A thousand thoughts and feelings flooded into his mind. He reached up and wiped his clouded eyes. "I love you," he whispered. Holding her close was comforting. He pulled her closer, tighter, and as he did an odd thought came to him.

It was nothing. Less than trivial . . . but he did wonder how she was able to get her captors to provide her with the shampoo she always used, the one she'd used in Mexico and Arizona. After they kidnapped her, no one had come for her things. He still had them. But it was nothing, of course. There were countless explanations; coincidence, or possibly the fact that she was an important hostage and was given a choice of personal grooming products. All that mattered was that they were reunited, and that she was safe.

"I love you, too," Ann whispered, kissing his neck between words. Suddenly, he remembered there was another man in the room. They disentangled, but Thomas still held Ann's hand. He saw that she was crying.

The man was impatient looking. He was thin and about 6'2". He had black, fifties-law-enforcement hair. It was slicked back and Thomas could still see the rows the teeth of comb had made. "Let's make that phone call, McAlister. They're waiting in Mexico City."

"Who are you?" Thomas asked.

"Peobles, FBI."

"Okay, Peobles. Let's do it."

Thomas had moved the phone to the end of the table nearest the second door. He pushed the button for speaker phone, got a dial tone, and entered the number he'd been given. One ring and it was answered.

"Hello from Mexico City." It *was* the cowboy. He'd gone to Mexico City himself. Evidently he wanted no more mistakes.

Peobles said, "He's here, sir." Thomas was looking at Ann. She was clearly glad to see him, but she seemed distracted. She had her arms crossed in front of her, and she was watching Peobles' every move. Like one business person might watch a peer in a meeting. She seemed to be waiting to see what was going to happen. It occurred to him that maybe she thought he had a special plan. Maybe she was ready to act on his cue. If so, she'd be surprised to see that he had none. He really was trading the Ark for her.

Thomas heard his name. The cowboy was speaking to him. "All right, McAlister, tell us where to go. And no runaround."

Thomas glanced once more at Ann. She was staring at the telephone. "First, I want your name. I don't think that's too much to ask."

"You're speaking to Special Agent DJ Warrant."

"Are you at the airport, Special Agent?"

"Yes. We have a chopper out on the apron ready to go. Scuba team, Egyptologist, Bible scholar, Bible, instant carbon dating, everything. Just like you said."

Thomas focused on the voice. It was distracting having Ann nearby. "First of all, shut the chopper down. You won't need it. Now listen carefully. Write this down. Short-term parking. Section A-12. Light blue Aerostar minivan. The crate containing the Ark is in the back of the van. The top of the crate can be pulled off by hand. Underneath the lid you'll find cotton filling material. I used it because I cut the top off of the original clay casing. Under the filling is a small metal box. Give the box to your Egyptologist. Inside, he'll find a wood sample wrapped in plastic. I scraped that sample off the Ark. He can use that for dating. It's real. You'll see that when you date it. There is nowhere else on earth that I would be able to find 3300 year old acacia wood. If you don't believe me, I also put a razor blade in the metal box. You can scrape off a new sample. If you want to take the crate apart and see the whole thing for yourself, you can, but I advise against it. The key to the van is on the right front tire. Did you get all of that?"

There was a pause, while DJ finished writing down the instructions. "You *bastard*! A chopper, a scuba team! You fucking bastard!"

"Hurry up and get to that van before it gets stolen, DJ."

DJ's voice roared through the phone. "Cut the chopper! Follow me."

Thomas asked Ann if she wanted to sit, but she shook her head. He asked her if she wanted a bottle of water. Still, no. After about ten uncomfortable minutes DJ's voice crackled, "I found the key! I'm going to unlock the back door. McAlister, if you have this thing booby-trapped, you're a dead man!"

"There's no trap."

He could hear the rattle of the keys and the squeak of the hatchback being opened. Arturo had rented the van at Avis under a false name, then retrieved the Ark from his brother's ranch, where they'd hidden it in an old cenote. Thomas had given Arturo detailed instructions on when and where to leave the van, so that it would only be unattended for a few minutes.

DJ wondered how wise it would be to take this crate back to Washington unopened. "Doctor Nelson, over here. Come on, man. Move! You're the Egyptologist. Can you date this thing from McAlister's sample? Or should we open it?"

"I do not think we need to open it here, Mr. Warrant. First of all, this parking garage does not have *any* of the characteristics of even of the most primitive laboratory. It is not . . . secure. Secondly, if you believe anything that you read in the Bible, *anything at all*, then this is not an artifact you want to fiddle with. The powers this container are said to posses are so immense as to be indescribable. And I agree with Dr. McAlister: there is nowhere else on earth that he would be able to get a 3300-year old piece of acacia wood, but then again, Dr. McAlister has proved very resourceful. So, I—"

"Get to the point, Nelson."

"My recommendation is that I quickly scrape a new sample from the top of the Ark, and date *that* sample. Is that acceptable?"

DJ liked the idea. By dating their own sample, they could be sure they were getting the real thing. Plus, he had a gut feeling that McAlister was giving him the real one. He could hear it in his voice. The man would never risk losing Ann.

"Do it, Nelson." Then to Thomas, "Hey, McAlister . . . we're going to shave a new wood sample and use that for dating. Any reason why we shouldn't do that?"

"That's fine. Just tell Nelson not to take too much or he'll scar the box."

DJ didn't pass that along. At this point, he didn't care if Nelson carved his initials into the damn thing.

For the next three minutes, there was complete silence on both ends of the phone. Peobles was getting jittery. Thomas noticed he had the skittish habit of pressing on his jacket, below his left breast, to make sure his sidearm was still there. Most men do that with their wallets and don't even know it.

Suddenly Peobles blurted, "Status from Mexico, please." Thomas smiled. What jerks these guys were.

DJ took his phone off mute. "We're dating it, Peobles. Keep your shirt on."

Three more minutes passed. Then DJ's voice blasted into the conference room. "It's real! I repeat, Peobles. It's the real thing."

Ann looked at Thomas, searching his face. She was shocked. Had he given it to them. No tricks? "Y-You gave them . . . the r-real Ark?"

Thomas looked her in the eye and nodded, confirming what she already knew. He had made the ultimate sacrifice for her. Fame, fortune, redemption, all the things that Thomas needed badly, were all gone. All for her.

Thomas stood and Peobles, a bit too quickly, said, "Hold on, Thomas." Then more calmly, "Sit back down a second. I want to give the team time to clear out of the parking lot. We need to make sure you don't have a little ambush up your sleeve."

"Sure, why not. Ann? Join me?" Thomas pulled out a second chair, but Ann declined.

"I need to speak with Agent Peobles for a minute. In private. It won't take long." Peobles and Ann left the room together, leaving the door to the conference room partially open.

They were talking in hushed voices and seemed to be arguing about something. They must've gotten to know each other pretty well during her captivity. Maybe Peobles had been in charge of Ann. Either way, they were arguing like brother and sister. Their familiarity disconcerted Thomas and he felt a sickness begin to rise in the pit of his stomach.

Ann stepped back in the room and shut the door with deliberate care, her back to Thomas. She pressed her forehead against the door. Thomas stood, waiting for her to turn and run to him. This was the moment he'd been waiting for. This was everything. He yearned to feel her pressed against him. Firm. Soft. So warm and alive. But she didn't come to him right away. She stood by the door with her back to him. Standing straight. Rigid.

"Annie? Hey, Annie, what's wrong?"

Still, she made no move to face him. She was looking down at something in her left hand, holding it close to her chest. Thomas didn't know what to do. He didn't know why she was acting so strangely.

"Annie?"

Suddenly, in one smooth, professional motion, she whirled and there was an explosion. A milli-second later he was lifted and thrown backward, with such force, such overwhelming speed and power, that he immediately, sickeningly, knew that he'd been shot at point-blank range. He landed on the carpet with a thud.

Ears ringing, eyes closed, Thomas could feel the trickle of blood running down between his arm and shoulder. It felt like someone was running a feather slowly across his side. No pain. Had he not known it was blood, it would've tickled.

His eyes fluttered open, and the first thing he saw was a yellow pencil stuck in a ceiling tile. It looked like it was a mile away. The pink eraser swam in and out of his vision. What the hell happened? Should he move? Pretend he was dead? *Think, Thomas!* What about Ann? What was she doing?

He was staring at the ceiling in shock. Not real medical shock. Rather, self-induced downtime, until his brain could figure out what to do. No precedent.

There was ringing in his ears and he saw movement on the other side of the room. He raised his head and saw Ann lowering her gun, staring at him with the blank, detached gaze of a hardened killer.

The look on her face took him back to a childhood field trip to a dairy farm. He'd never forgotten the detached way the farmer had looked at his dairy cows while explaining his business to the class. The cows that Thomas had formerly considered members of Old Macdonald's Farm had become machines that needed to produce X number of gallons per day, or they got eliminated, and replaced by better machines. He'd seen, and understood with great clarity, that the farmer had a job to do and that he'd separated his emotions from the job, so that there was no link. Ann had the same look in her eyes now. The way the dairy farmer had looked at the cows. Detachment. He never would have guessed she was capable of that expression.

And then suddenly something flickered behind her eyes and she turned and went out the door. He looked back at the ceiling. How long had the pencil been there? Who had thrown it? When would gravity cause it to drop? What in the hell had just happened? Thomas prided himself on his preparation, but in the million iterations on this exact exchange that he'd done, he'd never, ever planned on this outcome.

He lowered his chin to his chest and saw blood. He still couldn't feel the wound. It was like an extremely powerful person had come up behind him, put a hand on his left shoulder, and yanked him back as hard as they could. His breath became short and then he felt adrenaline surging through his body.

He remembered when President Reagan had been shot. Reagan hadn't known he'd taken a bullet until ten minutes afterwards. He had said he felt cold and clammy. *That's how I feel.* Reagan had almost died on the table during surgery. He'd lost a lot of blood. *Why isn't someone from the club coming to help me? If I stay here, surely I'll go into shock!*

And that's what would've happened had he continued to lie there, if he hadn't heard Ann's voice coming from outside the room. *Focus, Thomas. What was she saying?*

Faintly, through the door, he heard, "It's done. He's dead. Bring in the cleaning crew." Authoritative and convincing.

But it was clear she was trying too hard. *I don't believe her and neither will Peobles. He'll come back and, like the good agent that he is, put a bullet between my eyes. Then it will be done. Then he'll call the cleaning crew.*

But there was something rising deep within Thomas. From depths which he'd rarely, if ever, felt an emotion before. A dormant, animalistic section rarely used, seldom needed. A place that, after a few more generations, a few more mutations, would probably cease to exist.

His breathing increased and his chest swelled. His adrenal gland fully dilated. All pain and fear was gone. Suddenly he was filled with a flash of white hot anger — no, fury.

Without even thinking he sat upright. He was tempted to walk right out into the hallway, reach into Ann's blue blazer, pull out her pistol, and shoot both her and Peobles. How dare a couple of squabbling, amateurish government agents try to kill him. Shit, he was probably the first person she'd ever shot. So much for fair play. So much for love, and the future. He'd get even. He'd show every stinking one of these bastards who they were messing with.

Adrenaline, driven by black hate, coursed through his veins. Every nerve tingled. He looked at his wound. She had missed his heart and hit his left shoulder. It felt heavy, but he still had limited use of his arm. He rolled over and pushed up with his right arm. There was a small pool of blood on the floor. He felt dizzy, but the adrenaline brought clarity back. Two plus two still equaled four.

His head swung to the door. He could hear Peobles say, "Fine. I'll confirm, then we leave!"

Ann had lost the argument. Thomas went into survival mode. The thought of picking up a chair and slamming it into Peobles, as he walked through the door, crossed his mind, but he was in no shape to fight. He couldn't be sure that he could knock Peobles out on the first try. Plus, there would still be Ann to deal with. The new robotic Ann. The Ann with no feeling. No emotion. Detached Ann, capable of nightmarish acts. She'd shot him once. She'd do it again.

He moved as quickly as he could to the door on the other side of the room. The one to the service hallway. He turned the brass handle and was out and moving toward the stairway he had seen earlier. Then he stopped. It was a primary corridor and was probably being watched.

Thomas was about to go back the other way, but before he turned, he scanned the end of the hall and there, in center of the wall, was a large gray panel. He shuffled over to it, occasionally leaning on the wall to keep his balance. He yanked the knob and the panel rolled upward like a garage door, revealing a large, ancient dumbwaiter. He heard a door opening behind him and without a second thought, he dove into the dumbwaiter, falling heavily against the far wall. Lightening bolts of pain shot through him, and on the horizon, over the lip of the shaft he saw Peobles, with what looked like a .44 Magnum, aimed right at him.

CHAPTER 31

Thomas wondered if the bullet was still in his shoulder. What caliber would a girl like Ann use anyway? He fumbled with the chains on the inside wall of the shaft. He was losing dexterity in his left arm. He pulled one chain and the tray started to descend. But to what? Peobles saw him now and was running towards the dumbwaiter, frantic, gun drawn. Thomas loosened his hold on the chain, allowing his weight to carry the dumbwaiter down at little less than a free fall.

He was falling fast now and the light entering the shaft was getting farther and farther away. On his back, looking up, he saw the silhouette of someone looking down at him from where he'd entered the shaft. It was Peobles. Suddenly, flames spat from the barrel of Peobles' gun. Thomas's eardrums almost exploded, as the sound of the .44 Magnum reverberated in the shaft. Another shot, and Thomas felt a tug on the tray he was lying on. He looked down and saw a hole the size of a quarter. His own blood, which had been pooling in the tray, began running smoothly through the hole. Peobles meant business. He clearly had orders to kill.

Figuring he had to be near the bottom of the tunnel, Thomas let go of the chain. A second later, the tray slammed into the bottom floor. Before Peobles could fire again Thomas rolled out onto a terra cotta floor. He could hear the sounds of a commercial kitchen, before he saw the faces of the startled workers. The clanking of pans ceased and all motion stopped as they watched him roll out and stand up, blood dripping from his fingertips. He had to keeping moving.

One of the men, the dishwasher, pointed to his right to a greasy door that looked like it might lead out to the alley. Thomas took three steps, opened the door, and was greeted by a sliver of sunlight in a typically narrow Manhattan alley. It was the one behind the Harvard Club that he had photographed yesterday. Behind him, he heard the kitchen resume its normal din before the door slapped shut.

Thomas figured that Peobles, or whoever was running this operation, would handle his escape in typical government fashion. The same way they handle Presidential security. Starting with the Harvard Club, they would set up a series of circles, each wider and less secure than the one before it. They would search these and contain each circle, slowly squeezing in, slowly isolating him.

In this situation, where they probably didn't plan on his escape, they probably hadn't set up the surveillance circles. But they had agents in the area, and they would set them up quickly. The circles would be relatively tight, because he was wounded and they knew he couldn't travel fast on foot. And, since it involved DJ, they would be relentless. He had to get as far from the Club as possible as quickly as he could.

He stood in the center of the alley and surveyed his situation. From the Polaroids he knew the layout of each of the surrounding streets. He had to think fast. Any minute, Peobles would be in the kitchen, and someone would point to the door he had just come through.

The entire alley was lined with back doors to restaurants and retail businesses. Trash was piled high. There were many hiding places. Thomas walked over to the door directly across from the kitchen. It opened easily and led to the receiving area of some kind of paper and office supply store. Thomas took one quick look over his shoulder, to check for a trail of blood, and then went inside.

He moved quickly toward the front of the store, hoping it would place him on the street one block away from the Harvard Club. He passed a bathroom, reached in, took a handful of paper towels and continued on, stuffing them under his shirt where the bullet had entered. He went right out past the desk, where employees were helping customers with copy and printing requests, through a small retail area, and out onto the street.

He needed to get to his hotel. His car was only two blocks away, but driving in Manhattan would be like going to his own funeral. By the time he got to his car and entered traffic, he'd be within the FBI's net. No car. He stood in front of the copy store cycling through options. This was the key decision. It might mean staying alive or not.

The lunch rush was long over and three yellow cabs came into sight, with their lights out. He hailed one. "Start the clock, but don't go anywhere yet." He couldn't go anywhere cloaked in blood. His blue blazer was soaked through, a sticky mess, and he needed medical attention. The hospitals would all be on alert. He had to buy something to wear over his bloody shirt, so that he could get into the Plaza, to make phone calls. The dizziness was worsening. He would've fainted from the blood loss already, if he weren't so filled with anger.

He'd traded fair and square. True to his word. He gave them the most unique treasure in history, and they'd somehow gotten Ann to shoot him. *But how?* It didn't matter now. He would get to a phone and seek revenge. The seeds of an idea were already beginning to appear.

Three doors from the copy store was a sporting goods store. "I'm going to run into that store and pick something up. Here's a twenty. I'll see you get plenty more if you wait." He dashed out of the cab and into the store, quickly bought a Cincinnati Reds jacket, and wore it out of the store. If the people behind the counter had noticed he was bleeding they hadn't shown it. As he dove in the waiting taxi he hoped they weren't calling the police at that very moment to report a badly bleeding man.

"Plaza Hotel. As fast as you can get me there."

There was a dull, prickly throb in his shoulder now. He gritted his teeth and the thought of revenge was all that kept him from passing out.

» » « «

"I *confirm*, Agent Warrant. This wood came from the real Ark!" Dr. Nelson said too loudly into DJ's ear.

DJ smiled. He had it. Finally. He echoed the words to Peobles in

New York. And now, all he had to do was wait. McAlister was simply too dangerous to leave alive. He had devised a scheme to have Thomas shot so that it would look like self-defense. One of the agents on site, Peobles, would make it look like a domestic dispute between Ann and Thomas, in which Thomas became enraged and dangerous. Peobles would testify that Thomas had tried to kill both him and Ann, in a jealous rage. They would plant a gun on McAlister.

DJ lowered the hatch, leaned against it, and lit a Marlboro. He was the winner. Too bad McAlister wouldn't be around to see that he'd won. Best of all, he'd made Annie kill the bastard. What a shock it must've been, when his lover pointed the gun at him and fired. What a terrible last image.

DJ turned to peer through the back window at the Ark. They'd have it loaded on the C-120 in less than ten minutes. They had the full coop- eration of the Mexican government. The report would be easy. Straightforward because this was the outcome the President had wanted, had authorized. He smiled. He hated lengthy paperwork.

His radio crackled and a the sound of fast breathing came through. Then, *"DJ, DJ, come in! DJ, come in!"* It was Peobles.

He swung into action. Ready for the worst. "DJ here."

Peobles was running. "Subject has escaped! Repeat, subject *has escaped*! We're in pursuit. We've formed a tight perimeter. Goddamn it, DJ, *he got away*!"

DJ stood up and roared, each word ascending by at least an octave, "Goddamn it! God-fucking-damn it, Peobles! What happened?"

DJ could hear Peobles yelling commands to other agents. "He's shot once. Point-blank. Bleeding bad. I think I may have hit him again. Tighten it, tighten the circle. Everyone come in two blocks. Check everything, people. *Everything*. We're in pursuit; I'll update you when we have him."

"You better get him, Peobles. You goddamn better get him, or it's your ass!"

DJ hit the Aerostar, making a deep dent below the back window. His heart was pounding so hard he could barely breathe. Nothing like this had ever happened to him before. Had he lost his touch? Was this guy superhuman? He switched frequency on his radio, and began barking orders to the team that was standing by on the airstrip. "Steve, come in, come in, *Steve*!"

"Steve here."

"Steve, we're on our way to the runway. I want your men on Full Alert!"

"Ten-four, sir. Full alert!"

"*Full* alert!. Guns drawn, safeties off. Got it? No fucking around. Don't let anyone but me and the team near that plane. Especially no Mexican officials. McAlister may be up to something. They've had trouble executing the mission in New York. Hold tight, I'll be there in two minutes."

"Got it, sir. No one gets near us."

"Ten-four. Out."

This made four times the bastard had gotten away. DJ broke out into a cold sweat. Somehow he knew Peobles would not catch Thomas. Peobles would pull the team in too tight, and McAlister would break through. Hell, right now the son-of-a-bitch was probably riding a broomstick, on his way up to meet their C-120 head-on.

How could they have missed him at point-blank range? In such a confined area? Suddenly, the full implication struck him. He had committed conspiracy to murder and the only person who could testify against him was still walking around. He had to get McAlister at all costs!

He turned to Elmo, who had been watching and listening as the mission unfolded. "Get me a list of the names of every friend, family member, or acquaintance of Thomas McAlister, and their last known address and phone number. Sort them by proximity to Manhattan."

Elmo turned his computer screen to face DJ. Anticipating DJ, he already had the list waiting.

CHAPTER 32

Just as Thomas was stepping out onto the apron of the Plaza's entrance, he saw two men in dark suits exit a white van and rush through the hotel doors. He jumped back into the cab, reached for his cell phone, and said, "Take me to the Dakota! An extra fifty, if you get me there in less than five."

While they drove, Thomas dialed his dear old friend and favorite anthropology teacher, Dr. Taylor. Taylor, as he called him, had contributed greatly to Thomas's decision to become an Egyptologist and had served as mentor throughout Thomas's career.

The typical first impression of Taylor was that he was senile. After knowing him, it became apparent that he was an eccentric genius. He was always one level deeper and two steps ahead. His ability to be in front of normal thought patterns disconcerted most people. Thomas simply viewed it as what it was, ultra quick intelligence. If he opened his mind around Taylor, allowed his thoughts to flow freely, unencumbered, he could usually stay up with him.

Taylor had retired to live in Manhattan after making millions on corn futures. Now he served as primary consultant on Egyptian antiquities, to both Christi's *and* Sotheby's. Despite their being competitors, he was too good for both not to have access. So, like most eccentrics, he got paid to do what he enjoyed.

Taylor's phone rang its usual fifteen times before he answered it. Taylor had no answering machine but he occasionally had a secretary in who answered the phone for him. When the secretary was not working, he felt that if someone really wanted to talk to him, they'd let it keep ringing.

"Dr. Taylor."

"What happened to that cute girl you had answering your phone for you?"

"*Thomas!* Oh, my dear Thomas, I'm hearing such nasty things about you these days. Word is you're on to something of great importance. She ran away with a girlfriend. They went West. I'm sure I'll never see her again. Shame. Pretty girl, natural switchboard talent."

"Taylor, I'm in town and I need a favor. A big one. I want to warn you up front: it's an illegal one."

"If it's a favor for you, I'm in. Don't think twice, Thomas."

"I need to hold a business meeting at your house tonight. And I need to stay a few nights in your guest bedroom. My previous plans have been . . . jeopardized."

"Sure, sure, of course, yes to all of it. What time?"

"Can I come over right now? As I said, I'm improvising."

"It'll be fun. I'm getting lonely in my old age."

"This meeting tonight. There may be as many as six of us, could be several rough types."

"I can be rough. I'll leave if you want. Just make sure none of the rough types steal anything."

Thomas smiled. "I really appreciate this, Taylor. I'll see you any minute. We're crossing Central Park."

"I'll tell the doorman to let you right up."

» » « «

Taylor was considerably shorter than Thomas. His gray hair was receding at the corners and he wore it straight back. He always looked as if he'd been facing a strong wind, like Charlie Watts. Somehow, it was the best possible look for him. He was wiry thin and slightly stooped, but his eyes glowed friendly-blue. For people he liked, that is.

Thomas literally fell through the entrance of Taylor's apartment.

"Thomas, you're injured!" Taylor held him at arm's length. "Unless they're making Cincinnati Reds jackets that bleed. Where is it? Your arm? Here?"

"Yes, yes, it's that arm. I need a doctor. I'm pretty sure I can get a doctor over here."

"Jesus, you're all sweaty, and shaking. Hurry, come into the next room and lie down. If you fall, I won't be able to carry you."

"I've been shot. I think it was a .38. Maybe nine millimeter."

"Jesus, Mary, and Joseph! Sit, sit. What can I get you? Water? Brandy?"

Thomas sat down, trying to collect his thoughts, trying to stay calm. Seeing Taylor's reaction reminded him how serious his situation was. It wasn't the pain that bothered him the most. It was the thought of complications; major arteries cut, loss of blood, infection. "Do you have any orange juice?"

While Taylor was getting his drink, Thomas staggered to the bathroom. He gingerly removed his blazer and then tore off his shirt and tossed them in the bathtub. He ran water in the sink and grabbed a green towel to wet and clean the wound. Taylor burst in, saw the wound, and instantly turned and walked out. Seconds later, he returned with a first aid kit.

Thomas's voice wavered. "Taylor, it's much worse than I imagined. More than you or I can deal with." Because of his time in the field, Thomas was accomplished at administering first aid for things like scrapes, mild concussions, snake bites, and scorpion stings, but he was out of his league with this gunshot wound. He laid a cold cloth over his shoulder and pulled out his cellular phone. As he dialed, a bright red circle formed in the middle of the cloth.

He had memorized two New York numbers, Taylor's and Drew Montgomery's. Drew had already loaned him $20,000. He felt relatively sure he could also provide what he needed now. He tried Drew at work and got lucky. Drew was not on the trading floor and was available to take calls. Accomplished traders like Drew only traded for two hours in the morning and two hours in the afternoon. In between they had lunch and socialized. Drew and guys he traded with had rented a conference room, with a pool table and wet bar, for their mid-afternoon breaks.

Thomas felt bad for interrupting Drew at work. But only for a minute. The guy was a multimillionaire.

"Drew Montgomery."

"Drew, it's Tommy. Sorry to bother you at work."

"No problem. You almost missed me. Getting ready to go make a buck. What's up? How's your trip going?"

"Listen, Drew, is this a secure line?"

"Secure? It's a land line, not a cellular, and it's not a portable phone, if that's what you mean. Why?"

"Forget it. Drew, can you get out of there early today? I wouldn't ask, if it weren't serious. I need your help."

"Sure. This hasn't been a spectacular trading day."

"I'll owe you big for this. Here's what I need. Do you know any doctors? Like . . . ER types?"

"I know a trader who used to be a doctor. He wasn't making enough to pay off his medical school loans. I don't know him real well, but we're friendly."

"Can you get him to leave with you today?"

"I can ask. Someone hurt?"

"Yeah, me. It's bad." Thomas looked down and saw fresh blood seeping though the gauze bandages Taylor was trying to apply to the wound.

"I'll ask him. If he can't get away, I'll call my guy. He'll make a house call, if I pay him enough."

"Good. The second favor I need is . . . well, I need a criminal. A professional thief and some people to help him." Taylor shot him a worried look, but kept bandaging. "Do you know anyone like that? Even a friend of a friend."

Drew chuckled. "I see what you mean about the secure line. I've been a trader in Manhattan for ten years. Of course I know thieves."

"But do you know any *professionals*. Good ones, who know all the latest technical stuff?"

"I know what you mean. I've got someone in mind. I don't know this guy personally, but I know someone who does. The guy did time. Do you mind if they're ex-cons?"

"No. I prefer it. I won't be asking them to fill out a job application. I need you to get your doctor friend and have him bring medical supplies. Whatever he needs for a serious gunshot wound to the shoulder. Get him over to Taylor's apartment, in the Dakota, fast. The sooner the better."

"Go ahead. I'm taking notes."

"Good. But when you're through, burn them! Get the thief, and anyone else he trusts to work with him and meet us at Taylor's apartment. Come soon, especially the doctor!"

Drew said, "What else?"

"That's all. Just stay as far away from this as you can. It's not romantic, and it's not going to be legal." Thomas knew that if Drew saw this as an adventure, he'd never be able to keep him away.

"Will you be all right until I get there?".

"Yeah, the bleeding has slowed down. Right, Taylor?"

"Whatever you say."

"One more thing, Drew. If they ask, tell all of these people that I will pay them well."

"Will do." Drew replied.

"Oh, yeah, and one last thing," Thomas added, "Let the doctor know that I'm not sure, but I think the bullet may still be in my shoulder. He may need some different tools for that."

"Jesus man, what have you gotten yourself into?"

CHAPTER 33

After they had his shoulder bandaged tightly, Taylor led Thomas back to the living room.

"Say good-bye to that Reds jacket, Thomas. At least you had the sense to drop it on the hardwood floor, and not one of my Persians." Taylor picked the jacket up, careful not to touch the bloody part, and put it in the garbage.

Even with his pain and anger, Thomas couldn't keep himself from marveling at Taylor's artifact collection. It had always impressed him. Taylor had started collecting before many of the national treasure laws were enacted in foreign countries. He had so many artifacts he rotated them every three months. His apartment was like a museum. In fact, many museums around the world held artifacts on loan from his collection.

Thomas slumped in a leather chair. "I think I'm ready for a whiskey." He normally didn't drink whiskey, but he was starting to feel cold and hollow, and knew whiskey would feel warm when it hit his stomach.

"Whiskey, Thomas? Really?"

"Yes, whiskey, Taylor. I think I've earned it. Not only have I been shot by the woman I love, but a few weeks ago I was fired from Arizona."

"Any fool can see you've been shot, but you're joking about losing your job, Thomas."

"I wish I was joking. But, it's true. Washington sacked me."

"That's really quite hard for me to believe. You were all they had going over there. Had you stolen something? Slept with his wife, maybe?"

"I was teaching unapproved material. Washington told me they wanted to teach me a lesson. Speaking of sleeping with someone, I'm seeing a girl named Ann. At least I was. Until she shot me. She's the Mayanologist I wrote you about."

Taylor brought the drinks. "My God, a Mayanologist! Does she practice Santerria?"

Thomas winced, as he reached for the drink. "That's Haiti and you know it!"

"Bloody sacrifice, Thomas? Holding beating hearts up to the moon?"

"You're closer than you think!"

"Tell me, has she figured out what that Mayan ball game that they used to play was all about?"

"You dirty old man! No! No one has ever figured out exactly what they used to do on all those ball courts. Can I talk now?"

Thomas took two sips of his whiskey. It created a tight warmth in his throat and he felt it flow down to his stomach.

"Proceed."

"First of all, I'd be remiss if I didn't tell you that fake Etruscan vase on the foyer table is abominable."

Taylor registered shock. "How did you know? *I* barely knew it was fake!"

"You knew. You just didn't want to admit it to yourself. Throw it out, or give it to one of your silly New York interior designers. My God, Taylor! Has our throw-away culture finally infiltrated your apartment?"

Taylor rose from his chair and took the vase into the kitchen. Thomas heard the thud as it hit the bottom of the trash can. He raised his voice. "I need to tell you what I'm up to. Listen, okay? No commentary."

Taylor yelled back from the kitchen. "Okay, but you're taking all the fun out of this visit."

"I've found the Ark of the Covenant and the Ten Commandments. The *real* Ark of the Covenant. I held the tablets in my hands a few days ago."

"Yeah, and the vase I just threw away was really the holy grail."

"No, I'm serious, Taylor! The clue that led me to it was in Egypt. My good friend Martha Stevens helped me, you remember Martha, from the Amenophis find. The Ten Commandments are the reason they shot me. The FBI is looking for me right now. They may come here."

Taylor looked in from the kitchen. "Are you serious?"

"Completely. I've got a bullet wound for Christ's sake."

Taylor came into the room and sat down across from Thomas. He was slowly shaking his head, digesting what he'd heard. In a low, inward voice he murmured, "I knew the Ark had to be somewhere and if anyone could find it, it would be you, Thomas. But I thought Moses broke those tablets."

"Moses broke the *first* set. He made a second set later."

"Really? Didn't know that. My God, this is what dreams are made of. I'd trade everything I've ever discovered, or bought, to have a find like the one you're talking about. Tell me more. What about the Ark?"

"I don't have the big golden box everyone thinks of when they think of the Ark. I have the second one God ordered made. A simple wooden one described in both Exodus and Deuteronomy. Moses hid it, because the Ten Commandments in it are different than the ones he told his followers. He didn't want to get caught in a lie, by showing his people the real ones. I found it, Taylor, and the minute I took it out of the ground, our government showed up and snatched it right out of my hands. Fortunately, I had a few warning signs that someone was spying on me so I had planted a fake Ark."

"So the government stole the fake?

"Yes, that's right. But they also took my girlfriend, Ann. The Mayanologist."

"They kidnapped her? Whatever for?"

"I would have said they kidnapped her, until she shot me today. Point-blank. No emotion on her face. Now I have to wonder if she's working for the FBI."

"Did they have her long enough to brainwash her against you?"

"I don't know. I don't know how long that takes. I suppose."

"Hmmph." Taylor reflected. "Too bad you don't know where they took the fake Ark."

"I do. They took it to the National Museum of Art. I was supposed to trade the real thing for Ann today. I decided to give it to them, to get Ann back. I set up a meeting at the Harvard Club. Ann was there, with an FBI agent. She was acting odd, but that could have been for any number of reasons. I gave them the location of the real Ark and after they had it in their possession, Ann shot me. Just like that. She raised her gun, and shot me."

Taylor stared at him for a full minute. He could tell by Thomas's voice that he was as upset about losing Ann as he was about losing the Ark. "How'd you get out of there?"

"She stepped out of the room, to tell the FBI guy she had killed me. I heard her say that. 'He's dead.' I jumped up, dove into an old dumbwaiter, ran out of the club's kitchen, bought that jacket to hide the blood on my clothes, and jumped into a cab."

"I can't believe this all happened to you today. It sounds like a Bogart film. What are you going to do now?"

"When they stole the fake, they took it to the National Museum. I had put a GPS tracker in the crate. I think they'll take the real one there again. I'm going to get it back."

Taylor's mouth dropped open. "Are you mad? Thomas, seriously. You're a professor! A world-renowned archeologist. Not some hot-shot daredevil detective!"

"I'm also sitting here wounded and plenty pissed off. They not only took my find, they intended to kill me. I'm not going to wait around like some sitting duck so they can come and finish the job. I'm going to go get what is mine."

"That's a maximum security museum you're talking about. And it sits less than a mile from the Pentagon. It's a clear felony. You know that, right?"

"You're only right if you leave out the part about them taking it from me first."

"You're not well, Thomas. You've lost a lot of blood."

"I am well. I have to be well. Tonight they'll be bringing it into the country from Mexico. Tomorrow is Saturday. They won't get a group together to open it until Monday. Sunday is my only chance. After Sunday, I can't be sure where it will be taken. They'll probably move it Monday or Tuesday."

"You're probably right."

"Getting it back will put me in debt. Can you find a good home for it? At a good price?"

"Are you sure you want to sell it?"

"I'll have to. But only to the appropriate buyer. Very discreet, very high-end. You know what I mean. Someone who can appreciate this type of thing. Someone who will never sell it or reveal its presence. Highest confidentiality levels, of course. And I want access to it, once a year. Can you do that?" Thomas knew that Taylor was dialed into a world so rich, so decadent, that few even knew it existed.

"It'll be one of the easiest jobs I've ever had. Once I establish provenance, that is."

"Give them a sliver of wood for dating if you have to. This is important. And tell them that I can take them through the entire string of events that led to its unearthing."

"Say no more. I'll keep you posted. This is all assuming you get it back, of course." Taylor drained his glass. He was smiling as he tried to determine how to calculate the commission on a priceless item.

There was a long, uncomfortable pause. "Speaking of money. How do you plan to pay these guys? *If* they agree to do the job?"

Thomas adjusted his position to make sure his wound wasn't leaking out onto the chair. "Actually, I was planning to ask you for a loan. Against the sale price, once we sell it."

"You can have the money. You know that, Thomas. But what if you don't get the Ark back?"

"I'll get it."

"And if not?"

"I'll get it. If I don't, I won't pay the guys that help me as much. I'll make that part of the deal. So, if not, I'll owe you, but not as much. You can garnish my wages."

"You don't have any wages."

"Well . . . if I don't get the Ark back, I'll have to get a job."

Taylor leaned forward and narrowed his eyes. "Just don't get caught! If you go to prison, I'll never get my money back. When do these thugs show up?"

"I'm not sure they'll come at all. As soon as Drew can round them up. Can I ask one more favor?"

Taylor rolled his eyes. "You show up here with a hole in your shoulder and expect the world. What do you want now?"

"I need you to find a payphone and call my rental car company. Tell them where my car is parked. They charge a little extra to go pick it up, but under the circumstances, I think I'll pay."

"Just write down all the information. I'll go right now. I'm going to pick us up something to eat. Any requests?"

"You're a saint, Taylor. I'll take some kind of soup, a chicken sandwich with everything, as big a pickle as you can find, extra salty potato chips and . . . anything else that looks good."

CHAPTER **34**

Two hours later, Thomas heard Taylor's intercom system buzz. It was the Dakota's security guard. Drew had taken longer than Thomas had hoped.

"Mr. McAlister, your guests have arrived. Would you like to come down for them? Or should I send them up . . . unescorted?" Thomas assumed it must be a pretty seedy bunch. Both he and Taylor had already told the guard that they were expecting a large group and to send them up immediately, unescorted.

"Please send them up, Mr. Paxton. Thank you."

The group that entered Taylor's penthouse a few minutes later was not the typical Dakota party assemblage. Thomas ushered the men into the living room. There were six of them. Drew, the doctor, and the four men that were supposed to be professional thieves. Drew and the doctor split off from the group to help Thomas and the four other men sat down. Drew introduced the four as Ethan and his friends. Aside from Ethan, who was well dressed, clean-cut, and looked like John F. Kennedy Jr., they were a motley crew. The friend of Ethan's who'd entered first had long, grungy, Rastafarian style dreadlocks. The smell of incense wafted out of his loose fitting sweats, which he wore with old compressed flip-flops. The next had a crew cut and bore a striking resemblance to Robert DeNiro in later scenes of *Taxi Driver*. And the fourth had short, squarely cut blond hair and looked like the standard blue collar worker: flannel shirt, khaki work pants, and steel-toed boots. He would've been normal except that he carried a little brass spittoon in his left hand and every time someone referred to him he sucked the saliva out of an enormous piece of chewing tobacco in his cheek and spat it with great celerity into the little spittoon, thereby answering every question directed at him with a little 'ting'. Taylor appeared from cleaning up the kitchen and didn't bat an eye. He'd seen much worse. Thomas took Drew and the doctor into Taylor's bedroom.

"I've been shot in the arm with a pistol. I think the weapon was a .38. An automatic. She was about ten feet from me when she fired."

The ex-doctor nodded and instinctively headed toward the private bathroom located off of the bedroom where he began to wash his hands at the sink. "I've seen similar wounds. Though it's been awhile. Are you dizzy?"

"A little. Less than before. I think the food helped."

"Would you say you've lost a lot of blood?"

"I don't know. I did bleed heavily for a while. But it's leveled off now. Drew, will you tell your friends I'll be awhile, but that it will be worth the wait." The doctor removed the flannel shirt Taylor had draped around Thomas's shoulders and began to cut away the gauze bandages.

"My name is Lance, by the way. Hell of a name for a doctor, huh? Why don't you lie on the floor. Wait, I'll put a bath towel down first."

He knelt beside Thomas and began prodding. "You've got a fairly common gunshot wound. I used to see a lot of them in the emergency rooms I worked in. I think I can safely say that the bullet is still in there. Nothing vital has been damaged. Whoever shot you either really liked you or they were a bad shot. I'm going to give you a local anesthetic and then take the bullet out. As far as I can tell, it's sitting in the trapezius muscle, between the clavicle and the scapula. Are you allergic to any medications?"

"No."

"Okay. I'll sanitize it, stitch it up, and bandage it. Your neck and upper back will be very sore for a while, but with low to moderate activity for a few weeks, you'll be good as new. I brought some antibiotic cream, and an oral antibiotic. I'll put the topical on before we bandage you up. Put it on every time you change the bandages. Every four or five

hours. Only use the oral if it gets infected. I'll leave you extra bandages
and cream. Ready?"

» » « «

Forty-five minutes later, Thomas emerged from the bathroom feeling
much better. He'd finished another whiskey and his arm was still numb
from the local the doctor had given him.

The group of men surrounding Drew were having an animated discussion, with Drew in the middle, doing an obvious imitation of a drunk girl.
The guys were laughing and drinking. They'd found Taylor's bar.

Thomas approached and waited until Drew was finished before interrupting.

"I'm sorry to jump right in, but I'm not feeling well and the doctor
says I've got to get some rest as soon as possible. But I want to have
plenty of time for this meeting."

The one with dreadlocks said, "Where were you hit?"

Thomas was taken back. "How did you know?"

"Your color. That particular shade of pale. I was in the Gulf the first
time. Seen it many times."

What an odd skill. "I'm impressed. In the shoulder. Bullet's out."

Thomas sank into one of Taylor's brown leather chairs and Drew
handed him a glass of orange juice that contained a large dollop of
whiskey. "I'm an archeologist. I unearthed an artifact that I value very
highly. Earlier today, that artifact, my artifact, was stolen from me. To
rub salt in the wound, the woman I love, and who I thought loved me,
shot me. Point-blank. Apparently she's working for the other side. She's
either been with them all along, or they've got some kind of leverage
over her. Or they brainwashed her, or something. I don't know which .
. . I-I don't know which, yet." Thomas paused, looked down, and took
a deep drink.

Ethan, the smart-looking man in a black turtleneck and sport coat
cleared his throat and said, "You found the tomb of Amenophis a few
years ago, right?" He had a heavy British accent.

Thomas was impressed. He hadn't expected any archeology aficiona-dos in this group. "Karl Johnson led the expedition but, yes, I found the tomb. And I got most of the publicity, due to the technique I used to find it. Currently, I've been working on another find and I was successful." It was treasure far greater in magnitude and importance, but Thomas decided not to share that information. They might be tempted to steal it from him. "My new find has a lot of historical significance." Thomas took another drink. The anesthesia was starting to wear off and his arm was beginning to ache.

The men were still, hanging on his every word. This was the stuff childhood dreams were made of. "About a week ago, I found what I was looking for in Mexico. I hadn't had it out of the ground for more than ten seconds when a group of people swooped in and took it from me. Although I've never seen one in action, they looked and acted like a Special Forces team. Luckily, I was expecting just such an attack, and had removed the original the night before and replaced it with a fake. The GPS tracking device I planted in the frame of the fake tracked it to Washington D.C." Ethan nodded, acknowledging Thomas's shrewdness.

"Government," the man with the crew cut said disgustedly.

"Do you know where in D.C. they took the fake?" Ethan asked. He was clearly their leader.

"They took it to the National Museum of Art."

Ethan nodded again.

Thomas continued. "They kidnapped my girlfriend at the same time they stole the fake. They were holding her hostage, until I agreed to give them the real thing."

Ethan interrupted again. "Did she know it was a fake?"

"No. I didn't tell her," Thomas acknowledged. "Today, we traded. I gave them the real treasure in exchange for the safe return of Ann. But, as I've already told you, something went wrong. Somehow, they got her to shoot me. She shot me and they got the treasure. I think she was supposed to kill me, but I got away. They're looking for me."

The Rastafarian spoke up. "So, you think they're going to take it to the National Museum of Art again, and you want us to help you get the object back?"

Thomas nodded. "Yes. And it needs to be taken back before Monday. I think they'll move it after they've examined it."

Ethan stood up and began pacing. "What makes you think they'll take it to the same place?"

"There's no reason why they wouldn't. I put the GPS in the frame of the crate, not in the object itself, so I don't think they ever found the tracking device. They have no reason to think I know where they took it the first time. And I think the guy I'm dealing with would've told me if he'd found it."

"He might not have mentioned it on purpose. So that you'd think they'd take it there again."

"Maybe. There's also another reason. The museum is close to all of the Washington officials they might want to involve. They were comfortable using the National Museum the first time. I think they'll use it again."

Ethan continued. "What if they *did* find the device and are waiting for us?"

"I don't think they think that I'd try very hard to get it back, especially not wounded. But, hey, anything is possible. It's a risk. With any operation there is a certain amount of risk. Right?"

Ethan nodded, as did some of the other men in the room. He stopped pacing and leaned against the back of one of Taylor's chairs. "Thomas, this is like buying a house. We have to know the price you're willing to pay for our services, and you have to know the price we're asking for them. Because we may not even be in the same ballpark and then we're wasting each other's time. So at the risk of sounding offensive, let's talk price first. Okay?"

"All right."

"You want us to break into the National Museum and steal an object from the government. A museum that is so close to the Pentagon, it surely has updated security systems. And we have no more than twenty-four hours to prepare."

"Correct. But not just an object, it's *my* object."

"Okay, we're clear on that. I've worked with all of these guys before." He motioned to the other men in the room. "I know what they do and how much they'll take for a job like this. I will serve as their negotiator, to save time."

"This job is a felony, so you're asking us to risk a minimum of fifteen years of our lives. It's a felony directly against the government and judges always side with the government, so we're really risking twenty to twenty-five years."

Thomas interrupted. "I don't plan on us getting caught!"

The man's face flushed red, a momentary flash of anger. "Thomas, *you* don't plan on anything!" He calmed himself. "You don't have a plan, because you're an archeologist and you don't know how to plan something like this. If we do it, *I'll* plan it, and part of my plan is realizing that if I get caught, I'm screwed for twenty-five years. That's an important variable. When it's that long, my price goes up. Simple economics."

Thomas grinned. Ethan had the essential ingredient to make this operation a success: passion. "Keep in mind, I'm going with you. I'm taking the risk, too. I'm not hiring you to go in alone. You might steal the fake. So I'm right there with you."

"How many men will it take to carry this object?"

"Two can carry it. Three would be easier. Either way it will be cumbersome."

"Then you need me, two break-in men who will also serve as carriers, and one good security system man, like Mack over there. So you need four, plus you'll be there. I have to tell you that in your shape and with no prior experience, you're more of a hindrance than a help. Our price is one hundred thousand per man. Four hundred thousand total." He leveled his stare at Thomas, ready for a debate.

Thomas drained his glass. Drew quickly got up, so Thomas wouldn't have to, and refilled it.

"Ethan," Thomas said, "you and your men have been around some. You've been involved in a lot of illegal activities. I'll bet you've spent a lot of time bickering about money, too. You're used to it. As you say, I'm only an archeologist, but I'm willing to bet your rock bottom price for the job is probably fifty thousand per man. That's if you're hungry right now, which I have no way of knowing. In the mind of a professional thief, like yourself, one hundred thousand is out of the question. It's only a starting point. To use your analogy, it's like the initial asking price of a house. No one in their right mind would pay you that. Seventy five thousand is what you expect to get, and fifty is rock bottom."

Ethan tried to stifle a smile. Thomas's assessment was dead on.

"Here's the deal, guys. You get me into that goddamn museum and get my treasure back, I'll give you your hundred thousand apiece. On top of that, I'll give you *another* twenty thousand apiece . . . if we get in and none of us get caught. If we don't get the treasure you get nothing. If we go in and it's not there, I'll give you half: fifty thousand. I'll pay you well, if you do what you're supposed to do."

Drew interrupted. He didn't know Ethan well, and he was afraid Thomas had pissed him off. "So, Ethan, Thomas's offer is one hundred and twenty thousand per man, if you get the object back, and nothing if you don't, half if you go in and it's not there. Is that acceptable?"

Ethan stroked his jaw, estimating expenses in his head. "Yes. That'll do it." He put his empty glass on the tabletop. "Thomas, you need to get some rest and I need to put a plan together. I will meet you here at noon tomorrow, to take you through it. You're paying a lot of money, and I'll make sure you get what you want. But now, I have research to do."

Thomas nodded.

Ethan continued. "All I ask is that if you want to go with us tomorrow night, you're fit and ready to fly down to D.C. at midnight. We'll charter a plane, do the job, and, if all goes well, be back here before they know the treasure is gone. You need to be ready for a long, intense night. Come on, guys. Let's let this man get some sleep." They rose and headed for the door. "Thomas, I'll see you tomorrow at noon. Sleep well."

Thomas said nothing. He liked Ethan. Drew showed them out and then came back to talk to Thomas as he was getting undressed. "Do you know what you're doing here, chief? This isn't some liquor store robbery. I mean, I've heard of some heists, but I've never been this close to one."

Thomas said, "I lost my job. They just took the biggest archeological find of my life, and my girl. Those two things were all I had left. You ask me if I know what I'm doing here? *Hell* no, I don't!" He looked at Drew and a faint smile appeared. "But Ethan seems to."

» » « «

The fact that Ann, the woman he loved, had shot him, was eating him from the inside out. No one saw it, except Taylor, who heard the occasional waiver in his voice, saw the occasional hand tremor. Luckily, there was the work of organizing the break-in, and his driving desire to get the Ark back. *Otherwise, I don't know what would become of the poor man, Taylor thought.*

Taylor was right. Underneath the eternal optimism, he was hurting. Ann had damaged him in every way. Physically, yes, but emotionally it was ten times worse. And as hard had he tried to stay focused on the task at hand, his normally disciplined mind wandered. Her image seeped through; her quick turn, played back in slow motion, turning, raising the gun. Smoke. Impact. Being flung backward. Had he seen the bullet? Surely not. But he imagined it coming towards him, high and tight. Like a little lead fastball. And then her angelic, deadly face, and the detached eyes. How was he to do it? How could he simultaneously hate someone he loved? What twisted emotional condition had resulted from being in love with Ann, only to be betrayed by her? *They must've coerced her, brainwashed her, threatened her. That is the only way my Annie would've, could've, done what she did.*

Lying in bed that night, he opened his mind. Back to childhood, back to the child's question: if you had one wish, what would it be? If you could ask one question, no matter what it was, and get a truthful answer, what would you ask? Thomas knew his question without pause. Why? Why had she done it?

Could she have been working for the government the whole time? It was impossible. She had been at El Manati *before* Thomas arrived. The only way she could have been working for the government was if they told her to be on that hill before he arrived. But no one knew where he and Arturo were going that day. Hell, he and Arturo hadn't known until the day before. He had gone over and over it and it just wasn't possible. Thomas drew a deep breath. Unless . . . *Arturo had told them!*

Arturo could have called ahead, after they'd used the satellite photographs to find El Manati. Then someone could have planted Ann there, to wait for him. Her orders would have been to befriend Thomas, maybe even enter into a relationship with him: do anything to learn the location of the Ark. Had she purposely gotten him drunk that first night? But if Arturo *were* an agent, why send Ann? It didn't fit. Plus, Arturo had been referred to him randomly, by Dr. Ozgood. Accepting this theory would mean that Ozgood was in on it, too. Nonsense. Arturo was completely trustworthy. Ann couldn't have been placed on the hill that day. She was there on her own. She was not an agent.

But that didn't help him figure out how the hell they got her to shoot him. She'd handled the gun like a professional. She'd braced her right fist with her left hand, like police do. That required training. He had heard her use the words "cleaning crew" outside his room at the Harvard Club. Professional terminology. Those weren't skills and terminology that the average Stanford trained archeologist possessed. Yet they'd had many archeological conversations and her knowledge of the Maya was deep, too deep to be anything other than real. The conflicts with Ann's numerous and seemingly disparate traits had Thomas completely perplexed.

CHAPTER 35

Taylor was supposed to wake him at nine o'clock, but after five minutes of trying, he had given up and let him sleep. Thomas finally woke up on his own, at eleven o'clock.

Every muscle in his body was sore, and he had a mild hangover. After a hot shower he put on a fresh bandage, and trudged into Taylor's kitchen. Taylor had grapefruit, a large cup of coffee, fresh squeezed orange juice and two English muffins waiting for him. "You look better than you deserve to."

"It's this spa. Drinks. Hot showers. Breakfast, prepared conscientiously. I'm eternally grateful. And I'm feeling much better. Amazingly better."

Taylor looked skeptical.

Later, he was in the guest bedroom when he heard the doorbell ring. It wasn't quite noon, but he could hear Ethan talking to Taylor. Taylor was making up a reason to go out and run a quick errand.

Thomas emerged. "Good to see you. How are we doing?"

Ethan started right in. "I have about thirty minutes to take you through this and then I have to go. We're having trouble getting one of the D.C. public works maps. I want you to feel comfortable with the plan, but I can't stay and answer a hundred questions."

Ethan placed two large blueprints on the long glass coffee table. "This is the original blueprint of the National Museum. It was designed by John Russell Pope and finished in 1941. Nice building."

"It's all right."

"And here is the latest major remodeling and addition. Done by I. M.

Pei & Partners, completed in 1978. Paid for by you and me and headed by none other than your pal, current director George Valmer."

"Aren't these blueprints top secret? How did you get a hold of them?"

"Yes, they are classified. I have my ways. The originals were available but hard to find and the addition done by Pei gave us big problems. But we got it. The additional money you gave us helped. Anyway, as you can see, Valmer added a three-story addition on the back. The top story is his office and reception area. Notice the great view he gave himself." Ethan pointed to the office. "The treasure might be here." He tapped the blueprint.

"The middle floor has become an extension of the modernism gallery and the basement floor, here, is a conference room. Another potential place for your treasure."

Thomas pointed to a shaft running along all three rooms. "What is this?"

Ethan smiled. "Very astute. That is our transportation. An elevator shaft. You enter from the back. UP takes you to Valmer's office. DOWN takes you to the conference room. The elevator is an Otis. It's heavy-duty, private, and easy to use. I wouldn't be surprised if Clinton had used this set up for his little escapades. The Monica-vator, or something like that." Thomas was reminded how much the English love scandal. "Looks good, Ethan, but can you get us in?"

"Here's the plan. I'm not going into great detail, but trust me, I know what I'm doing. We pick you up at midnight. We drive an hour to Essex County Airport. It's a smaller business airfield in New Jersey, two miles north of Caldwell. We fly to D.C. in a Lear 35. We arrive outside D.C. within twenty minutes. We drive to the museum, get the crate, and we're out of there in minutes. Back to the Lear, and then back to New York."

"What about the museum's security system—"

"Don't ask questions, don't get in the way. Just stay by my side. I need you beside me when we find the crate. That's all you're needed for. The less you know, the better. If you get caught, you don't know anything. I like to do things a certain way. A job is like a fingerprint. If things I do were repeated to the right law enforcement people, they'd know this was my job. So trust me. You're paying me a lot of money for a two-day job. Let me earn it"

Thomas decided to trust him. It would allow him to start concentrating on other things. "I understand, Ethan. I'm going to trust you. Just get it right!"

"In my mind, I've already got the treasure. You identify your crate, we carry it to our van, take it back to the airport, load it into the Lear, and thirty minutes later, we're back in New York City. The whole operation will take less than four hours."

"I hope you've got some contingency plans, in case things don't go as planned like—"

"They will. And I do. I'm leaving now. My guys will be in front of the building at midnight. In a dark blue van with no windows. When we return from D.C., we will drop you and the box here. My men will help you carry it in, but what you do with it after that is up to you. We'll have done our job." Ethan was out of the door and on his way to the elevator before Thomas could ask any more questions.

CHAPTER 36

For dinner that evening, he and Taylor ordered in from Smith and Wollensky's. With one of the best steaks he'd ever eaten, he also had a huge baked potato, broccoli and a sizable wedge of chocolate cake.

"Your body sure does heal in style," Taylor chided.

A legend, Taylor, like Thomas, had been fortunate enough to discover a very large, very rich find early in his career. Taylor's was before most governments had laws governing how the treasure would be divided. He was able to sell most of the artifacts to the highest bidder. Only a few friends knew he had kept a few priceless pieces. He had shown them to Thomas once. Large, solid gold Egyptian statues of RA, lapis lazuli jewelry, and beautiful emerald insects. "I couldn't bear to part with them," Taylor had said. "They cast a spell on me and I knew I would own them until I die." Thomas remembered thinking that was the true definition of priceless. Taylor's fortune had allowed him to do whatever he wanted with the rest of his life; teach, appraise, and play in the corn and wheat futures market.

As midnight drew closer, Thomas got up to change clothes. He'd had a pair of black pants, a black turtleneck, and black shoes delivered from Macy's. He was in his room dressing when Taylor entered, carrying an assortment of boxes. He put them on the bed and began opening them.

Thomas peered over Taylor's shoulder. Each box held a different pistol, except the last, which held a collection of knives. From left to right, there was a Walther PPK, a snub-nosed .38, a 9mm Berreta, a Sig Sauer, and a WWII issue Colt .45 automatic. They were all set in velvet and accompanied by two clips, except the snub-nose, which had speed loaders. The final box had a hunting knife, a double edged combat knife, a nice bone-handled machete, and a Swiss Army Knife. Thomas stared in awe.

"Take your pick," Taylor said.

"Taylor . . . my God, I had no idea you had these. You've got an arsenal here!"

"I live in New York. I've to keep up with the common thief. I've picked these things up through the years. Never really needed them. Except once in Shanghai. Did I ever tell you about that time that I—"

"Yes, yes. You've told me now a hundred times! My God, Taylor. Do you really think I should pack iron? I left my .32 in Mexico, with Arturo."

Thomas picked up the big Sig Sauer. It felt good in his hand, but heavy and cumbersome.

"A few of those characters that were here last night were pretty seedy. I recommend the Sig Sauer."

Thomas picked up the Beretta next. It felt perfect. "I do love a Beretta. It'll only wind up causing trouble. I'd never shoot anyone anyway, at least not where we're going. I think I'll take a knife." Thomas picked up the Swiss Army. "This is a given." He dropped it into his pocket.

Taylor shrugged. "Keep in mind your first stop is not necessarily the place where you'll end up. I know you trust Ethan, but what about those other guys? You don't know them. What if you get caught? It could happen, you know. The government agent you're dealing with has already stolen from you and had you shot. None of this is going into FBI files. What would stop him from taking you somewhere, tying cement shoes on your feet, and dropping you into the East River?"

"You make a good case."

"What do you have to lose? You only use it if things go wrong."

Thomas conceded, "Okay . . . I'll take the Beretta and one clip." He picked up the machete. "Now look at this baby. This is nice. Too cumbersome for tonight. But I could use it in Mexico."

"It's yours."

Thomas swung right, then left. A deep pain shot through the left side of his body and he tried to hide the wince. "This is more like what I'm used to lately. Arturo showed me a lot of little tricks down in Mexico. I've got to get downstairs." He put the machete back in the box.

"Good luck, and be careful. Oh, and Thomas. Watch the double cross. Remember, you don't know these guys."

"Thanks, Taylor. I'll be back later tonight. I'll have the Ark with me but don't wait up. I'll need you to be sharp the next day. If you think of a good place to hide it leave me a note on the kitchen counter. Again, sorry about all this." But he knew that secretly Taylor was enjoying all the intrigue.

Down on the street the blue van was nowhere in sight. He shrank back into the dark into the shadows and tucked the Beretta down into the small of his back. He checked his watch again. It was five minutes past midnight. He hoped nothing had gone wrong. Negative thoughts. What if the government had traced him to Ethan, or rounded up all the top thieves in New York, to thwart just such an attempt? Ethan had said that he was well known to some investigators.

After three of the longest minutes of his life, a blue Dodge van, with a commercial grade suspension, pulled up to the curb and turned on its hazards. The passenger window lowered and someone whispered, "Thomas?"

He hurried to the curb and the side door of the van flew open. He reached back and brought the Beretta around to the front of his pants, clutching it with white knuckles under his shirt. He didn't see Ethan!

A man from inside the van barked, "Get in. Let's go!"

"Where's Ethan?" Thomas hissed.

"He's at the airport. Get in!"

He used his left arm to pull himself up into the van and flashes of white-hot pain burned through his field of vision. There was one man in the very back seat, and one in the passenger seat next to the driver. The door flew shut behind him and he took the gun out. It was dark and he couldn't see any of the men's faces well. He searched for one he recognized from the other night.

The guy behind him said, "Relax, man, it's us." Thomas recognized the accent and slid the gun back into his waistband.

"What the hell are you doing with a Beretta?" The man asked.

"I liked it more than the Sig Sauer."

"What are you going to *do* with it?"

Thomas was surprised. "You don't know?"

"Would I ask, if I did?"

Thomas said, "I was going to blow your fucking heads off if you weren't who you said you were."

After that, the drive to the airport was silent.

CHAPTER **37**

At the airport, the driver took them right out onto the tarmac up to the jet, where Ethan was waiting on folded down stairs. The engines were already warm and they were in the air within five minutes. Ethan looked like the quintessential thief, as he paced up and down the center aisle of the Lear in black slacks and turtleneck.

Once in the air, he reviewed the plan. "The other men and I have been over this many times, Thomas. We'll review it once for you, so that you know what is happening, but there will be no changes. Remember you're along for the ride, until we get into the museum. We are going to be moving very fast. You'll be with me. Just move with me, and be there when I need you. Never, ever talk. The other men and I have personal communicators and a few other signals that we use."

He picked up a headset with both voice and ear components and showed it to Thomas. "At the professional level, stealing is an art. A dance. We have everything synchronized, based on exact traffic routes in D.C., architectural building plans, etcetera. Here's the plan." He pulled out a street map of D.C. and the plans for the National Museum of Art, both the old building and the addition, and ran through the game plan. His thoroughness was impressive and comforting. He had contingency plans, including a safe-house in D.C., in case things went sour.

The part that impressed Thomas the most was Ethan's ability to acquire secret information. All of the architectural plans, electrical wiring grids, and the information about the security systems at the museum were labeled top secret. He even had the guard schedule. If 90 percent of any successful operation was planning, Thomas felt they had a very good chance of success.

Ethan finished and waited for Thomas's reaction. Thomas said, "We spend no more than two and a half hours in D.C., get out with the treasure, and are back in New York twenty minutes later. An hour after that we're back at the Dakota. Sounds fine to me."

» » « «

The jet touched down five minutes early at College Park Airfield in Maryland, outside the limits of Washington D.C. Once they rolled to a stop, the five men jumped out of the plane, leaving the pilot to deal with airport check-in.

The men strolled to the parking lot, where another blue van waited. They piled into the van, which was rolling before the side door was shut.

After they were on the road, Ethan said, "Driver, we're five minutes ahead of schedule. Get us flush on the way there." He glanced at Thomas. "In this business, being early is as bad as being late."

Thomas peered out the window. He noticed they stayed on major streets but avoided the highways. "Why are we staying off the highways, Ethan?"

"Almost every major highway in this country has video cameras looped into patrol offices. Here in D.C., it's worse. Some of the small roads are filmed, too. Intersections are especially bad, because they can get a still image of you. The patrol offices usually save the video for two days, sometimes four. After we make our play, they'll be looking for us on those videos. That's why even our front window is tinted."

It was almost two in the morning as they approached the museum. As the operation became more real, Thomas found himself getting more nervous. It was one thing to talk about such a big break-in. It was entirely another to be involved in one. Why had he left so much to Ethan? Why had he been sleeping, when he should have been preparing? It never crossed his mind that the sleep had been restorative. Instead he berated himself for being lazy. Should he call the whole thing off? One block north of the museum, they pulled into a park and two of the men got out of the van and left on foot. It was too late to call off the operation now. While they were pulled over, the driver got out and placed a magnetized sign on the side of the van that read *Federal Heating and Cooling*.

They drove around for another five minutes, to give the men who'd gotten out time to reach the museum. Then the driver took them to the receiving entrance, located at the rear of the museum.

"Won't they be suspicious of a heating and cooling van showing up in the middle of the night?" Thomas whispered.

Ethan didn't bother looking at him. "Museums with priceless pieces of art must maintain tight temperature and humidity tolerances. Systems need constant tweaking. When the temperature or humidity goes outside the acceptable range, it triggers an alarm at the heat and air company. Normally, they call ahead, but it shouldn't be a big deal for us to show up unannounced. This is the same color and style of van that Federal uses. No more talking until this is over."

Five minutes had passed and they pulled into the parking lot of the museum. They rolled smoothly back to the receiving area. There was a ramp down so that when semis backed in, the edge of their trailers would be even with the loading dock. There were two well-lit guard houses. One on each side of the dock. Both had windows made of bullet-proof glass and both manned. Neither Ethan nor Thomas knew that the usual Pinkerton men had been replaced with marines, under DJ's orders.

Over each guard house were cameras covering the dock area. Anyone coming or going would be seen on monitors, both in the guard houses and at the main security station in the basement of the older part of the museum.

Ethan knew and did not mention to Thomas that the museum had recently replaced their old Brinks security system with a new Honeywell Fortress5000 system. The Fortress5000 was a much better system, especially at motion and temperature detection. Fortunately, the loot they were stealing was probably in a conference room or office and not out on the museum's public display floor, where most of the masterpieces were. Normally, temperature and motions detectors were used only for the main floors, where the really expensive, high-profile items were kept. So, they had to worry about approach, entry, exit, doors, windows and cameras, but not temperature and motion, which made the job easier. Ethan knew the Honeywell system well and would soon exploit some of its weaker points.

The van reached the dock. Ethan and Thomas hid on the floor in back. The security guards would see only one silhouette. That of the driver.

The driver made a lazy U-turn and began backing up, so that the rear of the vehicle would face the dock. It was proper maintenance vehicle procedure, when a company had something to fix and needed to access tools in the back of the vehicle.

The driver stopped the van about five feet from the dock, equidistant between each guard house. Thomas felt his heart rate increase. From his point of view, this was the most dangerous part of the operation. He had no idea how Ethan planned to get them past these guards. He hoped their excuse was good enough to warrant being behind the museum at night. He felt the van shift as the driver opened his door to get out. Without moving his head he strained to see Ethan, but couldn't.

Still facing the floor, he heard the driver hail the guards. His nose was half an inch from the floor of the van. He smelled grease. He couldn't see the two guards who came out of their shack, dressed in black uniforms rather than the khaki ones the regular Pinkerton men wore. The driver of the van noticed that the uniforms were not tan, as they should have been, but did not even pause. "Just getting my work order," he said, while opening the passenger door.

The light behind the guards created long menacing shadows, accentuating their bulky M-16 machine guns. The driver reached into the van and extracted an envelope. He held it out, toward one of the guards.

DJ had brought these marines in to replace the under-skilled, low fire-powered Pinkerton men. The marines were formidable in battle, but the 60-minute briefing they'd received for this assignment did not cover all of the museum processes. It didn't transfer the knowledge that the

Pinkerton men had acquired from doing the same job night after night for fifteen years. By replacing Pinkerton with his own men, DJ had compromised a well oiled system.

The Pinkerton men would not have looked as ominous as the marines did in their black assault uniforms, but they would have never allowed the driver of an unannounced repair van, however familiar, to walk around or open a passenger door before they had a full explanation as to why they had not been notified by the scheduler at the main guardhouse. The correct process for all unscheduled service personnel and vendors was to detain them, then thoroughly check credentials. The Pinkerton men also would have noticed that the driver of this Federal Heating and Cooling van was not Mel, their buddy of ten years, who always worked nights for Federal.

The two skilled fighters didn't know any of this. Instead, the guard on the left leveled his M-16 and said, "What's the problem?"

As the driver began to speak, there were two barely audible thumps, one from each side of the loading dock. The well aimed tranquilizer darts hit the marines in their necks. Ethan's men had used the quickest tranquilizer known to man, one derived from a sedative used by the Tapirape Indians in the Amazon Basin, that instantly rendered prey immobile and unconscious.

The guards had fallen under the cameras, out of their view. The driver talked on, as if nothing had ever happened, for the sake of the cameras. He was gesturing and laughing and carrying on, as if he were having an animated conversation.

As he did, the two men who had fired the tranquilizers rushed forward. They stayed close to the building until they reached the cameras. Once under them, they removed small irregular stepladders from their backpacks and adjusted them to the proper height. They then removed long tubes that looked like telescopes and, in unison, clamped the long devices to the end of each camera lens. With these special lenses, the cameras would transmit to the main guard house whatever was in their last frame of view. They would do that for the next fifteen minutes, after which an alarm would sound because a small sensor in the brain of the camera would realize that for fifteen minutes nothing in its field of view had moved. Not a leaf, not a bug, not the repair van. The motion sensor in the camera was to guard against these freeze frame devices and was based on the principal that no one could get in, and out, in fifteen minutes or less.

Face down in the van, Thomas saw none of this. Suddenly, there was a tap on the side of the vehicle. "Put your ski mask on and follow me." Ethan was up and out the side door before Thomas had even rolled over.

He scrambled out of the van and saw that the driver, the two other men they had dropped off earlier, and Ethan were all clustered around the door to the receiving dock. It was located next to the guard house on the left. As Thomas moved toward the door, he noticed the marines, dressed in black, on the ground. He double checked to make sure they were still breathing. He wondered how they'd been neutralized so quietly. He noticed that the cameras overlooking the dock had strange-looking extensions on them. Amazing. Drew and his team were professionals all right.

The cluster of thieves around the door was quiet and intense. Then there was a muffled pop, the door opened, and they poured into the museum. He picked up his pace, but couldn't quite reach the door before it closed. Just before it clicked shut, it opened again and Ethan angrily pulled him in.

They were in a small hallway with an armored door directly in front of them. Thomas caught a glimpse of a key pad with an electronic sensor. The man in front turned back toward Ethan, who reached into his pocket and pulled out something the size of a credit card. The man held the card against the sensor and, miraculously, the door clicked open. A second later they were standing in the large, clean receiving area of the museum.

Thomas was astonished. They were in. They had broken into the government's most exclusive museum in less than five minutes. The lights were not on, but the red glow from the exit signs provided fair visibility. Despite the dimly lit hallways, everyone but Thomas seemed to know exactly where they were going. It was as if they had been in the museum before. He had to sprint to reach them. He caught up with them by a new-looking freight elevator. One of the men pulled the top half of the elevator door up, using a canvas strap, and the bottom half of the door disappeared into the floor.

They entered the elevator. Two men slapped large pieces of felt on the edges of the elevator doors, then pulled them shut. There was a nice, quiet thump when the edges of the doors met. Ethan immediately hit a button labeled B and the elevator began its decent into the basement. After fifteen slow seconds, the elevator stopped and, once again, the doors split, half going up and half down into the floor. They stepped out into a wide hallway, clearly part of the new construction.

Ethan motioned toward the two doors across the hallway from the elevator. He tried the knob but it was locked. One of the men stepped forward and held a small device to the keyhole. There was a click, the man turned the knob, and the door swung open, exposing a dark room.

The men advanced slowly, as their eyes adjusted to the dim light provided from the corridor. Fuzzy shapes began to appear, a large conference table, chairs, other doorways along the other walls, and . . . Thomas's heart skipped a beat. There, in the middle of the conference table, was a large black rectangle. And, although his eyes were still adjusting, he could easily tell it was the same size and shape as the crate that held the Ark.

He moved towards it, aware of the other men converging around the table. At any moment he expected a door to open, government agents to flow into the room, M-16's at the ready, but nothing happened. Ethan handed him a Maglight. Thomas knew what to do. It was the only reason they'd risked bringing him.

He glided around the table, to the side that brought him closest to the crate. When he was only inches from it, he shone the light on its corner. He was looking for the 3000-year old, crudely fashioned nails that held the crate together. The wood looked the same. He thought he recognized a large gash on the side of the crate, but not until he saw the dete-riorating spike, the one that might have come from the ancient foundry in Deir el-Medina, did he know that he was seeing the crate that held the Ark. He searched for the corner from which he'd cut his sample. *There it was.* He nodded to Ethan and gave him the universal sign for okay.

The two men assigned to carry the crate had been watching. They immediately moved in front of Thomas, lifted the case from the table, and hurried back to the double doors. Like a perfectly choreographed dance, the doors were waiting open for them. They were through the doors, up the elevator, and out onto the loading dock within two minutes. Thomas checked his watch as they piled into the van. The entire operation, from the time they'd pulled into the loading dock until that moment, had taken five minutes. That meant they had ten minutes to get as close to the airport as possible before the museum cameras recognized that nothing in their sights had moved, triggering the internal alarm.

Thomas knew that the minute the alarm sounded, an emergency process would begin. They would isolate the problem, determine whether it was a false alarm, and then notify George Valmer and whoever else was on their emergency call list. Valmer would probably call DJ. That would take another five to ten minutes.

Ethan had done some additional calculations. If DJ was good, he would have all flights from all area airports detained and searched. The logistics of that would take at least fifteen minutes. Airports had to be called, official explanations provided. So, the total, minimum, they would have to escape would be thirty minutes. It would be a close call. Thomas prayed they weren't delayed getting back to the airport, and that the Lear wasn't surrounded with red flashing lights when they reached it.

CHAPTER **38**

DJ had traveled back to Dulles Airport with the Ark, on the same day that McAlister had given it back to him. He'd personally led the escort from the airport to the National Museum and did not rest until the Ark was placed in Dr. Valmer's private conference room under lock and key. They had not opened the crate. After Dr. Valmer's hand picked Egyptologist had conducted his dating analysis in Mexico, he had ordered the crate to remain locked in the conference room until Monday morning at ten o'clock, when everyone who had been at the original opening would convene to repeat the process. As a precautionary measure, DJ had replaced all of the museum's perimeter guards, the Pinkerton men, with experienced marines. Once the marines were in place, he relaxed. He had the Ark locked in a maximum security museum under the noses of some of the best marines from Desert Storm.

DJ was thirty minutes into a much needed REM sleep when the motel phone beside his bed began its annoying ringing. At first the sound entered his dream, and the red phone was in his canoe, ringing as he paddled across a lake. It was the same lake as the one in the picture on his cubicle wall. But then he noticed that the phone cord ran off the boat into the lake, and this startled him, because he knew he should've had that cord plugged into a cigarette lighter. Shocked at his oversight, at not having a lighter installed in the canoe, DJ finally realized the phone was ringing for real. He sat bolt upright, breathing hard, with a very, very disturbed look on his face.

"What?" he growled into the mouth piece.

"Agent Warrant, this is Oliver Handman, Central Desk security officer at the National Museum of Art. You are third on my trouble call list, sir." The man sounded young and nervous.

"What's the problem?"

"Break-in, sir. We're not sure what, if anything, was taken."

DJ started to lose control. White noise. He couldn't form a thought. Didn't know what to do. He took a deep breath and tried to reel himself back in. *But still, the anger, the unbridled fury, was rising.* He had been in crises before and he knew how to act.

"Son, I have two questions for you, and I need exact answers. Got it?"

"Yes, sir."

"How long has it been since the break-in occurred? If I'm third on your call list, it can't have been long."

"Well, the problem is, sir, it was a professional job. They took out the perimeter men and used high tech camera attachments to freeze the lenses. The cameras aren't set to identify the attachments for twenty minutes. I was alerted about five minutes ago. It has taken me that long to get through my emergency check, re-check procedures, sir."

"So we've lost twenty-five minutes. *Damn it!*" It was McAlister. The sneaky son-of-a-bitch was trying to steal back the Ark!

"Get down to Dr. Valmer's personal conference room in the basement immediately. Find out if there's a large crate on the table."

"Yes, sir, but I have to make two more notification calls first, as part of my calling —"

DJ cut him off. "Forget the procedure. You go *now*, Handman, or you'll be spreading manure with the grounds crew next week! And you run! I'll hold."

"Yes, sir." DJ heard the click of the man's shoes, while he grabbed his cellular phone to dial Elmo. He held the cellular phone against one ear and the hotel phone against the other.

Elmo answered. He was in the room next to DJ's. Right away Elmo sensed a tension in DJ's voice. He could tell there'd been trouble. "Pull up the contact list for stopping flights in and out of D.C.!"

Thirty seconds later, Elmo said, "Got it."

"Start calling. I'll be over in a few minutes to help. I'm waiting for someone on the other line. I want *all* air traffic in and out of Washington D.C. stopped. Have authorities check every plane for Thomas McAlister and the Ark. Send them all his picture."

"I'll start now."

Elmo had detected an odd tone in DJ's voice. He'd known DJ's dislike of McAlister was intense, ever since the day in Mexico when he had hit him without cause. DJ didn't usually do things like that. It seemed that with McAlister DJ had met his match. He had been frustrated for weeks. Never had they had so much trouble with one man. And now, just as soon as they'd gotten the Ark back, they'd lost it again. But this time Elmo had heard something in DJ's voice that he'd never observed before. Fear. Cold fear. If DJ didn't deliver the Ark this time, there was going to be trouble, and trouble for DJ meant trouble for Elmo. He put his computer aside and picked up the phone. He dialed the first number on the screen, the head of Airport security at Dulles.

» » « «

A little over four hours after picking Thomas up at the Dakota, Ethan's men carried the crate out of the hotel's service elevator and down the hallway and into Taylor's apartment. Thomas directed them to the guest bedroom.

Back in the living room, Thomas shook hands with each of the men and then handed Ethan a black Coach briefcase. "The cash is in here, including your bonuses. Thanks for a job well done. Most professional. And thanks for not asking what's in the crate."

Ethan shrugged. "Not my business. Be careful. You have it back, but this is probably not over."

As he was shutting the door, Thomas added, "Nice meeting you, Ethan."

Ethan briefly turned back, smiled, and said, "My name's not Ethan, and we never met."

CHAPTER 39

Thomas had to work quickly. He still had no idea where he was
going to hide the Ark. He was sure that it was only a matter of hours,
minutes even, until DJ found him. It's one thing to steal the wrong treasure, as DJ had originally done. Psychologically, he'd never really had
anything of value. But it's different when the real thing is taken. He'd cher-
ished it. Savored it. Told his superiors about it. This time, the pain of loss
would be tenfold. The result would be an all-out, emotionally driven
search.

While Taylor slept, Thomas spent the next part of the night carefully taking the crate apart, nail by nail, board by board. With the removal
of each board, he became more alert and more curious. He knew the
crate had been built by either the Egyptians or the Olmec. From an archeologist's perspective, it would have been interesting to find only the crate,
with nothing inside. The proper way to disassemble something so rare
was in a laboratory, to ensure the retention of every microscopic sliver
of wood. Thomas documented the structure on graph paper as he disassembled it, including the size of each piece, where the nails had been
placed, and other significant marks and indentations. He didn't like the
fact that he was doing this work in the field but he had to get the Ark
out of its huge, cumbersome crate so that he could hide it.

Both the Maya and the Egyptians were creative cultures, but he had
never seen anything like the clay container that held the Ark. It had
amazed him in Mexico, and it had the same effect on him this time.
Between the clay shell and the Ark was tightly-packed hay. The hay had
held up well over the years and was still thick and protective. As Thomas
removed more boards, he wondered if this hay were from the same fields

as the hay the Egyptians mixed with mud, to be stomped into building blocks by Hebrew slaves.

Moses had enclosed the Ark in a casing of clay, to protect and seal it, and had used the hay as someone would use tissue paper around a gift. He then had it fired in a kiln using only enough heat to set the clay. Ingenious.

After disassembling the crate, Thomas began to gingerly chisel down the ancient clay encasement. It was brittle and fell away easily. Soon he could see the plain wooden sides of the Ark. The acacia grain was clear and beautiful.

He fought off his desire to further examine the Ark. It was getting late and by now DJ would be mobilizing to pay him a visit. Thomas assumed Drew and Taylor's apartments would be among first places DJ would look. He began working faster.

Knowing that he wouldn't be able to preserve the clay casing, he threw archeological training and convention aside and approached its removal like a child on Christmas morning. He worked until six o'clock in the morning. His shoulder was sore, and the bandages, long overdue for a changing, were soaked through with fresh blood. He changed the bandages, fixed himself an early breakfast, took two multi-vitamins and went to sleep.

It was a long, dreamless sleep, from which he was awakened at four that next afternoon by the doorbell. He heard Taylor in the living room and suspecting who it might be, he quickly rose, splashed water on his face, draped a flannel shirt over his shoulders, changed into a worn out pair of jeans, put a baseball cap on his uncombed hair, and went out into the kitchen.

He was pouring milk on cereal as Taylor escorted their visitors into the living room. He heard DJ's deep gravely voice, heavily accented, and grinned to himself.

DJ and two other men had just taken seats in Taylor's exquisitely decorated living room when Thomas entered, cereal bowl in hand. "Special Agent Warrant, I believe. The one who sucker punched me in

Mexico, and had me shot two days ago. I should probably leave the room before you throw a grenade at me." Thomas turned back toward the kitchen.

"No, no, don't leave, Mr. McAlister. Stay. We've got a lot to talk about."

Thomas smiled and said, "Well, that's mighty governmental of you, DJ. Thanks."

Taylor was hovering, enjoying the spectacle immensely. "May I get anyone a drink? I'm absolutely parched."

Everyone accepted at once. It was obvious they wanted drinks so that they could stay longer. Taylor prepared himself an early cocktail, gave Thomas an orange juice, and the government men Diet Cokes.

For several seconds, no one spoke. Finally, DJ broke the silence. "I'm here to pick up what you removed from the National Museum last night, McAlister. If you give it back now, there will be no charges filed."

There was a pregnant pause. A slow smile crept over Thomas's face, and he was about to say something when one of the younger government agents spilled his Diet Coke all over Taylor's glass coffee table while reaching f———

all over the table and threatened to ——— aylor dashed off to the kitchen and ———chief, which he used to stop the ———ned with a stack of hand towels ——— top the spill.

———nmered, clearly embarrassed. "If ——— end me the cleaning bill."

———est that the cleaning bill for the ———s entire annual salary, when he ———o laughter. He belted out a deep, ———)h, my," he finally sighed. "I've ———hen!"

———o damned funny?" DJ asked.

———l cackling, he yelled, "The spill

reminded me of an old joke about government agents. I heard it a long time ago. Trust me, you wouldn't think it humorous."

Thomas gave Taylor credit for coming up with such a rapid response. The old man was still mentally spry. He knew exactly why Taylor was laughing, and it made him smile, too.

DJ looked like he hadn't believed Taylor's answer.

Early that morning, after Thomas had removed the Ark from its crate and clay casing, he'd searched the entire building for a place to hide it. He'd even gone up to the roof, and down to the basement. No place looked secure enough. The Ark was just too big.

While he was eating breakfast, at six o'clock in the morning, he had turned on the television. A home shopping show was selling knives. The second item they offered was the best machete he'd ever seen. Bone-handled, with a hand-forged steel blade made in Spain. He had to have it for Arturo. He had placed his bowl on the coffee table, so that he could search for a pad of paper and a pencil, and when he did, he froze. He'd found his hiding place. Taylor's coffee table was not really a coffee table. It was a large Bedouin trunk on which sat a thick rectangle of glass. It was an artifact transformed into a functional piece of furniture. The Bedouin chest was roughly the same size as the Ark. He and Arturo were the only people who could recognize the Ark. No other human since Moses had seen it.

Thomas had built a fire in Taylor's fireplace and burned the crate and the hay that had held and protected the Ark. It grieved him deeply, but keeping it around would've given him away. Figuring out where to put the pieces of the clay case was the next problem. He ended up putting them into two of Taylor's large Greek urns. The clay looked like it had been put there by an interior decorator.

Finally, he'd taken the glass off the Bedouin chest, put the chest at the foot of his bed, draped some clothes across it, and then replaced the Bedouin chest with the Ark. Topped with the glass piece, it looked like an ordinary piece of furniture. There was very little chance anyone would ever believe the simple coffee table in Taylor's living room was the Ark of the Covenant. It was the perfect hiding place. Literally under the agents' noses.

Taylor, who had noticed that his chest had been replaced by what could only be the Ark when he was cleaning up, was still chuckling and wiping tears from his eyes, when he returned to the living room with a small wet towel, to wipe away the last of the stickiness.

DJ watched him as he worked. He was becoming impatient. "McAlister, I'll say it again. I'm here to get the Ark. I know you took it last night. I have proof."

"I have no idea what you're talking about. I gave you the Ark two days ago, right before you had me shot. If you've lost it, that's your problem. I'm no longer involved."

"Where were the two of you last night?" One of the other men removed a pad from his inside jacket pocket, ready to take notes.

Thomas shook his head, bored with their behavior. "We were right here, watching the video *Fast Times at Ridgemont High*. It's still sitting on the VCR over there." He pointed across the room to the armoire that held the television.

"You can prove that?"

"Yeah, Phoebe Cates has nice breasts."

"I meant, can you prove that you were here?" DJ was not used to insubordinate behavior.

"Not only was I here with Taylor, but I talked on the phone, too."

"To whom?"

"Drew Montgomery." DJ made a note.

Taylor spoke up, "I don't mind a little drop-in entertaining on occasion, gentlemen, but unless you have a search warrant, I'm going to have to ask you to leave. After all, this is my home."

DJ countered. "We do have a warrant issued from a New York District court at 9:00 a.m. this morning. If you don't mind, we'd like to start our search right now."

"Show me the document first, Mr. Warrant. If it's authentic, then by all means search away, gentlemen. But think twice before you break or damage anything. I know former Secretary of State William Bennet well. We went to Harvard together, and he obtained diplomatic permission for me to get into certain African and Asian cities many times while he was in the Senate. He commented on the value of many of my artifacts just last month, when he was here for dinner. I'd hate for him to hear that any of his agents broke anything."

DJ rolled his eyes and said, "Go easy, men."

The three men spread out, each taking a different section of the house. As they searched, Thomas poured himself another orange juice.

Thomas and Taylor relaxed on the couch, while the men searched every room, all over the roof, and in the basement storage areas.

When they were out of the apartment, Taylor expressed his astonishment in a quiet, reserved voice. "That's it, isn't it?" He gazed underneath the glass at the solidly built, weathered box.

Thomas heard a quiver in Taylor's voice. His old friend was deeply moved. "Yes," he said. "That's it. Beautiful in its simplicity, isn't it?"

"It isn't glowing or anything."

"No. It hasn't done anything weird since I've had it."

"The crate?"

"Burned. I saved the interesting clay encasement though." The agents began returning from their fruitless search. "I'll show you more, after they leave."

The men reentered the room. The two younger ones sat down, and began sipping their watery Diet Cokes again. Taylor didn't offer to bring them new ones. DJ continued his search in the living room. He opened cabinets and looked in the armoire. He even got down on his hands and knees to feel under the couches, in case Thomas had disassembled it. Finally, he returned to his chair and sat down. His left knee was literally inches from the Ark.

By law, DJ could ask Thomas anything he wanted. And by law, Thomas didn't have to answer. There were many reasons DJ didn't issue a warrant for his arrest. The government had stolen the Ark in the first place, the government had tried to assassinate McAlister, and an arrest would make everything public. Arrests were matters of public record. Nobody in the government, especially the President and those around him, wanted the public to know that the Ark had been found. DJ tried another line.

"Thomas, look. This problem is not going to go away. I have been instructed to find this thing at all costs. Do you hear me? *At all costs.* Do you know what that means?"

"At what level of government did this authorization come from?"

"The highest," DJ said automatically.

"Then, DJ, I guess you'd better define 'at all costs' for me. Why don't you define it for me, for my friend Taylor, and for the tape recorder I've got hidden in the plant on the coffee table?" Thomas retrieved the recorder and held it up to DJ's mouth. "Okay, we're ready. Exactly what did you mean when you said you needed to find this thing 'at all costs'? Did you mean that to find it, you might have to shoot me a second time, Agent Warrant?" And what did you mean when you said it was authorized at the 'highest level' of government? Does that mean the President?

DJ shook his head. He saw in Thomas's face a man who was never— not now, not ever—going to voluntarily tell him where the Ark was hidden. He knew from his profile that Thomas was stubborn. The records showed that on many occasions, in published material and in public, Thomas had challenged modern archeological theories to the temporary detriment of his career and image. He had a long history of making his stubbornness pay off. No, he was not going to get anything from the man. He would have to resort to other, more covert measures. The only thing that had happened here was that McAlister, by pulling the tape recorder out of the plant, had proven once more that he was a talented opponent. It infuriated DJ.

His face reddened and he glared at Thomas with intense, spine-chilling hatred. With gritted teeth, he hissed, "Fuck you and your tape, McAlister." Then, much louder, eyes still fixed on McAlister, "Let's go, men. It's not here."

Taylor showed them to the door. DJ couldn't resist one last snipe. "I'll see you soon, McAlister."

Thomas was draining the last of his drink when Taylor returned. Taylor switched off the tape player and said, "Congratulations! Good show. What are you going to do now, Thomas?"

"Find Ann."

CHAPTER 40

Thomas had found, lost, and re-claimed the most important, historically significant artifact in not only the history of archeology, but in the
world, and all he could think about was Ann. He had suppressed his
desire to search for her while he was reclaiming the Ark, but now, with
it safely disguised as a coffee table in Taylor's apartment, he could start
his search. The problem was he had absolutely no idea where to begin.

Realizing that she might be working for the government, he was
more intent on finding her than ever. He wanted to get the explanation
he deserved. He knew she loved him. Knew it! And as time passed, he'd
become more and more convinced that she had been forced to shoot
him. Coerced. Faced with no alternative, he believed she'd shot him in
the safest place she could. The only way to find out was to find Ann. This
would be the most important search of his life. Unfortunately, this time,
there was no riddle to guide him.

Thomas spent the next few days roaming Manhattan, wandering
from one favorite place to the next. Sometimes he thought of Ann, and
sometimes his mind was clear, only reflecting the images around him,
like Jimmy Stewart after Kim Novak's death in the movie *Vertigo*.

After four days of relatively aimless meandering, he found himself
breakfasting at the Plaza. Sipping real orange juice and eating improba-
bly fluffy pancakes. Slowly, almost imperceptibly, he was beginning to
form a plan. His search would start with basics. Ann had given him her
full name, where she'd grown up, and where she went to both undergraduate and graduate school. If all three were bogus, he would scan
graduate school rosters for archeology graduate students who had special-

ized in the Maya. One thing he knew was that she was a trained Mayanologist. Her knowledge had been too deep not to be real.

After breakfast, Thomas wandered for hours until he reached Union Square Café. Over perfectly prepared orange roughy, he realized that Ann had told him very little about herself. Had it been intentional, or was it his fault for not showing more interest?

Towards the end of the day, he stopped at the best tavern in Manhattan, PJ Clarke's. He sat at the bar stool closest to the old phone booth. He'd been walking all day, and it felt good to sit and relax. He recognized the bartender as one who had been there many years and without a word spoken a Bass Ale appeared in front of him. He nodded, and the bartender moved away, aware, like any bartender worth a damn, that he wanted to think rather than talk.

The last couple of days Thomas had been trying to play back every conversation he had ever had with Ann. He wanted to remember every detail, no matter how insignificant. It was hard, because in trying to recount the conversations, he kept seeing images of her face. He remembered thinking she was beautiful from the moment he'd seen her, after he had fallen on the cactus, when she had crouched over him to remove the spines. Even in that reflected light he'd been able to tell that her face was unusually perfect.

Later, they'd argued about who had fallen in love first, each saying that the other had been first. But, ultimately, late one night, in a voice as soft as a child's, Ann had admitted that she knew she'd fallen first. That something inside her had clicked at the bar that first night.

Because of their limited time together, and his desire to know her, he realized he remembered most everything she'd ever told him. And now, with a second pint of Bass in front of him, he was trying to remember the four or five specific things she'd told him that still remained elusive. They would float up, just out of reach, drifting close, before moving quickly away again. He wasn't even sure that any of these elusive tidbits would help. They might be no more than trivia. But he had to recall them. They might lead somewhere.

He tried thinking about what topics they might relate to. Nothing. He tried not thinking about them. Nothing. He tried using techniques that had helped him remember things in the past; chronological or sequential recognition, context and association. Finally he did recall one of them. In Phoenix, they had rented a Land Rover Discovery identical to the one Ann already owned, to evade whomever was looking for them. Ann had used a travelers check rather than a credit card. At the time, it was no big deal, but now it was a potential lead. He could return to the car rental company and ask to see the check. Maybe he'd learn that it was issued under a different name.

He had one more beer and, feeling slightly buzzed, decided to end the day at the Met. Several artifacts from his digs had become part of the museum's permanent collection so it held a special place in his heart. He also wanted to get a look at his favorite painting, the one he'd been looking at before going to the exchange a few days earlier, the *Joan of Arc,* by Dupais.

He reached the Museum and found that it was closed due to a VIP Behind the Scenes party. People dressed in formal evening wear were filing in. This was a night for large contributors to go behind the scenes and see the museum holdings that were not normally on display.

Thomas kept his Archeological Foundation Member Card in his wallet. It entitled him entrance into any museum anywhere in the world for free. The Met let him right in. He was wearing jeans, but luckily he'd taken a sport coat before leaving Taylor's earlier in the day.

The museum was only moderately crowded, and Thomas moved around easily. As he made his way closer to *Joan of Arc*, he floated slowly through the crowd, observing the Manhattanites who had bothered to pay enough to become VIPs. Very important people in the eyes of the Met. They were an excited, severely pretty, talkative group. Dressed to whatever the height of fashion was in their social circle. Thomas liked looking at them. They were fun to watch. Trying so hard. Knowing so little about the objects surrounding them.

He reached *Joan of Arc* and sat on the bench directly in front of her.

He became immediately absorbed in the painting, picking up where he left off the day he traded the Ark for Ann. It was a painting that he'd gazed at countless times, but he had new and different observations each time. This evening, his eyes were drawn again to the colors; the muted flowers, the red apples on the tree behind the main subject. Apples, spaced sparingly so as not to overwhelm. They were perfect.

Thomas looked at one apple, directly above and to the right of Joan of Arc's head. It had the deepest color of them all. It was not really red, but rather a deep, muted tone. Not maroon either. But what then? Thomas challenged himself to come up with a name for the color. He tried to remember all the reds in the large crayon box he'd had as a child. Not red. Not maroon. Not burnt sienna. Not fuchsia.

It was the color of something he'd seen recently. *But what?*

Then, at lightening speed, it hit him, and in remembering, he brought back one of the elusive memories of Ann that he'd been trying to recall all day! The color of the apple was the same as the deep red Mexican Hot Sauce that Ann had used in Mexico. The one she carried in her purse, that he had tried the first morning when he'd been so hungover. It was her favorite. She was a hot sauce fanatic. She had made a point of saying how she always carried her own bottle because the brand was so hard to find. She'd said she liked the hot sauce so much, she ordered it by the case from the distributor.

Thomas smiled. His first lead. It was such a minor fact she didn't even catch herself. Never even regretted saying it. But it was the single most important thing she had ever told him. It was the only mistake she'd made in what had been a perfect ruse.

Thomas's stomach tingled as he walked back to Taylor's apartment through Central Park. He had a spring in his step. *This could be it. But, damn it! I can't remember the name of the hot sauce distributor. She'd said it. I remember her saying it.* He could picture her reading it off the back of the bottle she had taken out of her purse. *What was it?*

He called Arturo and explained that he may have figured out a way to track down Ann. Arturo like the idea. He didn't remember the brand of hot sauce that Ann used but he was able to provide the phone number of the Hotel Mercado. They had used the same brand. He then called the hotel and got Jose on the line. It was good to hear his voice again. It brought back memories of falling in love with Ann and of searching for the Ark. He described the bottle of hot sauce and told Jose he needed the address listed on the label. His pulse quickened as he waited. He was getting so close, much sooner than he'd ever thought possible.

Please have it, Jose!

"Senor McAlister, I have a bottle right here in my hand. Are you ready?"

Thomas breathed a deep sigh of relief. Thank God. "Yes, ready, Jose."

After writing down the address, he repeated it back to Jose, letter for letter. Salsa Picante, Hot Sauce. Distributed by Farmer Bros. Co., Phoenix. It was too late in the day to call the company now. He would call tomorrow.

Taylor was in the living room having a night cap when Thomas came out of the guest bedroom. "What are you having there?"

"White Russian. I decided against Cognac tonight. You look like you've already had a few. Up for one more?"

"You have to ask me if I'm up for a White Russian? Pour away, my friend. Plenty of ice."

"How was your day?"

"I had a revelation!"

Taylor shot him a concerned look. "You might not want to use that word, while standing so close to the Ark of the Covenant."

"You're right," Thomas said glancing nervously at the coffee table. "Anyway. I figured out how I'm going to find Ann!" He took a long sip of the drink, sank onto the couch, and explained it to Taylor.

"You're basing your entire search on hot sauce?"

"The whole thing," Thomas said confidently. "I just hope the company will give me her address. Otherwise, I'll have to break in to their offices to get it."

"Again? Another break in?"

"Yep."

"Well, at least you can be sure of less security."

Thomas grinned. "I don't know. It's was pretty good hot sauce."

CHAPTER **41**

The next day, when Taylor was out running errands, Thomas called Farmer Brothers.

He had no idea what Ann's real name or address might be, but he thought he knew a way to get both of them. He would act like he didn't know exactly what kind of sauce he was looking for. That way he might be able to get the person to read the names of the people who had ordered it to him. He didn't know what he was listening for, but intuition told him he'd know her real name when he heard it.

The receptionist answered on the third ring and transferred him to the sales rep who handled special requests. "Mary Jean. How may I help you?"

"Hi, Mary Jean. My name is Thomas McAlister and I think I could use your help with something."

"I'll try my best."

"My fiancée loves a product your company distributes. She likes it so much she orders it by the case and carries a bottle in her purse. I always tease her about it, but I'd like to buy some for her as a surprise. I'm afraid I don't know the exact name of the hot sauce. Do you make more than one kind? I do know that she's ordered some within the past six months. Would that help?"

"Many people buy our products directly from us, especially when they purchase by the case. I have one old gal calls me every month. Says she hates to grocery shop. Did you say you didn't know the product name?"

"All I know is that it is a hot sauce. She uses it every morning on eggs."

"That's probably our Salsa Picante. You say it's a hot sauce, right?"

"Yes, the stuff is really hot. She made me try some once and it burnt my mouth."

"We distribute two versions. Medium and the Hot. Do you know which one she likes?"

"No. I'm not sure which." Thomas continued. "Do you get a lot of special orders?"

"Enough to keep me busy here full time. I do special event orders and consumer orders, too. Just taking consumer orders takes 40 percent of my time."

"That's a lot. You must be very busy. Let me ask you. Is there a way you could go through the small orders for those two hot sauces for the last six months? If you can quickly read off the names of the women who purchased, I'll tell you when I hear her name. You do keep track of that information don't you, Mary Jean?" Thomas knew Ann used the Hot. But he didn't know what name she used. He needed Mary Jean to read the names.

"Yes, of course. We keep all the records right here. I created the system myself. They don't have me on a computer yet. They offered to get me on one of the old ones, but I told them no. I told them I'd keep hand writing orders and filing them myself. I asked them, what if the electricity goes out while I'm on the computer? What if the computer goes on the blink and we lose all our records? No, I keep all files myself."

"That makes perfect sense."

"I got these files by product. I'll start with the Hot, and read you the names, from the most recent to six months ago. You tell me if you hear her name. Okay?"

"Yes, that will be fine. I can't begin to thank you. My fiancée is going to be so surprised."

After listening to four months of names, he hit pay-dirt. An Ann *Davenport* had purchased two cases four and a half months ago. That had to be his Ann. Good technique. Use an undercover name that rhymed with your real name and you'll be more likely to respond immediately, without giving yourself away.

"That's her! I knew she ordered from you!"

"I guess she likes the Salsa Picante. Too hot for me. Would you like to buy a case then?"

"Oh, yes, I definitely want to buy a case. And Mary Jean, can you give me the address she used for the delivery? I want to make absolutely sure we've got the right Ann Davenport."

"You want your own fiancé's address?"

"No, of *course* I know where she lives, but I want to make sure we've selected the *same* Ann Davenport. You never know. I don't want to buy her the wrong kind, or worse, buy some other Ann Davenport a case."

"It's against policy to give addresses over the phone, but you sound nice enough. You're not one of them serial killers, are you?" She laughed nervously at the thought.

"No, ma'am. I can promise you that."

"We sent it to 12 Magnolia Lane, New Haven, Connecticut." Thomas smiled and shook his head. Yale! She'd gone to Yale! No wonder she was such a strong Mayanologist! She studied under Michael Coe.

"That's my Ann. Thank you so much, Mary Jean! You don't know how much I appreciate this."

"Don't you want to place an order for the hot sauce?"

"Oh yes, yes, sorry." He gave her Taylor's name and address and thanked her again.

So Ann was Ann Davenport and she lived in New Haven! She was a Yale graduate and probably taught there! Now, with the sudden knowledge of her location, he had to decide if he really wanted to confront her.

CHAPTER 42

By the end of May, Thomas had been watching Ann for two weeks. The first time he saw her, walking out of her house on a beautiful New Haven morning, he almost got sick. He hadn't anticipated such a strong physical reaction. But seeing her, being physically close to her, brought back the strong emotional and physical attraction. When a man followed her out of the house, and kissed her good-bye, it was too much to take. His stomach knotted, convulsed, and he put his head down on the edge of the steering wheel, feeling physically sick, from being in love and knowing that something had gone terribly, uncontrollably wrong.

After a day of observing her, he discovered someone else following her. After three days, he determined that the man she had kissed was living with her. After two weeks he understood her schedule. Ann's routine was out of the house by seven every morning, always followed by the white Ford Taurus, driven by the man who was tailing her. She would park in the faculty lot at Yale, drop by a bakery for a bagel and coffee, sometimes a chocolate donut and coffee, and proceed to her small professorial office on Yale's campus. On Mondays, Wednesdays, and Fridays, she taught a class called "The Ancient Maya," at nine and ten o'clock in the morning, and again at one o'clock in the afternoon. On Tuesdays and Thursdays, her Archeology, Astronomy, and Mathematics course was at eight and eleven in the morning. When not in class, she usually stayed in her office, reading or grading, then left for home around four o'clock. She shopped for groceries on weekends and usually cooked at night. At least Thomas thought she did, because she and the man rarely went out.

The people who were following her worked in three shifts. Morning

Guy came at six and was relieved at three by Afternoon Woman. She followed Ann home and was relieved at eleven by Night Guy. The followers never talked to each other. One would drive up, and the other would pull away. After close observation, Thomas realized there was only one time when she wasn't being watched. Morning Guy usually left her every Monday, Tuesday, and Wednesday between nine and ten, to eat breakfast. Sometimes he went to the bakery she frequented, and then his detours were short, but more often he would go to a nearby Denny's for something more substantial. Thomas sat a few booths away from him one day, to get a closer look at him. He was definitely wearing a gun, and was probably a government agent.

These little breakfast trips gave Thomas an hour or so to get to her. He began plotting a way to get her out of class. What worried him was that Morning Guy didn't always go to breakfast. And even when he did, if he went to the bakery, it only took about twenty minutes. In the end, Thomas decided to play the numbers and assume Morning Guy would not start a diet on the morning of his attempt.

Since there was so little time involved, he would need to learn Yale's process for pulling a teacher out of class. Did they use an intercom or a messenger? If they used an intercom, she would be alone on her trips to the phone and back. If Yale used teachers assistants to take messages to faculty, she would walk to the phone with the messenger and only be alone on her way back to the classroom.

Thomas positioned himself at a phone bank between the classroom of a teacher he didn't know, named Teal, and the main office. He placed a call on his cell phone and told the receptionist that he had a private, emergency phone call for Dr. Teal. Thirty seconds later, a young female graduate assistant headed toward Room 4-C, Teal's classroom. About a minute later, Teal and the assistant hurried down the same hallway, on their way to the office. Thomas hung up and waited. Two minutes later, Teal returned to his class, visibly frustrated that no one had been on the line. Good. The school did not use an intercom system. He would get Ann on her way back to her classroom.

Thomas surveyed the path between the office and Ann's classroom during her Monday schedule and found a few opportunities. There was a classroom that was not used at nine, but it had a window on the door. There was a supply closet, but it was kept locked, and there was a men's bathroom. The bathroom was out; anyone could walk in at anytime. The supply closet was locked. The classroom was his best bet. It was relatively small, with windows on one side and the door on the other. With the lights off, no one would be able to see into the room.

He planned the ambush for the following Monday. All campuses, even Yale, were a little somber on Mondays. Hopefully, Morning Guy would eat a particularly large, greasy breakfast that day.

Over the weekend, he made plans. It was difficult, because he didn't know how Ann would react when she saw him. If she answered all of his questions to his satisfaction, maybe he could leave and go back to New York. That wasn't what he wanted, though. He wanted her back. He now realized that if she had been brainwashed, or coerced into shooting him, there might still be a chance for the two of them to trust each other again.

Monday came all too soon. He dressed like a student, in jeans, loafers, an old polo shirt, and his Arizona baseball cap. He drove to the school early and parked a few blocks away.

From his parking place, he walked to a park bench where he could observe the bakery Ann frequented. She arrived on schedule and just like every other day, the minute he saw her, his throat constricted and his breathing became shallow. Through the bakery window he watched her reading the morning paper while she ate, then watched her take the short walk back to her office.

Thomas checked his watch. At exactly nine he knew she was beginning her Monday curriculum. He remained on the bench and waited for Morning Guy. At nine-twenty, right on time, Morning Guy walked into Denny's. Perfect.

Thomas went directly to the vacant classroom and took out his cell phone. He dialed the number for Yale's Department of Anthropology and told them that there was an emergency message for Ann Davenport, and that he must speak with her immediately. Like clockwork, he heard the graduate assistant rush past his classroom to pull Ann out of class. He heard the two of them walk briskly back to the office. He caught a glimpse of her worried face.

Thomas moved into position. He quietly opened the door to the empty classroom again and left it partially open. He took a small mirror from his pocket and angled it just right, so that he could watch the hallway for Ann's return.

His heart quickened. He felt like a kid picking his date up on prom night. *What am I doing here? I haven't seen her in weeks! I'm the last person she expects to see. What if she screams and fights?* Suddenly, he considered canceling the plan. Ann could have contacted him through Arturo if she'd wanted to. She hadn't. She didn't even care to know if he was alive. For all he knew she had a husband, maybe even a child.

She rounded the corner at the end of the hall! Aside from her, the hall was empty. *I can't do this! He closed his mouth and took a deep relaxing breath. I have to do this, or I'll never rest again. I love her and I know she loves me. Someone made her shoot me.*

He could hear the brittle click of her heels on the marble floor as she got closer to the doorway he was hiding in. He pulled his mirror back, and then catastrophe struck. He held the mirror around the edges, between thumb and forefinger. As he stuffed the mirror into the front pocket of his Levi's his thumb caught on the little watch pocket that all Levi's have, just inside the right pocket. He squeezed his fingers together but rather than grasp the mirror more firmly, it shot out of his hand onto the silent marble, ten yards in front of Ann. The mirror bounced and shattered, glass spreading out in a circular motion from the point of impact.

The sound of her footsteps stopped. Thomas broke out into a sweat. Instinctually, he moved backward and flattened himself against the wall of the class room. Frozen.

Silence.

He heard Ann take two steps. She was trying to figure out what had hit the floor in front of her. She could see the open door of the class-room and that it was dark inside. She began to get frightened. Classes were still in session but the hallway was quite and deserted. Someone had obviously been waiting for her. Watching her. It began to make sense, because there had been no one on the phone call she'd gone to answer.

Reluctantly admitting to himself that his surprise attack had failed, Thomas pushed himself away from the wall and moved into the doorway. As he walked into view, the bill of his baseball cap obscured his face.

Slowly, he raised his head. "It's me, Annie." Then, like deja-vu, he saw that Ann had a gun drawn and pointed right at his heart. He remained calm. He had been through this once before, and he had lived. He looked down at her index finger, the one on the trigger, and it was not yet white from the pressure of pulling. Not yet.

"Are you going to shoot me again, Annie?"

Ann had never been more shocked in all her life. Tears immediately flooded her eyes and spilled down her cheeks. Her gun began shaking convulsively. Still trembling, she lowered the gun and started to collapse. Thomas caught her before she reached the floor.

He grabbed her around the waist and pulled her into the classroom, closing the door with one foot. He pulled her close and buried his face in her hair. She was shivering and he held her even tighter, as if there was something broken inside of her that he was trying to squeeze back together. Now he knew she still loved him. He could feel it.

She was crying uncontrollably and he worried that she would be heard by someone in another classroom.

"Oh darling!" She kissed him, her face wet with tears. "I'm so glad you came. So glad you're all right."

"I had to come, Annie. You've never left my mind. Ever."

She buried her face in his neck, and then pulled her head back so that she could see his face. She gazed into his eyes, knocked the hat off his head, and vigorously ran her fingers through his hair, as if he weren't real.

"You must go, Thomas! They're watching me all the time. Even now.

They're out there somewhere. Please go, darling! For me."

"Don't worry, Annie. I've been here for two weeks, watching them watch you. We're safe right now, until about ten o'clock."

That reminded Ann what a careful planner Thomas was. It was what she needed. "Thank God you're all right, Thomas. I didn't realize how much I missed you, how much I needed you . . . ." Her voice trailed off, as her lips approached his. If she's lying, she's the best actor alive, Thomas thought.

She kissed him firmly, forcing their lips together by putting her hand on the back of his head. He understood that underneath the calm relaxed exterior he'd witnessed the past two weeks there was a person under enormous stress.

They kissed with increasing passion and Ann pressed her body into his. Without another word spoken, Thomas knew what she wanted. He wanted it, too. His hand found the edge of her skirt and he slid it up on to her hips. He swung her around so that her back was against the blackboard, resting her partly on the chalk holder that jutted out from the wall. Her vice-like grip around his neck held her perfectly suspended against the wall, legs spread, craving union.

It was as if they'd never met, yet known each other forever. They were completely in tune to each other's needs and preferences, kissing wildly, tongues on fire, thrashing; hands exploring. They were meeting again, and in the most personal way, telling each other that they were still in love.

They were done, spent, leaning heavily on the blackboard, still coupled, when suddenly the class bell sounded, ending the nine o'clock period. It was ten o'clock! What had seemed like five minutes had consumed forty-five. Morning Guy would be back any minute . . . *if he wasn't already*!

"Oh, my God!" Ann said, frantically arranging her skirt. "My class!"

Thomas picked up her panties and shoved them into his pocket. Ann grabbed the gun, which she had set on the chalkboard ledge, and slid it back into a holster under her skirt.

"Who's that you're living with?" Thomas asked.

"My brother." An acceptable answer.

"You have to go, now!" Thomas said.

"I know! I'm going to cancel my nine o'clock class on Wednesday at the last minute. I'll meet you here, a few minutes after nine. Okay?"

"We have a lot to talk about, Ann."

"More than you know." Without another word, she rushed from the room.

Neither one of them saw Morning Guy when they exited the room.

They met the following Wednesday in the same classroom, and there Ann explained the unbelievable turn of events that had ultimately led her to shoot Thomas.

She was Dr. Ann Davenport, an expert in Mayan studies. She had been hired by the FBI a year ago, after she had finished graduate school, as part of a program designed to assist Mexican authorities in stopping the looting and export of pre-Columbian treasures into the United States.

"In March," she explained, "a group of high-ranking government officials called my program director, and eight other women working on my program, into a conference room in the San Antonio office. They said that they had data that indicated one of the largest importers of illegal pre-Columbian antiquities was moving into Mexico and that he was targeting a very old site. A crown jewel. We were all upset that someone would attempt it, but excited about the opportunity to stop it. It validated our jobs. The officials didn't know what site would be targeted; in fact, they didn't know much about archeology at all. They just knew the approximate date of the site."

"They told us the treasure this importer was seeking would have been buried around 1300 or 1350 BC, give or take 100 years, and they asked us for our opinions on what the richest and most active sites were during that time frame. They gave us two other criteria. The site had to be the dominant center of the culture for that period, and it had to be within fifty miles of the eastern coastline. We all agreed it had to be Olmec. They wanted the ten most likely locations. They were all in Veracruz, and we ranked them one through ten. Then they assigned each of us to one of the locations. We were to go to the site and set up camp, as though we were conducting a minor excavation. They placed me at El Manati, the one we agreed was most likely to be the target. You know the rest of that part of it."

"That's what you were doing when I saw you at the site that night that I fell on the cactus?"

"Yes. No one had any way of knowing if this renowned thief was going to show up at their site. The officials told us they'd be watching all ten sights. Of course the thief was you, but none of us knew that, nor did we know that the search you were conducting was perfectly legitimate. Once we made contact, we were to try to befriend the thief and, if possible, assist him in his work. And . . . well . . . you showed up on my hill."

Ann leaned forward and kissed Thomas. He didn't respond. She backed away, brushed a strand of hair from her cheek, and continued.

"In the beginning, the assignment sounded dangerous, but I was happy to do it. We all were. The way these government officials explained it, we were going after a known criminal. When you showed up, you looked like you could be a smuggler, so I thought you were. After all, you were sneaking up on me in the dark. That night at the bar, when Jose said your name, I was shocked. Thomas McAlister. You weren't a site robber. You were a credible, well-known, highly respected archeologist. The officials had lied to us." She paused. "It was the first of many lies."

Ann sighed again. "When I found out who you were, I started to get suspicious of them and their motives. I realized I didn't know any of them and, in retrospect, I realized they'd been very vague about the whole operation. Something was wrong. Once I learned you were working with Arturo, that cemented it for me. I had been fed faulty information, and I was being used. Arturo is a living legend among Mexican archeologists. After that first night, when you'd gotten drunk and confided in me about your firing from the university and your discovery of the Ark, I stopped being on their side. I swear to you, this is the truth, Thomas. Everything I did and said to you from that point forward was real. My love for you, my excitement over your project . . . all real."

Thomas shook his head in doubt. He turned to stare out the windows on the far side of the classroom.

"I can prove it," Ann said, clutching his arm. "Listen to me. After you located the Ark and we went back to Arizona for supplies, they asked me where the treasure was located. They asked if we'd found the right spot? They'd been watching from a distance the whole time. While we were away from the site, they were going to dig it up themselves and take it. I didn't tell them that you'd actually located the position. I told them you needed more *detection* equipment. Not *extraction*! They would have gone in and dug it up with bulldozers, if I'd told them you'd found it."

"Arturo was there," Thomas said, his voice flat.

"Thomas, one man wouldn't stop these people. We're talking about the FBI. You remember the number of agents that swooped down on us. I kept telling them the deal was off. I told them that they had it wrong. You weren't stealing. You and Arturo were respectable archeologists. At first, I thought they would listen, then I realized they didn't care. I didn't tell them that I was in love with you, but they guessed. They saw us on the roof of the hotel that night. I told them I would have nothing more to do with any of their plans. Said I would tell you about their plans if they didn't leave me alone. I wanted to be with you and go back to my old job, which I loved. That was when they took my mother."

"What? Say that again."

"They took my m-mother." Her mouth firmed and Thomas could tell she was close to tears.

"They kidnapped your mother?" Thomas asked, in true disbelief. "Your employer, the *government*? Come on, Annie, you expect me to believe *that*?"

"They still have her, Thomas! They claim *they* didn't actually do it but that they were in contact with the group that did. Either way, I know Hargrove orchestrated it. They threatened that this volatile group would kill her, if I didn't shoot you. They were desperate, Thomas. They know how suspicious, how cautious you are, and I was all they had! That's why I . . . s-shot you. They *made* me do it." Tears welled in her eyes. "They said they'd kill my mom and get my brother next." Her lower lip began to tremble. "I didn't know what to do. Thomas, they are all the family I have." She started to cry. "I t-tried to do it in a place that wouldn't . . . h-hurt you."

"That day, when we took the Ark out and they came and stole it . . . I didn't know they were going to take me, too. I thought they'd have what they wanted, my mother would be okay, and you and I would be together. That's all that mattered to me. They took me forcefully that day. Thomas, please believe me. I swear it on my life."

Thomas asked. "Why would they take you? As far as they were concerned, they had what they needed. They thought they had the real Ark. Why would they still need to take you?"

"I-I guess they thought they might still need me. I don't know."

"What did you say? Didn't you fight them?"

"They said they would only keep me from you until everything settled down. They told me it would probably be a week. Then they found out they had confiscated a fake! They were shocked. DJ Warrant was livid. He had been humiliated. This was the first case he had ever lost, he said. I laughed at them. I told them they could never outsmart you. But they said they could, because they had me. I was their leverage. I told them I would *never* help them. And that's when they took my mother." Ann's voice lowered to a whisper. "I still don't know where she is, Thomas. They let her call me once a week, so that I know she's all right. All she ever says is, 'Do what they say, Annie. Do what they say.'"

Tears spilled down Ann's cheeks again. "I couldn't go back. So I came back here to teach. We're all taking a breather, I suppose. I just don't know if I can ever go back, knowing what that agency is capable of."

"They still have her? Your mother? And you have no idea where she is?"

"I've been a good little government employee, especially after obediently shooting you. So they're bringing her back Saturday. At least that was the plan. The latest I heard was that they think you've stolen the Ark from them *again*. They're not altogether sure you were involved, because the job was professionally handled. Some of them don't believe you'd be capable of such a difficult heist, especially injured, but nevertheless, they're not sure . . . so they're watching me. They're telling me they might need me again. Oh, Thomas, are you sure they're not watching *you*?"

"I took some pretty evasive moves before I left New York."

Thomas was glad that she hadn't asked him if he was the one who had stolen the Ark. It showed him that she truly didn't care about the Ark, only about him. If she was still working for the government, she would want to know.

Her story was believable. They'd worked her into a very tight spot. She'd do any thing to protect her mother. He trusted her. Almost fully. Only it was hard for him to forget the cold look in her eyes when she'd pointed the gun and pulled the trigger. So, he would wait and watch and listen to her, before giving up that last glimmer of doubt. As long as she didn't ask him questions about the location of the Ark, he felt they might be all right.

He understood what had happened. He saw the psychology behind every action. First, she was doing her job. Then, she was keeping her mother alive. Yes, she had shot him, but as despicable as that action was, it hadn't been lethal. If you looked at that act alone, objectively, she had tried to minimize the damage by aiming for a safe area of his body. And he'd heard her declare that he was dead, when she knew he probably wasn't.

"Listen, Ann," he said. "We have to get out of here. Far away, while things cool down."

"I want that more than anything, darling, but I have to make sure my family is safe. I will not leave them in danger."

"If we all want to stay alive and be left alone, then your brother and mother are going to have to go away, too. We all have to disappear. Our government will not give up until they have what they want or can't afford to keep looking for it anymore. We need to disappear until they decide to re-deploy resources. On your way to class on Friday, stick your head in this classroom. I'll be here. Give me an envelop with three photos of you, three of your mother, and three of your brother. Head shots. Okay?"

"Are you going to get us fake identification?"

"Yes, licenses, passports, and credit."

"All right. I can do that. After that, when will we meet again?"

"Next Wednesday. One week from today. I'll need you for a full hour. Can you have your students do some work at the library or something? "

"Yes, but I won't tell them until that day, in case the agent following me has befriended one of them. I'll send them to do some research. They'll love me. Half of them will go to a bar." She paused, then said, "Are you sure you can pull this off, Thomas? I mean, you're a great planner, but you're an archeologist, not an international spy."

"I can do it. I'm becoming an expert at making things disappear."

She tilted her head and smiled at him. He would have loved to know what she was thinking. Was she wondering if he was the person who'd made the Ark disappear from the National Museum?

CHAPTER 44

Wednesday, Ann brought the pictures. Thursday, Thomas sent them to Drew, who was having Ethan make the new ID cards. Thomas had the thick, comforting envelope in his pocket the following Wednesday, when he shut the door to their classroom meeting place.

"Did the government return your mother?" He already knew the answer because he'd continued to watch her, but he asked anyway.

"Yes, thank God. She's very stressed, mostly from worrying about me, but they didn't treat her badly."

"They're not good at torturing people. Just killing them."

"They call that wet work." It was disconcerting to Thomas that she knew that.

"Now listen closely, Ann. You can't write this down and you need to remember all of it. Your brother and your mother are going to an island off the coast of Washington state called Whidbey Island. It's a beautiful place. I've arranged for them to use a nice house for the next six months. They leave next Wednesday morning. The plane reservations are made." He handed her the tickets, and the new identification cards. "This is important. Tell them they should do nothing to prepare for the trip, other than pack items they already own. They are not to buy anything new. That is so important. It would tip off anyone who was watching them. They should pack the night before or day of the trip, and call a cab an hour before going to the airport. They can buy whatever else they need when they get there."

"What about money?" Ann asked.

"The house is covered. There's an insured car in the garage. I've included passports, and a bank account number for a checking account in both of their names. They've got a Visa card for the account. There's plenty of money for them to live on. You and I will be able to watch the balance and the transactions on the Internet, to make sure everything is going all right."

"You've been busy," Ann said. "I don't know how you do it."

"Are you clear on everything? Buy nothing, do nothing, until Wednesday. Call a cab, go to the airport, get on a plane, and have fun. Your mom will love the place and your brother's career is portable. All a writer needs is a laptop."

"You're amazing. As usual, you've thought of everything. I wish they could meet you. They would love you as much as I do. What about us, Thomas?"

"We leave on Wednesday, too. We'll meet here at nine in the morning, as usual. From that point on, you'll have to trust me."

"You mean you're not going to tell me where we're going? You don't trust me, do you?

"Annie, I trust you, but you're vulnerable. Between today and next Wednesday, they could discover I'm in New Haven and sequester your mother again. They could force you to tell them where we're going. They could decide to give you a shot of sodium pentothal, and ask you a series of questions about my whereabouts and plans. What you don't know, you can't tell them. Let me handle this for us. It will be safer."

"Okay, Thomas. It's reasonable. I'll be here next Wednesday. What should I bring?"

Thomas stroked her cheek. "Just your pretty little self, Annie. If you want, you can slip a string bikini in your purse."

They met the following Wednesday, in the same classroom. Thomas hugged Ann tightly, then gave her sunglasses and a scarf to tie over her head, so that she wouldn't be as recognizable. Without taking time to look around, they walked briskly to his car. Thomas was counting on no changes in the routine of the agent watching her.

Thomas drove west on highway 34 for the next hour. They passed a sign that said Dansbury City Limits. He slowed considerably, looking for a specific turnoff. When he found it, he drove half a mile and then pulled into a grass parking lot next to a Quonset hut. It wasn't until Ann slid out of the car that she heard the humming of a single-engine airplane.

Thomas left the key to the car under the floor mat, and they ran to the plane. As he rounded the corner of the building, he half expected to see a wall of government men blocking their getaway. But that wasn't the case. The only person watching was Arturo, who had flown up from Mexico with his brother Esteban, in their Cessna. They would fly Thomas and Ann across the border. A sub-machine gun was casually slung over Arturo's shoulder, but there was no one in fast pursuit, no one to challenge their departure. They had apparently made a clean getaway. Thomas shook hands with Arturo, Ann hugged him, and they climbed into the airplane.

With little hesitation, Esteban whipped the plane around so that it was facing into the breeze, and throttled up for takeoff. Ten hours later, after stopping at a small strip in Alabama to refuel, they pulled into Arturo's driveway. They planned to stay with Arturo one night, before continuing to their final destination. Maria had prepared a celebratory dinner.

The last time they were all together was before they'd gone back to El Manati to get the Commandments. Although it had only been about a month ago, those early days had assumed a special dream-like quality for Thomas. They discussed what Arturo had been doing since they left his country. He'd been visited by government agents twice: once before Thomas traded the Ark for Ann, and once after it was taken from the National Museum. He said they hadn't been around recently.

Ann was curious. "How did you know when the Ark was stolen, Arturo?"

"Thomas told me."

"How did you know, Thomas?"

"DJ Warrant visited me at the apartment I was staying at in New York. I was staying there as a guest, until my shoulder healed. He accused me of stealing it." Thomas changed the subject, "Arturo, any feel for whether or not you're being watched?"

"No, no, my friend, I wouldn't have let you come down if I thought I were. Their visits to me were always at the university in Mexico City. They do not know of this ranch, because it is in Maria's name and married women in Mexico do not take their husband's surname. I don't believe they would bother to do the research, since I am not their target."

With that, the tension dropped. They drank margaritas and ate Maria's incredible dinner. She'd fixed enchiladas, beans, and rice because she knew they were Thomas's favorites. They did their best to avoid topics like the Ark, the government and, for the most part, even archeology.

Near the end of the meal, Ann turned to Arturo. "You've got to tell me, Arturo. How did you and Thomas ever mange to switch the fake Ark for the real one?"

It was one of those odd moments, when everyone has stopped talking and, in the silence, the question seemed glaringly loud and out of place. Arturo glanced at Thomas who said, "What was that, Ann?"

Ann shrugged. "It's just something I've always wondered about, during these past weeks. How did you switch the fake for the real? It must've been incredible to coordinate and plan. I was with you almost every minute, darling, and I didn't know about any of it. I didn't even suspect."

Thomas didn't like Ann's interest in the Ark, but realized he was probably being overly sensitive. It was a legitimate question. One she had probably been wondering about, ever since she had been taken. With a beer bottle in his hand, he pointed to Arturo and nodded.

Arturo said, "Thomas deserves all the credit. Somehow, and I still don't know how, he knew we were either being watched or followed. Maybe he's the most paranoid guy in the world, I don't know!"

They all laughed, and as Ann took a drink, she studied Thomas through her bangs, which had drifted down over her face. *Which was it, Thomas? Did you know? Or are you the most paranoid man in the world?*

Arturo continued. "From the minute he found the Ark, he knew he wanted to take it secretly and replace it with a fake. Maybe he even knew *before* he found it. I don't know. When he went back to Arizona with you, he had a man craft a copy, using exact biblical description. Then he had the guy reverse a vacuum cleaner on it to make it look old." Arturo's wife smiled and looked at Thomas.

As Arturo told the story, Ann was also watching Thomas. His whole world seemed to operate about three months ahead of everyone else's. Like a winning chess game, where the moves are made mentally, long before any pieces are played. *What other cautious, preemptive moves did he already have in motion?*

Arturo went on, almost laughing at the deep level of chicanery. "So, Thomas and I went out the night before we were set to unearth the Ark, took the real one out, and slid the fake in. The *coup de grace* was that Thomas had the foresight to put a GPS tracking device in the crate that held the fake Ark. After it was stolen, we traced its trip to Washington D.C. Yeah, we knew exactly where it went, to within a few feet."

Ann was shocked. Her face showed it. Thomas hadn't told her that. She had been with him almost the whole time in Arizona and he had never mentioned anything about having a fake Ark created *or* a GPS tracking device. This meant he knew where DJ had taken the Ark. She swallowed a gulp of her margarita. That meant that Thomas could be reasonably sure that the real Ark had ended up back at the National Museum, after he'd traded it for her.

Arturo continued. "To know who took that Ark was important. Yes. But we didn't know how important until after we gave them the real Ark for you, Annie."

Thomas shot Arturo a look. Arturo was saying too much. A tension rose in the room. Ann was putting two and two together when Thomas said, "Yes, well, that's as far as the story goes because we know who took it, DJ, but now he's lost it. And even the political pressure we were going to try to exert won't work now." He looked at Ann. "A friend of mine knows Senator Kennedy and former Secretary of State William Bennet."

Ann nodded, but she was thinking about what Arturo had said earlier. Why had it been so important to know where the Ark was taken if they hadn't planned on acting on the information? Clearly, Thomas didn't want to talk about it. She was slowly learning the extent to which he did not trust her, or anyone. Or was it just her? She wondered where they were going tomorrow. What did he have in store?

They stayed up talking until one o'clock in the morning. Thomas and Arturo traded a few archeological stories. Finally, Maria announced that they should all find their beds. Morning would come all too soon.

This was the first time Thomas and Ann had slept in the same bed since she had been taken from him in Mexico. They resumed their passionate relationship with ease. It was as though they had never been apart. Ann lay exhausted next to Thomas, realizing it was already three o'clock.

She sighed. "I love you, Thomas McAlister. And I will spend every minute of every day, from now to eternity, teaching you to trust me as much as you do Arturo."

CHAPTER **45**

They got a late start the next day. After lunch, Arturo drove Thomas and Ann across a field to his brother's Cessna 206. Only this time, he didn't board the plane with them.

As they taxied down Arturo's gravel landing strip, Ann put her mouth to Thomas's ear and asked, "Where are we going?"

"Still a surprise!"

She held onto Thomas's hand during takeoff. Long afterward, she was still holding his hand. After an hour in the air, the drone of the engine put her to sleep, head on Thomas's shoulder.

Thomas stroked her hair as she slept. The past few days had been his happiest since she had been taken from him in Mexico. There was a time in Manhattan when he thought he might never see her again. That made having her next to him now a sweet experience. And wasn't that what life was all about? Feeling happy, fulfilled, and content? Shouldn't that drive all decisions? If I'm happy, I'll keep Ann by my side. If I'm happy I'll stay with this person . . . even if she shot me. Especially if she shot me to save her mother.

He was convinced that she no longer had any allegiance to the government. Especially with her family safe and sound. She was on his side now. Yet he'd also learned to never be 100 percent sure of anything again . . . including commitment. But he was happy, and it was because of her. He couldn't begin to fathom the guilt she must feel, and he reminded himself to be sensitive to that.

He knew that much of the information Arturo had divulged last night was news to her. He'd felt her eyes on him, as Arturo talked about his preparation. He knew she was remembering their time in Arizona. They had been together almost every minute. She was wondering when he had ordered the fake to be made. Wondering when he had purchased the GPS and made arrangements to have it built into the crate. And, of course, she was wondering whether he was the one who had stolen the Ark from the National Museum. She would conclude that he couldn't have masterminded and executed such an elaborate plan. Not an amateur. A seriously wounded amateur.

It was all right with him, if Ann wondered about those things. However, he didn't want her to start asking questions or showing undue interest. Particularly in whether or not he'd taken the Ark. He would tell her some day, when the time was right, but not right now. Asking before he was ready would cause him to believe that she was still working for the government.

As they were flying over the Bay of Pigs, Ann awoke. There was a Russian MIG fighter jet flying less than two hundred feet from their right wing and another off their left.

Ann immediately exclaimed, "Oh, my God, they've found us!"

"They're Cuban. Russian-made, of course."

"What are you saying? If we're in Cuban air space, they'll shoot us down!"

"They only shoot at you when they don't expect you. They're expecting us. These are our escorts."

"*Escorts?* What are you talking about, Thomas? Don't tell me you know Castro!"

"I had an Egyptian assistant during the Amenophis find. His name was Shakir. We became very close on that dig. Shakir's brother owns a large tobacco farm and cigar-rolling facility on the island's northern coast. Have you ever heard of Montenegro cigars?"

"No." Ann was peering nervously out the plane's small windows, clearly concerned.

"He distributes them all over the world. Not directly to the States, of course, but a fair number of them find their way there anyway."

"Okay, Thomas, so he owns a farm and there are two MIGS following us. What does all of this mean?"

Thomas heard her frustration. Ann was a strong-willed woman, used to making her own decisions. She didn't like being toted around without knowing where she was going.

"I told you we were going somewhere to relax for a while, Annie. I wanted us to be in a place where we could be alone, with no worries about DJ or the government or being followed. I'm so tired of all that right now. We need to be together for a while. The two of us. If this is ever going to work. We're going to stay in Cuba, on Shakir's brother's property. It's on the beach. This the only place in the world where we could be truly left alone."

"This isn't on *our* terms, Thomas. It's on *your* terms."

"Just give it a chance, Ann. For me? For us? Please."

» » « «

Cuba is the one of the most beautiful islands in the Caribbean and Ann loved it. Shakir's brother, Neferu, was a retired Egyptian oil baron who had become friends with Fidel Castro not long after the revolution in Cuba. His estate included several cottages on the beach and, although they were small, they were modern and luxurious. For the first month, they spent every minute together. It was like their first month together in Mexico, but better. They relaxed on the beach, explored ruins, went scuba diving, danced at night, sometimes alone in their cabana, and sometimes in local clubs, and they made love daily.

Thomas had completely stopped keeping track of time. Had he continued to keep track of it, he would have realized that it was exactly thirty days after they arrived that he had become interested in a new research project. He had been reading a book about the history of medicine, which described the four Tantras of Tibetan healing. The Tantras were translated into pictorial form in the seventeenth century. This famous pictorial version was called the *Blue Beryl*, and it was said that whoever possessed it could heal anyone of any ailment. Including old age. The odd thing was that the books cited hundreds of witnesses to the healings, some with excellent credentials. There were seventy-four paintings in all, each describing a different Tibetan medical technique or cure. The *Blue Beryl* had disappeared in the 1950s, when the Chinese occupied Tibet.

The mystery of the Blue Beryl intrigued him, and when he and Ann visited the Cuban library, he checked out all the books he could find about the history of medicine and Tibet. When he found Ann's eyes on him, he shrugged. "One more thing you'll have to learn about me, Annie. When I get interested in something, I'm a voracious reader. I need to read every source on the subject. Don't worry, though. I will always have time for you. You know you're my ongoing research project."

CHAPTER **46**

Unable to hold on to the Ark, or find it again, there simply was not enough activity on the case to keep DJ Warrant, and all of his resources, assigned to it full time. Despite DJ's protests and promises to find the Ark and deliver it safely, he was reassigned.

The simple little surveillance job had turned into the worst case DJ had ever worked on. Ultimately, it got him demoted. It wasn't an official demotion. He was simply no longer given the high-profile assignments. He was given jobs reserved for less capable agents and for those who were biding time until retirement. Desk jobs. For DJ, this was worse than being fired. He had never been a team player and was not well liked by his peers. When he suddenly fell from grace, they were not shy about letting him hear about it. Even Elmo, who thought he'd work with DJ forever, had become ostracized. Guilt by association. Lately, Elmo had been thinking about putting in a request for a different partner.

The case of the Ark was left open, but no full time resources were assigned. The museum thieves were never found and since the only object taken wasn't even a part of their official inventory, the FBI couldn't discuss it with anyone.

After DJ learned that McAlister had found Ann and disappeared, he pleaded with his superiors to let him have a covert team to go get the Ark. He told them McAlister was the key to finding the Ark. He knew he needed only one hour alone with him to obtain the location of the Ark. His requests were denied. He'd lost favor, and the last thing the government needed was an international incident coming from an attempt to kidnap a man in Cuba who wasn't officially charged with anything.

After a month of fruitless attempts to convince his superiors to let him go get McAlister, DJ was assigned to surveillance of a prostitution ring. Prostitution assignments were the lowest of all. DJ knew there was not, nor would there ever be, any real attempt to stop hooking. All the government was interested in was giving the appearance of doing something to stop it. Beyond that, they didn't really care. In fact, many government officials used prostitutes regularly.

Elmo knew that he and DJ had been demoted and he was more than a little upset about it. He had hitched himself to DJ while he was a shooting star, and now it appeared as if DJ had burned out. Elmo had to get away from DJ. He was younger and couldn't afford to go down in flames so early in his career. He was single, had never been married, and had no kids. At thirty-five, he had amassed a small fortune of just under one million dollars. He kept a small efficiency apartment in Quantico and, since he was always traveling, he had no other living expenses. He never ate out, or went to movies, and he rarely bought new clothes. He owned a very old, well-maintained Honda Civic, with a mere twelve thousand miles on it. Research had told him that it was one of the most reliable cars ever made. And it had been.

Most of the time, when he wasn't working, he researched stocks. Often, during the day when DJ didn't need him, he went on-line to make adjustments to his positions. He had done well during the bull market years, and he was nearing the amount he had calculated he would need for his very early retirement in Paradise. He planned to travel the globe, to search for the perfect place to live in luxury, on peanuts. From pictures he had seen, he thought that place might be Tahiti.

The problem was that early retirement meant many years with no income, and he needed to make more money *now*. If he could receive two more substantial salary increases, he calculated that he could retire in three years. He needed the significant increases that he and DJ had historically been awarded, which were now a thing of the past. With nothing but regular assignments, they would only get small salary increases. That is, if they got any at all. He had become like the other agents that he'd always overheard complaining about their pay. Regular increases would extend his retirement date, and he didn't like that. He could only put up with the pretentious, hot-blooded DJ if it meant he'd make more money. He had very little, if any, loyalty. His relationship with DJ was parasitic, much like the Ramora eel, which attaches itself to the belly of a shark for sustenance. When the shark gets sick, the Ramora detaches itself and goes in search of a better shark. Maybe it was time for him to detach from DJ.

Elmo was sitting at DJ's desk, waiting for him to return from lunch. Today he would tell DJ he was putting in for a new partner. He was nervous. He was pale and would sometimes, without warning, begin to shiver convulsively. The sides of his laptop computer, which he was rubbing now, were worn to a high gloss. Beads of sweat collected on his lip.

DJ came in, saw Elmo, sat down, and began looking through the planner that was sitting open on his desk.

Without looking up he said, "What's up, Elmo?" Since the prostitution assignment, he had become snappy and short with Elmo.

Elmo was sure DJ could hear his heart pounding. All of the air was sucked out of the room. He swallowed and said, "I . . . I have something I'd like to talk to you about."

DJ stopped paging through his planner. He looked at his watch and said, "Hold on one minute. I have an important call that I *have* to make."

DJ picked up his phone and dialed a number. Elmo watched him. He noticed that DJ had used an odd area code that he'd never seen before. It piqued his curiosity. He quickly opened his laptop. It had been on standby, so the screen illuminated immediately. Elmo double-clicked on an icon called TELEPHONY. It was a search engine on his hard-drive that functioned as a worldwide white and yellow pages directory. It also had an area code search function. He could enter any area code and it would tell him what city or country the code was for.

Elmo had only seen the area code of DJ's call, not the entire number. He entered it and clicked SEARCH. In an instant, the word Cuba appeared. *Cuba? Why on earth would DJ be calling Cuba?* Elmo thought he was privy to everything personal and private that DJ had going on, but he had no idea why DJ would be calling Cuba. Certainly it had nothing to do with the prostitution ring case they were working on. The only reference to Cuba Elmo had heard recently was that it was rumored to be where Thomas McAlister had gone with Ann. *But that couldn't be it.* Elmo paused. *Or could it? Could DJ have a line on the Ten Commandment's Case? Could he be calling Ann Davenport?*

Someone picked up on the other line. DJ said, "It's me."

The other person said something and DJ replied, "I understand. Call me when the timing is better."

Elmo was very curious. Obviously DJ had called someone in Cuba, and it had not been a good time for the other person to speak, which meant that there had been someone else present. Maybe it was Ann, and McAlister had been there.

DJ looked up and said, "What's going on, Elmo?"

Elmo froze. His mind was still in Cuba. He was mentally divided. Half of him was ready to tell DJ he was quitting as his partner, the other half was wondering if DJ had something going on in Cuba related to McAlister. Maybe he had a contact in Cuba. There was even the chance that he was back to working with Ann.

The mere fact that DJ was still working on the McAlister case gave Elmo hope. DJ was still the best agent in the FBI, despite his recent failure, and despite what everyone was saying about him. He still had his special knack of being able to figure out things and synthesize data. If DJ could apply all of his skill, intuition and mental power, there was a chance, a good chance, that he could recover the Ark and the Commandments. If he could get the Ark back, he would be fully redeemed. He would rise from the ashes and become a legend. He would have personally solved a case that the agency had abandoned. And solved it without governmental resources. Full and total redemption.

Elmo was rattled back by DJ's deep, impatient, nicotine-laden voice. "Well? What did you need to talk to me about?"

Elmo had a decision to make. Maybe this wasn't the best time to part ways with DJ. If DJ did find the Ark, and Elmo had separated from him, Elmo would become the laughingstock of the bureau. He would become the brunt of their jokes; the agent who set the record for the worst timing to ask for reassignment in the history of the agency. He made his decision.

"I've got that data you requested on how the East Coast prostitution ring is importing Russian women. I'll send it to you via email, so you can look at it when you get time."

"That's it? That's what you've been wiggling around in your chair about? Send it to me, Elmo, and find something to do. You're a nervous wreck." DJ began rearranging papers on his desk.

"Looks like they're paying off someone in immigration." Normally learning about a government official who was on the take would get DJ's attention, but not today. His thoughts were definitely elsewhere.

"Okay, good, send me the file. Anything else?"

Elmo paused. He considered asking about Cuba, but something stopped him. DJ would need his help soon enough. "No, nothing else. Thanks."

CHAPTER 47

Washington D.C. The Oval Office

The President of the United States had met and forgotten more names and faces during his four year term than in the previous forty-five years of his lifetime. But when DJ was escorted into his office, the President remembered him instantly. He'd never forgotten DJ; he'd even thought about him from time to time. The agent had made quite an impression on him during their last meeting. DJ was the epitome of a man. A man's man. Tanned skin, nicely graying hair, stoic face, tall, a solid build. He was a cross between the Marlboro Man and Hemingway.

The man who entered his office today looked ten years older. Only weeks ago he'd held himself erect, and now he was slouching. Unused to failure, the Commandments Case had taken its toll on him. A real man is bothered by failure, the President thought. He doesn't forget the one that got away. It eats at him, until it manifests itself physically. Very different from the political animal, like me, who spins failure so that someone else gets blamed.

The President welcomed him with a handshake. "DJ, good to see you again. Betty, two whiskeys, please." He'd read in DJ's file that he drank whiskey and he wanted to have a drink with this man.

"Thank you, sir, and thank you for agreeing to meet with me."

"No problem, DJ. Your message sounded somewhat urgent and to tell you the truth, after the whole McAlister affair went sour, I've been wanting to hear your story firsthand."

Betty brought them their drinks and left the room. The President raised his glass, "To Moses. A man with a lot of foresight."

DJ didn't feel like toasting to his failed assignment, but he was not about to slight the President. "To Moses," he said. The whiskey tasted good. Maker's Mark.

"What can I do for you, DJ?" The President asked.

"You've denied my requests for a continued search for the Ten Commandments, and I'm absolutely certain I can still find them. I want to change your mind."

"Our initial concern was that McAlister, or whoever stole them from the National Museum, would make them public, but that has not happened."

"True, but it could at any time, sir. It's still a time bomb waiting to explode."

"Sure, I still worry about it. But what am I to do? I read your requests personally. There is no new evidence. You have nothing new to offer."

"Sir, I do now. I'm convinced that McAlister is the person who stole the Ark from the National Museum. Two weeks ago, I found a GPS tracking device hidden in the crate that held the fake Ark. I learned that McAlister had the fake made in Phoenix, then planted the GPS. He was able to trace the location of the fake from the minute we confiscated it in Mexico. When he made his trade for Ann, he knew we'd take it to the same place, the National Museum. You see? We had excluded him from our final list of possible thieves, based on the fact that he couldn't have known where we had taken it. But with his GPS reading, he would've known."

"It's an interesting piece of new evidence, DJ. If nothing else it shows a new level of extreme foresight on the part of McAlister. But it's still conjecture. It's still circumstantial evidence. Not enough to convict on and not enough to deploy another team. Your boss, Hargrove, has too many other crises requiring resources right now. Does this still worry me? Hell, yes. But without some new facts . . . ." The President was shaking his head.

"There's more." DJ took a deep breath. He was now going directly over his supervisor's head by supplying the President with information he had not yet told Hargrove.

"Yes? What is it?"

"I've got someone who is close to McAlister."

"That's rich. Your last report said that McAlister was rumored to be in Cuba."

"Yes, sir, the person I'm referring to is with him in Cuba."

"Who is this person?"

"Ann Davenport."

"Ann Davenport? Isn't she the agent who you used last time? And didn't she fall in love with McAlister?" The President opened the file in front of him and began to skim it.

"Yes, sir. They fell in love. She's the one who shot him at the Harvard Club."

"It says here they're back together again. They're together in Cuba for Christ's sake, DJ. They're probably romping on the beach as we speak. What makes you think she'd ever help you again? Is she even still on active duty?"

"She's still active. I'm almost positive she'll get the information I need."

"Almost? *Almost?* What's gotten into you, man? Why do you think she'd walk across the street for you?" The President was showing his frustration. "If I made decisions based on *almost*, I'd have been run out of here a long time ago. Have you got anything or *not*? Why do you think she'll help us?"

DJ was silent. He uncharacteristically chewed his bottom lip. He'd hoped that it wouldn't come to this. That this level of detail would not be necessary. Not because he was about to violate a confidence, but simply because he didn't like talking about it. But the President had humbled him, and he hadn't argued well.

Another minute passed. DJ continued to stare at his drink. Finally, he raised his head and, for the first time in as long as he could remember, he had tears in his eyes. "Mr. President, I can get her to work with us because Ann Davenport is my daughter."

CHAPTER 48

Ann slowly replaced the receiver, tapping it several times while staring into space. She checked her appearance in the mirror and then left to join Thomas on the beach. He was sitting on a towel, cold Carta Blanca resting against his left thigh, totally focused on a passage about the painter of the *Blue Beryl*, Sangye Gyamtso. Ann came up behind him and kissed him softly on the cheek.

"How's your mom?" Thomas asked. This was the time of day that Ann's mother usually called from her new home off the coast of Washington State.

"She's doing well. You were right. They're liking it there. My brother had just walked in from shopping and she was going to help him unload, so she told me she'd call back later."

"Good. I'm glad they like it. It's important for them and for you."

"You seem pretty absorbed today. Is that one of the books you got from the library the other day? Let me see what my competition is."

Before Thomas could protest, she had snatched one of the three books stacked on the towel. "Hmm. "*Studies in Tibetan Medicine*. Going to Tibet?"

Thomas didn't mind her curiosity about the books. This would be a new project. One that shouldn't interest the government. But still, once in a while, when she was running indoors to get the phone calls from her mother, he'd fight with his demon of doubt. Was she talking to someone else? Was someone other than her mother calling her? She had been on the phone more and more, and the calls had increased to a daily rate, but they were always from her mother, or brother. She always told him about the conversations, what both her mother and brother were doing, and how they liked it on Whidbey Island.

But, ever watchful, it did seem that she always arranged to receive or make her calls when he was running errands or on the beach. He had begun to wonder if there were stores in Cuba, like there were in the States, that sold phone recording equipment.

Stop it! He refused to let these paranoid thoughts creep in. He reminded himself to get over his tendency toward paranoia. He must not let the feeling of distrust rule his relationship. Everything was fine as long as she showed no interest in the location of the Commandments. That was how he would regulate his trust. She wasn't asking about the Ark, so it didn't matter how much she was on the phone.

Ann picked up another of the books. "I've never seen this one. *Medical History Across Ancient Cultures*. What are you into this time, Thomas? The theme is medicine. Are you already starting your next . . . what should I call it? Treasure hunt?"

"No time like the present. Only, I'm finding it a little hard to retain information in this environment. A topless girl on one side of me. A cold beer on the other. Blue ocean in front of me. Tropical sun above."

She put the book down, straddled him, and kissed him softly for a long time. Then she looked at him and said, "You know, Thomas, I've never told you this. I know you're the one who stole the Ark from the National Museum . . . after you traded it to them for me."

His heart sank. His breathing stopped. Fear poured through his body. "Really?" he said, trying to act uninterested.

"Uh-huh. As soon as Arturo said you had placed that tracking device in the original crate and that you knew where they'd taken it, I knew."

Thomas rolled onto his side, forcing Ann to roll off his lap. "Really?"

"Yes, I mean, come on! I'm no dummy. It was stolen two days later. Who else could have possibly known it was there? And the thieves didn't take anything else. You'd think they would have taken something, with all those priceless treasures sitting around everywhere. If they were professional art thieves, they wouldn't have been able to resist. But you. You could resist. You found some of the artifacts that are in that museum. You didn't want the art. You only wanted what was yours."

She was right. Thomas felt sick. Why was she bringing this up now? Did it have something to do with the recent increase in phone calls? Thomas prayed she wouldn't ask a direct question as to where the Commandments were. She knew the topic was off-limits.

"How did you know it was stolen *two* days later? And that nothing else was stolen? I never told you that."

Her hesitation was barely discernable. "Before you came to me at Yale, I had gotten a call from the government. They told me that the Ark had been stolen two days after its arrival and that nothing else was taken. That's when they warned me to keep an eye out for you."

Thomas rolled over onto his back and squinted against the glare of the sun. He followed the course of a particularly fluffy white cloud. It seemed so far away. "What if I did take it back, Ann? What difference would it make?"

She turned toward him and smiled. "Well . . . that would only leave one question to be answered."

Thomas was screaming at her from inside, pleading with her not to ask it. He knew she wouldn't. She didn't care where it was.

"No, Ann. There are no questions left. I can't think of a single one."

"Oh, come on, Thomas, stop being such a tease. You can tell me."

"Tell you what?"

"You know what, silly. Where you hid the Commandments!"

CHAPTER 49

One week after asking Thomas where he hid the Ark, Ann came
home from the grocery store to an empty beach house. She'd only been
gone an hour and a half. The minute she entered the bungalow, she knew
something was different. It was not just quiet. It was still. The silence was
eerie. She didn't even have to go to the bedroom to check his closet. She
knew she was alone. She knew Thomas was gone.

She walked back to the open door and listened to the coastal breeze.
The beach looked so different now. So lonely. With two people in the
house, the breeze and the beach had been exciting; now, it was nothing
but sad. Tears flooded into her eyes and she made no attempt to wipe them
away. It was her fault. She had made her choice. She surveyed the room
and noticed the letter Thomas had propped up on the library table he'd
used as a desk. That confirmed it. She stayed in the doorway a long time,
mustering the strength to cross the room. *Wait a minute, Ann. You're
listening to your guilty conscience. Maybe he's just run back to the library
for more books.*

She rushed across the tile floor and snatched up the notepaper, unfold-
ing it with shaking fingers. When she saw that it was a long note it
confirmed what she already knew. He was gone.

Dearest Ann,

*By the time you read this note, I'll already be back in the
States. Don't try to catch me. You can't and it wouldn't matter
if you did. I have so much I want to say and despite having had*

a few days to organize my thoughts, I haven't been able to. When it comes to you, my thoughts have never been logical or even sequential, and now is no exception. I am left to ramble like the love-struck, thrice-betrayed idiot that I have been. And now, in my final act of this relationship, an avalanche of emotion is weighing me down, making each letter, each word, each breath, a difficult task.

I suspected you were consciously working against me, not just brainwashed, after you shot me that terrible day in New York. It was all so professional, even the way you held your gun. I didn't want to believe it, though. When you explained it away so perfectly, with such a plausible story about your mother being kidnapped and threatened with death, I eagerly accepted your story. There were always little things that bothered me . . . like your hair smelling of citrus that day at the Harvard Club, the little .22 in your skirt at Yale, and all of the phone calls you've been making to your mother recently. But, Annie, even those, in aggregate, did not make me doubt you. My love for you never wavered. I was true to the end.

One of the things I agreed upon with the man who rented me the house on Whidbey Island was that he would check on it once a month, to make sure everything was all right. The man checked on the house a week ago, Annie, and no one was there. As you know, no one had ever been there. The door was still padlocked shut. Your family never went to Washington. You lied to me every day. So, I became suspicious about all the phone conversations you've been having recently with your mother.

Very early into this adventure, Annie, I decided that even if I never found the Ark and the Commandments, I'd still found my treasure. You. You became everything to me. I loved you. My mission had been successful before I'd even started. I'd found my true love. God, it was great, Annie. I'd found you! A gem. A diamond. A girl who could make a man want to do good in this world. It's taken me a long time, too long, to learn that my diamond is a fake, my pearls, cultured. The jewel that I once prized above all others, mere costume glitter. You're lucky, Ann, that I was able to get the real treasure back, the Ark and the Commandments, or you'd be getting a lot more than a good-bye letter.

I know DJ is your father. I know you had your name changed from Warrant to Davenport when you entered the FBI, so you wouldn't be given preferential treatment. When you call your father today, tell him that I no longer have the Ark and the Commandments, they've found a safe, secret home.

And tell him this, Annie . . . I've got so much on you, your father, the FBI, and even the President that I know none of you will ever bother me again. As proof of that, and justification for leaving you, I've left a present for you in the drawer of the table. It's a copy. If anything happens to me, the originals go to the Attorney General, and the media, of course.

I wish things hadn't turned out the way they did. Amid all your lies, perhaps you can take comfort in this one bit of truth. You broke my heart.

Thomas

Her tears had already smeared the letter, but Ann carefully refolded it. They'd want to see it later. It was evidence. She pulled out the desk drawer. Inside was a tape recorder, an old, heavy Panasonic. It had been a popular model in the seventies and was probably the best Thomas could find on the island.

A tape had been left inside the machine. She ejected it and read the label written in Thomas's handwriting. ANNIE AND DJ. It was dated six days ago . . . the day after she had asked Thomas the location of the Ark. She shoved the tape back into the player and wiped the tears from her face. The sides of her mouth involuntarily turned down, as she fought off more crying. Her future was being handed to her.

She raised her hand and gently pushed the PLAY button. The spindles began turning. She didn't bother to check the volume. She knew Thomas would've pre-adjusted it. She heard a hissing noise, then the sound of a standard dial tone, followed by someone dialing. It seemed like a lot of digits. A phone rang. After four rings, a man answered.

Male Voice: DJ Warrant.

Ann: It's me.

DJ: Is he there?

Ann: No. He said he was going to the library. He should be gone for at least an hour.

DJ: How are you holding up?

Ann: Not great. This isn't getting any easier. You're putting me in a very tough place. I told you earlier today—

DJ: Annie! Annie, I know all that *we're in love* stuff. We've been through it before. Just hang in there. You've got to hang in there. We're almost home.

Silence.

DJ: Did you get a chance to ask him about the Ark? Did he steal it? Where has he hidden it?

Ann: I asked him again yesterday. Nothing I did worked. He was silent. I asked him again and he said he didn't want to talk about it. The subject was closed. He won't confide in me.

DJ: Couldn't you read between the lines a little? Or couldn't you shame him into telling you? You're an archeologist. You helped him find it! You deserve to know!

Ann: It's not like that with him. He doesn't have that kind of an ego. And, let's not forget, Dad, he may not be ready to fully trust me again, after New York.

DJ: Annie, you have to get it out of him. *Force* it out of him! You have to! Get him drunk. Drug him, like the first night you met. Do whatever it takes! Hold a gun to his head!

Ann: What wrong with you? I'm not one of your case monkeys! I love him! I'm not going to drug him! I'm about ready to call this whole thing off. We're not going to get anywhere. You don't understand how resolute he can be. He's through with the Ark. He's already thinking about his next project.

DJ: Ann, Ann, listen to me, honey. You have to wind this up so we can get on with our lives, too. I cannot . . . I *will not* retire with this failure hanging over my head. Think about *me*, Annie. I don't deserve to be labeled a fucking failure by my peers. You know how it is with the FBI. Hargrove and the guys are treating me like dirt. After the *career* I've had. You and I are teammates on this. Case partners. If we don't get this done, we will never have a chance to get to know each other again.

Ann: Get to know each other *again*? What the hell do you mean "*again*"? You left Mom and me when I was two years old, you bastard. I never knew you the first time! There is no *again* here! There's only the first time.

DJ: I meant *again* from *my* perspective, Annie. I've always felt like I knew you. I can understand how you wouldn't feel that way. Look, I'm sorry about the past. I've been on the road for the FBI all my life. If I can retire with pride, I'll be the father you never had. Trust me, Annie. Okay? I can't do it without your help. The President has given me permission for one last try. He'll have my head, as well as my badge, if I don't come through.

Ann: Dad, I really think we're pushing things here. He's going to suspect something. He's too clever not to. And if we lose him here, then we've lost him for good. Plus . . . I mean, haven't you already had your chance with Thomas?

Silence.

DJ: No. This is not over yet. You will help me finish this.

Ann: He's going to suspect. I don't think he has yet, but what do I tell him when he does? What then?

DJ: Ann, you shot him and he forgave you. Do you think a few phone calls are going to make him stop trusting you?

Ann: Damn it! How could you bring that up? I was under duress. I would've never, ever done that on my own and you know it! I was forced. So don't you dare flippantly say I shot him as if I had a choice.

DJ: You're right, you're right, calm down. You were following an Executive Order. There was no way for you to refuse. What I meant by what I said was that he trusts you fully. That's all. Okay? Find out where it is and let's get past this, okay? I don't like putting you through this any more than you like doing it. I understand that you're having trouble with this. I know it gets confusing when you're working undercover. I've been there, honey. Just remember your job. Always remember your job.

Silence.

DJ: Okay, Annie?

Silence.

DJ: Annie?

Ann: I hear you. I'll . . . try.

DJ: Atta girl. Let's plan to talk again in a few days. When you get a few minutes, give me a quick call to let me know what's happening. And be careful. Are you using the sniffer I gave you?

Ann: Yes, I used it before I called today. This phone is not bugged.

DJ: Good. Don't take anything for granted. You're a professional, but he's as tricky a man as I've ever come across.

Ann: He's not tricky. He's smart. It's one of the many things I like about him. I'll call soon. I've got to hang up now. Good-bye . . . Daddy.

DJ: Good-bye, Annie. Take care of yourself. I'm proud of you.

The tape continued to run, but it was only filled with silence. She wondered how long Thomas had been recording her conversations. It didn't really matter anyway. That conversation encapsulated everything he needed to know.

All she'd ever wanted was a father. A dad. She'd watched the other girls getting picked up and dropped off at school by their fathers and it hurt. She had cried herself to sleep a thousand nights, wishing her daddy would come home. Every Christmas and every Birthday of her life, every time she saw a shooting star or found a penny, she'd made the same wish. *I wish my daddy would come home.* And now, she'd thrown away the most important relationship in her life in her attempt to get closer to her father. Trying to please him had cost her the man she loved. And, in losing Thomas, she would most probably lose her future with her father. Now that Thomas was gone, her father wouldn't need her anymore. She put her head down on the table and cried. And didn't stop crying for a long time.

CHAPTER **50**

Washington D.C. The Oval Office.

DJ mumbled unintelligibly to himself, occasionally shaking his head. Director Hargrove, sitting only a few feet away from him, nervously spun his pen as he always did before meeting with the President. Neither man looked at the other. Neither was in the mood for conversation. Each considered the other a failure, at least as far as the Ten Commandments project was concerned. And at that moment, it was the only project that mattered.

Based on a briefing he'd received from Director Hargrove, the President had asked both of them to come to his office for a short meeting. Ten minutes or less, he had said.

When the President entered the room, he was smiling, but when he saw DJ and Hargrove his face turned stern.

"Good afternoon, gentlemen." They both stood but the President made no move to come around his desk to shake hands. "Sit." They sat.

"I have read your briefing on the Commandments Case. It stinks. Hargrove, you brought me this matter and stressed its urgency. DJ, you were responsible for it being carried out at a tactical level. I'll be damned if I can understand why we can win world wars and send men to the moon, yet we can't confiscate a little chest from an archeologist." He rubbed his face, and then took a deep breath, trying to keep his temper under control.

Hargrove nodded, DJ just sat, staring forward, focusing somewhere beyond the President.

"You both know the current evaluation system for government

personnel is heavily based on the input and opinions of your superior officers. Correct?"

Hargrove nodded.

"I've asked both of you here to personally let you know what action I'm taking. You're both career men. I feel I have no alternative other than to write a negative evaluation, a demerit, into both of your records." He looked from one to the other. Both were stone-faced. But, below the facade, nervous tension was boiling. There was nothing worse than a Presidential demerit on a government employee's record.

"Hargrove, you were ultimately responsible. But as you and I both know, the failure of the project lies with DJ. *That*, in my estimation, is where the real responsibility for the failure of the case lies. With DJ." Without moving his head, DJ looked directly at the President.

"You had responsibility for making this campaign a success, DJ. You were a respected veteran and because of that were allowed special latitudes not given to just any field agent. In a sense, you called your own shots. And you failed. I'm not saying the entire burden lies on your shoulders, but in my estimate 90 percent of it does. The record will reflect that."

The President continued. "Your primary mistake was so juvenile, so elementary. Time after time after time you continued to underestimate your opponent. You were outfoxed and outmaneuvered again and again. This was a case study in the dangers of underestimating your opponent. Why, we should use it at Quantico."

DJ was furious. He'd never, ever had a berating like this in his entire life. The fact that it was from the President was professionally incomprehensible. He was witnessing the death of his own career. If anyone else were doing this to him, even Hargrove, he might retaliate, but the problem was, the President was right. Every word he said was dead-on.

"You came to me, to personally beg for another chance, assuring me you could end the project in mere days . . . because you were using your daughter as bait! You could *guarantee* success, you said. You said nothing could go wrong. And what happened?"

The President opened a manila folder on his desk and read directly
from DJ's final report, "'The target of the investigative surveillance
detected the undercover nature of the agent, with whom he was having
a relationship, and permanently terminated the relationship. We now
believe the Ark has been sold, and is unrecoverable.' What the hell is
that? Why didn't you just say that McAlister found out his lover was
your daughter and still on your payroll? Now McAlister is off licking his
wounds and your daughter is so brokenhearted she wants to quit the
Bureau. How many lives did you fuck up during this unsuccessful inves-
tigation?"

The President waited for an answer, but DJ said nothing. He sat still,
like an oak tree on a windless day. But his mind was racing. He knew if
he moved, even twitched, it would be to hurl himself over the desk and
grab the neck of the man across from him. He could almost feel the soft
skin on the pads of his fingers, the cords in the man's neck that he would
squeeze and savagely rip away from the cartilage that held them in place.
He dreamed of giving the President a powerful, solid, even animalistic
head butt on the crown of his forehead to stop the inevitable squirming.
Then Hargrove spoke up.

"Sir, in DJ's defense, he did everything he could, more even. It's one
thing dealing with the criminal mind, and quite another—"

"*Save it!*" The President slammed his hand down on his desk. "I
don't want to hear anything more about McAlister or this case. That
will be all, gentlemen."

Hargrove protested the curt dismissal. "Mr. President, won't you
give DJ a chance to speak on his own behalf?"

The President raised one eyebrow. "DJ, do you have anything to
say?"

DJ barely heard the question. The President's voice was muffled and
indistinct. It was as if he were underwater, looking out at them from
inside an aquarium. Something had happened. He was so angry, and
he'd suppressed it for so long, that a minute ago he'd felt a little pinch,
somewhere deep within. A tweak. Nothing major. Not yet. But somewhere

deep in the recesses of his soul, a reserve of hate had been opened. He'd always known it was there. He'd called on small portions of it from time to time. It had been easy to govern, to turn off. But now, the little door was off its hinges, the filter gone, the dam punctured. And it was bringing forth a blackness, a focused hate, that had never been allowed out before. Even as he sat there he felt it begin to flow. He would nurture it now. Increase its pace, little by little, until the torrent was unstoppable.

Hargrove and the President stared at DJ, waiting for an answer. An uncomfortable amount of time passed and, still, he said nothing. Finally, the President rose from his desk. "Our meeting is over."

Hargrove rose at the same time, but DJ remained seated. Hargrove tapped his shoulder. "Warrant! Snap out of it! The meeting is over!"

DJ followed his boss out of the office. The President was no one to him now. Before today, the President had represented the United States, a country that DJ had loved serving. Republican or Democrat, he had always respected the Office, and the man who worked in it. But not anymore. None of it mattered anymore.

Now, with hate swelling inside him, he only had one objective. One singular goal that was forever burned into his brain. Having the hate unleashed was refreshing. He would get revenge. Sweet, simple, hate-filled revenge. He would focus, like a laser beam, on the person responsible for his demise: Thomas McAlister.

When DJ got back to his desk, he tore the picture of the serene lake off his bulletin board, wadded it up, and threw it into the trashcan. He replaced it with a picture of Thomas McAlister. McAlister, not the lake house, would be his new retirement goal. He refused to retire with his reputation in ruin while the man responsible went unpunished. He would stay in his current position until he was on top again, and he would nurture the hate, the fury, that was now flowing so freely within him to bring McAlister down at all costs, no matter how long it took.

CHAPTER 51

The only difference between Cuba's public telephone service and that of the United States was that, long ago, Cuba's had been updated with a technology that allowed conversations to be recorded from the central office, at the mere flick of a switch. After the revolution, Castro had insisted on it. It was no longer necessary for the secret police to plant "bugs" into individual phones. The revolutionary government could listen at will to conversations deemed important, and they often did. If civilians had the right connections, and enough money, they could listen too.

Shakir, Thomas's host, had the needed connections. The recording device tied to the telephone line at the beach house where Thomas and Ann were staying was turned on, at Thomas's request, the day after Ann asked him where the Commandments were hidden. The nice thing was that ordinary bug sniffers didn't work on this system. That was how Thomas was able to get the recordings of Ann, and that was why her bug detection device didn't work.

After the listening device was installed, Thomas found that almost every time Ann said she was calling mother, she was really calling her father, DJ Warrant.

Thomas wasn't sure what hurt him more, losing Ann, or coming to terms with how gullible he'd been. His consolation was that he'd figured it out and, in the end, it hadn't cost him the true treasure . . . the historical one.

Once he had listened to the recording of Ann and DJ, he'd made arrangements to return to the States alone, immediately. He couldn't bear to spend another hour with Ann. He left the note, and flew back in a private plane which, by filing as an academic transport flight, had permission to land in Florida. The next day, he had leased a 35-foot Sea Ray and started up the East Coast, taking the Intercoastal Waterway. The recording would keep DJ, Hargrove, and everyone else off his back.

It took a few days but, eventually, the pressure of always having to look over his shoulder, and be two steps ahead, subsided. He started to remember what life was like before the search for the Ark had started. Though there were aspects of the last few months that he'd enjoyed, he was ready for a break.

Despite being a sailor by nature, a motor boat with its shallow draft and faster speed was a better choice for heading up the Intercoastal. He motored at a leisurely pace and stopped often, at isolated locations, mooring at marinas only when he needed more groceries, gas, beer, or books. His cash reserve was running low, because of the chartered flight and the two-month lease on the boat, but he'd have enough to enjoy a short break before reaching New York City.

Thomas was docked at a small well-kept harbor in Elizabeth City, North Carolina, when he received the e-mail message. It was the second email he'd received from Taylor that week. Unlike the first one, which had no title, this message was entitled, "CONGRATULATIONS!" Thomas smirked. There was little in his current life that would justify congratulations. In the period of a few months, he'd lost his job and one of the people that mattered most to him; Ann.

There were bright spots, of course. His friends had been inordinately kind, helping him interpret the Moses Riddle, locate the site of the Ark, excavate it, and snatch it back from the clutches of the government. As low as he was, he still had those things, and the Ark, of course. At least he thought he did, until he read Taylor's email. Thomas clicked on the word CONGRATULATIONS to open the message.

Dear Thomas,

I was going to send you one of those silly electronic cards, but given my computing skills, it would've taken much too long. I wanted to get this information to you as soon as I could.

Not more than an hour ago, I sold your treasure. The deal met all of your criteria regarding price, security, purchaser and visitation rights. The client approved of annual visits for you. I'll save telling you who the client is until you arrive. Be assured I used my finest contacts and was able to locate the crème de la crème, as they say. I even surprised myself a little!

The two numbers following this epistle represent the sale price and the number of the Swiss bank account into which the currency will be deposited by day's end. Rest easy, son. This adventure is over on a high note of success. You may not know it now, but it was worth every bit of grief. I look forward to seeing you again. Take your time, though. Learn to relax again. Oh, yeah, and don't spend it all in one place.

Taylor

Thomas had accumulated a huge amount of debt during the past couple of months. He glanced down at the sales price number. He looked up. Stopped. Focused. Then looked back down again. His mouth dropped open. Then, he counted zeros, to make sure he was reading it right. It was a fantastically large, almost silly number. He laughed aloud. The laugh sounded foreign and he realized how tense he'd been. He hadn't smiled or laughed in weeks. He'd been so consumed with Ann and DJ, and with worrying about the safety of the Ark and, lately, with his dwindling bank account, that he'd never stopped to consider what would happen if the Ark actually sold.

If the numbers in the e-mail were correct he could immediately repay Drew and Taylor, and include generous bonuses. Both of them had loaned him the money to pay Ethan, and given him money for other expenses. That alone was a huge burden lifted. He would also be able to handsomely compensate Arturo for his vital help. Arturo was far too proud to accept direct payment, but he wouldn't be able to stop Thomas from setting up a trust fund for each of his children, to help out with college.

In addition to taking care of other people, he could now realize his own dream. Ever since Washington had fired him, and ever since he'd started the quest to find the Moses Riddle, he'd been thinking about what he might do with the rest of his life. A fascinating, gripping idea had taken root. He was considering launching a campaign to try to find the world's ten greatest lost treasures. He'd started a list, and was even doing a little research already. So far, he had estimated that even the least expensive expedition would cost more than he could afford. *Until now.* Now, with the money he'd made from the sale of the Commandments, he could afford to search for all of them. He only had to decide which treasure to investigate first. And, actually, it would only be nine treasures. He'd already scratched the first one off the list.

As sweet as the money was, it would not restore his reputation among his peers. Since the entire find and subsequent transaction was private, no one would ever know he had found the original Ten Commandments. There would be no professional redemption. The funny, insular academic world would still consider him an outcast.

He put that thought aside. Right now, nothing mattered but what he was going to have for dinner in the way of celebration. Thomas thumbed through the CDs on the shelf in the main cabin, and selected a Cheryl Crow favorite. On deck, he could hear lively sounds coming from a small harbor restaurant. It sounded inviting. He decided to go there for cocktails and dinner. Later, in the restaurant, the crowd cheered him as he bought everyone a third round of drinks. Yet, even in celebration, he couldn't help but think how preposterously lonely one could be while standing in the middle of a large group of people.

CHAPTER 52

Thomas tied up at Laurence Harbor and took a train into Manhattan. He was eager to see Taylor again, and he swept him into a heartfelt hug at the door of the apartment.

"The Caribbean wasn't all bad, Thomas. Your color has improved and I don't detect that little tremor in your hands that you had during your last visit."

"Excuse me, Taylor. On that visit, I had an open gunshot wound. That didn't help the little tremor."

They moved into the living room.

"It was deeper than that. You were unsettled mentally. How'd that wound heal, by the way?"

"Great. It's a small pink circle, the size of a quarter. Not sore at all."

Thomas noticed that the Bedouin trunk was back in place as the coffee table again. "You didn't waste any time getting this out of the bedroom."

Taylor smiled and said, "I tried something else for a few weeks, but it simply didn't go with the rest of the room."

Thomas laughed. "Yeah, there aren't many rooms that piece of furniture would go well with. It's very hard to . . . match. So, where did you place it?"

"I'll tell you during dinner. I'm in the middle of making Spaghetti al Cartoccio. That's a clue, by the way."

"Is the clue that you're cooking? Or that you're making an authentic Italian dish?"

"The clue is that it's a central Italian dish. If you can't figure out who I sold it to from that, you need to look for new work." Taylor raised his voice, to be heard from the kitchen. "How long are you going to stay and what can I plan for us, Thomas? Last time we didn't have much fun. There is an excellent off-Broadway play that—"

"No, no, Taylor. No plays. No late nights chatting with New York glitterati. I'd rather take in a few movies, read a lot, and hang out a little. My boat trip up the Intercoastal was just phase one of my R and R campaign. I hope you won't mind. I need to lay low and figure out what I'm going to do with the rest of my life. I'm not ready to go back Arizona."

"Afraid our friend, Mr. Warrant, might be waiting there for you?"

"I hadn't even thought of that, but I'm glad you brought it up. We need to watch our backs for a while. That man is as unforgiving as cold steel."

"You're welcome to stay here as long as you need to, Thomas. You're no imposition at all. If you promise to stop moving my furniture around, that is."

Thomas dropped into one of Taylor's large enveloping arm chairs and randomly paged through a book he picked up off of the coffee table. "Feels good just to sit," he yelled into the kitchen.

They were silent for awhile, both men thinking about DJ Warrant. Finally, Thomas put his head back and closed his eyes. He felt the stress of the travel, of getting to Taylor's, recede. It was over. Done. He had engineered the treasure into safe hands and had a nice full Swiss bank account to show for it. His mind floated to thoughts of the future but he quickly slammed the door. Not yet. He needed a palate cleanser. He had no desire to think about what he would do next. None.

Then Taylor came back in the room. He set a glass of red wine in front of Thomas and started back toward the kitchen. He rounded the corner and then stood in the doorway. "By the way, Thomas, I spoke with my Chinese friend the other day."

Thomas drew a blank. He leaned his head back and looked at the ceiling. "Who?"

"You know. You told me to ask around about the Blue Beryl, and I told you I had an old friend who was born in China. I thought he might be a good person to ask about it."

Thomas swirled his wine, only half interested. "And?"

"He told me an interesting story."

"Come on, Taylor, out with it. Don't play your cat and mouse game with me tonight."

"He told me he knew of an old healer who had the ability to cure the blind. To correct their vision. Many people have told my friend that it works. People walk away with their sight restored."

"Taylor, I can turn on the television or walk down Forty-fifth Street and find people who say they can heal the blind. It's usually a hoax. Hell, it's always a hoax."

"My friend told me that this man can really cure the blind. I believe him. The old healer uses a page that was evidently torn from a book a long time ago. He said there were many pages, one for every ailment. But he only has one page. He says the book was called the *Xi Chi Chuan*. That's Chinese, of course."

Thomas rolled his eyes. Taylor knew that he didn't speak Chinese. "Okay. What does Xi Chi Chuan mean?"

"It means . . . ." Taylor said, peering around the corner, "*The Blue Beryl*."

Thomas rose from his chair and strode into the kitchen. "Now that, my friend, *is* interesting. Where is this old healer located? Did he say?"

"Yes. The old healer is in Tibet."

Thomas considered the idea that a page from the Blue Beryl might actually have been preserved. Though only one page, if it were found, and if it did contain some type of revolutionary medical information, its value would be priceless. One healing page alone would be worth millions to any of the large pharmaceutical companies. What appealed to Thomas, was that with a little practical detective work and applied archeology, where there was one page, there may well be more. He smiled. Tibet. The land with the mysterious fusion of Indian and Nepalese influences, Hinduism and Buddhism. It would be weeks before he would be physically ready for such an expedition, months before he would be in the right mental frame of mind.

Yet when Taylor went to look for Thomas, to tell him that dinner was ready, he found him in the library, acutely focused on, solemnly studying, a map of Tibet.

The End

THE MOSES RIDDLE
CIPHER CHALLENGE:
$5,000, OR ANCIENT TREASURE.

Since you've read a book involving a riddle, I thought you might like to try to solve one. But, beware, before you get to the riddle, you must decipher the ciphertext used to encrypt it.

What is the contest?

The Moses Riddle Cipher Challenge is an opportunity for readers of the Moses Riddle to test their riddle-solving, cipher-cracking skills to win a prize worth $5,000. The winner can either chose a cash pay-out or a cache of ancient Egyptian treasures valued at $5,000. Deciphering the ciphertext will generate a riddle. Solving that riddle will generate three code words. You must correctly identify all three code words. Clues that can be used to solve both the cipher and the riddles are contained in The Moses Riddle text.

How do you claim the prize?

No purchase necessary. Contestants may enter as many times as they like. The first contestant to identify all three code words will win their choice of either $5,000, or a cache or Egyptian treasures valued at $5,000. Taxes, if any, are the sole responsibility of the winner.

All claims must include three code words, the contestant's name, address, phone number and e-mail address (if applicable). All claims must be sent by registered mail to: The Moses Riddle Cipher Challenge, P.O. Box 9082, Winnetka, IL 60093. The winner will be the first to send the three correct code words, based on postmark date. The winner will be notified within 28 days by regular mail, phone, or e-mail. All updates on the Challenge will be posted on Mr. Kingsbury's web site: <u>www.huntkingsbury.com</u>.

The winner will be required to claim the prize and to execute an Affidavit of Eligibility and Promotional Release within 28 days of the date notice is sent or the prize will be forfeited. If Winner is a minor, a parent or guardian may execute the release. If the prize notification or prize is returned undeliverable, the prize will be forfeited and may be awarded to another winner.

If an entry contains at least one correct code word, Mr. Kingsbury will respond to the contestant within 28 days by regular mail as to which of the code words is correct.

Incomplete or illegible entries will not be honored. Mr. Kingsbury is not responsible for late, lost, misdirected, damaged, illegible, incomplete, incorrect, misrouted or postage due entries. Mr. Kingsbury is not liable for printing, typographical, or other errors contained in the ciphertext. Entries become the property of Mr. Kingsbury and will not be returned.

What is the contest duration?

The contest duration will be determined by Mr. Kingsbury, based on progress made in the first year. If, after one year, no one has solved the cipher, Mr. Kingsbury may, at his discretion, provide clues on his web site.

Who is eligible to play?

This Challenge is open only to legal residents of the United States. By submitting an entry, the contestant agrees to be bound by these Official Rules. Entry constitutes permission for use of the winner's name, address, likeness, biographical data, and contest entry, for publicity and promotional purposes, with no additional compensation (except where prohibited by law).

Mr. Kingsbury shall have no liability and shall be released and held harmless by contestant(s) for any damage, loss or liability to person or property, due in whole or part, directly or indirectly, by reason of the acceptance, possession, use or misuse of prize or participation. Any and all disputes, claims and causes of action arising out of or connected with this contest, or any prize awarded, shall be resolved individually, without resort to any form of class action, and exclusively by arbitration. Claims, judgments and awards shall be limited to actual out-of- pocket costs incurred, including costs associated with entering this contest, but in no event attorney's fees. Offer void where prohibited and subject to federal, state and local laws. This prize is not transferable.

How will you know who won?
Winners will be posted to Mr. Kingsbury's web site. Good Luck.

Sponsored by:

Mr. Hunt Kingsbury
c/o Bimini Road Enterprises,
P.O. Box 9082,
Winnetka, IL 60093.

THE MOSES RIDDLE
CIPHER CHALLENGE:

264 89 37 246 149 140 425 91 376 458 412 299 19 52 312 114 69
397 20 10 93 283 181 462 111 326 203 301 96 293 315 6 153 159
210 223 411 250 164 390 174 371 421 46 379 255 457 380 62 207 137
134 252 490 389 13 233 277 105 66 395 251 50 227 294 350 454 410
478 486 3 188 100 130 279 399 55 216 400 322 73 5 284 455 453
168 402 76 385 493 393 320 58 387 211 34 41 199 266 197 244 177
28 30 370 105 144 121 276 118 347 360 461 11 99 8 217 170 14 435
395 181 359 60 222 5 47 126 331 406 7 481 9 150 309 381 3 51 229
414 32 204 20 200 153 301 405 118 210 293 101 156 21 57 193 34
253 136 319 201 55 213 323 367 62 77 233 25 130 6 85 470 10 455
129 496 415 480 191 153 18 295 29 258 492 68 490 312 272 103 257
349 375 111 122 170 121 71 195 17 344 22 483 310 463 319 67 323
237 41 394 277 148 113 331 441 106 99 462 299 288 424 109 177 235
474 426 469 123 36 354 93 73 161 284 451 271 280 484 489 65 231
81 62 406 209 262 51 290 67 131 116 286 186 95 303 32 5 106 281
36 74 196 50 34 110 277 68 64 74 203 42 247 15 209 12 89 224 105
19 295 199 179 221 273 81 237 145 229 34 4 56 204 200 58 94 103
230 147 95 66 173 226 273 116 140 296 284 35 68 281 40 98 13 107
61 126 87 129 83 42 240 119 287

Acknowledgements

I'd like to thank the following people for all their help and assistance: Nancy Johanson, Ann Collette, Bob Aulicino, Angela Washelesky, Susanne Kirk (and her anonymous assistant), Jack Matosian, Kit Williams, Doug and Dina Isern, Carolyn Patterson, Dana Roeser, MaryAnn Atkinson, my mom, Winnie Kingsbury, and wife and children for their encouragement and patience.

Hunt Kingsbury lives in the Chicago area with his wife
and three children. He is a graduate of TCU University (BA)
and Loyola University (MBA). *The Moses Riddle* is his first novel.
He is currently working on the second novel in the
Thomas McAlister "Treasure Hunter" Adventure Series.